P9-DXG-369

A PLUME BOOK

# THE DISMANTLING

BRIAN DeLEEUW is the author of the novel *In This Way I Was Saved*. Born and raised in New York City, he is now a screenwriter living in Los Angeles.

---

### Praise for *The Dismantling*

"With its high-tension plot and atmosphere of unease, *The Dismantling* is a morally ambiguous thriller in the grand tradition of Graham Greene and Patricia Highsmith. It has smart things to say about memory, redemption, and what it's like to live in a world where everything is for sale, but it says them by telling a gripping story."
—Christopher Beha, author of *Arts & Entertainments*

"Intense, spare, and unflinching, DeLeeuw's *The Dismantling* treads risky, ethically nuanced territory, exploring the nature of absolution and revenge, the lies we tell our families, and the honesty we can find with strangers. A psychologically insightful, gripping novel."
—Michaela Carter, author of *Further Out Than You Thought*

"While this is a fast-paced, engaging thriller, it is also much, much more. It is, at its heart, a fully and tenderly rendered exploration of loss and shame and the deep yearning for some manner of redemption."
—Thomas O'Malley, author of *This Magnificent Desolation*

"A whip-smart modern noir. Brian DeLeeuw's writing is as keenly intelligent as it is eerily propulsive."
—Jennifer duBois, author of *Cartwheel*

CALGARY PUBLIC LIBRARY

JUN - - 2015

ALSO BY BRIAN DELEEUW

*In This Way I Was Saved*

# The
# Dismantling

*A Novel*

## BRIAN DeLEEUW

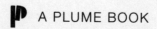 A PLUME BOOK

PLUME
Published by the Penguin Group
Penguin Group (USA) LLC
375 Hudson Street
New York, New York 10014

USA I Canada I UK I Ireland I Australia
New Zealand I India I South Africa I China
penguin.com
A Penguin Random House Company

First published by Plume, a member of Penguin Group (USA) LLC, 2015

Copyright © 2015 by Brian DeLeeuw
Penguin supports copyright. Copyright fuels creativity, encourages diverse
voices, promotes free speech, and creates a vibrant culture. Thank you for
buying an authorized edition of this book and for complying with copyright
laws by not reproducing, scanning, or distributing any part of it in any form
without permission. You are supporting writers and allowing Penguin to
continue to publish books for every reader.

P REGISTERED TRADEMARK—MARCA REGISTRADA

LIBRARY OF CONGRESS CATALOGING-IN-PUBLICATION DATA
DeLeeuw, Brian.
The dismantling : a novel / Brian DeLeeuw.
    pages ; cm
ISBN 978-0-14-218174-4 (softcover)
1. Organ donors—Fiction.   2. Transplantation of organs, tissues,
etc.—Fiction.   I. Title.
PS3604.E4437D57 2015
813'.6—dc23              2014029836

Printed in the United States of America
10  9  8  7  6  5  4  3  2  1

Set in Sabon

This is a work of fiction. Names, characters, places, and incidents either are
the product of the author's imagination or are used fictitiously, and any
resemblance to actual persons, living or dead, businesses, companies, events,
or locales is entirely coincidental.

For Alex

A secret is the hoard inside the maze of lies.

—Colin Harrison, *Manhattan Nocturne*

In all, the ultimate fetish is the idea of life itself as an object of endless manipulation.

—Nancy Scheper-Hughes, *Commodifying Bodies*

# ACKNOWLEDGMENTS

Thank you to Richard Abate and Melissa Kahn for sticking with this project far longer than might have seemed reasonable. Thank you, also and profoundly, to Liz Stein for your willingness to take a gamble and your tenacity in seeing that gamble all the way through.

Thanks to Katie Arnold-Ratliff and Christopher Beha, both of whom read many more iterations of this novel than anybody should rightly be subjected to. Your suggestions and guidance were indispensable, as always, and you are as good friends as you are readers. I'm also grateful to my friend Dr. Lauren McCollum for generously sharing the story of her own liver donation.

And thank you, finally, to the Corporation of Yaddo for providing the welcome time and space to complete a crucial portion of this book.

# The
# Dismantling

## One

SIMON looked again at the girl's photo on his screen. There was no denying it: she might as well be Lenny's younger sister. Besides the Mediterranean coloring, there was a certain leonine quality to the face, the strong jaw, canted eyes. The photo was from the shoulders up, the background a tan stucco wall presumably somewhere in Los Angeles. She looked directly into the camera, smiling with her mouth only. He wondered if she was an actress, or trying to become one. She was young enough; pretty enough too, or nearly.

*I hope I've understood your company's website correctly,* her first e-mail had begun. *I'm twenty-two years old. I don't smoke. I don't drink. I live a healthy lifestyle, or as healthy as you can in LA when you don't have much money. This has been a difficult year for me financially, which is why I'm interested in the kind of deal I think you're offering. Please be in touch with more of the specifics. Yrs., Maria Campos.*

Simon had replied, through Health Solutions' encrypted server, in the usual manner: direct, impersonal, detailed. He told her that if her blood type was a match, she would need to undergo some tests—first blood work, a physical, and a CT scan in Los Angeles, and then if these were satisfactory, liver function tests at the hospital here in New York. Next would be the screening interview. After all that would come, if she passed, the surgery itself and a few days of in-patient follow-up. Then she could go back home, and that would be the end of it. If she was still interested, she should send him the record of a recent physical examination, a photograph, and a phone number. He didn't mention money yet.

The next morning she had responded: *Before I wrote, I thought about what you might need, so I got these records ready. The photo request is weird—this isn't a date—but here you go. You can reach me at 562-820-1980. Please advise the next step. Yrs., Maria.*

Simon had looked at the attached photograph and medical records; then he'd looked at the photograph again. He'd hardly been able to believe his good luck.

SIMON pursued an obvious strategy in the winnowing of transplant applicants: it's easier to convince the hospital's social workers that people who look as though they belong together—which really means looking as though they have roughly the same amount of money—are involved in an altruistic partnership. If the recipient is a pasty rich guy from Connecticut, then flying in a donor who doesn't speak English, from, say, Brazil, is probably not going to be particularly convincing. And if they look physically enough alike, as if they might be first or second cousins, it all becomes even easier. Now, finally, after a week and two dozen applicants he'd been forced to toss aside—wrong blood type, wrong attitude; too old, too sick, too fat—it appeared he had the perfect candidate.

The next step was securing Peter DaSilva's approval, which was the reason Simon was sitting in the Health Solutions office at nine on a Sunday morning. This was a rare in-person audience with his employer, who preferred to communicate via cryptic text message or hurried calls from one of the five boroughs' remaining handful of public pay phones. DaSilva was half an hour late, but at last Simon heard a key slide into the lock, and then the door swung open and in he walked, Yankees cap perched loosely on his cinderblock head, black blazer draped over his bulk, laptop bag slung over his shoulder. Peter DaSilva was a droopy-eyed, corpulent man who always seemed on the verge of falling asleep. He nodded at Simon and slumped onto the couch, where he lit a cigarette and rubbed at the pouches under his eyes. He looked as though he should be permanently installed on the bleachers of a horse-racing track somewhere, preserved in the amber of stale cigarette smoke and fried food. But there was something about this shambolic persona that set his patients at ease as he led them and their families—in his other, legitimate job as associate transplant coordinator at Cabrera Medical Center—step by arduous step through the emotionally brutal transplant process, as he played the roles of advocate and counselor and confessor. He exuded calm. It wasn't exactly an act—more like camouflage. Because Simon knew that Peter DaSilva was very good at what he did—both his coordinating job at Cabrera and also as the shadow proprietor of Health Solutions—and he didn't get to be that way by not paying attention.

"So, who is she?"

Simon lit his own cigarette and turned the monitor to face the couch.

"Hmm." DaSilva exhaled smoke through his nostrils like a cartoon bull. "I don't see the resemblance."

"You . . . what?"

"I'm fucking with you. Nice break, for once. What's the age difference?"

"Seventeen years."

"Maybe we go with a second cousin angle. That should satisfy social."

"She already e-mailed me her records." Simon handed over a printout. "Take a look. Compatible blood. No underlying conditions. Healthy. Young."

DaSilva flipped through the pages. "A hundred and thirty-five pounds? I hope her liver's fat and happy. Lenny's a big boy."

"I'd say it's worth pursuing anyway, wouldn't you?"

"She's in Los Angeles?"

Simon nodded.

DaSilva took a binder off the bookshelf, flipped it open to a tabbed page. "Here's the number of a lab in Glendale. Tell her to go for the usual screening package."

"So I should call her?"

"Does Lenny have a secret twin I don't know about? No? Then I don't see the point in waiting for anybody else. Just do me a favor: when you talk to her, make sure she's not a mopey jerk-off. One per pair is enough."

"Lenny was that bad?"

"Let's just say his attitude didn't inspire confidence. I don't want him doing any improvising in the psychosocial, okay? Everything he says should be something he's heard coming out of your mouth first."

"You know I'll do my best to prep him."

DaSilva stubbed out his cigarette and stood up. "That's all I ever ask."

THE search for a donor had begun eight days before, when Simon pulled his rental car into Howard Crewes's driveway at the terminus of a quarter-mile cul-de-sac tucked within a gated development off Route 1. Simon had stepped out into the late-summer haze, feet crunching on gravel, and squinted up at the house, a blinding-white neo-Georgian. This, apparently, is what a decade in the NFL buys you: brick chimneys, black-tile roofing, Ionic columns flanking your front door. Crewes had called Simon that morning and disclosed that he'd been "guided" to the Health Solutions website and wanted to speak with somebody from the company in person. Simon had known about Crewes for years before he received the man's call. He was the Bruiser back then, an enforcer at strong safety for the Jets, accused cheap-shot artist. But now he was just a middle-aged man living by himself in a big house in the middle of New Jersey, and he was, Simon had to assume, dying.

Simon had walked up the path and rapped the knocker, a brass lion's head. A tall, stooped black man with a head of receding salt-and-pepper hair opened the door. He wore a crisp blue dress shirt tucked into tailored khakis, a pair of leather slippers on his feet. It was Crewes, looking some years older than he'd appeared in the most recent photograph Simon had found online, new tributaries of wrinkles creasing the landscape of his face.

"You must be Simon Worth," Crewes said, squinting against the glare.

"Yes, sir." Simon wondered what the man thought of his appearance, of his bland gray suit, his nondescript white-guy's face and salesman's smile; whether Crewes had expected somebody flashier or more rugged looking, or at least a few years older. Simon was twenty-five, but he knew he looked about five years short of even that.

"Come on inside."

Crewes turned, limped across the foyer. The lights were dim; the air-conditioning roared. Sunlight filtered through tall bay windows to reveal the improbable scale of things: acres of oak flooring, a cavernous fireplace. There was very little furniture, nothing on the walls. Crewes led the way to a study in the back, all mahogany, velvet, and brass, which appeared to be the only room on the ground floor in regular use. He waved at a club chair and installed himself behind a leather-topped desk.

"Don't be offended," he said. "But I gotta admit you guys were my last choice."

Simon nodded; this was typical client throat clearing. "We usually are."

"You understand I tried to do this the right way. The legal way. I asked family. Close friends. Hell, I even asked other guys from the team. But either people weren't interested, or the ones who were didn't match up right."

"And now let me guess: the transplant centers are telling you to get on the list and wait. As though you had all the time in the world."

"Worse. You ruin your liver drinking? Forget it. Don't even bother with the list."

"Six months clean." Simon shook his head ruefully. "UNOS won't consider you otherwise. Most units won't either."

"I've been made aware of that, yeah."

It was a familiar story, but what Simon saw when he looked at the man didn't fit. As discreetly as he could, he checked for the usual signs of liver failure: jaundiced skin and eyes, whitened nails, the crooked stiffening of flexion contracture in the fingers. He saw none of this. Crewes's shirt lay flat across his belly, no sign of the telltale bulge of fluid in his abdomen. Simon hadn't thought somebody this desperate would be able to hide it.

"The drinking," Crewes said. "We do things your way, will it be a problem?"

"I can't make guarantees yet. But if there's any possible way around it, we'll figure that out."

Crewes leaned back in his chair, clasping his hands behind his head. "I know what you're thinking: why does this sick guy look so healthy? Or maybe I'm flattering myself, maybe I don't look so great either. Anyway, this isn't for me. This is for Lenny. Leonard Pellegrini. He's a guy I played with, a teammate; a friend too, or at least he used to be. He's messed himself up, bad enough that he's going to die if he doesn't do something about it. If he doesn't do . . . this."

"And you're . . . funding everything?"

"Funding. Organizing. Making sure the thing happens." Crewes sighed regretfully. "I'm not a match, or else I'd just donate myself."

"A gift."

"A gift, yeah. Lenny can be an asshole, but that doesn't mean he deserves to die. You see this house." He pointed up at the ceiling, then swung the finger down to his own chest. "I'm the only one living in it. I can guess how much this is going to cost, but what else am I saving my money for?"

The arrangement was unorthodox, but Simon didn't think that was enough of a reason to turn Crewes down. "I need to speak with him before we go any further. In person."

"I figured. I'll drive you out to see him tomorrow. I just wanted to check you out myself first."

"And?"

"You're a real live human being, which is a start. You people screw me, you're the one I'll be looking for."

He stood up: the meeting was over. He stuck out his hand, and Simon took it, Crewes's grip firm and rough as a brick.

Driving home on the Turnpike, Simon thought again of the play that had briefly made Howard Crewes the most infamous football player in America. He'd seen it live on television a dozen years before, as a thirteen-year-old kid sitting alone in the den of his father's Rockaway Beach home. He remembered gangly Alvin Plummer running his pattern to the middle of the field. Flying out of the left side of the screen, Howard Crewes led with his head. Plummer was focused on the overthrown ball; he didn't see the hit coming. The temple of Crewes's helmet met the crown of Plummer's. The second man's head snapped down and to the side as though on a well-oiled hinge. The two men collapsed to the ground. Crewes got up; Plummer did not. Trainers huddled over the receiver, his fingers curling into odd, baby-like fists. A golf cart crawled across the turf. Medics parked it near Plummer, assembled the gurney and backboard. Crewes stood, hands on hips, his back to the felled man. Simon remembered feeling as though he were witnessing something, in this raw moment before the imposition of a palatable narrative (tragedy, contrition, redemption), that he was not meant to witness: the unadorned fact of a man lying crippled on a field and the man who had crippled him turning away.

Simon dropped the car off at the rental agency in Long Island City and took the subway to Roosevelt Island, that sliver of land tossed carelessly into the East River between Manhattan and Queens.

He lived on the cheaper side of his apartment complex, facing east, toward the southern end of Astoria, rather than west onto a foreshortened slab of Midtown. His view from the twelfth floor looked straight across a narrow band of river onto the Astoria power station, its four candy-striped smokestacks rising higher than Simon's own building, higher than any building on the island.

In the apartment, he went to his computer to search for a clip of the play on the internet. Plummer had been paralyzed from the neck down; he'd nearly died. Simon remembered learning about this in the sports pages the following day and finding his own confused adolescent feelings to be incommensurate with the reality of what had occurred. He knew sadness was the appropriate emotional response, but he'd found it difficult to think of Plummer as an individual existing off the field, as a person rather than a player; before the injury, he hadn't been notable enough for anybody to interview, and when Simon tried to think of his face, all he saw was the shadowing helmet and face mask. Years later they'd trot Plummer out, in his wheelchair, to various functions—hall of fame inductions, stadium dedications—but the trickle of appearances slowed and then stopped, and Alvin Plummer again faded out of the public imagination until he died, just a few months ago, of some kind of lung infection, a delayed complication of his paralysis.

And now, in one of the NFL's occasional paroxysms of brand management, the hit seemed to have been wiped from the internet. Simon clicked from one YouTube clip to the next, sifting through dozens of brain-rattling hits from pro, college, and high school games. He wanted to see how his memory of the injury matched its visual record, but he couldn't find Crewes and Plummer. He stopped instead on some of the high school clips. They had a snuff-film feel to them: ripped from shaky handheld footage, climaxing with a laid-out body, coaches kneeling over the injured player while the other team's kids—fifteen- and sixteen-year-olds—jumped around and slapped each other on the helmet.

In the comments section people wrote things like "That dude got raped!!!" and "OWNED." Simon watched a few of these, the collisions replayed in lascivious slow motion. It was difficult to look away, but finally, overwhelmed by a greasy sense of complicity, he forced himself to close the window.

On the following humid and colorless morning, he waited down the block from the Health Solutions office, at the corner of Sixty-Second and Second, chain-smoking Parliaments until a black Lexus with tinted windows pulled up exactly on time and emitted three short blasts of its horn. Inside, Crewes wore a black cardigan and a pair of circular, purple-tinted sunglasses that gave him the appearance of a dandyish, late-career jazzman. He acknowledged Simon with a nod before he pulled away from the curb, cutting east and accelerating across the Fifty-Ninth Street Bridge, the Roosevelt Island tram dangling in the murk outside the window like some giant tree-borne fruit. They swooped down onto Queens Boulevard and exchanged one eastbound highway for another until, forty-five minutes later, Crewes exited the Southern State for local roads. Soon they were in Leonard Pellegrini's town, a collection of single-family clapboard homes, strip malls, and auto dealerships wedged between its wealthier bayside neighbor and the Sunrise Highway.

Crewes pulled onto the weedy yard of a small yellow house. He got out of the car without comment, and Simon followed him across the yard and up the porch steps. Midday was shadowless, without contrast; no visible sun, just a high, white brightness. Crewes opened the screen and rapped on the front door, which was yanked open quickly enough to suggest their arrival had been watched.

"Yeah?" A sunburned nose surfaced out of a sea of freckles. The girl was sixteen or seventeen, streaky blond hair pulled back into a tight bun.

"Lenny here?"

She looked at Crewes, then Simon, then behind them. "Why are you parked on the lawn?"

"It's where Lenny tells me to park. So I don't block the garage."

"Bullshit," she said, then blushed.

"Look, sweetheart," Crewes said, "why don't you tell him I'm here. Howard. He's expecting me."

She seemed about to tell them off, then reconsidered. "Wait," she commanded, before disappearing into the darkened recesses of the house, letting the door bang shut in their faces.

"Who's that?"

Crewes shrugged. "Who knows? Lenny's lived around here his whole life. A lot of people still want to help him."

The door opened again, and the girl, looking pissed off, said, "He's in the kitchen." She marched by them and picked up off the grass a bicycle Crewes had nearly run over, wheeling it onto the sidewalk before pedaling around the corner and out of sight.

"Let me start the talking." Crewes took off his sunglasses. "You take over whenever you think it's best."

Simon nodded. He didn't like sharing control of the situation like this, but he wanted to observe Crewes and Lenny, to better understand the dynamic of their relationship, before he made his pitch and asked his questions.

The inside of the house was dim, as Crewes's had been, but any similarities ended there. Simon's general impression was of mildew and unleveled floors. Leonard Pellegrini sat at a Formica table in the kitchen, swirling a glass of what appeared to be Coca-Cola on ice. He glanced at Simon, then continued to inspect his drink. "Nancy said there were two of you."

"You know who he is," Crewes said.

"The organ grinder."

"Don't be an asshole, Lenny."

Simon fixed a neutral smile onto his face. So: it appeared Leonard Pellegrini hadn't agreed to any of this yet. It would've been helpful if Crewes had let Simon in on this little fact. The man downed half his drink, the glass a toy in his hand. He was enormous, six foot five or six and wide as a car, and yet his bulk seemed inflatable, as though he'd been drained of all substance.

"Have a seat," he said. He reached out and opened the refrigerator without getting up, grabbing a can of Coke and refilling his glass. "Soda?"

"You got Jack in yours," Crewes said. "I can smell it from here."

"Not true." Lenny assembled his features into a hurt expression. "I really resent that, Howard." He winked at Simon as though they were schoolmates goofing off in class. His hair fell across his face, and he brushed at it distractedly.

"Let's have that soda."

Lenny reached into the refrigerator, pulled out another can. Then he reached under his chair and came up with a fifth of Jim Beam. "Told you it wasn't Jack."

"I came here to save your ass," Crewes said, "and you want to fuck around."

Lenny just smiled into his drink. In the fluorescent light of the kitchen his skin was waxy and sallow; acne scars flecked his cheeks and forehead. His legs emerged from his mesh shorts like a pair of weather-ravaged marble columns, a pink scar running down the middle of each knee.

"They bother you much?" Simon asked. Crewes shot him a quick glance. "The new knees."

Lenny ran his fingers across one of the scars as though he'd just noticed it. "Not that new anymore. Howard, buddy, what'd I say about all this, huh? What'd I tell you?"

"What you said wasn't worth hearing. You know what your problem is? You have no sense of yourself anymore. You were a professional football player, Lenny. That's something just about nobody gets to be. You should respect that. But instead you sit in this kitchen five miles from where you were born and drink yourself to death like you don't have a choice." Simon got the impression that this speech was as much for his benefit as Lenny's. "It's like the good part of your life never happened," Crewes continued, "and you just woke up eight years later, fatter and with two titanium knees."

"And arthritis," Lenny said.

"And arthritis."

"And the headaches."

"We all get the headaches."

"Not like I do."

"Maybe not."

"Did Cheryl find him?"

"I did. But it's nice you remember you still have a wife. Do I need to remind you about your kids too?"

Lenny suddenly turned to Simon. "So who would it be? Some sad fuck from Mexico?"

Simon suppressed a flinch. Lenny's attention was flavored with hostility and bitterness, his entire personality expressed as a challenge. "I can guarantee the donor will be American."

"Oh, good. The homegrown poor."

"Whoever he is," Crewes said, "he'll be a lot less poor afterward."

"That doesn't mean I have to feel good about it."

"The donors," Simon said, trying to gain control of the conversation, "they come looking for us. They know what they're getting into. We tell them exactly what to expect. Maybe you've read stories about what happens in other countries. Careless doctors. No follow-up care. Shady brokers." He allowed himself a small smile, sinking into the familiar patter—all the easier because he believed it to be more or less true—and feeling it temporarily muffle his anxiety. "That's not what we're talking about here. Our transplants take place at a top New York City hospital, with top surgeons. It's as safe as this surgery can be. Which, by the way, is very safe."

"You're not mentioning the fact that it's illegal."

"But I don't think it should be. Neither do all the people we've helped who'd still be waiting for a legal transplant when they're dead."

Lenny shrugged, unmoved. "Maybe that's how things were meant to go for those people." He grimaced as he stood up, his hand straying to a stomach that Simon now noticed was swollen and bloated looking. He limped out to the back porch, carrying the bottle of Beam with him. Crewes motioned for Simon to stay put before he followed Lenny outside.

Simon looked around the kitchen, which was small and neat, though he couldn't imagine Lenny was the person who cleaned it. Stuck to the refrigerator was a note that read, in loopy, optimistic handwriting, "Every Tues 1 PM: session w/ Jen. Every 2nd wknd: Greg and Dani. Sunday AM: CHURCH." He sat at the table, fiddling with Crewes's can of soda. He didn't like how he was being forced to persuade Lenny of the moral viability of Health Solutions' entire business model. This meeting was supposed to be about his evaluation of Lenny as a recipient, not a referendum on the ethics of how he'd spent the last eight months of his life; he was ambivalent enough about that already without a gravely ill potential client piling on. He could see the two of them through the window, leaning against the porch railing. Crewes pointed back at the house—at Simon maybe—but Lenny wouldn't look.

Crewes came back inside a few minutes later.

"He'll come around," he said, walking through the kitchen. "You did all right."

CABRERA Medical Center had always been the second of Roosevelt Island's two hospitals: second built, second choice, second rate. Silver River Memorial, at the northern tip of the island, was a solid, geriatrics-centric public hospital that knew what it was and didn't try to be anything else. Cabrera, down on the island's south side, past the Fifty-Ninth Street Bridge and the pustular tennis bubble, had been conceived in the 1970s as an oncology center to challenge Sloan Kettering, yet it had somehow ended up, thirty years later, as a repository for the overflow of gunshot and car-crash victims from Long Island City, Astoria, and Greenpoint. The buildings were shabby; the manner of care chaotic. In 2005 the facilities were purchased by a national hospital chain whose first order of business was the construction of a new transplant wing. Before it could become the money maker the chain was betting on, the first thing this new wing needed was surgeons; these it now had. The second was patients (or, perhaps more accurately, "clients"); these the hospital's administrators were still working on, which put the unit under enough pressure to churn out transplants that its surgeons weren't inclined to look too closely at whatever donors their coordinators fed to them.

Not long after Simon had learned all of this from DaSilva, he got to see the transplant wing for himself. On his first day after moving into an apartment building near Silver River Memorial, he walked the perimeter of the island. It wasn't much of a walk: the island was only two miles long and less than a quarter mile wide. After crossing beneath the bridge and its deep pool of shadow, he was presented with his first view of Cabrera: a long, squat central building streaked with soot and bisected by three smaller wings. (Later, looking down on the hospital from the tram, he'd thought it resembled a giant stitch sewn into the land.) He kept walking south along the riverside path, past a group of young men in wheelchairs—all smoking cigarettes and staring at the river, bundled under blankets, not speaking—past a cluster of willow trees, a parking lot, and then there it was, the new wing: a weird, asymmetrical structure, like an oval with a dent in one side, constructed out of turquoise glass and steel. According to DaSilva, the building had been designed in the shape of a kidney, although this seemed too ridiculous to be true and was likely just Peter fucking with him. It was as though a small chunk of one of the new condos springing up like weeds in Williamsburg had somehow ended up here, flicked aside like a bitten nail. A glass-sided sky-walk ran over the parking lot, connecting the new wing to the old hospital. A group of nurses burst out of the main building and headed toward the riverside path, breath steaming and hands flashing as they produced cigarettes, lighters, gum, candy bars. Simon stood and watched as the light drained from the sky, the new wing glowing, doctors rushing back and forth across the skywalk, the wheelchair-bound patients quiet and shadowed under the willows by the river's edge.

Eight months later, and Simon had still not set foot inside Cabrera. He did his work in his apartment or at the Health Solutions office, a small room in an anonymous building in the East Sixties, off Second Avenue. The building was filled with small-scale independent businesses—dentists, physical therapists, tax accountants, the kind of operations that didn't require more than a room or two. There was no company name on the office's door, only the suite number. It was more important that their room appear to be a functioning office than actually be one, and so the space exhibited a sense of the generic, like an IKEA display: a blond-wood desk, a bookcase lined with medical reference texts, a Barcelona Couch, desktop PC, printer, fax machine, ergonomic chair.

Eight months, and he'd already put together a dozen deals; all kidneys and all medically and financially successful. This case with Lenny was his first liver, and livers, DaSilva told him, were where the real money was. It was the more expensive surgery, the more valuable organ. (Also the more risky surgery and grueling recovery, for both donor and recipient.) Liver transplantation was the field in which Cabrera Medical Center had decided to make its name and its fortune, and so it was the field on which Health Solutions would now focus. In addition, the few other domestic brokers DaSilva was aware of traded exclusively in kidneys, which made livers, he said, the definition of an opportunity.

So far Health Solutions had not been, for Simon, a particularly difficult job, at least not operationally. (Morally was perhaps another question.) The donors were always enmeshed in some pedestrian sort of financial trouble, and what concerned them were the hard figures: the payout, the time away from work, the insurance ramifications. *Is the surgery safe?* they'd sometimes ask, and Simon would tell them yes, it is. They'd nod, as though they hadn't researched this themselves before they found the courage to send an e-mail to the contact address listed on the slickly designed and factually scant Health Solutions website. That their sale might buy someone ten or twenty more years of life was understood as a kind of bonus, a renewable interest on their payout, the kind of thing they could turn to for some small measure of consolation when the new money ran out, which it nearly always did, DaSilva admitted, and often sooner than they expected.

Simon had found the buyers trickier. Some of them wanted to know everything about their donors; they wanted to be told exactly how their money would transform these people's lives. Others wanted to know nothing and seemed to prefer to think of the purchased kidney as the miraculous product of a lab.

When he first took the job, Simon wondered how he would possibly locate donors. Recipients he understood. These people talked to each other; there were message boards, forums, as well as old-fashioned word of mouth. Theirs was a community that traded in the currency of hope. Besides, Peter DaSilva had access, through his coordinating job at Cabrera, to two of the relevant waiting lists: the United Network for Organ Sharing's and Cabrera's own. He knew who needed a liver or a kidney, who wasn't going to get one anytime soon, and who could afford to pay a lot of money not to wait any longer. When someone fulfilled all three criteria, he might offhandedly direct the candidate to one of a few online message boards populated by the transplant community, where, under pseudonymous handles, Simon posted testimonials describing how a friend or a spouse or an uncle had found the answer to his transplant troubles by contacting the good folks at Health Solutions. That DaSilva himself was involved with this company—was, in fact, its proprietor—never occurred to the candidates, which was, of course, exactly how he wanted things.

Donors though? It wasn't as if Simon could just walk around Times Square, waving a wad of cash. This wasn't Chennai or Manila in the nineties, where whole neighborhoods of young men, he'd heard, would suddenly exhibit the exact same scar in the exact same location on their torsos. During his first meeting, before DaSilva had finished explaining how Health Solutions worked, Simon imagined he'd have to fly to Brazil, Turkey, Syria, Moldova, offering a few thousand dollars and a trip to New York City to whomever was willing to part with a kidney. He'd imagined skulking around the worst neighborhoods of New York like a drug dealer or a pimp, trawling for the desperate, the easy marks. He didn't know if he could bring himself to do it. The exploitation was too frank, the moral ambiguity of utilitarianism shading into the self-evident amorality of raw, unfettered capitalism.

But it turned out none of this was necessary, not anymore. Not in 2008. It turned out that plenty of people in what one might think of as the middle class—or people who were once in that class or who wanted to appear to be in that class—were open to the idea. Why not sell something that cost you nothing to own in the first place? It was a kind of entrepreneurship of the body, a utilization of previously untapped resources. These weren't people in need of food or shelter. These were people in need of a car, college tuition, debt relief. Simon's very first client wanted LASIK and a nose job; why not, she reasoned, let one surgery pay for two more? As the spring of 2008 slipped into summer, and now turned to fall, the list of people—American citizens, no less—who might be interested in the company's services grew longer and longer, and Simon's e-mail inbox began to brim with the kind of inquiries he'd feared he would have to sift through the most wretched corners of the third world to find. As the jobs accumulated, Simon's ethical queasiness over his role in these transactions was calmed by his donor-clients' embrace of a wonderfully mutable philosophy of self-empowerment, a worldview that made easy room for the conversion of flesh to cash, for the literal capitalization of the self. These people knew the score, knew what they were getting into, at least as much as they could without having gone through it already. Who was he to stand priggishly in judgment of them or of himself?

Also, he was making badly needed money—and fast—which didn't hurt.

IMMEDIATELY after visiting Lenny, Simon told DaSilva about Howard Crewes's role as sponsor and planner. He also told DaSilva that Lenny was still drinking. But Peter didn't think this would be a problem: "Can this Crewes guy really pay?"

"He's got the money, yeah."

"All right." DaSilva's voice came through the pay phone clear and strong, Bronx street traffic fulminating somewhere behind him. "Then unless Leonard Pellegrini dies before I can get him into the OR, we'll make it happen."

"Peter," Simon said. This attitude seemed unusually aggressive for DaSilva, who for the last eight months had preached nothing but risk management, turning aside dozens of candidates, both donors and recipients, because of one irregularity or another. Maybe the success of the last run of deals had emboldened him, or maybe landing a lucrative liver job was incentive enough to bend his own rules. "The guy's an alcoholic. There's no hiding it. Forget six months. It probably hasn't even been six hours since his last drink."

"What did I say? I'll get him in there. Those regulations are too conservative anyway, you know they're just there to protect the hospital's ass. Just make sure he tells Klein he's been clean four or five months and I'll do the rest."

"What about the piss test?"

"I said I'll fix it. Worry about your own job."

And so a week after his excursion to Long Island, Simon sat in the office, scrolling through a batch of applicant e-mails. Crewes had called Simon the day before to inform him that Lenny was going forward with the transplant. He was doing it, Crewes had said somewhat melodramatically, for his children's sake, not his own. Crewes and Cheryl, Lenny's estranged wife, had returned to Lenny's house the day after Simon's visit, and they'd sat with him in the kitchen, turning the screws and refusing to leave until he deigned to allow them to help save his life. It was now the morning of Lenny's physical exam at Cabrera; Lenny and Crewes were due at the office any minute. Lenny was scheduled to undergo a battery of laboratory tests—liver function, electrolyte levels, blood typing, coagulation—as well as radiographic studies of his liver and an EKG. The point was to determine his general fitness for surgery, as well as what sort of characteristics Simon would need to look for in his donor. Simon hoped DaSilva hadn't exaggerated his ability to massage these test results, or at least to place them into some kind of more favorable context (which most likely meant emphasizing Lenny's financial solvency by proxy), since Simon was fairly sure the machines would paint an internal picture of widespread alcoholic waste and ruin.

The two men buzzed from street level. Simon let them into the building and waited in the hallway. They exited the elevator, Lenny stuffed into a pinstriped suit like a parody of Mob muscle, Crewes wearing black slacks and a fitted purple sweater, and it was as though the hallway had suddenly shrunk, squeezing in around them. They carried a presence beyond their height and weight, a *largeness* that must have been a residue from their playing days. It wasn't arrogance or swagger. It was almost the opposite: a carefulness as they made their way down the hall, a delicacy of motion, as though they were afraid of damaging anything with which they might come into contact. As Simon shook Crewes's hand, he thought of Alvin Plummer's body, lying broken on the turf, and was immediately ashamed of the thought.

He ushered them into the office and sat them on the two chairs facing his desk. He explained the tests, and then asked if the hospital had been in touch regarding the day's schedule. Lenny said that the transplant coordinator, "a guy named DaSilva," had called a few days earlier to introduce himself. "He said he'd meet me in the lobby and escort me through the procedures."

Simon nodded. "You'll be in good hands." He wrote the name and address of a diner on a slip of paper and slid it across the desk. "When everything's finished, Howard and I will meet you here for lunch. It's just a few blocks from the hospital."

Lenny looked at him very seriously throughout this conversation. Beads of sweat puckered on his upper lip; he slipped a gold wedding band on and off his finger. Under the suit jacket, his white shirt was stippled with moisture. Was he nervous? Maybe, but Simon didn't think that was it, or at least not all of it. Then he realized Lenny probably hadn't taken a drink yet that day, or maybe for the last few days, as though he could trick the hospital's instruments into believing his body to be clean and blameless. *Well, good,* Simon thought. *Better to start late than never.* At least he'd have a week of practice at being sober before the screening interview.

They left Crewes's Lexus parked on the street and rode the tram across the river. The tram car lifted out of the station and swung above the traffic on First Avenue, climbing alongside the bridge's vaulted underbelly. As they rose above York, they drew even with the higher floors of an apartment building; Simon caught a glimpse of a cat sunning itself in a window, a curtain tangled in the needles of a cactus. They crested the midsection of the bridge, and he pointed out the curve of the United Nations Headquarters a dozen blocks downtown, the ruined smallpox hospital at the southern tip of the island. Back on the ground, he led them toward Cabrera, stopping a few hundred feet from the entrance. Clusters of nurses and staff sat on the grass outside the hospital, eating their lunches in the sun, smoking, laughing, their scrubs pink, baby blue, lime green—pieces of candy scattered across the lawn. Simon shook Lenny's damp hand, told him he'd be fine. Lenny nodded, saying nothing; then he walked away, stolid and deliberate.

Now Simon turned the monitor back around to face him, the last of DaSilva's cigarette smoke drifting across the office. He stared at Maria Campos's fake smile and wondered what particular variety of financial misfortune could have pushed her to this decision. She was so young; usually it was the middle aged, the overextended and overleveraged, whose cagey, probing e-mails piled up in his inbox. He'd have to be careful not to reveal his curiosity. He didn't want to risk scaring her off, and, besides, DaSilva paid him not to pursue these things, to leave the inessential questions about his clients' lives unasked.

He dialed her number. Just as he was sure it was about to go to voice mail, she picked up: "Yeah?"

"Ms. Campos?"

"What?"

"It's Simon Worth, an associate at Health Solutions." For a few long seconds, he listened to her breathing, the faint murmur of a television in the background. "We've been e-mailing."

"Simon," she said. "Right." Her voice was raspy, as though she'd just woken up.

"I'm calling to tell you that our initial evaluation of your candidacy is positive."

"That sounds like a good thing."

"It is. We'd like to do some testing to assess your compatibility with our client. I have the number of a lab you can visit for some additional blood work and liver imaging. Is that something you want to do?"

"Livers are worth more," she said, "aren't they?"

"I'm sorry?"

"I looked it up." Her voice straightened, sloughing off its sleepiness. "Liver transplants, they cost more than kidneys. So a piece of liver—a piece of *my* liver—it's gonna be worth more than a kidney, right?"

"In theory, yes."

"In theory? Either it is or it isn't." She paused. "I'm sorry. I just need to know if this is worth it to me before we go any further."

"If you qualify—and I can't make any promises yet—but if you qualify, we can offer you $150,000." Silence. "Plus we'll pay for your travel, which includes two weeks in a Manhattan hotel."

"One fifty." Her voice was neutral, but Simon thought he heard a tremor of the effort required to keep it that way.

"Yes. You would receive $5,000 in good faith when you arrive in New York. The rest follows the operation."

"I'm not trying to be rude, but how can I be sure this isn't a scam?"

"You can't. But what would we get out of flying you across the country and putting you up on our dime?"

"Not that. I mean how do I know you'll pay me the rest after the operation?"

"I suppose you can't know. But think of it this way: we don't want anybody angry with us. The way we arrange things, everybody wins. The hospital. The recipient. You, the donor. Everybody's happy."

"I've never been to New York."

"You'd have $5,000 and two weeks to see how you like it."

"Yeah," Maria said. "So what's the number of that lab?"

Simon gave it to her.

"They're ready for me?" He could sense her eagerness and at the same time her attempt to suppress it, as though she could take or leave what he was offering. "When can I call?"

"Today, if you want."

"Today is all right," she said. "Today is good."

## TWO

THE next evening Simon waited in the fluorescent bowels of Penn Station, under the LIRR departures board. He was on his way to Leonard Pellegrini's house, where they would begin preparations for the Cabrera psychosocial interview. Simon had suggested meeting in his office, but Lenny said he didn't like taking a train into the city—he wasn't driving these days—unless he had absolutely no choice. Looking around Penn Station, Simon couldn't blame him. The place—low ceilings, crappy food, horror-show lighting—would depress anyone. At 6:15 p.m. the station was crowded beyond even what he'd expected. Each time a track number appeared on the board, a portion of the waiting mass of commuters detached itself and stampeded toward the track entrance, a riot of elbows and briefcases and shopping bags. When his train's number came up, he waited until the rush had cleared and was rewarded with a standing-room spot next to the lavatory, its stale, uric smell wafting through the train compartment each time somebody wrestled open the sliding door.

After an hour, he stepped out of the train and into the failing dusk. Headlights sliced though the parking lot's busy shadows. His taxi driver nodded at the address and sped over the Sunrise Highway and past a high school, the football field's goalposts glowing white against the sky. At Lenny's house all of the lights were out. Simon opened the screen and knocked on the door. He waited, then knocked again. The door was locked. He dialed Lenny's number on his cell phone, and he heard the ringing in his ear and its echo inside the house. He stepped back onto the porch and looked up at the second-floor windows. The curtains were pulled tight; if Lenny was in there, he didn't want anybody to know it. Simon sat down on the porch steps. Ten minutes passed, then fifteen. *Screw this guy,* Simon thought. *Why should I help him when he can't even be bothered to help himself?* As he was dialing a taxi to take him back to the train station, a black Lexus swung around the corner and pulled to a stop in front of the house. The driver's-side window rolled down; Crewes's head popped out.

"I drove as fast as I could," he said. "Lenny just remembered about you. Shit, man, you gotta tell me about this stuff. You can't expect him to remember."

"Where is he?"

"Get in. I'll take you."

They quickly left Lenny's town behind, heading north on the Cross Island Expressway. Crewes drove fast, weaving in and out of traffic, Al Green pleading on the stereo. Fifteen minutes later they exited the highway for a new town. Here, large houses were set back from the road; hedges shielded the properties from each other. Crewes drove up a gravel driveway and parked behind six or seven other cars. The house was large, not as big as Crewes's, but older, more solidly built. A brick chimney rose out of a shingled roof; lights blazed in every window.

Simon looked at Crewes. "Where are we?"

"Don MacLeod's house." Simon knew the name; MacLeod had played fullback for the Giants during the early nineties, one of those players reliably cited by announcers for the integrity of their "fundamentals." "Once a month," Crewes said, "some guys, some retired players with the same problems as Lenny, they come over with their wives. Etta MacLeod hired a therapist to lead some discussions. Sessions, I guess you call them."

"The same problems? You mean drinking?"

"Can be. But more the headaches. The moods. The screwed-up marriages. Get your bell rung enough times while you're playing, and these things seem to go together."

"So what are you doing here?"

"You think he would come if I didn't show up at his door and drive him? He and Cheryl went once, when they were still living together. He hated it. Said he was being condescended to. Said it was humiliating. So they never went again. But I knew if I could get him here, she'd come too. That's her car right there." He pointed at a maroon Honda. "I drive him, hang out in the car during the meeting. When the session's over, I'll come in, have some coffee, and talk to Don. Reminisce about the time I popped his helmet off in a preseason game."

"You're not allowed inside during the meeting?"

"Of course I'm allowed. But I don't come here for myself. It wouldn't be right to sit there and watch, like it's some kind of show." Crewes checked his watch. "We'd just arrived when he remembered he was supposed to be meeting with you. This will be over in fifteen minutes. If he doesn't want to do it now, you can reschedule with him in person. He'll remember it better that way."

They stared at the house in silence for a few minutes, like cops stuck on some desultory stakeout. Simon again felt as though he'd lost control of the situation, this job still refusing to fall in line with the choreographed procedures of his first dozen.

Crewes said, "I'm guessing you've never come across anybody so resistant to having their life saved, huh? But you have to understand what it is for somebody like him to accept help. Asking for help can make you feel like you're too weak to do it yourself, right?"

"I guess sometimes it can."

"Well, it can for Lenny. And for a lot of us. I didn't even know what was happening to him until one of the other guys organized a dinner, a team reunion. This was last year. Lenny and I were close when we played together, and we stayed that way for a while after he retired. But over the last few years he drifted away from me. Turned out he drifted away from everybody. I thought he might be at the dinner anyway. When he didn't show, I wanted to talk to him, but I couldn't get him on the phone. I kept getting his wife instead."

Simon sensed that Crewes had been waiting to tell somebody, anybody, this story. It was something Simon had often run into over the last eight months, this compulsion on the part of his clients to reveal their circumstances and motivations and exigencies, to present their narratives. Part of it was that Simon already knew what was most difficult to tell anybody else—that they were willing to purchase another person's organ to save themselves—and part of it was that they seemed to seek a generalized absolution it cost him very little to grant. Still, even though it was sometimes difficult not to care, he tried his best to remain uninvolved, to preserve, like Cabrera's surgeons, a layer of professional distance, all the while hoping he never appeared as callous and mercenary as he sometimes felt himself to be. He was not a judge, but not a friend either; he was a facilitator, a middleman, grease for the wheel, oil for the cog. He would listen to his clients if they wanted him to, even offer an opinion if asked, but his involvement in their lives usually ended the moment the recipient checked out of the hospital and the donor received his cash. Through all of this, he was discovering the moral absolution that strict professionalism offered to its most zealous adherents, a condition, he'd come to realize, second only to freely circulating cash in the essential qualities of a functional modern capitalism. That such detachment—especially justified as it was—happened to suit his own natural personality did not escape his notice either.

"His wife?"

"Yeah. Cheryl was still living with him at the time. She kept feeding me all kinds of bullshit. 'He's fishing.' 'He's fixing the car.' 'He's napping.' 'So why can't he call me back, Cheryl?' Finally she slips a bit and says he's sick. She wouldn't say how. So I drove out there to see for myself. The drinking was obvious. He didn't try to hide it. Painkillers too. He didn't even seem surprised that I showed up. It's funny, because all he needed to do was get on the phone once and lie to me for a few minutes and I probably wouldn't have thought about it twice. But he didn't."

"She left him?"

"I wouldn't say she left *him*. But she left, as in she moved out. She wouldn't live with him anymore, mostly because of the drinking. Once they knew his liver was failing and he'd made it clear he wasn't going to change a damn thing about his behavior, she refused to sit there and watch him slowly kill himself. And I guess there were other things too."

"What other things?"

"These headaches, man. He'd hole up in his room for days. Pull the shades, lock the door. Wouldn't talk to anybody, wouldn't eat anything. He said it was like his head was being crushed in a vise. Like his brain was too big for his skull. I got the idea that he lashed out at Cheryl during these things if she tried to help him."

"The kids live with her."

"Yeah. Gregory and Daniela. Six and three. Young. Like I told you before, I think they're the only reason he agreed to this. Anyway, after Cheryl moved out, I started driving up there more often. I thought it might help. But it was hard to tell if he wanted me there or not. He didn't seem to care one way or another."

The front door of Don MacLeod's house opened, and a rectangle of light spilled out onto the steps. A large silhouette paused in the doorway, a shorter, slimmer silhouette standing by its side for a moment before disappearing back inside the house. The larger silhouette stepped forward onto the lawn, and Simon saw it was Lenny, his shoulders hunched inside a jean jacket.

He limped over to the car as Simon and Crewes got out. "Sorry," he said, unconvincingly. "I got the dates confused."

"It happens," Simon said.

Crewes put a hand on Simon's shoulder. "Why don't you wait out here for a minute. We won't be long."

Crewes and Lenny walked up the stone path and through the open doorway. Simon's eyes followed them through the window as they moved across the living room and paused to talk to a wiry blond who appeared to be in her late thirties. She looked from Crewes to Lenny, and then, frowning, out the window to where Simon stood by the parked cars. He knew she couldn't see him, looking out into darkness from a bright room, but still he felt exposed. It was outrageous that he'd been forced by Lenny's forgetfulness into such a semipublic appearance. The fewer people in Lenny's life who saw his face, the better; an ideal number, in fact, would be zero. The three of them turned and disappeared through a doorway in the back of the room. Simon could see a sliver of kitchen, the flicker of bodies moving across the doorway. It was the wives, of course, who had made all of this happen, who had pulled these men out of their private miseries, who had forced them to see that their battered bodies and brains were not something to be ashamed of or denied but instead something that needed to be shared with others who suffered as they did.

A few minutes passed, and then Lenny and the blond woman reappeared in the living room. They exited the house and headed toward Simon, the woman leading with spiky, irritated steps. She reached him first and stuck out her hand. "You must be Simon," she said. "I'm Cheryl Pellegrini."

"Simon Worth." Her fingers were cold, her skin dry; her bangs gripped her forehead like a claw.

She looked him frankly in the face. "I thought you'd be older."

"Sorry to disappoint you." He winced internally; he didn't mean to sound peevish.

"If you can do what Howard says you can do, I don't care if you're twelve." She glanced back at the house. Lenny stood a few feet behind her, staring off into the hedges. "Howard's going to stay for a while and visit with Don. I'll drive you both back to the house, and you can talk with Lenny about whatever it is you need to talk about."

Simon nodded. He hated how thoroughly his original plans had been derailed, but what could he do about it now? Demand to drive Cheryl's car himself? He sat in the backseat of the Honda, as though he were their child, while Cheryl accelerated, yanking the gearshift like she was trying to snap it in half. She asked Lenny what he'd thought of that evening's session.

"It was fine," he said tonelessly.

She wrenched the car into third and pointed out that he'd been there, after all, and therefore maybe he'd formed some more substantive opinion.

"Okay," he said. "I could live without Don's name-dropping. Who cares that he still talks to all these guys? We were all in the league. We were all there. It's like he's still trying to kiss his coach's ass fifteen years later, and the guy's not even in the room."

Cheryl nodded rapidly. "That's what you took away from the meeting. That's what you'd like to discuss."

"I don't want to discuss anything. You asked me the question."

"You don't try," she hissed, swinging the Honda out into the passing lane. "You don't even fucking try." She flicked her eyes at the rearview mirror. "Simon's thinking he didn't sign up for this. Well, Simon, I'll tell you what, you're gonna earn your commission with us."

Cheryl jerked to a stop in front of the house, speeding off as soon as Simon stepped away from the car. Lenny unlocked the front door and walked straight to the kitchen. They sat at the table. Lenny poured himself a glass of Jim Beam and offered the bottle to Simon, who declined.

"I hope you enjoyed that little performance," Lenny said.

Simon made a noncommittal noise.

"Cheryl's problem with me," Lenny continued, as though answering a question Simon hadn't asked, "is that I'm an ungrateful person. I don't appreciate her. I don't appreciate our kids. Now I don't appreciate Howard and what he's doing for me. The thing she doesn't understand about Howard is that he wants this to work more than I do. It ain't just coming out of the goodness of his heart."

"No?" Simon said, trying to seem as neutral as possible without causing offense.

"The thing with Alvin Plummer happened during my last season with the Jets, when they were draining my knee every damn week. We were playing in Philly. As soon as it happened, we all knew it was bad. You can't see that hit and not know. The man's neck . . . I was on the sideline fifty yards away, and I knew something was seriously fucked up. They took Plummer to the hospital by UPenn. Howard went up there late that night. He didn't tell anybody about this until much later. What happened was the family wouldn't let him in. Plummer's mother stood there in the lobby, looked him in the eye, and told him to get the hell out. He never talked to Plummer, not then, not ever."

Lenny sipped at his drink and waited. When Simon kept quiet, he continued, more heatedly now: "Don't you get it? Plummer finally croaks, so now Howard's flailing around, looking for something—*somebody*—he can fix. It's just money. He's got enough of that. Sure, I'm grateful," Lenny said, "sure. But that doesn't mean I don't think paying somebody for a piece of their liver isn't fucked up. It doesn't mean I don't see why Howard's really doing this. What Cheryl wants is for me to bow down and kiss Howard's ring. And that's not something I'm gonna do." He knocked back the whiskey and poured himself another one. "But, okay. Why should you give a shit. Let's talk about what you came here for. You've found my donor."

"I might have," Simon said. "She seems like a good candidate so far."

"She?"

"Gender doesn't make a difference. I'd like to tell the hospital you're cousins. Second cousins."

"You're kidding."

"It's the easiest way. Look." Simon pulled a printout of Maria's photo from his jacket pocket and laid it flat on the table.

Lenny looked at the photo. "I guess I see it. So what's the problem?"

"What do you mean?"

"You said 'might have.'"

"She's smaller than a typical donor for someone your weight. But so far the imaging indicates that her liver is large enough to work."

"And what about this?" Lenny waved the empty whiskey glass in front of Simon's face. "I've been trying to cut back, but, you know, old habits die hard and all."

Simon clamped down on his irritation. "The less drinking you do over the next week, the better. But what's most important is that you tell Cabrera's social worker you gave it up months ago."

"That shouldn't be too hard. I've been lying to Cheryl about it for years."

Simon outlined the narrative. Lenny's father was Maria's mother's cousin. Maria and Lenny may have always lived across the country from each other, but they share memories of childhood reunions, barbecues in Syosset and Bay Shore. He gave her a tour of New York City when she visited after graduating from middle school; he arranged for tickets to his games whenever the Jets traveled to the West Coast.

Simon wrote key names and plot points on a legal pad and tested Lenny's retention. It was slow going. Lenny's memory was erratic; facts slipped out of their rightful places, unbalancing the story. Fifteen minutes in, Lenny started to fidget like a kid stuck in detention. Simon asked him again to characterize his relationship with Maria.

"Close," Lenny mumbled.

"Please," Simon said. "Can you try to elaborate?"

"This is stupid," Lenny said. "Don't sit here and drill me about shit that's not even real."

"I'm trying to help."

Lenny stood abruptly, upending his chair. "Screw your help. Howard's too."

Simon sat very still, the pad perched on his lap. "We can stop for the night."

"You condescending *shit*."

With the back of his hand, Lenny knocked his glass off the table. It clattered across the linoleum and into the wall, spinning on its side, like the needle of a busted fuel gauge, before coming to rest.

Simon placed the pad on the table next to Maria's photograph. "Would you like me to leave?"

Lenny rocked onto the balls of his feet, leaning across the table. Simon could see competing emotions rush across his face, see his mind spinning. The lid of his left eye fluttered; his breath smelled of whiskey and coffee. For a moment, Simon was sure he was going to be punched, that his jaw would be broken. Then, as suddenly as it had seized him, the tension left Lenny. He went limp, slumping against the wall.

"Do whatever you want," he said dully.

"I'll leave. That's enough for now." Simon ripped the top page off the pad and pushed it across the table. "The day after tomorrow?"

Lenny shrugged, his hair falling over his eyes. He didn't look up as Simon stood and backed slowly into the kitchen doorway. Simon waited there for a moment, and when Lenny still said nothing, he turned and crossed the living room to the screen door and the porch beyond, his pulse twitching in the hollow of his neck.

Two weeks later Simon waited for Maria Campos in one of JFK's shabby baggage claim areas. It was eight thirty in the morning; she was due any minute, off the last red-eye from LAX. As the waiting limo drivers checked their phones and sipped their scalding coffees, a new load of passengers slogged down the hallway from the arrival gates, and he saw her then, walking slightly apart from the main flow of passengers, dragging a small roller bag. Her long, dark hair was crazy with static electricity; a pair of large purple sunglasses covered half her face. She stopped near the baggage carousel and looked around. Simon moved to greet her, but then something held him back. She had no way of recognizing him, and he wondered how he would appear to her. A bland, starched white guy of average height and average build, hair a desiccated blond nearly the same tone as his skin; a face lacking specificity, his overall physical appearance an act of collaboration with whomever was doing the viewing.

She frowned, set down her rolling bag, checked her watch.

He wondered what would happen if he just left, if he slipped out of the terminal and never answered her calls or e-mails. She would eventually take a taxi to the hotel near Times Square and sit in her room and wait. She had no one else to call; he hadn't even told her where the operation was going to take place. Maybe she'd be furious about wasting her time; maybe she'd be relieved not to have been forced to go through with it. Maybe she'd take it as a sign and stop seeking the quick, radical fix to her money problems, whatever they were. Or maybe she'd just find another broker.

He let go of the fantasy and approached her. She saw him coming and offered a speculative, noncommittal smile, pushing her sunglasses up onto her forehead. Her eyes were slick black pebbles, dark enough to show no difference between pupil and iris, heavy purple half circles anchoring them into place above her cheekbones. Her fingers picked at the cuffs of her baggy sweatshirt, the nails unpainted, bitten low. Despite the smile, her body seemed coiled, ready to run.

He stopped a few feet in front of her, at what he hoped was an unthreatening distance.

"Maria Campos, right?"

"Who are you?"

"Simon Worth," he said. "From Health Solutions. I'm here to pick you up."

The black eyes stared at him, as though weighing the reality not just of this statement, but of the proposition of his entire existence. Then her smile softened, even as her fingers continued to worry the sweatshirt cuffs. "For a moment I was afraid this was a trap." Her voice was sandpapery, her cadences stoner slow. "Like, just kidding! You're under arrest!"

"No trap. Just a guy who should've taken a cab instead of the AirTrain." She stared at him blankly. "What I mean is sorry I'm late. Ready to go?"

They retrieved her checked luggage—a large, overstuffed duffel bag—from the carousel. Simon shouldered the bag out to a taxi, wondering why she'd bothered to pack so much.

As their cab crawled out of the JFK loop, he asked about her trip.

"Weird," she said. "It was my first time flying."

"Really?"

"My family wasn't the vacationing type." This with acid sarcasm.

"How was it?"

"Fine, I guess."

"It didn't bother you?" he said. "Being up in the sky like that for the first time?"

"I thought it might freak me out. But it didn't, not at all." She shrugged and looked out the window. When she spoke again, it was after enough of a pause that Simon was for a moment unsure what she was talking about. "It wasn't that big a deal."

Their cab accelerated out of Jamaica, past the Maple Grove Cemetery, its carpet of gravestones unfurling below the Van Wyck. He noticed her hand gripping the door handle, white knuckled and trembling. She let go, as though she'd felt his eyes. A short time later, the Manhattan skyline came into view through the front windshield, all the iconic profiles set into detailed relief against a crisp blue autumn sky. Maria leaned toward him, and he smelled something familiar, some sugary perfume girls used to wear at his high school. She stared at the skyline fiercely, as though she were trying to burn the sight into her memory. He'd often wondered if the never-ceasing flood of photographs and film appearances of New York's most telegenic landmarks had drained the reality of the place of its impact or surprise. Looking at Maria, at the way she was inhaling the skyline with her eyes, told him that this wasn't necessarily the case, that the brute presence of the city was still more than capable of impressing.

Times Square, however, was its usual catastrophe. The taxi fought through a scrum of tour buses and pedicabs and deposited them in front of the Royal Crown on Forty-Fifth Street, just west of Eighth Avenue. Inside, the maroon lobby was dim and smelled of dusty radiators. The Royal Crown was a relic, a musty vision of what a grand Midtown hotel was supposed to be. It was also, for some unexplained reason, where Peter DaSilva preferred to put up Health Solutions' clients. Maria's room was small, a queen bed taking up half the space, the TV hidden inside a cabinet. It was clean though, and quiet twenty-nine stories above the street, with a clear view running west across Forty-Fifth.

Simon set her bag down. "Is this okay for you?"

She stood at the window, looking down at the street. "Yeah. It's good."

"Here." He took a padded envelope from his messenger bag. "Your advance." He placed the envelope carefully onto the bed.

She turned away from the window and glanced at it.

"Five thousand in cash," he said. "Take a look."

She opened the envelope and looked inside. She stared down at the cash for a moment, then looked back up at Simon and nodded, expressionless.

"You must have a lot of questions about how this is all going to work," he said.

She shrugged. She looked suddenly exhausted, a blurry copy of the woman in the photograph.

"Did you sleep on the plane?"

"Not a minute."

"Get some rest," he said. "Tomorrow morning we'll go over everything."

He had a scrap of paper in his pocket with the address of Health Solutions' office written on it, but on an impulse he grabbed the notepad and pen on the bedside table and wrote the name and address of a café on the Upper East Side.

"We'll meet here for breakfast. Ten o'clock. Okay?"

"Okay."

"You can call me," he said. "If you need anything."

"Okay," she said again. She sat down on the edge of the bed and put her hand on the envelope.

THE next morning Simon sat waiting at a table by the window of the café, a sun-drenched place not far from his high school, St. Edmund's, which was the only reason he knew it existed. He'd arrived early and found the café still sitting smugly in its plum spot two blocks from the Metropolitan Museum. He'd peered through the window at the diners, neighborhood types and tourists visiting the museum. The former were mostly women and mostly bottle blond, all knobby wrists and severe clavicles, gold bracelets heavy as manacles. He'd never been inside before, only walked past, and so when he sat down and looked at the menu, he was not prepared for the appearance of an eighteen-dollar goat cheese omelet.

He couldn't afford this place, but the café's expensiveness was part of the point. It was the same reason he'd chosen this neighborhood, with its air of sobriety and permanence; he wanted Maria to feel confident in the people to whom she was leasing the use of her body. He had the strong impulse, stronger than with any of his prior donors, to set her at ease, to make her as comfortable as the situation allowed. Part of it was that she'd traveled to New York alone; the donors almost never did that. Another part of it, probably, was that she was young, very near his own age, which he supposed made it easier for him to identify with her and with what she was going through. The remainder of his motivation he couldn't quite account for yet, which bothered him perhaps less than it should have.

At quarter after ten, he spotted her hurrying across the street in a battered black leather jacket, half of her face hidden behind the same bulbous purple sunglasses. She rushed by the window without seeing him, then stopped inside the door, scanning the room. He waved, and she sat down opposite him, sweat glistening on her forehead.

"The subway," she said. "I messed up the transfer." She glanced around the restaurant. "This is where you do business?"

"I thought it would be more pleasant than my office."

"So you're making an exception for me?"

"Most donors don't show up alone," he said carefully. "They bring their mom, their husband, whoever. Since you're here by yourself, I thought it might be nice to make things a little less impersonal."

She frowned. "I don't want your pity."

"That's not how I meant it."

They sat in uncomfortable silence until the waiter stopped by and rescued them. Simon ordered coffee and a croissant while Maria flitted around the menu, finally settling on a cheddar and ham omelet with a side of sausage, white toast, and strawberry jam. Their orders in, Simon asked what she was planning to do that afternoon.

"Walk," she said. "I can't do that at home. If I want to go for a walk there, I have to drive somewhere else first."

"Where's home?"

"Los Angeles."

"Yeah, but where?"

"Torrance."

"What's it like there?"

"It's a place to live. I don't hate it. I don't love it either."

He reminded himself to be careful, not to ask too many questions. "I've never been to California."

"I've lived in every Los Angeles neighborhood you've never heard about," she said. "I say LA, what do you think of?"

"Hollywood. Beverly Hills."

"What else? The other side of the coin."

"I don't know. South Central? Watts. Compton."

"It depends on what movies you've been watching, right? What music you've been listening to. They don't make movies or songs about the neighborhoods I grew up in. Not because they're so bad, but because they're so boring. Shabby, but mostly homicide-free. Nobody wants to hear about that."

"Your family, they still live in the city?" *Stop it*, he told himself.

"My mother's dead. My father lives in some shithole in the Valley, rounding up illegal immigrants to mow people's lawns. Prune their topiaries. It's the best job he's ever had." Her tone was more ironic than hostile, as though her father were too absurd a subject to merit actual disdain. "I don't really talk to him. I guess you could say we're estranged."

Their breakfast arrived, and Simon told himself that he wasn't really interested in her background, that he was just doing his due diligence for Health Solutions. Maria demolished her omelet in less than two minutes. Outside on Madison Avenue, a Pomeranian lifted its leg and pissed on the wheel of a parked Mercedes. Simon sipped his cup of coffee, which cost five dollars and was excellent.

"How many people know you're here?" he asked.

"How many know I'm not in LA? Five or six. That includes my boss at the bar. He thinks I'm visiting my aunt in Bakersfield. How many know I'm in New York? Two. My son and my sister, who's looking after him while I'm gone. Not that my son has any idea what New York even is. How many know what I'm *doing* here? None."

"Your son." Simon tried not to sound surprised. She was so young, and the medical records she'd supplied hadn't mentioned anything about her having given birth, although it wasn't a certainty that they would.

"Yeah."

"How old is he?"

"He's three."

"And what's his name?"

"Gabriel." She paused. "You want to know why I'm doing this, right?"

"You don't have to tell me that."

"But that doesn't mean you don't want to know."

"What's important is that the team at the hospital thinks *they* know. It doesn't matter what I think."

"And you have a story for them?"

"Part of one, yes."

He told her about Lenny: first, the extent of his illness, and then the outlines of his—and her—fictional extended family.

"Second cousins? Couldn't they just look that up and see it's not true?"

"That's not as easy as you might think. But don't give them a reason to and they won't even try."

She picked at her toast, nodding. "Well, in case you want to know anyway, I have a job pouring drinks for cheapskate alcoholics and a son whose father wants nothing to do with him. It's not any more complicated than that."

He tried a joke: "You also have a dear cousin in need."

Her face split into a smile. "And I've been possessed by the spirit of giving." Her teeth were white and straight except for the top right incisor, which was crooked and marbled gray, like an old gravestone. She closed her mouth. He wanted to ask her to keep smiling, so he could see the tooth again. He liked how its irregularity reshaped the rest of her face, the flaw making the whole more appealing.

"This guy," she said. "Leonard."

"Lenny, yeah."

"Lenny. How long would he have left? Without me."

"A year. Maybe less. And it wouldn't be a good year."

She considered this for a moment, although he couldn't quite parse her reaction. "So what's next?"

"Tomorrow morning you'll go to the hospital to meet the transplant coordinator and surgical team, and they'll take another look at your liver. Thursday we'll prep together some more. Friday you'll meet Lenny. And then Saturday's your psychosocial exam."

"The screening interview."

"Yeah. That's when they make sure you're not getting paid, among other things. I'll tell you what to say. I'll show you the exact questions they're going to ask. You'll be fine."

"And if I pass?"

"*When* you pass, they'll schedule the surgery. It'll be no more than a few days later. They don't see the point in waiting."

She nodded. He could see her counting off the days in her head: less than two weeks until payday. "What about you, Simon?"

"What about me?"

"Health Solutions. It's not your company, is it? You're not the one running the show."

"Why not?"

"You're too young, for one thing."

"I've heard that before. Anything else?"

"It just doesn't seem like the kind of business you'd want to build for yourself."

This sounded like flattery. "That's a strange thing for someone in your position to say."

She shrugged. "So then tell me: how did you end up doing what you're doing?"

"We're not having this conversation."

"I'm not supposed to ask questions?"

"Donors ask all sorts of questions. Just not about me."

She shrugged again. "I'm a curious person."

"And this is my dream job."

"Uh-huh." She smiled, and there was the tooth again, like a chip of concrete wedged into her gum.

## Three

THAT evening Simon rode the A train out to the Rockaways for his biweekly dinner with his father, during which he would continue to spin out the lie that he was still enrolled in medical school. He'd kept this up for nine months now. The first time he'd seen his father after his official withdrawal from school, they'd sat around the kitchen table, eating pork chops and red onions grilled on the rusty outdoor Weber, drinking bottles of Stella, and talking about the rapidly tanking stock market. Simon had felt at each successive moment as though he was going to make his announcement, but then that moment would pass by unexploited, and the next and the next, and soon enough they'd finished their dinner, and Simon found himself on the train back to Roosevelt Island, entirely sure that during the following visit he would speak, that at the next dinner he would unburden himself and offer a full and convincing explanation. Of course no such thing happened, not that next visit and not on any other visit either. But still there was no avoiding the dinners. The simple truth was that his father did not have anyone else, and although Simon had to admit he was now a liar, he refused to be a delinquent son.

The ride out to the Beach 116th Street station was as interminable as it had always been, the train wending its way under the entire borough of Brooklyn before crossing Jamaica Bay and delivering Simon onto the spit of the Rockaways. It was on this train ride—it was *because* of this train ride—that he had first come to distrust his father's decisions. He'd just turned twelve when Michael Worth determined that a stretch of promenade above the FDR Drive would be the best place to inform his two children that their small family was moving from Yorkville to the farthest reaches of southeastern Queens. Exley Chatham, the brokerage firm at which Michael was a vice president, had imploded in tandem with the Japanese currency market a few months before. Simon remembered his father looming like a scarecrow as he outlined in his mild North London accent why his children would be required to take the subway for an hour and a half to get to school that fall. Michael's chest and arm hair were white as milk, and when the sun slipped out from behind one of the East End apartment towers to backlight him, the fuzz on his body glowed as though he were swaddled in tiny white-hot filaments. He was, as usual, wearing a pastel Polo shirt open at the neck—this one, Simon remembered, lime green—and, also as usual, smoking a Parliament, and all of this—the fiery hair, the shirt, the cigarette, the accent, the chopping motion of his hands as he delineated the concept of square footage—combined to form a sort of ur-Michael figure, the concentration into one moment of everything that made Simon's father his father.

When Michael asked if there were any questions, it was all Simon could do to shake his head. Amelia, though—his younger sister, ten years old, fifty-five bony pounds swallowed up by a pink sweatshirt—said, "We're poor now, aren't we?"

"Shut up," Simon said, but Michael just laughed as though he were choking.

"Not yet," he said. "Poor*er*—well, I can't argue with that."

Yet when they moved into the house on Beach 113th Street, on the last weekend of July 1995, Simon and Amelia were too astounded by the amount of space they could now call their own to think about much else. Two floors! A crawl space! A porch! (Concrete, but still.) It was bounteous, an abundance. They could walk to the beach in five minutes: how could their move be understood as anything other than an improvement? (And, of course, when Simon was a bit older, he understood that they weren't in fact poor at all; they'd merely slipped from the upper to the lower confines of that infinitely elastic American category, the middle class.) But then the school year began, and their days became bracketed by bleary-eyed, impossibly lengthy subway rides; they seemed forever in transit, the school day itself only one stop on some never-ending, laborious journey.

On the night before school resumed, Michael had sat Simon down in the kitchen after Amelia had gone to bed. "I'm going to need your help, Simon," he said. "I've always been able to trust you to be responsible for yourself. Now you're old enough that I can ask you to share some responsibility for your little sister. Take her to school in the morning and bring her home in the afternoon. If I'm not back by dinnertime, order something to eat—pizza or whatever you like. I'll leave some money by the phone. Help her with her homework. Keep an eye on her. Be there for her when she needs it. I'm going to have to stay on later at work for a while, and it's going to take me longer to get home now too, so . . ." He regarded Simon very seriously, wreathed in blue smoke, the Parliament held loosely between two fingers. "Can I depend on you?" he asked.

Simon nodded. "I won't let you down."

"Not me," Michael said. "Your sister. She's your responsibility now too. Remember that."

"I will. I promise."

"Good," his father said. "This is what it means to be a big brother."

And what about St. Edmund's? A Jesuit education couldn't have held too much meaning for their atheist father. Simon had always assumed it was instead in deference to the memory of their mother, the daughter of first-generation Italian Americans, nine years dead by then of pancreatic cancer, and while alive a passionate if inconsistent Catholic. It was also possible that Michael Worth harbored a stubborn European distrust of the New York City public school system, and yet private school was as beyond his newly diminished means as a private jet. Whatever the reason, off to the Upper East Side Jesuits Simon and Amelia had been sent, and once he'd managed to wedge his children into the school, Michael was not going to let a little thing like the family's move to the hinterlands change his mind. The result for Simon had been a partitioned adolescence: school in Manhattan, home in farthest Queens. In each place he maintained the illusion that his real life—where you'd find his closest friends and his truest, most comfortable self—occurred in the other. For five years, the one thread that ran through it all was Amelia, and then she was dead and the whole thing—his doubly calibrated identity—collapsed like a gutted building, destroyed from within by her sudden absence.

The subway jolted out of the elevated Howard Beach station, and Simon was presented with a view of the weather-beaten little houses that backed onto a canal snaking into Jamaica Bay, the houses lifted on stilts above the turbid channel, Boston Whalers tethered to their back porches. They were rooted more in water than dry land, clinging to this far edge of the city like barnacles. A beached motorboat lay on the spongy ground by the side of the canal, "MERK" sprayed in pink bubble letters across its side. Simon watched the planes spiral into JFK as the train clattered its way over the water, the Edgemere and Arverne and Dayton projects—Rockaway's own serrated skyline—rising across the bay.

He remembered one night, the previous winter, when his tenure in medical school was beginning to fall apart. He'd gone drinking with his father at a loud, dingy bar on Maiden Lane, the kind of place where the decor, bartenders, and clientele hadn't changed much in thirty years. They'd been joined by Michael's old friends from Exley Chatham, fellow refugees from the company's 1995 collapse, who had all scattered after the firm's demise, most, like Michael, retreating from trading to the back office at any Wall Street shop that would give them a second chance. They called in favors from former classmates, former bosses, former employees, to get their new jobs. Most had lost the taste for trading, the taste for risk; they'd been burned too badly. Exley Chatham's bet had been on the continued resurgence of the yen. The firm had been highly leveraged, and when currency markets began to break in the wrong direction, Chatham had, in a bid to buy itself time to fix things, been less than forthright with its creditors about the precise status of its investments. Of course, they ran out of time, and things were not fixed; things were, in fact, broken more thoroughly than they would have been if the firm had disclosed its losses when they'd first occurred. But here, in this bar and a few others on Cedar and Pearl and John Streets, the old colleagues could sit together and drink as though the last twelve years had never happened, drink until they could barely stand; yet no matter how drunk they got, they always managed to stagger outside and flag a cab for Penn Station or Grand Central in time for the last train home to Roslyn, Pleasantville, Forest Hills.

And they got drunk that night, Michael most of all. Simon remembered his father rising out of his chair every five minutes to propose another toast, his face flushed with pride as well as liquor—pride in his son, his diligent, quiet, melancholic son, who was going to be a doctor, his son who'd soldiered on despite losing the sister who'd meant everything to him. And here Michael had wavered for a moment, his friends looking down into their drinks, before he gathered himself and finished the toast and they all drank it down.

A few of Simon's old Rockaway friends sometimes asked him how Michael was. Well, how should Simon know? His father's routine had tightened with such stricture that it did not allow for much variation. He was Michael Worth—that's how he was. He left Rockaway at six in the morning, balanced a brokerage's books until five—a dull, moderately paid job, the best he could get on the Street with the taint of Chatham smeared over his résumé like dried shit—drank until seven, rode the train back home, then did it all over again. On the weekends there was tennis, if he could find a partner, and the ocean—his nominal reason for moving all the way out there in the first place—if it was warm enough. Otherwise there was always Derry Hills and the other Rockaway bars. And Simon too, of course, paying his twice-monthly respects, telling his twice-monthly lies.

After Simon switched trains at Broad Channel, his car pulled into the Beach 116th Street station, and five minutes later he was knocking at the familiar door, his father appearing with a burning cigarette stuck into the middle of his red-cheeked face.

"You should get a car, Simon," he said. "It would make your life easier."

"Want to buy me one?"

Michael grabbed his son in a rough hug, the glowing tip of his cigarette narrowly missing Simon's earlobe. "We're having roast chicken," he said. "How does that suit the good doctor?"

Simon followed his father toward the kitchen, glancing up the darkened stairway as he passed to the back of the house. He wondered again how often his father went upstairs, to the second floor and Simon's and Amelia's old rooms—if he ever did. Michael opened the oven, and the kitchen's air thickened with the smell of crisped chicken skin. He set the pan straight onto the table, the bird resplendent in a pool of its own juices, and poked at the breast with a pair of tongs. The table was set with two bottles of Stella, two chilled glasses, two carving knives. Simon and his father sat down and took turns slicing chunks of meat off the bone, a loaf of sourdough bread on hand to transport the meat from plate to mouth, a bowl of mayonnaise for lubrication. Simon kept up a difficult pace of eating and drinking, afraid that the moment his mouth was found empty, he would be forced to invent some new fantasy about medical school. But this was not the topic his father had in mind.

Michael cleared the plates and brought out a fifth of Jameson and two tumblers. He wanted to talk about the banks. They were all diseased, he said. Some might be cured, others put out of their misery. There was no logic here that he could see. Nobody knew what the hell they were doing. Simon listened, watching his father's face. The firm in the back office of which Michael now worked appeared to be safe for the moment, but who knows? It was ironic, he said, that avaricious, unchecked risk, the one thing he'd tried to avoid since Exley Chatham, might screw him over yet again.

Simon had watched, in real time, this excision of risk from his father's life. He'd been too young to understand much of it as it was happening, but even then he'd known a shift was taking place within his father, not just a shift of circumstance, but an internal shift, a shift of character. Michael Worth—the middle-class North London boy who'd won over a stubborn Italian American graduate student while on scholarship at University College London, arrived in New York a year later with his new and pregnant wife, torn into his first job trading bond debt at Chatham, seen his wife killed by pancreatic cancer less than a year after their second child's birth, and doubled and tripled his efforts at Chatham, becoming a vice president on the currencies desk just before the entire firm came crashing down—Michael Worth had turned away from the part of himself that had carried him this far. He'd turned away from jealousy and ambition and hunger. He understood Chatham's collapse as his own, and, financially, it was. And so he methodically carved away the aspects of himself that might ever prove a threat to the few things that remained for him: his children and his home. Exiled were his competitiveness, his impulsiveness, but exiled also were his energy and his desire. He became an attenuated Michael. When Amelia died, there was little left to give over to grief; his already narrow world simply became narrower.

Or so it appeared to Simon. How could he know what his father really felt? He might as well ask a tree or a rock or the ocean; he might as well not ask at all. Michael's life had become something that would have been unrecognizable to his younger self. And yet he seemed to have discovered some peace in the idea that there was nothing left to achieve, only the maintenance of daily ritual. He must have smothered his fantasies of what his life should be, of what it could have been; there was only what it was, and that would have to be enough.

His father was saying that what had happened to Chatham was now happening to everybody else, but for even stupider, greedier reasons and on a scale beyond anybody's comprehension. He filled the tumblers.

"Rest in peace, Lehman Brothers," he said, tossing the whiskey back.

Simon looked at his own glass, then drank it down.

Michael refilled the tumblers: "Rest in peace, Bear Stearns."

Down went the whiskey.

"Rest in peace, Merrill Lynch."

Only after the third toast did Michael allow himself a smile, and then Simon knew what this was all about. Let others suffer what Michael had suffered. This was a wake, but like all good wakes, it was also a celebration.

Sometime later, the whiskey bottle nearly empty, Simon stood up to leave. The kitchen tilted and pitched; he hadn't realized how drunk he was. It was exhausting to think of trudging to the subway, of sitting through the endless ride back to Roosevelt Island.

"You can spend the night if you'd like," Michael said, as if reading his thoughts.

"I have class tomorrow." The lie slipped easily out of his mouth.

"I'll drive you to Manhattan in the morning," Michael said. "I have a few things I need to do in the city anyway. How does that sound?"

Simon was too drunk and tired to object. The linen closet

smelled as though it hadn't been opened in years, and perhaps it hadn't. Upstairs a layer of dust coated the hallway's floorboards. In Simon's old room, his bed had been pushed into the far corner, the mattress bare and yellowed. His desk was in its old position, but on it sat a new desktop computer and three large ring binders labeled "RECEIPTS," "MORTGAGE," and "BANK." A metal filing cabinet that looked as though it had been salvaged from the street was wedged against the desk, and a rectangle of corkboard had been tacked to the wall.

But the conversion to an office had been abandoned halfway through. The bed was still there, and also Simon's bookshelves, lined with the spines of thirteen years' worth of a progressive Catholic education: *The Confessions of Saint Augustine*, Aristotle's *Poetics*, Caesar's *Commentaries on the Gallic War*, *Ethan Frome*, *1984*, as well as the usual lineup of battered science and math and Spanish textbooks, purchased thirdhand at the annual St. Edmund's book fair. Michael lurched over to the bed, onto which he dropped the stack of sheets and pillows, a cloud of dust billowing into the air.

Coughing, he thumped Simon on the shoulder. "Sorry about the clutter. Sleep tight." He closed the door behind him, his hacking following him down the stairs.

Simon made up the bed and pulled down the window shades. He turned on the desk lamp and turned off the ceiling light, and then he sat there, on the bed, in the half dark. His body was tired but his mind suddenly awake. The whiskey made it a useless, chaotic awareness, a head full of randomness. He took a book off the shelves and could make no sense of the words. He gave up, turned off the desk lamp, and lay back on the bed.

After a sleepless hour, he turned on the lamp again and looked around the room for some way to pass the time. He'd learned long ago that he couldn't force sleep, couldn't trick or trap it. He got out of bed and sat at the desk. He stared at his bulbous reflection in the computer's convex screen. He turned the machine on. There were no icons on the desktop. No files, no programs whatsoever. Simon searched the Start menu and found that his father hadn't even installed an internet browser. It seemed the impulse to use this office had died before the computer even arrived.

He stood up, his head pulsing from the whiskey, and crept as softly as he could into the hallway. He had not set foot in Amelia's bedroom since his father had stripped it clean of its contents, donating the clothes to Goodwill and junking everything else in a grief-fueled burst of efficiency a month after her death. The room was at the end of the hall. Simon paused for a moment before gripping the cool brass knob and pushing the door. It stuck in the frame, then released with a tearing sound. He stepped inside. The streetlights shone through naked windows. The room was entirely bare, nothing but a thick layer of dust on the floorboards and walls. He felt as though his presence were an intrusion. The dust he'd stirred up resettled onto his bare feet, and he sensed a familiar void opening up inside him, a featureless, bottomless pit of shame and self-loathing to be endlessly filled with his sadness, his anger, his guilt. Amelia was dead, and it was his fault, and nothing he could ever do or say would change that. Turning away, he quickly left the room, shutting the door behind him, not caring about the noise he made as he hurried down the hall and back into his own bedroom, where he collapsed onto the bed and fell finally into a sweaty and shallow sleep.

HE was sitting in the Health Solutions office the following afternoon, still tasting the whiskey in the back of his throat, when the desk phone rang. It was Maria, telling him that the tests had gone smoothly. Her transplant coordinator—she meant DaSilva, of course—had met her in the lobby and accompanied her throughout the day, from examination room to lab to imaging department. Simon hadn't been particularly worried about the tests—he knew from the results of the California exams that she enjoyed above-average health—but still, he was always relieved when a donor's first visit to Cabrera went off without a hitch; it validated his work up to that point, he supposed, and it was no different this time, with Maria. As she talked now, Simon pictured her going back to the Royal Crown, sitting alone in her room, anxious and stir-crazy, the surgery looming in her mind.

"I just wanted to let you know everything went fine," she said. "So—"

"What are you doing right now?" The words were out of his mouth before he could stop them.

"I'm . . . nothing. Heading to the hotel, I guess. Why?"

He wanted to pretend it was because she might need a distraction, but he knew that wasn't the entire truth. "I thought you might want to do something this afternoon." Silence. "That I might do something with you."

"Because I'm here alone," she said flatly.

"I just thought—"

"I told you already, I don't need your pity."

He flushed, and was glad she wasn't there to see it. "This isn't pity."

"What is it, then?"

"It's . . . courtesy," he finally said, then immediately felt stupid for saying it, the word bizarre and anachronistic to his ears.

She laughed—but, to his surprise, genuinely and without malice. "What did you have in mind?"

"It's your first time here. We can do whatever you want."

"I have no idea, Simon."

"There must be something you want to do."

He waited through a long silence before she said, "Okay, yeah. There is something."

What she wanted to do was see what her liver looked like—or, not her liver, but *a* liver. She'd noticed ads on the subway for an exhibition that displayed dissected and preserved human cadavers. Would he take her there?

"Where are you?" he asked.

"Outside the hospital."

"Take the F one stop into Manhattan, and meet me outside the station, on Sixty-Third and Lexington."

He hung up and waited ten minutes for her to cross the river. He knew that with this field trip he was straying into the unorthodox and probably inadvisable, but he was too hungover to reproach himself with any kind of conviction. By the time he walked around the corner, she was standing there, arms crossed over her chest. She'd dressed up for her visit to the hospital, a simple black cotton dress above a pair of black Chuck Taylors. She wasn't reading or listening to music or playing with her cell phone. She just stood there, staring across Sixty-Third Street—in the wrong direction— purse slung over her shoulder, tapping her foot like a caricature of the stood-up date.

He walked up behind her and tapped her shoulder. She jumped as though he'd pressed a lit match to her skin. "Jesus, Simon! Don't fucking sneak up on people like that."

"I'm sorry," he said, taken aback. "I didn't mean to."

She glared at him, on the verge of saying something more. Then she took a deep breath, as though deliberately expelling her anger. "Let's just go, okay?"

Downtown, they made their way through the cobblestoned theme park of South Street Seaport. The entrance to the exhibition was hidden between a J.Crew and a Sephora. Inside, a placard told them the cadavers were unclaimed dead from China, mostly homeless men. "We can't even manufacture our own dead people anymore," Maria muttered. The bodies were the color of Silly Putty, pink streaks simulating muscle tone. They'd been arranged into dynamic postures: conducting a symphony, shooting a basketball. Individual bones and limbs and organs were displayed in glass cases running along the sides of the rooms: bisected slices of lung, marbled like prosciutto; the coiled eyeless snake of a large intestine; a thumb swollen to the size of a soda can. They drifted through a room that exhibited feathery networks of veins, arteries, and capillaries extracted from their surrounding tissue, dyed bright red, and submerged in tanks of water, resplendent as tropical coral. In another room malformed fetuses curled in on themselves, innards spilling out of their mouths, unfused skulls lumpy and irregular. Soon enough, they arrived at the livers, which sat smooth and tan and dense in their case.

"This might be the dullest thing here," Maria said. Next to the healthy organ sat a larger and greasier-looking specimen. A placard identified it as an example of fatty liver disease. "Is this what Lenny has?"

"Not exactly. But similar."

She looked at it for a moment, then switched her attention back to the healthier example. "How much of this lump am I giving up?"

"About seventy percent."

"*Seventy?*"

"Since he's so much heavier than you, they're probably going to resect the maximum amount, which is about seventy. Don't worry, you'll be back at ninety percent within a few months. In a little over a year, it'll be full size again."

She touched her abdomen. He placed his fingers on her wrist, moving her hand up and to her right. "There."

"I can feel her kicking."

He smiled, but he could sense his heart skittering around his chest. He began to feel hot and nauseous, the gasoline taste of secondhand whiskey rising again in his throat. He desperately wanted a cigarette. He was thinking, unwillingly, of the dismantled bodies in the medical school's anatomy lab. The emptied chest cavity of his cadaver, the feel of her serpentine intestines in his gloved hands, the black nail polish capping her fingers. The liver display was located near the end of the exhibition and its exit, and he guided Maria outside as quickly as he could without seeming pushy.

As they rode the subway together to Times Square, she studied the map affixed to the car's wall. "Show me where you live," she said.

He hesitated, then pointed out Roosevelt Island. He instantly recognized that he'd just crossed another line he'd drawn for himself when he started working for DaSilva.

"Really? Right by the hospital?"

"On the other end of the island. But, yeah, not too far."

"Where in the city did you grow up?"

"What makes you think I grew up here?"

"Well, didn't you?"

"I did. But how can you tell?"

"Good guess." She dropped her eyes. "So, where?"

Where indeed? He paused, then pointed out the Rockaways in the far bottom-right corner of the map. "We moved here when I was twelve."

She studied the map. "The A train. End of the line."

"Yeah."

"That's a long ride."

"Depends where you're coming from."

"Manhattan."

"Yes. It's even longer than it looks. This map, it's not to scale. Manhattan is blown up. Or the other boroughs are shrunk, whichever way you want to think about it."

"That doesn't seem fair."

"It's just the way it is."

Outside the lobby of the Royal Crown, he asked about her plans for the night.

"I need to call my sister," she said. "She'll put Gabriel on the phone. Other than that . . ." She shrugged. "Room service. Maybe watch some TV then go to sleep early."

"Your sister," he said. "What did you tell her you were doing here?"

"I just said I had to go. That I had no choice. She knew I wouldn't have asked her to look after Gabriel if that wasn't true."

---

THE next afternoon Simon watched from across his desk, picturing the tiny tears and bruises deep in the man's battered ganglia, as Lenny tried to stitch together the story of his second cousin's generous gift. Lenny was thirty-nine years old, but Simon guessed that his brain more closely resembled that of somebody twice his age. He spoke slowly, as though testing how each word sounded in his mind before releasing it into the room, and he was sweating again even though the AC unit was running on full blast. In the chair next to him, Howard Crewes frowned, a man worried about the soundness of his investment.

"Let's start again," Simon said. "Just relax, okay? Now, what is your relationship to Maria Campos?"

"She's my second cousin."

"How did Maria learn about your liver condition?"

"Look at me. It isn't a secret."

"How long ago was this?"

"Last year. I was in San Diego with Cheryl and our kids. On vacation. We met Maria for lunch at this Mexican place in San Clemente. She knew already from talk in the family, but she hadn't seen me herself."

"Did you discuss your options at that point? With Maria, I mean?"

"No, not yet. I think she knew Cheryl wasn't a match though."

"But you spoke with her about it afterward."

"She called me a few weeks later," he said. "She wanted to know what I was going to do." He spoke in a monotone, as though these things were of no concern, as though they'd happened to someone else, which of course in a way they had. "I told her I would get on the list and pray."

"The UNOS list?"

"Yeah. But I also told her I might never get off that list alive."

Simon liked this line. He'd fed it to his second client, a middle-aged corporate executive whose kidney had been annihilated by hepatitis C. He remembered showing up at her mammoth suburban home, where she faced him across the dining room table in a pink cable-knit sweater, and wondering from what incongruous chapter of her past the hepatitis was making such a savage and unwelcome visitation. She never said; he never asked. He could sense her anger though, her anger that she should be found out and hunted down in this way by the exigencies of her youth. He didn't know if she ever used the line, and its corny machismo sounded better coming out of Lenny's mouth anyway.

"Maria called me about a month later," Lenny said. "She asked for my blood type. I said, what for. That's when she told me she wanted to donate."

Crewes groaned. "For Christ's sake, Lenny, you sound dead already."

"Please," Simon said. "Did you ever lead her to believe she would receive any compensation in return?"

"No." Lenny shook his massive head. "Absolutely not."

After the two men left, Simon stood at the window and lit a cigarette as he watched them limp their way up the block to Crewes's black Lexus. Would it matter if Lenny's performance in the actual interview was this horrendous? Would anybody care? DaSilva had managed to finesse Lenny's rickety body through the tests—had contextualized, cajoled, or outright lied enough to gain Lenny's acceptance into the transplant program—so Simon imagined that, short of assaulting his examiner or directly admitting the fact that the necessary portion of Maria's liver had been purchased, Lenny was probably safe, unconvincing zombielike demeanor or not.

He thought of what Crewes had told him about Lenny's "funks": the headaches, the moods, the rejection of the world beyond the four walls of his darkened bedroom. He imagined Lenny sequestered in his bed, head throbbing in time with his pulse, the engorged blood vessels of his brain jammed up against the cramped interior of his skull. Simon knew something about how migraines could cripple a life. His sister had suffered from them throughout her adolescence, although the word "migraine" only meant something to Simon later. When they were growing up, he and Amelia just called it "The Pinch." The Pinch meant a lot of things—visual glitches, nausea, numbness in her lips and tongue—but most of all it meant headaches, pulverizing, catastrophic headaches that lasted a day at a time.

Amelia hated talking about The Pinch almost as much as she hated the thing itself. She avoided the nurse's office at St. Edmund's, which always smelled of Lysol layered over the sweet, faint, ineradicable tang of vomit. She'd gone there with the first of her headaches one morning in fifth grade. The nurse had sat her down in a chair and given her two Tylenol. After an hour, it was suggested that she return to class. She hated having to say that, no, she'd rather stay, and actually, was there a dark and quiet room somewhere in which she could lie down? Saying these things made her feel shameful, weak; the nurse, an ancient nun named Sister Carolina, had no explanation for her suffering. Finally Simon was summoned out of algebra class and told to take his sister home.

He led her out of St. Edmund's, into the bright, slanting sunlight. She scrunched up her face, one hand covering her eyes, the other clammy and ice cold against his palm as he dragged her across Park Avenue, over to the subway on Lexington. They waited on the platform, the train's hot, stale breath rushing over them as it pulled into the station. She sat hunched in her seat, poking at her face, telling Simon she couldn't feel her bottom lip. After they switched trains at Fulton Street, she closed her eyes and stopped speaking. Simon sat next to her, still holding her hand, murmuring that they would be home soon, that she would be okay, but she didn't seem to hear him. She didn't seem to be aware of anything around her, turning her attention entirely inward. He looked at her face, the fine colorless down on her cheeks and upper lip, the sharp point of her chin. He reached out his free hand to stroke her forehead as the train burst out of the tunnel, sunlight slicing across the car. Amelia let go of Simon's hand and covered her eyes. At Broad Channel, he helped her off the train, and they waited on the platform for the shuttle, Amelia slumped against the wall.

Days later, centuries later, they arrived at the house. Inside it was cool and dark. Simon led Amelia up to her room. She lay on the bed, and he sat on its edge, holding her hand and talking, saying whatever came into his mind. He thought, without quite believing it, that if he let her fall asleep, she might never wake up. She squirmed against the mattress as he talked, and then suddenly she stood and pushed past him to the bathroom in the hall, pulling the door shut behind her. He stood at the door, his hand on the knob. He heard her retching, then the flush of the toilet. He withdrew his hand and stood in the doorway to her bedroom. He didn't know what to do. A few minutes later, she came out of the bathroom, limp and flushed. She slipped past him and collapsed onto her bed. She said she felt a little better and asked if he would please call Dad now. "Okay," he said, and he went downstairs to the phone in the kitchen. He stood there, leaning against the refrigerator, looking at the phone, then up at the wall clock. It was four thirty. His father would be leaving work in an hour, home an hour after that. He looked at the phone again, and then he went back upstairs and sat on the edge of his sister's bed and watched her drift in and out of sleep.

It was dark when he heard his father's key turn in the lock. He hurried downstairs and told Michael that Amelia was sick, that she'd thrown up, that she said it felt as though something inside her skull were drilling its way out.

His father put down his briefcase and frowned at the ceiling. "You brought her home from school?"

Simon nodded.

"Why didn't you call me?"

"I did. At the office. Nobody answered."

His father looked at him. "And you didn't leave a message? Don't bullshit me, Simon."

"I'm not."

Michael shook his head and walked up the stairs. Simon waited in the kitchen, turning the dials on the stove, watching the blue flames blossom and die. His father returned a few minutes later and put the teakettle on. He said it was a migraine and nothing to worry about; their mother had suffered them too, the entire time he'd known her. He brought the steaming cup upstairs, and Simon followed him and watched from the doorway as he placed the cup on Amelia's bedside table, drew the blinds, tucked her under the blankets. Michael placed a pill in her hand, told her to swallow it down along with her tea. Simon slipped down the hall to his own room and closed the door. He felt a gnawing sense that he'd failed his sister, that he'd been exposed as ineffective, dispensable.

One Saturday morning in December, during Simon's senior year of high school, Amelia woke up with the left side of her mouth and tongue entirely numb; by noon she'd vomited everything in her stomach, but still her brain remained incandescent with pain.

Simon sat on the bed as she thrashed around under the sheets. She told him again that he didn't have to stay with her.

"It's okay," he said. "You shouldn't be alone."

She abruptly sat up and glared at him. "No," she said. "It's not okay. You're not helping. I want to be alone."

"I thought you wanted me here."

"When did I ever say that?" She fell back against the pillows. "Please, Simon, just go."

She closed her eyes and turned away from him. He went into the hallway, closing the door softly behind him. He sat all afternoon in his room, trying to read, but instead he found himself staring at the wall that separated his room from Amelia's and picturing her suffering. She'd described it to him and he'd witnessed it himself so many times that he felt he knew its course, its cunning movement: the aura, the numbness, the lull, the arrival of pain, the hatred of light and sound, the nausea, the vomiting, the pain's slow abatement, and the collapse, finally, into sleep. He tried to align his imagination with what was happening at that moment on the other side of the wall. He was angry about what she'd said but more frustrated that he couldn't experience the pain along with her, frustrated because it was during these episodes that he felt most acutely how he could never know what it was like to be Amelia.

LENNY'S performance had been painful, but at least Simon didn't have to worry about Maria. She'd shown up at the office earlier that morning—still-damp hair piled atop her head, skin smelling of apricot soap—with no trouble understanding what Cabrera would require of her. She was expansive and emotional, her eyes widening as she described the "moment of clarity" she'd been struck with while sitting in traffic on I-5. She'd realized she had a "moral obligation" to help anyone she could. She described the San Clemente restaurant, its patio overlooking the Pacific. She described Cheryl's "tired eyes," young Gregory and Daniela's "devotion" to their father. She remembered, as a kid, tossing a football with Lenny at a family reunion in Long Island, how she knew even then that he was one of those lucky people who were able, if only for a brief while, to do the thing they most loved to do.

She was, in short, an entirely convincing liar.

Simon asked if she understood the risks of the operation, the unavoidable scarring of her abdomen.

"It's all right," she said. "I don't plan on wearing a lot of bikinis."

There was that sarcasm again, a way of talking that reminded him so much of Amelia in her teenage years, and again he tried to read whether it was a defense mechanism—an affectation—or an honest expression of not giving a fuck. Probably, he decided, a bit of both. Just like it had been with Amelia.

He handed her a photocopied sheet of paper showing one hundred stick figures arranged in rows of ten. Thirty-one of the figures, scattered throughout, had been stamped with black dots over their midsections.

"The social worker is going to give you something like this," he said. "About thirty-one out of a hundred donors have some kind of complication after surgery. Usually it's not anything serious— abdominal pain that lasts longer than usual, a bile leak, sometimes a minor infection. These things would be addressed at Cabrera before discharge. We'll also set you up with a doctor in LA, for follow-up."

"Why don't they just say thirty-one percent?"

"The idea is that percentages are too abstract. Just listen to the social worker. His name is Klein. Listen to him, let him talk. Pretend to think it over. Then tell him what he wants to hear." He passed her another sheet with a similar graphic, this time with ten dotted figures. "He'll show you this too. About ten percent of the people like Lenny who have this surgery die within a year. The idea is for you to understand there's some chance this won't save him even if the surgery itself is successful."

"And you want me to pretend to be upset?"

"I want you to look as though this is new information. Absorb it, then say you're comfortable moving forward. Be confident but not too brash. They want to see that you're committed but also that you're not some kind of martyr."

"Heroic donors."

He looked up at her, surprised. The phrase was a piece of hospital jargon, not something he thought was in common usage. The gray tooth winked as she smiled.

"You've been doing your research," he said. "Right: no heroes. Just autonomous, compassionate individuals. You see the difference, right?" He pushed another sheet across the desk. "Here's the last of these graphics. One thousand figures. Two are dotted. This is the 0.2 percent living donor mortality rate."

She glanced at the paper.

"No," he said. "Look taken aback. Nobody's mentioned *death* to you before. But then recover quickly. After all, it's a tiny percentage, and it's not going to happen at a hospital like this, to someone healthy like you." He caught her eye. "That's true, by the way. In case you really are worried and are just hiding it well."

"I'm not."

"You shouldn't be. Now, here are a few questionnaires. He'll give you these at the end of the interview, to make sure you've understood everything he's said about the surgery, the recovery, and so on. To demonstrate that you've been fully informed. Here's a pencil. You read the documents I e-mailed you? Then you shouldn't have any trouble."

He stared out the window and fought the urge for a cigarette as she filled in the bubbles. He had to admit he liked this part of the job. He liked being responsible for a process that provided measurable results, clear successes and failures. And he couldn't be too bad at it, because they'd all been successes so far. Every pair he'd selected and prepared had been approved by the hospital and come through surgery without any unusual difficulties. He could honestly say that he'd helped to save the lives of people who most likely would have otherwise died before their names hit the top of the UNOS list or else pursued a far riskier brokered transplant overseas, in South Africa or Turkey or the Czech Republic. (Thoughts like these assuaged periodic flare-ups of guilt about his role in the flow of organs from poor to rich, in the commodification, quite literally, of people's insides. Say what you want, he thought, there are individuals who would be dead now if it weren't for what he did.) It was true that he'd never worked on a liver case before. Also true that he'd never worked with an active alcoholic like Lenny—all the other clients who'd drank their kidneys to ruin qualified as ex-alcoholics, having logged time in AA or sobriety programs of their own devising before coming to him—but the surgeons had given their authorization, so he had to assume Lenny's condition wasn't something they couldn't handle. He also assumed that DaSilva had tampered with Lenny's records, giving Klein the impression that their patient had been sober far longer than the few weeks of half-assed abstinence the man could honestly put to his name.

Maria set down her pen. She'd had no trouble with the test; her score was perfect.

"You might want to throw a question or two," he said. "Just for appearance's sake."

"Really?"

"I don't want them to think you've taken it before. Answer something wrong near the beginning—the most important questions are at the end." He paused. "They're also going to ask you about the environment in which you'll recover. What they want to hear is that you have a strong support system. Can you tell them that?"

"I can tell them anything."

"Would you have to lie in this case?"

"It depends on what they're looking for."

"Relatives, friends. A husband, a boyfriend."

She paused. "I have my son."

"They'll see him as a stressor. Sorry, but it's true. You've told me his father isn't around. Is there a boyfriend?"

"Would it look better if there were?"

"Honestly, yes. Make him up if you have to. Talk about your close friends, your supportive boss. Talk about your sister. Here, I have a surprise for you." He handed her another sheet of paper. "That's your new savings account. For Cabrera's purposes anyway."

"This is fake?"

"Doctored. It's more suspicious if it looks like you really, really need the money. No offense."

"You want me to bring this in with me?"

"They'll already have a copy. They know Howard's paying for the surgery and your medical bills—all of that's fully legal, as long as none of the money goes directly to you—but there's still the financial strain of recovery and travel. Here's some evidence that says you can absorb it. This might seem like it's getting complicated, but remember they want to go through with this. All we have to do is make sure we don't give them a reason not to."

He sat behind the desk after she'd left, cracking the window and lighting a cigarette, and tried to imagine her at home, in Los Angeles, a city he envisioned as an endless sprawl of stucco bungalows pounded low by the merciless Western sun. He could find Torrance on a map, but it wouldn't mean anything to him. He tried to see it: the small, bright house, the toy-littered rooms, the afternoons spent at the playground. At night her sister would arrive to babysit, and together they'd put the kid, Gabriel, to bed, and she'd dress in her work clothes—jeans, black leather jacket, silver buckles and jewelry—and drive to the bar, its walls painted black, stools topped with torn red vinyl, neon beer signs thrumming in the window. He tried to stitch a life for her around these details, but he couldn't make it hold together; the thread of his imagination was too weak, or perhaps he'd simply not been given enough material to construct anything convincing.

## Four

FROM the moment Simon woke, early on the morning of Maria's and Lenny's surgeries, until late that night, he did little but sit on the couch and stare at the television, working through a pack and a half of Parliaments and two boxes of frozen pizza, sunk deep into the paradoxical mire of anxious torpor. Outside the apartment's windows, a blustery October Monday rose into view, the slate-gray river topped and speckled with whitecaps, before glumly sinking back into darkness eleven hours later. Lenny and Maria's meeting on Friday had gone as well as Simon could have hoped—Lenny taciturn, Maria wary, but both just cooperative enough. Lenny even summoned the graciousness to thank Maria in his own monosyllabic way. On Saturday, Maria had passed her interview with Klein without any difficulties. Simon had last spoken to her near midnight on Sunday, only six hours before she was due to begin her OR prep at Cabrera. She'd been reserved, with little to say, but she did not for a second betray any doubts or hesitations. She was committed. And then, for Simon, the waiting began.

As he sat in front of the television, cycling through the daytime wasteland of twenty-four-hour news, talk shows, soaps, and half-remembered movies from the 1990s, his mind circled obsessively back, as it often did, to the first months after his sister's death. It was as though he believed the solution to the cipher of his current life could be discovered in a careful enough examination of that raw and disorienting period, as though attentiveness to his feelings and actions then would provide some clarity to the foggy now.

He remembered that after Amelia died, he had felt his days, no matter how cluttered with incident, to be thin, insubstantial. There was the physical world, in which one event dutifully followed the next, but there was no corresponding private space in which those events carried any meaning. It was not that he was empty; it was rather that he was too full, that he was afraid he would displace his feelings for Amelia—love and sadness and grief and resentment and a thousand other less definable but no less deeply experienced emotions—as though emotional investment was a zero-sum proposition. He felt he had exhausted his capacity for caring about what happened to him, but that could not be entirely true, because he seemed to care enough about this lack of caring to want to do something about it.

He decided that practicing medicine would be his solution. He had the notion that he would—should—spend the rest of his life helping strangers. The idea was that caring for other people would be a useful substitute for caring about himself. He was aware, even at age eighteen, that this was a cliché. But didn't all clichés contain a measure of truth? Or was that too just another cliché?

He came to this decision near the end of the year he took off after graduating from St. Edmund's. He deferred his college scholarship upstate to surf his way down the Pacific coast of Mexico, then south through Guatemala, El Salvador, Nicaragua, Costa Rica. He got around by bus and hitchhiking. It was a highly irresponsible trip—he didn't have enough money to be spending even this little of it—but he found that people would let you get away with all kinds of irresponsible things while you were grieving, and nobody could question the depth of his grief. He and Amelia had been, as everybody knew, as close as a brother and sister could be. Not that he thought of the trip as getting away with anything. There was not much thought involved at all, only the compulsion to leave far behind the house on Beach 113th, this house that had somehow become smaller after the subtraction of one of its three inhabitants. He found himself running into his father in the kitchen, the living room, the mudroom, as though they were bats whose sonar had been scrambled. Amelia's absence was itself a presence that filled the house more densely and concretely than any object, more sinuously than any smell.

He booked a flight to Mexico City, taking along the majority of his savings, cash he'd accumulated from various summertime jobs. After two months of rattling down washboarded Central American dirt roads in the beds of pickup trucks, of sleeping in hostels and on the beach, of surfing nearly every day, pummeled by sun, pickled by salt, Simon ended up in San José. He rented a room in a Holiday Inn for a weekend, pulling shut the blinds and cranking up the air-conditioning. On the bus ride into the city he could feel a sickness welling up within him, and it was there, in that anonymous hotel room, that it overflowed, a furious fever that ripped through his blood like an electrical current, shaking him with chills that lifted his body off the bed, soaking him with sweats that pooled in the hollow of his chest. He took the last pills in a bottle of ibuprofen, and then he was left with no more defenses, with nothing to do but wait the suffering out.

He squirmed on the foam mattress, the thin sheets and scratchy bedspread twisted around his body. The light at the edge of the blackout shades brightened and dimmed. He left the bed only to urinate in thick, deep-yellow streams and to fill a plastic bottle from the bathroom tap. Languidly, distractedly, he wondered if he might be fatally ill.

Sometimes he slept. But more prevalent than sleep was a half-waking haze, fever dreams full of gaudy abstractions—fiery pinwheels, metastasizing blobs—sometimes interrupted by a figurative intrusion: a teacher's face, a palm tree, the inside of a subway car. These images lurched up out of the muck of his brain and then were quickly sucked back down again. Only once did an entire scene present itself. He had been woken by the sound of a moped backfiring. He closed his eyes and sank back down into the mattress, and then, as though a screen had been switched on, the clearest image of Amelia appeared behind his eyelids. She stood on one of the rock groynes that jutted out from the Rockaway beach into the ocean, wearing a purple windbreaker, her hair batted across her face by the wind. He was aware that he was standing on the beach, but the idea of his body seemed beside the point. The level of detail—glistening, granular—was beyond that of memories, beyond waking sight. He saw the stippled surface of the ocean. He could count each rock of the groyne, each container ship studded along the horizon. His attention did not have to be parceled out but could instead meet the entire breadth and depth of the scene at once. Amelia stood at the tip of the groyne, the ocean's spray whipping across her legs. She looked back at him. Her face was many ages at once. She was a little girl; she was a teenager; she was the young woman she'd never become. Her face did not flash from one age to the next but rather accommodated all the ages, in the same space, at once. When she smiled, it was many smiles and also one.

Simon opened his eyes, and this vision of his sister remained so true, so perfect, that he was sure for a moment Amelia was there in the room with him. Or rather, that the dim hotel room was itself unreal, an illusion, and the beach was what was real, the beach and the ocean and Amelia, and he was the visitor, the apparition. As though he had died and Amelia were still alive. He struggled to sit up in bed, the force of the vision and the hot weight of sickness grinding down on his body. The fever broke a few hours later. The next day he used the last of his money to buy a plane ticket home.

It was within a month or two of his return that the idea of becoming a doctor first occurred to him. He couldn't say when he initially thought of it—maybe during a conversation with his father or while watching some medical drama on television—but once he'd taken hold of the idea, he could not let it go. It was as though he'd always been working toward this goal without knowing it. He enrolled at the SUNY campus upstate the following fall and began taking premed courses. During his four years there, he passed all his requirements, not at the top of the class, but far enough from the bottom. He studied for the MCAT and did well enough on that too, and eventually he was accepted to a middle-tier medical school on Manhattan's Upper East Side.

He rented a one-bedroom apartment on East Ninety-Third Street, near York Avenue, not too far from where he and his father and Amelia had lived before moving to the Rockaways. Michael visited the apartment and noted the doorman, the elevator, the views onto the river, before wondering aloud at its cost. Simon lied, undershooting the monthly rent by $500. It was the summer of 2007, and the cost of things seemed malleable, practically beside the point. You only had to wait and whatever money you had now would surely multiply, like self-dividing amoebae, so why stress over such things? Simon took out $45,000 in loans for school and spent his savings from four years of part-time work at the campus bookstore on rent and prescription drugs—mostly Valium and Klonopin and Ambien—which were delivered to his new apartment by a baby-faced NYU freshman.

He didn't try to make friends at medical school; it happened only once and by chance, with a woman named Katherine Peel. She was black haired and pale skinned and five years older than him, a large woman who wore her largeness easily, sexily, as though it were a flattering dress she'd chosen for herself. Simon thought they understood each other immediately. He would have said their friendship was built on the platform of a shared pessimism, and on a shared response to that pessimism, which was to work obsessively hard against it, not in the hope of changing the world, or themselves, for the better, but instead out of a perverse personality defect in which despair and industry were inextricable. They thought this attitude would serve them well in their future residencies in the public hospitals of New York City, where good work had little to do with optimism. For Simon, it was as though rubbing against a surface as rough as his own had scraped away a layer of dead psychic skin, and he felt, briefly, in more direct contact with the world and with himself than he had since Amelia died.

THE night before he officially withdrew from medical school, he met Katherine at a bar near her apartment in Murray Hill. He drank too much that night, a sloppy cascade of whiskey and beers and more whiskey. He talked about how much he missed Amelia. He talked about his father, how he would never be able to tell him he'd left school, how he was too ashamed to ask him for help with his loans. He was aware, even through the enabling scrim of alcohol and self-pity, that his performance was bathetic, ridiculous, and that Katherine's response—to take him back to her apartment so he could drink himself the rest of the way into oblivion in private—was the correct one.

And so suddenly there they were, in her clothes-choked studio on East Twenty-Ninth Street, two glasses of terrible Spanish red wine and a pile of red capsules on the coffee table in front of them, Katherine explaining that the drug was the current hotshot painkiller in clinical trials, and she couldn't tell him how she'd gotten her hands on it, and it wasn't like the dirty opioids, and the word was that if you snort it, you're treated to the most delicious pharmaceutical high this side of morphine, and did he want to try it?

Yes. Yes, he did.

Katherine leaned over the table and cracked open two of the capsules and prepared the lines, her hair, dyed to the bluish-black shine of crow feathers, falling across her face. The contents of the capsules resembled dried clay, and the sinus burn was incredible. Nothing happened for a moment, and then a warmth blossomed

at the back of his skull and slipped down his neck, spreading out-
ward through his blood with the slowness and sweetness of maple
syrup dripped onto his tongue.

He leaned back in his chair and blinked at Katherine.

She gave him a dopey half smile: "I think we have a winner."

He nodded, lit a cigarette. He drifted away for a moment, closing his eyes and following the thin trail of heat down into his lungs.

He'd been called in front of the med school's disciplinary board
that afternoon. He'd arrived expecting to be excoriated and then
expelled; instead, they offered him a one-semester suspension and
a psychiatrist. They wanted to talk about his feelings. He sat in
his chair at the end of a long, polished conference table and
blinked at the cluster of gray heads at the opposite end. A woman
with hair the color and texture of steel wool sat at the head of the
table, chairing the committee. In a kind voice, she asked whether
he considered the school's opportunities for psychological outreach and support to be sufficient or, perhaps, too limited, either
by time constraints or, possibly, by the medical culture itself. He
said he wasn't sure. He asked them why they thought he might
benefit from psychological outreach. There was silence from the
far end of the table; then one of the doctors said that if Simon
wanted to offer an explanation for his actions in the anatomy lab,
they'd be happy to hear it. The woman at the head of the table
shot the speaker a warning look. "We don't expect our students
to be machines," she said. "We understand that the stresses of our
program can manifest themselves in a variety of ways." She told
Simon that the school would be able to roll over his spring semester loans to the following fall on the condition that he enter into
their psychological counseling program. He understood that an
answer was expected of him. He already knew he wasn't coming
back, but he said he'd think about it. The committee members
shifted in their seats as though a foul smell had wafted through
the room. He waited for somebody to say something more, and
when nobody did, he asked if he could leave.

"So, what are you going to do?" Katherine asked, pulling him back into the room. "I'm sorry." She waved a languorous hand as though to disperse her words. "We don't need to talk about this now."

"It's okay," he said. "I don't know yet. Lab tech maybe. Medical consultant."

She nodded, as though she believed he was already considering these jobs, as though he had any sort of a plan yet. "You'll have weekends, vacations. Time for other people. I'll be jealous."

"Of what?"

"You know. Your social life."

But of course she wouldn't in any way be jealous. Why should she be? There wasn't any aspect of failure to be jealous of. And, anyway, he currently enjoyed no social life to speak of, his isolation first self-imposed then self-perpetuating. He didn't see that changing simply because he was going to drop out of medical school and have some free time on his hands.

He moved from the chair to the couch next to her, bent over the coffee table, and snorted another line. The drug hit him faster and stronger this time. He was pinned back against the cushions by the heel of a firm yet gentle hand. He reached out to touch Katherine's knee, feeling the denim grow warm and damp under his palm. She didn't move her leg or push his hand away. The air in the room grew thick, tropical. He looked over at her. Her face was tilted away from him, her eyes half-closed, her lips half-smiling. With an enormous amount of effort, he lifted his hand from her knee to her neck, to the smooth skin there, white as bleached bone. She turned to him; he leaned into her. Her lips were hot and dry, and she let them rest against his for a few moments. Then she gently took hold of his shoulders and pressed him back into the couch. "No," she said, simply and not unkindly. She stood up and disappeared behind him, returning with a blanket. "Sleep here." He allowed himself to be guided into a prone position, allowed the blanket to be spread over his body. It felt good to be taken care of like this. She turned out the lights, and he heard rustling and then a sigh as she climbed into her bed on the far side of the room. She'd left for class by the time he woke up the following morning. When she called him next, a week later, it was to say she thought she might have found him a job.

He'd gone into his interview with Health Solutions knowing only what Katherine had told him, which wasn't much. Peter DaSilva was a childhood friend of hers from Riverdale, in the Bronx. She'd been close with his little sister; he'd been the obnoxious older brother, teasing and pranking his sister's friends. A big mouth, the neighborhood smart aleck. He was a natural hustler, she said, a schemer from birth, the kind of kid who sold loosies in the high school locker room and crafted fake IDs on his family's desktop. Early in his adult life, he'd discovered the health-care industry to be fertile ground for a wide variety of scams and side deals. He'd been, officially, a pharmaceutical sales rep, a health insurance consultant, a hospital administrative staffer, but he was now, in his midthirties, involved in "organ transplant consulting services" that "weren't totally legal," and he was in need of someone "discreet" with a "decent knowledge of medicine." Katherine had helped DaSilva out a bit during the company's first year—meeting with potential clients mostly—but his business was expanding, and he needed somebody more committed. Now that she was in med school, she didn't have the time to spare.

They'd met at an Irish bar in Bay Ridge. Simon still didn't know if this was near where DaSilva lived or if the location had been chosen randomly or even as an intentional misdirection. (Peter would prove remarkably adept at keeping the details of his life outside Health Solutions and Cabrera hidden from Simon, and he didn't probe for information about Simon's private life either. Simon recognized this as a smart business decision: the less they knew about each other, the harder it would be to link them in any investigation. It was possible, too, that DaSilva simply didn't *have* much of a life outside of his two jobs, that there simply weren't enough hours in the day.) It was early afternoon, and they sat at a table by the front window, milky January sunlight spilling across their laps, a slice of the Verrazano's underbelly hanging high in the window's upper corner. DaSilva—calm and terrifically fat, sipping daintily at the head of a pint of Guinness—seemed most concerned with establishing that Simon wasn't going to try to return to medical school. He needed "continuity." It was not, he said, the kind of job you try out and then drop right away if it doesn't agree with you. Simon told him he couldn't go back to that school even if he wanted to, and this seemed to be good enough.

When DaSilva explained what Health Solutions did, he made the company sound like a charity or an NGO, like Planned Parenthood or Meals On Wheels: an organization that provided a morally necessary service neglected by traditional institutions.

"Who are we," he wondered, speaking as one reasonable person to another, "to tell people what they can and can't do with their bodies? If we're honest with people, and they're willing to pay for a surgery and accept all its risks, who are we to tell them they can't spend their money like that?" He waited for an answer.

"I don't know," Simon said. And he didn't.

"I work in a transplant unit, okay? That's my 'legitimate' job, I guess you'd say. I'm a coordinator. I try to put the pieces together for donations. I try to get very sick people the organs they need to live. I see, firsthand, my patients dying because they can't get access to a kidney or a liver fast enough. Not enough young, healthy people crashed their motorcycles or shot themselves in the head this month, so, sorry, no liver for you. If nobody in your family's a match or healthy enough to donate, you're likely shit out of luck. It's a waste, and I'm sick of it. So those are the recipients. As for the donors, who are we to tell people they can't sell something that's already theirs?" He leaned in with the fervor of a true believer, or at least a very convincing facsimile of one. "Isn't it condescending to talk about exploitation, as though these donors—rational, adult human beings—can't make decisions for themselves? Why should we restrict their ability to better their lives? They know the risks. We don't mislead anybody. For Christ's sake, *they* come looking for *us*."

Simon wanted to tell him that the further prosecution of a moral argument wasn't necessary. He didn't know precisely where he stood on the issue of legalizing organ sales—he'd never had a reason to consider it before—but he did know that he harbored no opposition strong enough to prevent him from taking the job. He needed money, and he needed it quickly; if he could make that money while helping seriously ill people, then all the better. Yet DaSilva seemed to enjoy playing the provocative ethical philosopher, so Simon let him talk, nodding and frowning at the appropriate points. The whole time, he wondered how DaSilva could trust him with all of this information.

"You'll work on commission," DaSilva said. "You'll get 2.5 percent of the recipient fee for each successfully brokered pair. That might not sound like a lot, but if—when—you start making deals at $200,000 or $225,000 a pop, it'll add up. Let me ask you something: you have a way to pay off your med school loans anytime soon?"

Simon shook his head.

"Katherine put them at about $50,000. That right?"

"Nearly that."

"Debt's a motherfucker, huh? Tell you what: I'll clear your loan with the school the day you start working for me. I'll pay it all off at once, in your name, obviously. You'll owe me instead, with no interest, and guess what? Credit agencies aren't going to be calling *my* number anytime soon. And that means a clean slate for you."

"It doesn't sound like a bad idea."

"That's because it's not a bad idea. You like where you're living right now?"

Of course Simon liked it, but he couldn't afford it anymore without his stipend and loans. He shook his head.

"I own a place on Roosevelt Island, near the hospital," DaSilva said. "I'll rent it to you for a few hundred bucks a month. First two months free, until you start pushing through some deals. What do you think?"

There wasn't much to think about. How else could he clear his loans so quickly? He'd put in a year with DaSilva, maybe two, and then he'd be debt-free, able to start his life again unencumbered, on level ground. Besides, even if he didn't want to admit it to himself, he was intrigued. Maybe this was a way in which he could help people; maybe he'd found a task for which his particular combination of experience and temperament was well suited. And if it all seemed too good to be true, there was an obvious reason: it was illegal. This explained DaSilva's aggressive pitching—after all, how many people with Simon's medical knowledge and clean background would be willing to participate in a criminal enterprise, to assume all of its attendant risk? Sure, Simon was desperate but so too, he guessed, was DaSilva.

Anyway, Simon didn't harbor any strong objection to breaking the law per se—he did it all the time, didn't he, just like everybody else, every time he exceeded the speed limit or took drugs or even jaywalked? And, besides, he thought this might be one of those instances, like marijuana or stem cells, in which the law had fallen behind ethics or, at the very least, common sense. A crime was when you deliberately hurt somebody else, not when you broke an arbitrary rule. As for the risk, building any kind of case against Health Solutions would, the way DaSilva explained it, be both unlikely and difficult. The only illegal act was the exchange of money between recipient and donor. The recipient wrote a check to Health Solutions for "consultation fees"; the donor was paid, weeks later, in untraceable cash. And who was going to bring a charge anyway? If they did their job right, it was in everybody's interests—the donor's, the recipient's, the hospital's—to keep quiet, to protect the status quo. What good would a messy legal case do for anybody?

Yes, maybe his father had sworn off risk, but Simon wasn't required to follow his depressing example. In any event, it sure beat the hell out of registering with a temp agency. He moved into DaSilva's Roosevelt Island apartment by the end of the week and started searching for clients the following Monday.

And how had DaSilva known Simon wouldn't screw him? Maybe it was something Katherine had said, or maybe DaSilva just took one look at the crumpled figure sitting across the table and understood, with his hustler's intuition, that here was a broken young man, no more capable of fucking him over than of sprouting wings and flying.

FINALLY, just before three on Tuesday morning, Simon received DaSilva's text—"All fine. Hang tight."—and was flooded with relief.

Maria was a recovering inpatient at Cabrera now, out of his reach, and he heard nothing more until five days later, when he received a second text directing him to the Sixty-Second Street office. On the desk he found a clear plastic folder. Inside were two sheets of paper. On each was printed the location of a bank and a safe-deposit box number. Written next to one address was "45K," and next to the other, "100K." A small key was paper-clipped to each sheet. A third sheet of paper listed the name, address, and phone number of a doctor in Glendale. Simon bent down behind the desk, where a heavy metal safe was pushed against the wall. He spun the combination and reached inside, removing a tightly packed black plastic bag. Within the bag were banded stacks of bills, mostly hundreds, some fifties and twenties. This was his commission. He counted it out on the desk: $4,750. Half of the 2.5 percent of the deal fee he was technically owed, but they'd agreed that DaSilva would deduct fifty percent of the payouts until Simon's loan was cleared. Still, the figure was almost double what he'd earned on any of his previous pairings. He had to guess he was seeing here, in the inflated fee, the argument for shifting their focus to livers.

His cell phone buzzed as he stuffed the cash into his messenger bag. Another text from DaSilva: "Discharged AM. Drop off PM." Simon wrote back: "Confirmed." Five days was the earliest end of the donor's postsurgery inpatient window; Maria must be recovering quickly.

Simon cracked the window, lit a cigarette, and did a quick calculation: he still owed DaSilva about $10,000 on the loan. Two more deals like this one, though, and he'd be free and clear. As he tapped the cigarette against the ashtray perched on the windowsill, a gust of wind pushed into the office. The cherry of his cigarette came loose and was blown to the carpeted floor, still glowing, hot and orange, behind a stand supporting the fax machine. "Fuck!" He stubbed out the butt and dropped to his hands and knees, peering underneath the stand. The ember was burrowing into the carpet just beyond his reach. He grabbed a curled sheet of paper from the floor behind the stand and stretched to stamp out the ember with its folded edge.

He stood up and looked at the paper, which appeared to be some kind of wire transfer form filled out in DaSilva's bulbous, oddly childlike hand. Strings of account numbers and routing codes; a bank address in the Bronx and another, it seemed, in Cyprus; at the bottom, DaSilva's signature. A small burn hole marred the document now, an inch above the top account number. Simon folded the paper and slipped it into his inner jacket pocket. He'd return it and explain the burn hole to DaSilva when he next saw him; he assumed Peter didn't want something like that just floating around the office anyway.

Simon walked to the subway, messenger bag slung over his shoulder. His first stop was his own bank, a Chase on Delancey Street. He stacked the new cash into his deposit box, where it joined about $3,000 left over from his earlier deals, and peeled off a few hundreds, folding them inside his wallet. Next he took the 7 train to an HSBC in Flushing. He handed over his driver's license and the deposit key to the clerk, a Chinese girl no older than eighteen, her hair pulled back into a high ponytail, diamond stud in her nose. She scanned his license, glanced up at him. Then she disappeared into a back office, and he waited by the teller windows, fiddling with the strap of his bag. At the window nearest to him, he watched an old woman with a face like a dried date shove a stack of wrinkled bills under the divider.

"Sir?"

She was back, his clerk, handing him the key and his license, leading him down a hallway to a set of double metal doors. She unlocked the doors, and he followed her down a narrow row of brass-fronted boxes running up to the low ceiling. They stopped, and she slid the bank key into the upper lock of DaSilva's box. Simon slid his key into the lower lock; they turned the keys in unison. She removed the oblong box from its slot and handed it to him with a grave formality. He nodded, carrying the box to a small room at the back of the vault and closing the door behind him. He placed the box onto a plastic table, sat on a foldout chair. Inside the box were bundled stacks of cash, crisp and fresh, smelling of ink. He transferred the cash into his messenger bag, one bundle at a time. When the box was empty, he closed the lid and sat for a moment, trying to get his breathing under control. It still unnerved him, handling this much money; he didn't know if he'd ever get used to it.

He didn't know exactly how DaSilva manufactured the cash. The recipients made their checks out to Health Solutions, and Simon placed the checks into the office safe. DaSilva had never explained through what process of laundering alchemy those checks became the cash in this, and all the other, deposit boxes, and Simon thought it best if he didn't know anyway.

His next stop was a Bank of America in the East Fifties, a bright, low-ceilinged space installed on the ground floor of a brutalist office tower, and he collected the rest of the payment from the deposit box there without incident. Outside again, his bag heavy with cash, he watched the light fade from the sky with a certain finality. People rushed along the street, collars pulled tight; the days of lingering, of strolling, were nearly done for the year. The thought hit him: What if he just left? Took the $145,000 and split. He could hole up in some remote, cheap corner of the country, whittle away at the cash while he figured out what sort of a life he could stand to live. God knows he wouldn't be leaving very much behind, besides his father (and if anyone could understand such an abrupt withdrawal from a prior mode of existence, it was Michael Worth). He wondered how far DaSilva would go to find him, what sort of resources his employer had at his disposal. He wondered, not for the first time, whether DaSilva was an ambitious regular guy—an inveterate hustler, maybe, but no more—who'd stumbled upon a criminal opportunity too good to pass up, or a budding career criminal in deep cover. It was a long way from designing fake IDs to tampering with financial and medical records, violating medical law and ethics, and laundering hundreds of thousands of dollars at a time. The question was one of temperament or, to put it another way, of whether DaSilva was the kind of person who regarded intimidation and violence as the cost of doing business. Because that, to Simon, was a criminal: someone who considers anybody standing between them and what they want as an object to be eliminated in as expedient and permanent a manner as possible.

But who was Simon kidding? This line of inquiry was pointless. He wasn't going anywhere. He didn't have the balls, and, besides, he wouldn't be stealing from DaSilva—he'd be stealing from Maria, and he wasn't going to screw her over like that.

He took the shuttle from Grand Central to Times Square and walked the few blocks to the Royal Crown. On the twenty-ninth floor, he found the door to Maria's room and knocked. He heard a rustling, and the door opened partway, the lock chain pulling taut.

Half of Maria's face filled the crack, a single deep-black eye. She closed the door, and he heard the chain fall free, the door opening fully for him now. Maria retreated to the bed as he stepped into the room. The overhead light was off, the bedside lamp throwing an orange circle across the bed, the side chair, a swath of wall. The radiator gurgled and hissed in the corner. The heat was turned up too high, and there was an odd odor in the air, something sour and chemical. Maria gingerly lay back against the stacked pillows. On the bedside table stood a row of orange plastic pill bottles. The television played on mute, teenage girls screaming silently at each other outside a nightclub. Maria wore a baggy gray sweatshirt and flannel pants, her black hair falling lankly over the white pillows. She gave Simon a fatigued, drugged smile.

He sat down in the chair, the bag in his lap. "How are you feeling?"

"I'm feeling," she said, "just fucking peachy."

"Did the Cabrera people treat you okay?"

"I wish I could tell you, but I don't really remember." Her voice was thick, syrupy. She pointed at the bag. "Did you bring me a present?"

"Your money." He opened the bag, tilted it toward her to show the cash inside. "We've also arranged for you to see a doctor when you're back in California." He placed the sheet with the doctor's information onto the bed beside her. "It's important that you see him as soon as you get home. Okay?"

"All business," she mumbled.

"What?"

"Want to see the sutures?" She clutched at the hem of her sweatshirt. "I'll show them to you."

"I don't—"

She pulled up the sweatshirt. Her abdomen was flat, some faint stretch marks creeping above the waistband of her pants. He let his eye drift toward what she wanted to show him, the upside-down Y, its central branch beginning below her sternum and running through her belly button before splitting, the two prongs diving into the hollows of her hip bones. The cut was covered by medical tape, but he could see the shadow of the suture underneath, an eel slipping through murky water. The skin around the edges of the tape was red and puffy, an ointment of some kind glistening in the light of the lamp. She sat up straight, sucking in her stomach, the wound rippling with her breathing. He glanced up at her face, and she was looking down at her abdomen dazedly, the pink tip of her tongue probing the cracked corner of her lips, as though she couldn't quite believe what had been done to her. Then she lay back against the pillows, letting the sweatshirt fall. She winced and grabbed at her stomach.

"Jesus *Christ*." Her face screwed up in pain, and then she relaxed again, opening her eyes and staring at the ceiling. "He almost fucked it up. Him and his bitch of a wife."

"Who? Lenny?"

"Before I left, the doctors wanted me to go see him and say good-bye. Because we're so close and everything. I limp in, and that woman says, 'So this is her.' Like she's surprised."

"That's . . . Who was in the room?"

"The coordinator. And two nurses."

"The coordinator? You mean Peter DaSilva?"

"Yeah. She's sitting in her chair staring at me. Lenny—tubes running into his nose and mouth and stomach—he mumbled something to her. I couldn't hear what, but he sounded pissed. If you were in the room, you'd know she never saw me before in her life. You haven't heard anything about it, have you?"

"No."

She looked at him, her eyes suddenly lucid. "It's DaSilva, isn't it?"

"What is?"

"Your contact at the hospital."

"I don't have a con—"

"Simon. Please. The whole thing, it was too smooth. Somebody's greasing the wheels in there."

Simon shook his head.

"He didn't blink," she said. "He just stuck to the script, talking about what a fast recovery I'd made. What a blessing it all was. He knew what was going on. I could tell."

"That's just not the case." It seemed somehow obscene to lie to her as she lay there wounded and diminished on the bed, but he didn't see any other choice. "Sorry."

She sighed. "Whatever. Fine." She looked at the TV, turned it off with an irritated flick of the remote. "Just tell me I don't have to worry about it."

"About what?"

"The hospital coming after me. Or Lenny. Asking questions. Looking for this." She pointed her toes toward the bag on the floor.

"You don't have to worry about it."

"Okay. I want to get on the train on Monday and leave it all behind."

"That's what's going to happen." He looked around at the chaos of the room, socks and underwear hanging off the radiator, lotions and nail files and toiletries spilled across the bathroom counter. "I can take you to Penn Station if you want."

"I'll be fine." She pointed at the bag with her foot again. "I think I have enough cash for a taxi."

"Tell me you'll go see the doctor when you get home."

"I'll see him."

Simon stood, sweat pooling in the small of his back. Maria closed her eyes, and he thought for a moment she might have fallen asleep. He felt an impulse to sit next to her on the bed, to stroke her forehead, hold her clammy hand. A strand of hair stuck to her cheek, curled underneath her bottom lip. He stepped toward the door, and then she opened her eyes and said, "I forgot something when I was showing you the suture." She propped herself up onto her elbows, wincing again. "Look." She pulled the sweatshirt up and peeled off the top portion of tape. The incision was black and yellowish purple, puckered at its quilted junction like a pair of bruised lips, but that wasn't what she was trying to show him. She pointed to a chocolate-colored birthmark a few inches below her sternum that had been bisected by the cut. It was irregular, vaguely oval: a coffee stain, a dirty cloud. Simon leaned in closer as Maria tilted her torso toward the lamp. He could see that the birthmark's two halves had not been aligned properly during the sewing-up of her abdomen; one had been set a half inch or so higher than the other. The marred birthmark seemed in its asymmetry more grotesque than the scar itself, more unnatural, and abruptly, in one vertiginous moment, Maria's wound swallowed up the rest of the room, the rest of the world: the halved birthmark, the bruised tissue, the sheen of ointment.

He stepped back, bumping into the chair.

"Yeah, well. Like I said, I don't wear a lot of bikinis." She shrugged, let the sweatshirt fall again. "This"—she nodded at the money—"it's going to save my life. You don't even understand. Anyway. Take care of yourself, Simon."

HE couldn't sleep that night. After an hour, he rose from his bed and pulled open the shades, leaving the lights off. He watched a black rope of water uncoil as it slid past the river's near bank, and then he turned away, closing the shades and switching on the bedside lamp. He opened the bottom drawer of his dresser and removed a metal lockbox. He sat on the edge of his bed, in the lamp's pool of light, with the box in his lap. It was Amelia's. Simon had taken the lockbox and its contents during the two weeks between her death and his father's stripping of her room. He remembered pushing the door open gently, gingerly. He'd felt as though he were moving within a dream or a hallucination, an interval outside the normal flow of time, in which Amelia was absent, and upon his return to the real world, he would find her here, in her bedroom again, still angry at him and still alive. He discovered the lockbox under her bed, pushed into the far corner against the wall. He took it back into his room and solved the four-digit combination on his first guess. The code was her birthday; locking the box seemed to be a ritual, not an actual protection against anyone who knew her well opening it. Inside was a small red notebook held shut with a black elastic strap. His nerves sang: her diary. He opened the book to its first page to begin reading, but he found he couldn't do it. His eyes filled with sudden tears; the letters on the page blurred and swam. The dream ruptured. The notion that she was gone and that he could have saved her took on the heavy gravity of truth. He felt in his gut the first spasms of overwhelming guilt, like the probing tendrils of fever in the hours before it fully seizes the body. He closed the diary and slipped the elastic strap back into place, and he let himself cry.

He spun the lock now, lifted the lid, and took the diary out of the box, placing it on his bed. Seven years later, it remained un-read. He removed the other two objects and laid them by the di-ary's side. One was a woven hemp bracelet her high school boyfriend had given to her, the kind a kid might make at summer camp. The other was a series of drawings in ballpoint pen of a Venus flytrap, its exterior electric green, the lining a fleshy pink. The plant's mouth was opened wide and the fringe rimming the mouth had been exaggerated into fangs, each tooth tapering to a point dripping with saliva. Amelia's flytrap possessed a tongue as well, a thin, curling protuberance on the tip of which sat a small girl with wings, a Tinker Bell–like figure, her legs hanging over the edge of the tongue, her eyes looking dreamily off into the dis-tance as though unaware of the jaws poised above and below. The image had been drawn on a sheet of drafting paper in four itera-tions, each sharper and more complex than the next. These were sketches for a tattoo Amelia had planned to get inked onto the space between her shoulder blades. He had found them in her desk drawer, on top of a stack of discarded ideas—an octopus, a lotus, Mount Fuji and its reflection in a pool of water.

He'd brought the lockbox to college with him, and for a while he'd worn the hemp bracelet as though it were a fetish or a pathetic attempt at some kind of communion. The university had been built at the top of a steep hill, with a moribund upstate town at the bottom. During the winter, which never seemed to end, the road up the hill would ice over, and the students could choose between a freezing, laborious walk up from the town's bars or a ride chauffeured by the self-reportedly least drunk of their friends. This situation didn't concern Simon, who rarely left his room for anything other than classes and meals. He could purchase pot from a kid down the hall, and this was what he decided to do with his free time during freshman year, finishing his class work around midnight and puffing at a glass pipe shaped like a blowfish until he passed out. One night, in the middle of January, he sat on his bed, stoned and sleepless, staring into the open lockbox. The bracelet sat on top of the red diary. He took it out, retied the frayed knot. He lit the red candle that sat in a puddle of dried wax on his dresser, pressing a softened wad of wax onto the knot, sealing the bracelet around his wrist.

The next morning he heard that a car packed with six students had skidded off the road up from town as the driver, blind drunk, gunned it up the hill. The car had slammed into a tree. Four kids died, all freshmen; the driver chipped his front teeth on the steering wheel and walked away. The campus contorted itself into a frenzy of grieving, and for a time Simon felt as though his classmates had tuned themselves to the same pitch as his own private frequency of guilt and pain. The resonance rattled his bones, a bell struck inches from his ear. He applied a fresh dab of melted wax every morning, when he woke up, to ensure the bracelet's seal. Only when it was time to return to Rockaway for the summer did he take it off; he didn't want his father to recognize it. By the time he returned to school the following fall, the campus's grief had become formalized, had cooled and hardened into an object to be regarded at a respectful remove. The resonance was silenced. Back on his wrist, the bracelet looked idiotic; it had, after all, been made for a girl. He sliced through the wax with a penknife and dropped it back into the box, where it lay curled like a worm.

He sat on the bed now and looked at the three objects: diary, bracelet, drawing. This ritual of looking and handling took place in a realm somewhere parallel to everyday life. He tried not to think about Amelia in the daylight, in the company of other people. The brittleness he felt then, out in the world, the sense that he moved always across a field of thin ice beneath which lay cold black water—the sense that he *was* that field of ice—was replaced late at night, in private conference with these objects, but with what he couldn't exactly say. He conceived of it only as a *thickness*, a thickness of feeling. He needed this ritual because it reminded him of the pain that true feeling carried within itself—what intensities of pain were latent, buried like a land mine, within any love—and he thought that if he did not allow himself to touch pain in this controlled way, it might rush upon him at any moment in his daytime life and sweep him under.

And yet that wasn't entirely it. Within the pain flickered a sense of possibility. The pain told him that he was still capable of loving in the first place, capable of caring on a level deeper than the shallows of the everyday. The idea that he had exhausted or abandoned true and deep feeling—it could be disproven, reversed. There was an emotional stiffness to him, a kind of cramp, as though he'd twisted his capacity for love under the weight of his body and forgotten it there. He could extend the metaphor: the real suffering, and the real healing, would begin only when he untwisted the sleeping limb and allowed the blood, hot and screaming, to rush back in.

The drafting paper was growing brittle, the bracelet yellowing. The unopened diary, though, looked as new as the day he'd found it. He held it for a moment, rubbing its oily leather cover with his thumb. Then he placed it back into the box, closed the lid, and spun the lock.

## Five

A LITTLE less than a week later, Simon sat in the office, arranging a new pairing. The e-mails piled up, a steady stream of small miseries: a woman in Aurora, Colorado, facing foreclosure and offering one of her kidneys for "$100,000 (price negotiable)"; a man in a Phoenix suburb who wanted to know whether a case of gout precluded him from donating; a kid from White Plains who'd heard giving up a kidney might void the remainder of his National Guard commitment. They'd all found Simon's e-mail address on the sparse Health Solutions website. Most of them mentioned being directed to the site from comments and anecdotes on message boards like Living Donors Network and Transplant Friends. Some of these comments had been planted by Simon, some were left by actual former clients, and some, it seemed, were written by people with only secondhand knowledge of what DaSilva's company offered. Simon sifted through Cabrera's recipient waiting list and compiled the names Peter had marked with a "$," the lucky few who possessed the means to buy their way to the front of the line. He arranged these names by blood type and then began to compose his responses to the most promising of the aspiring donors, hoping for a few quick matches. He was typing one of these messages—this applicant a furloughed Michigan machinist with a problematic mortgage—when the desk phone rang.

It was Cheryl Pellegrini. She asked, in a forced sort of way, how he was doing. Fine, he told her, trying to keep his surprise at hearing from her out of his voice. And how was Lenny? He was pretty good, she said. In fact, he'd made a suggestion, which was the reason she was calling: why didn't Simon come out to their place for dinner? *Their place*. Lenny thought it was too bad, she said, that he hadn't seen Simon since the operation; he wanted to thank him in person. Unless they'd given the man a brain transplant as well, Simon thought this extremely unlikely. But, still, it was his responsibility to ensure that Health Solutions' clients were satisfied after their surgery, so he told Cheryl he'd be glad to eat dinner with them.

The next evening, he hurried to Penn Station to catch the train, and an hour later his taxi pulled into Lenny's driveway. He peered through the windshield at the little house. He could see movement in the kitchen, a backlit figure—it had to be Cheryl—bending over the stove. He paid his fare and made his way up the porch stairs. The screen door was closed and latched, the front door half-open behind it. He paused for a moment, looking through the foyer and into the living room. Bright light from a half-dozen new lamps opened up the space, raising the ceilings, pushing out the walls. He was still standing there, his knuckles poised to rap on the door frame, when a little girl barreled down the staircase in the center of the foyer, pulling up short as she saw him. She couldn't have been more than three, a chubby child dressed in nubby lavender pajamas. She put her finger in her mouth and cocked her head at him as though deciding whether to be upset by his presence. She turned around and said, "Greggy." A boy, a few years older, pale and doughy with a to-scale version of his father's squared-off head, joined her on the landing, saying, "I *told* you not to call me—" He cut himself off as he noticed Simon standing on the other side of the screen. "Mom!" the boy called out, not alarmed, just doing what he'd been told to do. Simon knocked on the frame—a formality now—as Cheryl Pellegrini rounded a corner into the living room. She quickly unlatched the screen door and waved Simon inside.

"You made it." She sounded as though she hadn't fully believed he'd show up. He didn't take it personally; he assumed living with Lenny had conditioned her to expect disappointment. "Lenny's in there." She jerked her thumb toward the kitchen. "Greg, Dani, stop skulking around and come say hello to Simon."

The children regarded Simon warily from the landing. Greg stood behind Daniela, one hand resting protectively on his sister's elbow. They were glum, serious kids, Simon thought, something of the hangdog about the pair already.

"What's this, kiddos?" Cheryl said. "Pretending to be shy?"

They came down the remaining stairs, jostling halfheartedly against each other. Cheryl took hold of their shoulders, propelled them forward. "Simon, this is Gregory and Daniela. Greg and Dani, meet Simon."

Simon started to squat down, then thought better of it halfway, ending up in a kind of tensed crouch. He never knew how to approach children, whether to address them as though they were dizzy, uninformed adults or to slip into kidspeak—"Hey, whatcha got there?" and so on—which he suspected even the kids thought was pathetic.

"Nice to meet you," he said, nodding.

"Are you a doctor?" Daniela said around the finger still stuck in her mouth.

"Not really. No."

"He's a friend of Daddy's," Cheryl said.

"From the football team?" Daniela asked doubtfully.

"Uh-uh." Somber Gregory shook his head with grim certainty. "You'd get killed."

"That's not nice," Cheryl said.

Simon laughed. "It's true though."

She pointed up the stairs. "Bedtime for real now, okay?" The kids registered a brief complaint before dragging themselves tragically up the stairs and down the hall.

Simon followed Cheryl into the kitchen, which smelled strongly of garlic and stewed tomatoes. Lenny sat at the table. He'd cut his hair. The floppy black mop was gone, and now a buzz cut hugged the contours of his monolithic skull, making him appear younger, soldierly. He looked up as Simon entered the room, his face thinner, the skin slack over his cheekbones. He spread his arms wide, his torso hidden within a giant green sweatshirt with "Property of the New York Jets" emblazoned across the chest.

"The new me," he said. "What do you think?"

"Looking good," Simon said, somewhat more passionlessly than he'd intended.

"So Cheryl tells me. Feeling pretty fucking good too." He nodded, vigorously, as though ready to prove it with a bout of arm wrestling or jumping jacks.

"He's still got some pain in his gut," Cheryl said. "But nothing worse than what they warned us about."

Simon wondered if she'd moved back into the house or if this was only temporary, a trial period while she helped Lenny regain his health. Both of them were behaving pleasantly enough, but he could sense tension in the room, the crackling of something left unsaid.

"The follow-up from Cabrera," Simon said. "It's been all right?"

Lenny shrugged. "That guy, the coordinator, he's checked in on us a few times. I've made it to all my appointments, believe it or not. There hasn't been that much for them to do."

"They've been fine," Cheryl said firmly. She turned to the stove, stirred a pot of softball-sized meatballs. "How's the girl?"

"The girl?"

"My heroic second cousin," Lenny said.

"She's back in California." They waited for him to say more. "In Los Angeles," he added.

"No, hey, I get it," Lenny said. "Don't worry—we're not going to show up at her doorstep with a fruit basket. But it would be nice to know she's not bleeding to death in the basement of Cabrera."

"Lenny!"

"She's doing fine," Simon said.

"Are you going to talk to her soon?" Cheryl asked.

"Possibly. I could if you'd like me to."

"If you do, tell her I'm sorry for how I was at the hospital."

"What do you mean?"

"She didn't tell you?" Cheryl said. "I almost gave everything away. They brought her into Lenny's room, and I said something stupid and—"

"'So this is her.'" Lenny flashed a hostile grin. "That's what you said."

"Thank you, Lenny." She poured the meatballs into a bowl and aggressively scraped the dregs of sauce out of the pot. "She barely blinked, so kudos to her. But it was very tense for a minute in there. The hospital people didn't seem to notice, thank God."

"Maria looked pissed," Lenny said. "Can't say I blame her."

"So you've said. More than once." Cheryl glanced over her shoulder at her husband, then turned back to the sink. "Look, I'm grateful for what she did, even if I know it had nothing to do with Lenny. That's not an easy choice to make, no matter how much money she got out of it. And her reasons for doing it don't really matter in the end, do they? Not to us anyway. Lenny got what he needed, and now he can start the rest of his life."

"That's right," Lenny said, again nodding mechanically, as though someone had pressed a button to activate his agreement.

Dinner was veal meatballs topped with sugary tomato sauce, Parmesan, and basil, with a side of sautéed asparagus and, for Cheryl and Simon, a bottle of juicy red wine. Simon chewed and sipped and talked, wondering why he'd really been invited here. It was Cheryl's idea, that much was obvious; Lenny didn't seem to feel the need to thank him for anything, and why should he? It was as though she'd wanted to put her husband on display. But why? He watched Lenny eat. The man cut the meatballs into tiny pieces, which he pushed around his plate and often abandoned before they made it into his mouth. He sipped his water. He spoke when spoken to, answering his wife always in the affirmative: yes, he was glad Howard had kept after him all those months; yes, he would be happy to return to the meetings at Don MacLeod's house in a few weeks; yes, of course, it was wonderful to be spending more time with Greg and Dani again. Yes, yes, yes, wonderful, wonderful said his mouth. His eyes said nothing at all.

They finished eating and sat in silence for a few moments.

"Well," Lenny said, "I'm stuffed. Everything was delicious, honey." He heaved himself up from his chair. "Hate to say it, but that's it for me. These pills knock you out. Simon, thanks for coming by. I appreciate it."

Simon stood up and took the hand that was offered to him, Lenny's fingers the size of cigars, his palm calloused and sweaty. He squeezed Simon's hand, then let it go and slowly made his way out of the kitchen, his heavy steps creaking up the staircase.

"Come on," Cheryl said. "I'll drive you to the station."

She led him through the living room and out onto the front lawn. The maroon Honda was parked on a tongue of concrete in front of the garage. They drove the mile to the station in silence before she pulled to a stop near the tracks. She turned toward him, the skin under her eyes dark and shiny, like the skin of a plum. A crease slashed down and away from each corner of her mouth.

"Thanks again for coming out here," she said. "I understand it probably isn't something you normally do."

"I don't mind," he said, "if you think it might have been helpful in some way." He tried to leave a question mark floating at the end of this statement, hoping she might give him some idea of why she'd wanted him here.

"Sorry he went up so early. He's been sleeping a lot. He's still on a lot of medication and . . ." She trailed off for a moment, then said, "I'll be honest, I was worried about the painkillers they gave him. That's part of how we got here in the first place, you know?

It seemed too much like the same crap all over again. But I guess there's no way around it."

"I'm sure the hospital took his history into account," he said, although given DaSilva's tinkering with the medical records, he wasn't sure of that at all.

"Yeah." She stared out through the windshield. "How did he seem to you? Really."

"Well, I'm not a doctor, but, physically, his recovery—"

"Come on, Simon." She straightened in her seat, suddenly irritated. "You know that's not what I mean, they can tell us that at the hospital. How did he *seem* to you?"

"I think he's glad he went through with it," Simon said carefully. "He seems happy to be with the kids again. To be with you."

"Yeah, I know that's what he *said*, but do you—oh, Christ! You're making me feel like I'm fucking crazy." She rubbed her eyes, then looked him straight in the face. Her expression was raw, overflowing with the need to be heard, to be understood. "Howard was over here last week, okay? I asked him the same thing, and he answered the same as you: 'He's glad he did it. He's happy to have you back. It's all fine. It's all great.' You have no idea how much I want to believe that. After all the shit we've been through, after the years I've spent watching Lenny drink himself into oblivion, his organs crapping out on him one by one . . . You think I *want* him to be lying to me now?" She shook her head sharply, as though trying to rid herself of the thought. "I can't talk about this with anybody else. Everybody thinks—miracle of miracles—he got his new liver off the UNOS list, from some poor kid who crashed his motorcycle and smashed his skull or whatever. They don't know how hostile Lenny was to the idea of saving his own life. But you do. So, please, I'm going to ask you this one time, and then you can forget I ever said anything: Can you honestly tell me you didn't notice anything fake about the way he was talking? Can you honestly tell me you think he believed in what he was saying?"

Simon could easily tell her he had no reason to disbelieve Lenny; he could tell her he'd noticed nothing to indicate her husband wasn't genuine in his optimism and gratitude. Pleading ignorance would be an easy means of disengagement. The establishment of a safe, blameless distance. And yet he found himself silent. She continued to search his face, the train station's halogens carving shadows into her cheeks, her eyes fervid and alert. She didn't want to be reassured; she wanted to be told the truth, even if that made her husband's new embrace of life a lie. But he couldn't be the one to tell her.

"I think he's doing all right, Cheryl," he said. "I really do."

She held his gaze for a final breath. And then, abruptly, her eyes shut down, their intensity snuffed out. She nodded, looked out the windshield again. "If that's what you really think," she said, and he heard in her voice that he'd waited too long to answer, that he'd given himself away. She knew he'd seen what she was talking about, and she knew that he was a coward for not admitting it. "Thanks again for coming out here."

"Good luck," he said, lamely, before he let himself out of the car and walked up the stairs to the platform.

Simon was back in the office late the following afternoon, continuing to sort through the Cabrera list, homing in, he hoped, on Health Solutions' next pairing. He tried to put Lenny out of his mind, those flat lizard eyes, that cheerful and utterly hollow voice. He and DaSilva had done what was asked of them, hadn't they? It wasn't their fault if it wasn't what Lenny truly wanted. Not their problem now either.

The desk phone rang again, disrupting the construction of his self-defense. Usually Simon considered the phone, like the rest of the office, more of a prop than a functional tool, and yet here it was intruding on him for the second time in as many days. He checked the caller ID: he didn't recognize the number, but the area code indicated the Los Angeles area. He hesitated, then thought of Maria and picked up: "Health Solutions."

"Peter DaSilva, please." A male voice, Mitteleuropean accent.

"He's not in. Who's this?"

A pause, then, "Who is *this*?"

"Simon Worth. Can I help you?"

"Simon. That's right. Peter mentioned you."

"Yeah?"

"It's Stan Grodoff, calling from Glendale."

Simon straightened in his chair. "Dr. Grodoff."

"Maybe you can help me with this. Your client, Maria Campos. She missed her appointment with me. Peter knows I don't like to chase after these people, so I'm going to let you do that now."

"I . . . I'm sorry. I don't know what to tell you."

"You don't have to tell me anything. I just thought you should know. Give Peter my best."

"I will," Simon said, but Grodoff had already hung up.

Simon's first thought was to call DaSilva, but he stopped himself. Maybe he could handle this on his own. He called Maria's cell phone, using the office line. It rang five times before going to voice mail. He hung up without leaving a message; then he took out his cell phone and dialed again. This time he left a message, asking her to call him, not mentioning her missed appointment with Grodoff.

The Royal Crown stonewalled him over the phone, so he showed up at the front desk and brandished the credit card on which he'd charged Maria's room. The clerk retreated, a manager replacing him to inform Simon that Ms. Campos had indeed checked out on the morning she'd been originally scheduled to leave. No, she had not extended her reservation with cash. And what was his relationship to Ms. Campos, if he didn't mind them asking? "Colleague," Simon muttered, already walking away.

He stood outside on Forty-Fifth Street and called Amtrak—she'd been scheduled to take the train back to California to avoid having TSA agents quiz her about the $150,000 in her baggage—which informed him that the status of its passengers was not public information, and, no, it did not matter that he'd paid for the trip. He called Maria's cell phone again and left another message, this time mentioning her appointment with Grodoff. He imagined her cooped up in her Torrance apartment, sweating with fever, too sick to take Gabriel to the playground, the boy scrambling all over the house, driving her batshit.

He ate dinner near his apartment, at a glass-walled sushi place installed on the ground floor of a new residential complex called the Octagon, which was named, rather unbelievably, after a mental institution that had once stood on the same ground and been made infamous by an outraged Charles Dickens on one of his American publicity tours. After drinking a carafe of hot sake to smother the little flame of anxiety that flickered in his chest, Simon walked home along Main Street, past the tiny old Episcopalian church tucked among the apartment towers. Nine p.m., and Roosevelt Island had emptied out and turned in—the stores shuttered, the few restaurants mostly quiet. What was Maria up to?

He let himself into the lobby of his apartment building, a pile of take-out menus strewn along the path to the elevator. Upstairs, he lay down on the couch, lit a cigarette, and turned on the television. He let the bad news wash over him, the graphs plunging into red, the anchors auguring further collapse; the campaign for the presidency was in its acrimonious and frantic final days. He decided that in the morning he'd tell DaSilva what had happened, making it sound as though Grodoff had only just called him. He got up to fix himself a whiskey, then lay back down to watch the CEO of the bank that employed his father explain how he couldn't be held responsible for the mistakes of employees whose jobs he didn't fully understand.

He fell asleep easily, as soon as he dragged himself from the couch to his bed, a small miracle he wasn't fully aware of until some hours later, when he was woken by his buzzing cell phone.

He checked the screen: the Health Solutions office number. Baffled, he answered before he was fully awake.

"Office." DaSilva's voice, icy, level. "Now."

"Peter? What—"

"Now, Simon." The line went dead.

A cold stab in his gut. It was five thirty a.m. He got up and dressed, half hungover, half simply dog tired. He walked to the subway, full of dread, running through a short list of feeble excuses.

When he let himself into the office, DaSilva was sitting behind the desk, a cigarette hanging from his lip, three crushed butts in the ashtray. Peter waited for Simon to close the door behind him. Then he said, "Where is Maria Campos?"

Simon stopped, his hand still touching the doorknob. "California?"

"California." DaSilva's voice remained, for now, as calm and uninflected as usual; his eyes betrayed nothing. "You're telling me California. Do you know that, or are you just saying it?"

"I don't know. No."

"No, what?"

"I don't know that."

"Until an hour ago, I didn't know either, and I didn't care, because I thought you had a fucking handle on things." DaSilva paused, regained his calm. "She's in the ICU at Abraham Medical Center. In Williamsburg. You know, *in Brooklyn?* They processed her tonight after somebody found her collapsed in the stairwell of some shitbox on South Tenth Street. Where she's apparently *living* now. Do you have any idea what I'm talking about?"

Simon gripped the doorknob so tightly his knuckles ached. "No."

"No. It's three a.m. in Los Angeles right now, which is the only reason I haven't called Stan Grodoff to ask him why his patient was admitted to a Brooklyn hospital with a bile leak and 103-degree fever. Can you help me guess what he's going to say when I do call him?"

"She never showed."

"And you know this how?"

"He called and told me."

"When?"

Simon stepped away from the door and dropped his head, the chastened freshman called into the principal's office for a stern dressing-down. "Yesterday," he said.

"Yesterday. And did you ever stop and say, hey, maybe my bud Pete DaSilva might be interested in this particular nugget of information? Did that ever cross your mind? Because, I'll tell you, I would've felt like much less of an asshole when some admitting resident from Abraham calls our unit, wondering whether we've recently performed a living donor resection on somebody named Maria Campos."

"Why would—"

"Why would what? Why would what?" DaSilva was hissing now, his anger escaping like pressurized steam. "Why would he think that? Maybe because a girl with a fresh transplant scar just washed up in his ICU half-delirious from fever, claiming, first, that she never had any surgery, then changing her story to say it took place two weeks ago in fucking *Israel*."

"You said no."

"What?"

"You said she hadn't been a patient at Cabrera."

"What the fuck do you think?"

Simon took his Parliaments from his pocket and got one lit. His hands were shaking.

"Here's what you're going to do," DaSilva said. "You're going to go down to Abraham when we're finished here and find out what the fuck is going on. She's got a biliary leak. It didn't rupture until after she left Cabrera. Grodoff would've spotted it five minutes after she walked into his office, but now we're dealing with the possibility of sepsis. They're probably blitzing her with IV antibiotics. My guess is they're going to go in through the mouth to see if a stent will work. She'll be there for at least a few days. Apparently she's living here alone and wouldn't give them a number for anybody to notify. Whenever they're done with her, she'll be pumped up with pain meds, and they'll need somebody to sign her out. Guess what? You're that special somebody. You're going to take her back to her apartment, and you're going to watch her until she's healed. I don't want her disappearing like this again. I want to know why she lied about going back to Los Angeles. It doesn't make any sense to me yet, and what I don't understand makes me nervous." He crushed his cigarette into the ashtray. "Anything else I should know? Or maybe you prefer I look like an asshole every now and then—I don't know."

"I thought I could deal with it on my own." Simon figured it probably wasn't the best time to tell DaSilva about his family dinner with the Pellegrinis. "I thought it was my responsibility. My problem, not yours."

"What a noble sentiment. Too bad it's bullshit. What you wanted was to fix your fuckup before I knew it had ever happened."

"Look," Simon said, suddenly tired of being lectured, "have I ever made a mistake before? In eight months of working for you, has anything like this ever happened?"

"One mistake is all it takes, Simon." DaSilva picked at a particle of food wedged between his front teeth and flicked it into the ashtray. He looked as though he hadn't slept in about a year. "We depend upon people's inertia. Their willingness to not pay attention, to look the other way. Nobody, except maybe some asshole journalist trying to boost his career, *wants* to discover what we're doing. The hospital administration, the police: what a fucking headache an investigation would be for those guys, right? Because it's a case without a victim. Somebody like Maria wants to keep her cash and shut up. Somebody like Lenny wants to keep his new liver and shut up. The surgeons and administrators want to keep their fee and shut up. But it only takes one little mistake to unbalance all that. One irregularity. Somebody asking why a transplant patient turned up at Abraham talking a bunch of bullshit about Israel. They trace her back to Cabrera—that could be the mistake I'm talking about. I'm not pissing on you because it's fun, Simon, okay? Health Solutions is a balanced, self-regulating system, but it is *delicate*. You need to understand that." He lit another cigarette. "I thought you did understand that, frankly."

This was the longest speech DaSilva had delivered in the eight months Simon had known him. Perhaps because his first dozen cases had gone so smoothly, and perhaps also because he so rarely saw DaSilva in person, Simon had nearly forgotten what kind of a risk his employer was taking, what kind of base-level paranoia and anxiety must always be simmering behind his mask of exhausted placidity. And yet, even as he was reminded of all of this, even as he saw these cracks in the mask, he still thought DaSilva was at least partly full of shit.

"We're supposed to be obsessed with not drawing any attention to the unit," Simon said, "but you force Lenny through?" DaSilva stared at him, his mouth hanging slightly agape. Simon's cheeks flushed—he'd never defied DaSilva before—but he pushed on. "It seems to me that enrolling an obvious alcoholic in the program counts as a mistake."

"The fuck it was. The surgeons would never have operated on him if they thought he couldn't survive the procedure."

"But I thought you altered—"

"Yeah, I can trim a few corners to get him past Klein, but I won't mess with his medical exam results. Never. That's the surgeons' call. I told you before: this hospital—this transplant unit— needs volume. That directive flows from the top down, and the surgeons are just interpreting it like everybody else. Besides, were there any problems with Lenny's surgery?"

"No, but—"

"Then why are we talking about it?"

"But what about Maria?"

"The bile leak? I told you, if she'd done what she was supposed to do—what you were supposed to make sure she did—then this wouldn't be a problem. So now, yes, *you* need to fix this, Simon. Get her out of Abraham. Supervise her recovery. Figure out why she lied and what she's planning to do next. Can you do all that?"

"Yeah." It helped that he also wanted to know the answers to these questions. "I'll handle it."

DaSilva nodded. "You're deep in this thing too, Simon. Don't fucking forget it."

## Six

SIMON found Abraham Medical Center south of the elevated J/M/Z tracks, the demarcation between the Williamsburg of cupcake shops and bike lanes and faux dive
bars and that of storefront *iglesias* and bodegas and, a few blocks
farther south, yeshivas and *shtreimel* hatteries. The line, though,
seemed to have lost its elasticity since the last time Simon had been
here, sagging now irregularly southward. As he walked down a
block of sooty tenements from which a ten-story glass tower protruded like a flipped bird, he decided he was going to set this situation with Maria right, deliver to DaSilva another two viable pairs,
and then get the hell out. He didn't like how exposed he suddenly
felt. Maria, Lenny, Cheryl, Crewes, now the staff at Abraham—it
was his face and name they'd point to if shit really hit the fan, if
DaSilva ever blew the whole thing up. And he didn't like the
way DaSilva was shifting the responsibility for Maria's situation so squarely onto his shoulders. Okay, he'd fucked up by not
checking in with Grodoff sooner, and maybe he should've told
DaSilva about the doctor's call right away. But how was he supposed to know Maria would lie like that? It had ambushed both
of them, and it was a problem they should be solving together.
Instead, DaSilva was isolating him, boxing him in. He didn't like
it at all.

He continued toward the BQE. The hospital was on the far

side of the expressway, a hulking white-brick structure set back from Lee Avenue. He dodged a Hebrew-lettered private ambulance and located the main entrance. He was directed up to the fourth floor, where he gave Maria's name to the receptionist, a pink-cheeked young woman with silver crosses dangling from her earlobes. She tapped at her computer, asked for his name.

"Simon Worth."

"You're the first to come see her." She checked a clipboard, scribbled a note. "She didn't give us a contact name or any number to call. I'm assuming she'll be happy to see you?"

"I'm her boyfriend," he said. The lie was spontaneous, thrilling.

The receptionist glanced up at him for the first time. "Just hang tight for a sec."

She picked up the desk phone, dialed a number. She glanced up at him again, and he realized he was leaning over the desk, crossing an invisible barrier into what she'd apparently designated as her personal fiefdom. He straightened up and backed away, shoving his hands into his pockets. Bells pinged, phones rang, the PA droned: the white noise of a busy urban hospital.

"She's not cleared for visitors yet," the receptionist said. "If you want to come back in a few hours—"

"I'll wait."

The receptionist frowned, then pointed at a row of molded plastic seats fastened to the wall.

He sat in one of the chairs and watched the business of the hospital unfold in isolated and harried bursts of activity. He closed his eyes and imagined Katherine Peel rounding the corner, Maria's chart in her hand. Then he imagined himself close behind, white coated, sober faced, holding forth to a gaggle of interns on the proper questioning technique for rounds. What a joke that was.

"Mr. Worth?"

Simon jerked his head. He must have dozed off, the short night of sleep catching up with him.

A gaunt-cheeked man in blue scrubs extended his hand: "Dr.

Rudich. I'm taking care of Ms. Campos. Diane tells me you're Maria's boyfriend?"

"Yes."

Rudich frowned at his clipboard, distracted. "And how did you find her here?"

"I'm sorry?"

"We didn't call you." Rudich looked up. "Neither did she, unless she's hiding a cell phone under her mattress."

"Her neighbors," Simon said, improvising. "I came to see her this morning and ran into some of them on the stoop. They said she'd been taken away in an ambulance and this is the closest hospital." He shrugged. "It was a good guess."

"Smart."

"What happened?" Simon said. "Is she okay? I don't—they didn't tell me much else."

"She's stable now, yes." Rudich seemed on the verge of saying more before reconsidering.

"Look, Dr. . . ."

"Rudich."

"Dr. Rudich. I've been out of town for a few weeks. In California. I got home last night. It's been a little while—maybe a week—since I talked to Maria. We were kind of in a fight." Simon looked down at his shoes, wondering if he was overdoing it. "I guess I'm asking . . . is this a sudden thing? Or has she been sick for a while and I just didn't know it?"

"Mr. Worth, has your girlfriend been to Israel recently?"

Simon raised his head. "Yeah. Last month. Why?"

"Did you go with her?"

"No. I was in California visiting family. Los Angeles."

"Have you seen her since she returned?"

"No. We talked, but I haven't seen her. Like I said, I just got back last night. Did she get sick while she was there?"

Rudich looked at him, tapping his pen against the edge of his clipboard. His eyes blinked rapidly behind frameless glasses. "Not exactly. She's had a procedure done, which she says took place there."

Simon tried to project the appropriate level of confusion, furrowing his brow, crinkling his nose. "What procedure?"

"It left her with a bile leak," Rudich said, ignoring the question. "We went through her mouth to place a stent. When we got a clear look at things, we saw that the duct tear was actually rather severe, and we had to go in laparoscopically to repair it." He shook his head. "Cleaning up somebody else's mess is always fun."

"What do you mean?"

"Ask her about this Israeli procedure, if you want."

Simon paused. He wanted to sound concerned, but not overeager. "Will she be able to leave today?"

"Tomorrow. She'll be on fairly heavy pain medication. You'll be the one signing her out?"

"Yes."

Rudich nodded as he led Simon down a hallway lined with empty gurneys. Doorways provided glimpses into windowless rooms, most of the patients hidden behind drawn plastic curtains. Simon glimpsed a few lying blanketed and entubed. Most were sleeping; the rest stared up at wall-mounted televisions, remotes cradled loosely in their hands.

"Here we are." Rudich rapped on a half-open door, stuck his head into the room. "Maria?" He took a few steps inside, Simon close behind him. "You have someone here to see you."

She lay propped up in the bed, her eyes closed. Her clothes— jeans, a gray sweatshirt, pink socks—were neatly folded inside a clear plastic bag, sitting on top of her black Chuck Taylors, on the seat of the room's only chair. A tube, its gauge the width of Simon's thumb, ran into the crook of her arm; a number of other tubes and wires disappeared under her gown. Her toes, the nails painted electric purple, protruded from the sheets.

"I doubt it," she said, her eyes still closed, her voice thick and drugged.

"Your boyfriend?" Rudich said.

Her eyes snapped open, her head bolting off the pillow. She saw Rudich first, then found Simon standing beside him. She stared at him, her body rigid. Slowly she relaxed, sinking back down onto the mattress, grimacing, touching her abdomen.

"Simon," she said. She looked away, color blooming in her cheeks.

"Are you all right?" Simon could feel Rudich's eyes on him; he forced himself to keep his attention on Maria.

"I don't know." She jutted her chin at Rudich. "Ask him."

"Could we speak in private for a moment?" Simon said.

"That's up to her," Rudich said.

She waved a hand. "It's okay."

Rudich glanced at Simon a final time before he slipped out of the room.

They stared at each other, Simon standing just inside the door, Maria breathing heavily, the pulse jumping in her neck. Simon broke first, turning away to place her sneakers and bag of clothes onto the floor. He pulled the chair closer to the bed and sat down.

"Boyfriend?" Maria said.

"Should I have said cousin? I thought you might be sick of that game by now."

She smiled, twisting it off into a grimace.

"I've been calling you," he said.

"I threw away my phone."

"Why?"

She didn't answer.

He leaned forward. "I went along with the Israel story," he said quietly. "I said I knew you'd been there but that I didn't know anything about the surgery. Why Israel?"

"I read an article," she muttered. "I don't know—it popped into my head. I hadn't planned for this."

"What did you plan for?"

She shook her head, looked away. "How did you find me?"

"I got a call," he said.

"You got a call? What does that mean?"

He ignored this. "I'll tell you something. If you boarded that train? If you visited that doctor in Glendale? Then, yeah, it's none of my business what you were planning. Why you needed the money. What you were going to do with it. I never pressed you about any of that because it didn't matter. It wasn't relevant. But now?" He paused, took a breath. Maybe he was going at her too hard. But the truth was that her evasions were pissing him off. "Do you know how many hospitals do live-donor liver transplants?"

"No, Simon, I don't."

"Three in New York City. About a dozen in the rest of the country. In the rest of the world, maybe thirty. You can't just turn up in the ER with that scar and not have people ask questions."

She stared at the ceiling.

"Maria. I need to know why you're still here in New York. And when you're planning on going home."

She said nothing.

"Maria?"

She snapped her head around. "I wouldn't be here unless the surgeons *you* sent me to hadn't fucked up. *I'm* the one who's suffering. *I'm* the one who's got a hole in her gut. Not you."

"If you'd gone to Dr. Grodoff—"

"*Fuck* Grodoff," she hissed. "And fuck you." She collapsed back into the pillows, her sweaty hair pasted across her forehead. She closed her eyes again, shuddering and clutching at her abdomen.

"I'm trying to help you," Simon said.

She shook her head.

"Your son," he said. "Is there somebody you want me to call? Maybe your sister? I can wire some of your cash out there, or . . . I don't know."

She shuddered again, this time with smaller, trembling movements. He realized she was laughing. She mumbled something he couldn't make out, and he leaned closer, asking her to repeat it.

"There's no son," she said.

"What do you mean?"

"I mean"—she quieted the trembling, spoke louder now—"there is no son. I've never had a child. Probably never will. No sister either."

"I don't understand."

"What's not to understand? You make up stories for people all the time. I made one up too. I figured if I was a single mom you might ask fewer questions about why I needed the money."

No wonder the life he'd imagined for her in LA felt so hollow, so incomplete; he'd assembled it out of faulty parts. "So you just lied to me?"

"Don't act so shocked. Isn't this whole thing a lie? Health Solutions and the rest of it?"

"We need to invent cover stories so—"

"Yeah, I get how it works. I'm just saying that you shouldn't be so surprised to find out you're not the only ones doing it."

His ears felt hot. He didn't fully understand why he was taking this so personally. "What else did you lie about?"

"Now is not the time."

"Maria—"

"Please." She pointed at her stomach. "Can we talk about this when I don't feel like there's a bag of broken glass in my gut?"

Simon looked more closely at the lines running into and out of her body: the saline drip, the antibiotic drip, the morphine drip, the catheter. Her pupils were dilated, the muscles in her face slack. He saw the plastic button held loosely in her hand, its cord running to the morphine drip. She watched him fidget in the chair, her eyes tracking a fraction behind his movements. She licked her lips.

"You know what?" she said. "I liked it better when I got paid to be a patient."

"I don't blame you."

"I want to get out of here." She lifted the button. "And I'm gonna take this with me."

"Tomorrow. I'll come sign you out."

"You're going to take me to my apartment?"

"Yeah."

She nodded. He watched her depress the button. "Who else knows I'm here?"

He hesitated. "Nobody."

"Liar."

"You're safe, Maria. I promise."

"You don't know what the fuck you're talking about," she said, the words slurring together.

She wriggled her body against the thin mattress, closing her eyes and turning her head away from him. He sat in the chair and looked at her. Her hospital gown had shifted with her movement, and he could see the side of one of her breasts, a pale swell of skin that rose and fell with her breath. He crossed and uncrossed his legs. He wanted to readjust her gown, to pull the pilled cloth tight across her chest and cover her up.

What was he going to tell DaSilva? She'd given him nothing, no real reason for not returning home to Los Angeles, no real reason for lying about having a son. (Or, rather, no clue as to why she would need to invent a lie at all.) He watched her breathe, the muscles of her face slackening. He wasn't going to get anything more out of her now. He bent down to her sneakers and the plastic bag stuffed with her clothes. As he lifted the sneakers up onto the seat, he noticed a flash of brass inside one of them. He reached inside: two keys hooked onto a safety pin, partially tucked underneath the insole. He glanced over at Maria as he pulled the keys free and cradled them in his palm. She hadn't moved; her head still faced the wall and her breathing was deep and steady.

These had to be the keys to her apartment. South Tenth Street, DaSilva had said. But South Tenth and what? He looked around the room and found her chart, tucked into a plastic holder affixed to the wall beside the door. He quickly scanned the top of the page, and there it was: "85 S. 10th St., #3B, Brooklyn, NY 11211."

He took a last look at Maria—passed out, tunneling deep into a morphine cloud—and slipped the keys into his pocket.

Outside, on Lee Avenue, Simon bummed a light from a man in a sheepskin coat who sat with his back against the hospital's wall, three empty Starbucks cups strewn around the man's feet, as though the sidewalk were his office. Simon walked north. He thought of the way Maria tensed when Rudich announced her boyfriend was there, her eyes wild and searching. She'd looked like a cornered animal, feral and desperate.

He turned off Bedford Avenue onto South Tenth. The block was near the river, on the northwestern fringes of Williamsburg's Hasidic community. Simon found number eighty-five on the north side of the street, close to a spartan asphalt playground. The building was old and solid, pale-tan brick with white trimmings and rusted orange fire escapes, free of the vinyl siding and ticky-tacky tar-paper roofing that plagued much of Williamsburg's housing. Simon shouldered his way through the building's outer door—wrought iron and glass—and stepped into a dim vestibule with a row of tarnished brass mailboxes mounted on one wall. He used the first key again on the interior door and proceeded to the stairwell, his shoes scratching on a layer of sandy grit. The lighting was poor, the fixtures grimy. He smelled frying onions and wet cement as he walked up the steps, black stone slabs with depressions worn into their centers. Leaking into the second-floor hallway was the syncopated thump of reggaeton, the outraged tones of talk radio. He walked up to the third floor and found 3B in the far corner, a worn plastic mezuzah affixed to the door frame. The second key turned in the lock, the deadbolt giving way with a satisfying thunk.

He stepped into a short, narrow hallway, closing the door behind him and sliding the lock chain into place. He flipped the wall switch; a jaundiced light issued from overhead bulbs. The hallway opened into a living room and kitchen area, an electric stove and refrigerator jutting from one wall along with a perfunctory strip of counter. The rest of the space was bare except for a single plastic folding chair. A white sheet had been nailed up over the room's only window. Next to the refrigerator was a tiny black-and-white tiled bathroom, and on the other side of the room, the door to the bedroom. Simon took two steps inside and couldn't go any farther: a king-sized mattress lay on the floor, sheets and blankets and pillows piled on top of it, an out-of-date, battered laptop nestled in the blankets, the mattress's edges flush against three of the room's walls. A small window was set into the wall above the head of the mattress, and a sheet had been nailed up here as well. He pulled the sheet aside and looked down onto a courtyard littered with toilets, air conditioners, and refrigerators in various stages of repair or decay.

Immediately to the right of the doorway was the bedroom closet, an open-mouthed cubby. Maria's clothes hung from a rod, jeans and sweatshirts and a few gauzy summer dresses. Her black leather jacket lay crumpled on top of the messenger bag he'd given her in the Royal Crown. The bag was empty. Next to it was a safe, squat and gunmetal gray, with an LED screen and a numerical punch pad on its door. So this was how she was protecting her money. He tested the safe's weight; it was very heavy, impossible for one person to carry.

He went back out into the living room. He wondered how she'd chosen this neighborhood, this apartment. Probably she'd heard the party line on Williamsburg—a place for young people to pretend for a few years they could be whatever they wanted to be—and thought it would be a suitable place for her own reinvention, if that's what this was supposed to be. She'd found a landlord who would accept cash, and she'd rented the place, unaware that it wasn't quite in the Williamsburg she was thinking of. He opened the refrigerator: a quart of milk, a few plastic liters of seltzer water; some take-out containers filled with what looked like Indian food. The kitchen cabinets and drawers were empty except for some clean plastic containers, a plastic fork, a few pairs of chopsticks. In the bathroom a family-sized bottle of ibuprofen sat on the bottom shelf of the mirrored medicine cabinet, along with a stick of deodorant, a tub of facial cream, toothpaste, and a toothbrush. On the second, higher, shelf rested a row of prescription pill bottles. Simon picked them up, examined the labels. They were the medications she'd been given upon her discharge from Cabrera, or, rather, they were refills she'd picked up at a pharmacy nearby. At least she'd done that much.

The place was depressing, but what else, really, had he been expecting? He was impressed that she'd made it as far as securing an apartment at all, not an easy thing for any twenty-two-year-old, let alone one who had only been in the city a few weeks while recovering from major surgery (although she did, of course, enjoy the advantage of having $150,000 in fresh cash on hand).

He returned to the bedroom, sat down on the mattress, and looked at his watch: it was nearly ten a.m. DaSilva would expect to hear from him soon, and still Simon had few answers. He lifted Maria's laptop and saw, buried in the sheets by its side, a flash of metal. He picked up the object and cradled it in his palm: a switchblade, slim and dense, the handle inlaid with a swirling mother-of-pearl design. He depressed the button on its handle, and the blade sprang free. "Jesus, Maria." He folded the blade and tossed the knife back onto the mattress.

He propped himself against the wall, Maria's computer in his lap. His fingertips played nervously across the cool, smooth cover; an internet connection stick protruded from the USB port. He didn't like doing this—picking through Maria's things, snooping like a jealous boyfriend. He'd never believed Health Solutions' donors owed him any sort of full explanation. He'd always tried to withhold judgment about their reasons for selling their organs or how they spent their money afterward. They could do what they wanted, as long as they were circumspect about the source of their cash; beyond that, it was none of his business. But Maria had been reckless. DaSilva was right: you couldn't just turn up in a hospital with such a fresh transplant scar and not risk exactly the kind of unwanted scrutiny he and DaSilva worked so hard to make sure their patients would avoid. He needed to know why Maria had lied to him, not just about returning to Los Angeles but also, now, about her fictional son and sister. Or, rather, he knew why she'd lied—to serve him with an easily digestible, appropriately unhappy cover story—but he needed to know what truth that lie was designed to conceal. He needed to know what she was planning to do once she was discharged from Abraham. He needed to know all this to get DaSilva off his back, yes, but also because, sitting there in the hospital room, he'd felt the first stirrings of a protective feeling for Maria, a half-remembered species of emotion that had doubled when he'd stepped into her bleak apartment. He wanted to help her, and he couldn't help her if he didn't know what she was doing.

He opened the laptop and tapped a key. The screen lit up, her e-mail account open and naked in the browser window. He'd start here. Scanning the list of received messages, he could see that she'd read all of them but, beginning with the day she'd arrived in New York, hadn't responded to any. He opened a few conversations from before that date. Most were banal exchanges with friends: scheduling dinners and movies, forwarding YouTube links and inside jokes. Moving further back in time, to early September, he saw his own messages, their whole cagey exchange.

He returned to the most recent message, from dalia.rodriguez@ gmail.com. "Please M," it read, "just an e-mail, a text, fucking something! Let us know you're OK. Whatever it is, we can help. I promise. xo, Dal." There were dozens of other similar, pleading e-mails sent from three or four addresses over the last few weeks, all unanswered.

Simon closed the browser window. Maria's desktop image was a black-and-white photograph of a man prone on the sidewalk, his faced smashed sideways into the concrete, long hair swept off his forehead, blood pooling beneath his busted nose. A revolver rested on the sidewalk in the foreground, the barrel pointing toward the man's head. He was quite clearly dead. Simon felt a jolt of dislocation before he was able to place the image as a Weegee, the murdered man some long-ago-doomed Lower East Side gangster.

Aside from the Weegee, Maria's desktop was strikingly bare: only two folders, one labeled "Memento," the other "Mori." Simon opened Memento first. Inside was only one file, a PDF of a death certificate. Name: Vanessa Campos. Date of death: August 1, 1999. Vanessa Campos had died two days short of her thirty-third birthday. Simon scanned down to the cause of death: respiratory arrest as a consequence of opiate intoxication. She'd been pronounced dead at her address of residence in Alhambra, at one thirty in the afternoon. He couldn't be certain, but Simon had to guess this was Maria's mother he was reading about. In 1999 Maria had been thirteen. Simon pictured her returning home from a routine day at school to find her mother's body already removed from the apartment, a social worker sitting on the porch prepared to deliver the news. Or had they sent somebody to her middle school to pluck her out of class? How did it work? Under "Marital status," the box for "Never married" was checked. What if Maria had been the only next of kin? She'd told him she was estranged from her father; perhaps that had been true even then. Did they make her identify the body? Could you do that to a thirteen year-old kid, drag her down to the morgue to stare at her dead mother?

Simon closed the file and clicked open the Mori folder. Inside was a list of about thirty JPEGs, each with a generic string of numbers for its title. He opened one at random: a photograph of a modest neighborhood—somewhere in Southern California, it looked like—palm trees bracketing small houses and tidy, fenced-in squares of lawn. The parked cars dated it to the late eighties. A young black man in a Los Angeles Raiders cap sprawled on the sidewalk, the fingers of one limp hand curled delicately over the curb. The cap had been knocked back so Simon could see that most of his forehead was missing, in its place a mash of reddish-white tissue. Blood stained the sidewalk beneath his head. A few other young men stood nearby, their faces scrubbed of emotion. A police officer was positioned between the group and the dead kid. A second officer stood closer to the body, looking down, his hands on his hips. Simon closed the file and opened another. This second one was clearly an official crime scene photograph. The victim—a white man in his twenties or thirties—wore a 1970s-style tan suit, the baby-blue shirt underneath soaked with blood. He was sprawled in what looked like a red leather restaurant booth, his sightless eyes staring up at the ceiling. Simon opened more of the files. A body covered by a tarp in 1980s Times Square, gawkers crowding the police cordon. A man at the bottom of a freshly dug ditch, his hands bound behind his back, a bullet hole in the back of his skull. Another Weegee, this one of a man laid out on his back, pageboy cap blown off his head, legs crossed demurely at the ankles, a pail of what looked like melons incongruously crowding the front edge of the frame. A CCTV still shot of a man crumpled on the floor of a convenience store, back pressed against the soda fridge, baggy white T-shirt bloodied, hand loosely gripping a pistol. One after another, a lurid catalogue of violent ends. Finally Simon closed the folder. He shut his eyes and the grotesque parade played across the inside of his lids. The photos had been taken over at least five decades. The victims were black, white, Hispanic, rich and poor—murdered in hotels, apartments, out on the street. They only had three things in common: they were all men, they were all young, and they had all been shot to death.

## seven

**B**ACK in the Roosevelt Island apartment that night, some-time closer to sleepless dawn than midnight, Simon sat up in the darkness and rested his head against the wall. The quiet in his bedroom was a black canvas against which the rain-drops spattering onto his window stood out like gobs of neon paint. Fragments of Maria's photos—a bullet-shredded torso; a gaping, forever-silenced mouth—flashed across his mind. He'd told DaSilva only about the e-mails he'd read, leaving out of his account the contents of the Memento and Mori folders. Peter had been impressed at Simon's ability to infiltrate Maria's apartment, less impressed at the volume of information he'd managed to un-cover. He instructed Simon to continue to monitor Maria's recov-ery, to pry for the truth whenever he sensed an opportunity, and to report back with everything he discovered. Simon agreed, although he privately considered the reporting to be optional; DaSilva didn't need to know everything.

Now his memory reached back to his sister's emptied room, to that dusty, stale space sealed off from the rest of the living world. It was Vanessa Campos's death certificate that had summoned Amelia to his insomniac mind. The thought of teenage Maria in the morgue, identifying her mother, blurred with the memories of his own visit, alongside his father, to the Queens County Morgue to view Amelia's bloated corpse, which had washed up onto the

Rockaway beach like any piece of trash. For years and years, he'd believed that to avoid thinking about the specifics of her death would somehow, over time, erode its pain, that it was useless, or worse, to relive events he couldn't change. But this approach, he now saw with a painful flash, had gotten him nowhere, gained him nothing. It wasn't just ineffective; it was cowardly.

And so he gave up trying to fight it off, and he sank into his memories of that April day: Walking to the train in the morning with Amelia. His sister angry with him, not talking, earbuds screwed firmly in place. Finishing her homework on the subway, or pretending to. She looked terrible—purple bags under her eyes, bad skin. She hadn't been sleeping much for weeks, and it showed. As soon as they arrived at school, she bolted for a group of her girlfriends. They'd been given the next day off, for Good Friday, on the optimistic theory that the students would attend services with their families, but just to be thorough, St. Edmund's ended Holy Thursday with a Mass of its own, in the old church on Park Avenue. Amelia sat with her class somewhere behind Simon. After Mass was completed and the students let out onto the street in an unruly throng, Simon looked around, but he couldn't find her. A few of his friends informed him that they were heading to Central Park to get high. He didn't want to go back to Rockaway alone yet, so he went along even though he already knew he wasn't in the mood.

It was drizzling, one of those fine-grained rains that seem less to fall than to hang suspended in the air. By the time they'd walked the four blocks to the park and up to the bridle path around the reservoir, they were soaked. One of his friends had hidden two wrinkly, needle-thin joints, wrapped in a ziplock bag, in a pocket of his backpack, and they passed these around under the shelter of an oak, doing their best to keep dry. Simon sucked fiercely at the joints, smoking more than his share, and by the time they were finished he was stupendously high. The other boys decided to see what was playing at the movie theater on Eighty-Sixth Street. He said he'd go with them, but then as they all left the park and re-emerged onto the street, he was seized by a horrible panic. He had a sudden impulse to be alone. The faces of his friends distended into grotesque, gargoyle-like masks. He knew, somewhere in the back of his mind, that he'd simply smoked too much, too fast. But that knowledge didn't change anything. He had to leave, immediately. He mumbled something about needing to meet his sister, and then he bolted.

As soon as he got on the subway, he knew he'd made a terrible mistake. If he'd just gone to the movie, he would've been fine. A dark theater is one of the better places to be dysfunctionally stoned; a packed subway car is not. The fluorescent lighting was an abomination. Simon was convinced he reeked of weed, and he tried not to look anybody in the eye. He was jammed up against the doors on the 6 train, somebody's messenger bag wedged into his crotch. The train was delayed between stations for a few minutes, and he thought he was having a heart attack. His palms were sweaty, he couldn't get his breath, and he felt his pulse thudding in his temple, his mind a rabid dog with its leash cut, snapping at anything within range.

By the time he switched to the A at Nassau Street, he was doing somewhat better. Getting off the train for a few minutes and walking across the station helped; he took the fact that he could walk as proof that he probably wasn't dying. The passengers thinned out as the train made its way across Brooklyn. Only two dozen or so people waited on the outdoor platform at Broad Channel for the shuttle to the peninsula. It was around six o'clock by then and nearly dark. On the ride across the bay, he watched pockets of rain skitter over the water and was fascinated by the way they spun and weaved like miniature tornadoes; he was calmed by his fascination because it took him outside himself for a moment, focusing his brain on something other than his own anxiety.

The house was dark and empty when he got home. He heated some leftover lasagna and sat in front of the television and watched a surfing video. Amelia came home about an hour after him, alone. She wore a purple windbreaker without a hood, and her hair was soaked and tangled. She looked around and asked why he hadn't turned on the lights. He shrugged. He felt his heart start up again, kicking the way it had on the train. She looked small and bedraggled and very tired. She took off her jacket and sat next to him on the couch. They watched the movie in silence.

He wanted to say the right thing to make his sister less angry with him, but his tongue felt fat and useless, like a slug in his mouth. The plate of lasagna leftovers, with its red smears of dried tomato sauce, suddenly seemed shameful to him and eating itself an embarrassing act. The sun set and the house became very dark, the blue glow of the television the only light.

Out of the long silence, Amelia said, "You need to stop."

"What are you talking about?"

"You know what."

"I don't."

"All of it. All the jealousy or whatever you want to call it. It's fucked up, Simon. You've got to let it go."

He said he wasn't jealous. He said he was trying to help her.

"Do you want me to hate you?" she asked. "Is that what you want? Because I can't understand why else you'd act like this."

What he'd done was confront her boyfriend, Ray Kippler, a freckled and loud-mouthed Beach Channel High senior. Their father may not have paid attention to what Amelia did with herself, but Simon did, and he'd decided that Ray was ruining his sister.

The first time Simon saw Kippler, he was at the beach with Amelia, on Labor Day, seven months before this conversation in the den. He remembered walking to the edge of the ocean, slipping under the crumbling waves, the sky overcast, the Atlantic the color of corroded copper. Underwater, he opened his eyes and watched columns of disturbed sand drift lazily upward. He pushed off the bottom, surfaced. He could make out, on the shore, his sister on her towel, knees drawn up to her chest. Another teenager squatted next to her, poking at the sand with a stick. Simon couldn't see his face at first, only a shock of bright blond, nearly white, hair. The kid stared at the sand as he spoke, as though afraid to look at Amelia. Simon understood the feeling: that summer his little sister had morphed into some entirely new creature, bronzed and spindly, a sudden and humbling inch taller than him. He'd walk into the living room, and she'd be huddled on the couch with two or three of her Rockaway girlfriends, under a pile of towels, their long limbs crooked and jutting like those of some giant daddy longlegs, heads bent toward each other in furtive conference. Whole fertile swaths of her life suddenly seemed to be hidden from his view. So, yes, sometimes he too was afraid to look at her, at this evolved Amelia, afraid to see in what way she was shedding her childhood self now—afraid because the more she grew up, the less she might need him.

He next saw Ray a month later, in October. Simon was in the habit, that autumn, of surfing before school. He would creep downstairs, to the silent kitchen, where he'd eat gummy white bread and slug orange juice straight from the carton. He'd grab his thirdhand board from the mudroom, a chunky 6'5" pintail with cracking epoxy and a permanent coat of dirty wax, and jog down to the beach in the silvery predawn to paddle out alone. One morning he left the house and turned toward the salt-heavy air, passing a few houses not unlike his own—two-story clapboard boxes with a car in the cement yard and three locks on the front door—before he crossed Shore Front Parkway and the boardwalk, and stepped down onto the beach, the cool white sand, fine as ashes, pooling over his feet.

He changed into his wetsuit, tucking his sweatshirt under the boardwalk, and inspected the ocean. The waves were shit, but at least he had them all to himself. Then he saw even that wasn't true. A small figure in a red wetsuit stood at the water's edge, white-blond hair bright against the dull morning. As Simon stepped closer, he realized this was the same kid he'd seen speaking to Amelia.

The boy turned and saw him. "Dude." He nodded, freckles spattered across his face. He was short and lean, and he seemed somehow to vibrate, energy effervescing out of his pores. His nose was so sunburned it appeared flayed.

"What's up." *Dude?* Surfing or not, they were still in Queens.

The kid frowned at the choppy lineup. "Sucks."

"It looks all right."

"I guess for up around here."

"Why, where're you from?"

"Florida," the kid said, still looking at the ocean. "Moved a month ago. My mom barely pulled her shit together to get us up here before school started."

"Beach Channel?"

He nodded again, then finally looked at Simon. "How come I haven't seen you there?"

"I go to school in Manhattan." Simon bent down and fiddled with his leash. "What's your name?"

"Ray Kippler," the kid said. "Are we surfing or what?"

Simon had learned to surf by reading magazines and watching the Rockaway locals. He'd started the first summer they'd moved to the peninsula, and he'd liked it immediately—the physical challenge, the sense of being alone and yet also connected by the invisible thread of shared desire to the other surfers in the lineup. By the time he met Kippler, he thought of himself as a decent surfer, at least above the Rockaway average. But it only took five minutes to see that Ray Kippler was on an entirely different level, not just from Simon but from any Rockaway surfer Simon had ever seen.

He watched from the shoulder as the Florida kid clawed into his first wave. Ray flattened his upper body against his board before he sprang to his feet, pumping down the line past Simon and launching a giant air, his arms spread wide, his red body and white board suspended against the gray towers and gray parkway and gray sky like some exotic species of bird, ripping himself out of the normal flow of time and motion in the manner of all airborne things. He landed cleanly in the flats and stepped casually off his board like it was no big deal. This went on for nearly an hour, Kippler tearing his waves to shreds while Simon watched, stunned, the enjoyment of his own rides compromised by how pedestrian they seemed in comparison. Finally Simon spotted his sister standing on the shore. He straight-lined a wave on his belly and trotted out of the shallows, shaking his wet head like a dog.

Amelia thrust his sweatshirt at him. "Jesus, Simon, you're not even wearing a watch."

"Where'd you find that?"

"Behind the same stupid pylon where you always stash it."

"You couldn't wait at the house?"

"Not when you're this late. Hurry up."

She glanced behind him and frowned. He turned around, and there was Ray, board tucked under his arm, grinning like an idiot.

"It's Ray," he said. "From the beach."

"I know," Amelia said. Was she blushing?

"Oh. Good."

"This is my older brother." Amelia tapped Simon's shoulder. "In case you hadn't figured it out."

Simon took his sweatshirt and jogged underneath the boardwalk to change. From behind a pylon he saw Ray say something to Amelia before giving her an awkward sort of salute and sprinting up the stairs to the boardwalk, the soles of his bare feet flashing ghost white before he disappeared somewhere above Simon's head.

A month later Amelia and Ray were dating, and by the early spring they were inseparable, locked into the cage of teenage first love, the rest of the world rendered irrelevant and blurry. Kippler now liked to come over in the early evenings, between Amelia's return from school and Michael's return from work. Simon would listen, kneeling at the wall between their two rooms, his ear pressed to the plaster, as Kippler crushed up his Ritalin pills and cut the powder into lines on Amelia's desk. Kippler and Amelia would snort the lines and smoke cigarettes and tune into Hot 97, and sometimes, as Simon listened, they'd move over to the bed. He could still hear them then, their talk growing quiet and throaty, punctuated by Amelia's laughter. He'd turn up his own radio to drown them out or ostentatiously slam his door and clomp down the stairs to watch TV in the den, but none of that helped. He knew what was going on anyway, and it was killing him. After a few weeks, after Amelia had started snorting Ritalin nearly every evening and most mornings before school, after she'd started cutting her afternoon classes to meet Kippler earlier, after bags started to appear under her eyes and flesh to drop off her bones, Simon could not ignore the fact that he was doing nothing to help her, and so he confronted Kippler on the beach, alone, and told him that he needed to stop bringing his pills around. Kippler laughed in his face and said, "Or what? And how do you know what we do anyway?" Simon had no answer. Kippler told Amelia, of course. This was a week ago; she'd barely spoken to him since.

Here, in front of the television, they could finally have the conversation Simon had been waiting for, the conversation he had, without entirely realizing it, been trying to provoke. But he was unable to translate his feelings into words. All the things he needed to say to her—how he was scared she wouldn't need him anymore; how he hated their father for making him do the work of parenting in his place; how he was jealous, not only of Ray and his claims on her attention, but of *her*, of her ability to be the sort of outward-facing person he secretly and desperately wanted to be—sank into the bog that filled his head.

Instead, he said, "What are you going to do when Ray gets tired of fucking you?"

She got up from the couch without another word. He heard her bedroom door slam a few seconds later.

Their father came home soon after that. He'd bought two rotisserie chickens at the grocery store, but Amelia didn't want any dinner, and neither did Simon, so Michael ate in the kitchen alone.

At eight thirty, Amelia went out. Simon was still sitting in the den, and he couldn't hear much of what she said to their father before she left. She didn't look into the den on her way out.

A few minutes later, Michael appeared in the doorway. He asked Simon if he was staying in. Simon nodded. His father nodded back. The surf movie had ended, the TV screen cut to black.

"Can I turn on the lights or are you sitting in the dark for a reason?" Michael asked.

"I'm fine."

His father nodded again. He waited a few moments. Then he said, "What's your sister so angry about?"

"I don't know. Maybe Ray?"

"Did they have a fight?"

"I don't know, Dad. Why don't you ask her?"

"She doesn't like to talk about that kind of thing with me."

"Have you tried?"

Michael let out an irritated puff of breath. "Don't be snotty."

His father went into his bedroom a little after ten o'clock. Simon walked upstairs with the idea that he would go to bed early himself, but he found he wasn't even close to being able to sleep. He felt terrible about what he'd said to Amelia, but part of him— the stubborn, aggrieved part, the part forever underappreciated and wronged—clung to a sense of its own sour righteousness. He slipped down the hall to Amelia's bedroom. The door was unlocked. He shut it quietly behind him and stood very still as he looked around.

He noticed a strange smell he couldn't identify until he spotted the incense holder and its worm of crumbled ash on the windowsill. The closet door was open, disgorging piles of dirty clothes. The desk was covered with textbooks, colored pencils, loose papers. He searched the room for traces of Kippler, as though Ray might have marked his territory by pissing on the carpet. He went through the drawers in her desk, and right there, in the top drawer, was a small plastic bag of about a dozen white pills. Also in the drawer was a smooth, rounded black stone, shaped like a swollen thumb, and a vanity mirror, both coated with white powder residue. He wanted to feel what Amelia felt; he wanted to understand from the inside what she'd been doing these last weeks. He put one of the pills on the desk and ground it with the stone until it dissolved into dust, which then stuck to the stone and the surface of the desk and was impossible to scrape into anything resembling a line. He brushed the dust into the wastebasket, and then he tried again, this time placing the pill between two sheets of paper. This method worked better, and he carefully tilted the paper and spilled the pile of powder onto the mirror. He divided the pile into two lines with Amelia's school ID and used a short length of straw he'd found in the drawer to suck one of them up his nose.

Simon had never snorted anything before, and the burn was vicious. He wasn't prepared for it. He reeled back onto the bed and sat on its edge, stunned. How did they do this? He stood up and quickly snorted the other line before he had any second thoughts. He tried to clean the stone and mirror even though his hands were shaking. He hurried back into his own bedroom. He sat down on the bed, then stood by the window, then paced back and forth across the floor. His mind accelerated, each thought tumbling out ahead of the next, but it was a linear sort of acceleration, nothing like being stoned, none of that awful sense of losing ownership of his thoughts. Instead, he was painfully in control, moving from thought to thought very, very quickly. He felt as though the top of his skull had been removed and a cool, mentholated breeze was caressing the exposed crenulations of his brain. Delivered by this speed and this focus was a clear imperative: he needed to apologize to Amelia, and he needed to do it right now. Waiting for her to come home would be disastrous. He latched on to the notion that if he didn't find her and tell her he was sorry and beg her to forgive him, something horrible might happen to her—that she would bring this horrible thing, whatever it was, upon herself intentionally to show Simon what a shit he'd been.

He didn't want his father to know he'd gone out, so he got down on his hands and knees in the hallway and put his ear to the floor. He didn't hear anything, not even the murmur of the radio Michael sometimes listened to while in bed. He closed the door to his room, leaving the light on, and slunk down the stairs, across the darkened foyer, and out the front door. He moved away from the house as quickly and quietly as he could, heading toward the beach. The drizzle had stopped, but every surface was covered with a glaze of moisture.

At the head of Beach 113th, he climbed the stairs to the boardwalk. A cold wind blew in from the ocean, and the moisture was starting to ice up. His heart jackhammered away; his mouth was dry as paper. Of course, he had no idea where Amelia and Ray had gone. He decided to look around the cluster of stores and restaurants on Beach 116th, near the subway. The streets were deserted. The pizza place was empty; so was the kebab shop. Everything else except for Derry Hills was closed. He pressed his face to the bar's window, the glass fogged up from cigarette smoke and the heat of the bodies within. Maybe Ray and Amelia had somehow managed to talk their way inside. He could see a crush of people against the bar, bellowing at each other under green tinsel and cardboard shamrocks left over from Saint Patrick's Day, and beyond to the booths and scarred wooden tables. Ray and Amelia weren't inside, and there was nowhere else to look. He thought they might be at one of Ray's friends' houses, but he didn't know where any of those kids lived. He walked back along the boardwalk, to the head of Beach 113th. It was after eleven. His nerves were thrashed, ragged. He leaned against the railing facing the beach, its metal encased within a sheath of ice. The night was overcast and he couldn't see the ocean very well. All he could make out were flashes of whitewater surging up out of the blackness and then expiring again just as quickly. From the wind and the sound, though, he could tell the waves were rough in a chaotic way, full of crossed-up whitecaps and currents.

The reasonable thing would have been to go home and wait for Amelia there, but the thought of sneaking into the house, of creeping around like a burglar, of sitting on the edge of his bed, straining to hear the click of the front door, made his skin feel tight and pinched. He decided, instead, to wait for her outside, on the boardwalk, where he could see a good distance both east and west, as well as north across Rockaway Beach Boulevard and down the barrel of Beach 113th to their house.

He didn't have to wait long. He saw them coming, far off down the boardwalk, from the west, Neponsit or Belle Harbor. They were riding Kippler's BMX, Amelia standing on the back pegs. He knew it was them from the cherry-red of the bike as it passed under the streetlights, and also from Amelia's laugh, which he heard in snatches, chopped up and scattered by the wind. Kippler struggled to keep the bike upright on the icy wood, and they pitched and wobbled as they approached. Simon's plan, if he could call it that, had been to peel Amelia away from whomever he found her with and speak to her alone. Clearly there was no way to do that now, yet he still didn't want to go back to the house. He only had about thirty seconds before they would see him. Without really thinking about what he was doing, he hurried down the stairs to the beach and hid in the space under the boardwalk, crouching against one of the cement supports.

The roar of the ocean echoed in the hollow as though he were wedged inside a giant conch shell. The distance from the sand to the boards above his head was about six feet, and the space extended back into darkness maybe a dozen feet before the level of sand rose to meet the boards and pinch it shut. Some light from the streetlamps slipped through the gaps between the boards. Submerged in the damp sand were crumpled beer cans, unidentifiable mounds of plastic. Freezing water dripped onto his head and inside the collar of his jacket.

He heard Amelia's laugh again—unchecked, goofy, the way he remembered it from when they were younger. The boards rippled above his head. He heard a rattle and thump as the bike tipped over and they spilled off, Amelia laughing louder now. There was a pause, and then the boards rippled again as they walked toward the stairs that led down to the beach. He pulled himself farther back into the shadows and waited for them to appear at the foot of the stairs. Kippler had his arm around Amelia, and they stumbled as they hit the lumpy sand. Their footsteps crunched on the crust of ice until they stopped to sit on the ridge of some frozen tire tracks about twenty feet in front of him. He stared at Amelia's back, at her hunched and narrow shoulders. They lit cigarettes, the smoke drifting back to his hiding place under the boards. Amelia took a swig off a small bottle Kippler removed from his pocket, coughing before handing it back. Simon's fingers started to turn numb; the muscles in his legs cramped. They sat for a while, smoking and talking, sometimes kissing. He wanted to know what they were talking about, whether Amelia was telling Kippler what her brother had said to her earlier that night. He inched up to the edge of the shadows and leaned forward, which was exactly when Amelia turned around to flick the butt of her cigarette over her shoulder.

She saw him. He knew she had. She paused for a second, her arm bent, the butt glowing between her fingers, her head turned precisely toward where he was hiding. Then she tossed the filter away and turned back to the ocean, and to Kippler.

Simon stayed where he was, frozen in place. They stood up and started to walk back to the stairs. He shrunk himself down, pressing his body into the sand. As they went up the stairs, he heard Kippler say he'd walk her to her house. She told him it was fine, that he should just ride home along the boardwalk; she said her brother might be waiting up for her and that it would be better if she showed up alone. Simon guessed then that she'd told Kippler what he'd said, and he was filled with a bottomless shame.

The tires of Kippler's BMX rolled over his head and off down the boardwalk. After a minute or two, he heard footsteps coming down the stairs. He stepped out of the hollow and met Amelia on the sand.

She stared at him. "What are you doing, Simon?" Her voice was defeated, dead.

"I want to apologize."

"For what?"

"For what I said earlier."

"Which time?"

"In the den," he said, "earlier tonight."

She nodded. "So you had to stalk me to tell me you were sorry. That makes sense."

He told her he'd had a feeling something terrible was going to happen to her if he didn't find her and apologize.

She nodded again. "Something terrible like kissing Ray or smoking a cigarette or having a drink? Something terrible like that?"

"That's not what I meant."

"No?" she said. "Then why don't you tell me what you did mean."

He looked down at his sneakers. He knew anything he said would sound absurd. Thoughts and feelings that had seemed natural and defensible to him would be, by the act of being hammered into words and spoken, rendered grotesque. So he swallowed, tasting the acrid drip of the crushed Ritalin, and said nothing. Amelia sneered and marched past him toward the waterline. He hurried after her, calling for her to wait. She spun around. "What do you want from me?" she hissed. Now her voice was alive, crackling with anger.

"I want . . ." He trailed off and stood there, staring at her, at her face screwed up into an expression of total contempt. The purity of her anger hit him like a slap across the face.

"You can't say it?" she said. "Fine. I'll tell you what you want. You want me to be a weak little twelve-year-old girl with migraines again. You want me to be helpless. You want me to need your protection, so you can feel like you have a purpose. Well, listen to me now: you can't have that anymore."

She walked away from him, toward the water. He followed her, his sneakers crunching across crab and mussel shells snarled in seaweed. Amelia stopped at the foot of the groyne. It jutted out about forty-five feet into the water, a narrow strip of concrete hemmed in on both sides by piles of uneven rocks fixed to each other with grout. She climbed up onto the concrete strip. She looked down at him imperiously from her perch on the rocks and asked if he had anything to say.

"I've only done any of this because I love you," he said.

She shook her head. "Possessiveness isn't love."

She started walking out along the concrete strip, her arms spread wide, placing one foot directly in front of the other, heel to toe, as though she were balancing on a tightrope. Patches of slick ice dotted the concrete. She walked out ten feet and then was surrounded by water on both sides. Waves slapped against the rocks, spray blowing over the top.

"Get down from there," he said, knowing it was the exact wrong thing to say and unable to stop himself from saying it. "Get down, Amelia, please."

She laughed and continued her walk out to the tip. He scrambled up onto the concrete. She turned around and saw him. She lifted one leg off the ground and bent it behind her like a stork.

"Uh-oh," she said. "Now the wind's going to blow me right off."

"Stop it." He approached her slowly, his sneakers slipping on the ice. A strong gust of wind really did blow then, whipping her hair across her face. She put her foot back down, but still she stood there, defiant.

He should have backed away. He should have backed away and stepped off the groyne and let her know that she wasn't being told to do anything. Instead, he stepped toward her. He stepped toward her, and he offered her his hand. The taunting smile disappeared from her face. "Get away from me," she said. She took a few steps backward.

"Amelia, please."

She shook her head. "Get away. I'll come down when I want to."

He took another step toward her. She stepped back quickly, her heel slipping on a patch of ice. She stumbled and one of her feet missed the concrete strip, plunging into a space between two of the stones. Her leg buckled, her ankle trapped at a peculiar angle, and as she tried to wrench herself free, Simon heard a pop, a dry cracking noise, like a twig snapping under a heavy boot. She cried out and reached for her ankle—an involuntary motion, a reflex—and the momentum of her reaching pitched her forward onto the rocks. Her foot popped free, but she wasn't able to find any grip on the icy stones and she slid into the water.

He rushed to the edge of the concrete and looked down. She was there, at the base of the groyne, five feet below him, hanging on to rocks slick with algae, barely holding her head above the waves. He'd been surfing in his thick winter wetsuit just a few days before; he knew how cold the water was. He knew water that cold feels like lead. It squeezes the air out of your lungs. It doesn't want you living in it. One of Amelia's hands slipped off the rocks, and her head went under. Somehow she pulled herself back up long enough to scream his name. But still he didn't move to help her. He was frozen. Panic seized his muscles, paralyzing him. All of this took about five seconds. Then a wave slammed into the groyne, and she was pulled away from the rocks and sucked under. Her head reappeared a few yards away, a shiny blot against the dark water. Finally he scrambled down the rocks and dove in.

The cold was like an iron bar slamming into his head. His jacket filled with water and he struggled free of it, trying to keep Amelia's bobbing head in sight. A line of whitewater rushed over him, and when he surfaced again, he didn't see her. He swam as hard as he could, his heavy clothes pulling him down. The water was pitch-black. He felt the rip running alongside the groyne pull him away from the beach. He screamed her name, and a blast of spray filled his mouth. Lifted by a swell, he saw the flash of her hair out near the tip of the groyne. The rip ran along the flank of the groyne, then bent around the end into deeper water. That was where she was being taken. He thrashed his way out, trying to stay near the rocks without being smashed into them. He tried to keep his eyes on her head, but he kept losing her in the chop. He finally reached the tip of the groyne and grabbed on to one of the outermost rocks. He braced against the current, raised himself up onto the rock. The ocean stretched out in front of him, black and cold and empty. He was shadowed from the lights of the boardwalk; the darkness was total. He screamed her name. Nothing. His body was shaking violently. His vision kept contracting and expanding, as though his pupils were beating with his heart. He held on to the rock, his hands numb and bloody. He screamed until his throat was raw. His grip started to loosen as a warmth began to spread through his limbs. He was still aware enough to recognize this as the beginnings of hypothermia. He stopped screaming. He felt sleepy, distracted. He used the last of his concentration and strength to haul himself up over the rocks and onto the concrete. He lay there, his cheek pressed against a patch of ice. He recognized that the ice was cold, that he should move, but these facts didn't seem to directly concern him.

Then he heard something. It was his name. Ragged, blown to bits by the wind, but he heard it. He dragged himself up and looked out into the ocean. He stared long enough for the black water to start pulsing in front of him, to take on weird curves and bulges. He yelled for Amelia, but his voice was gone. He didn't hear her again.

He didn't remember much about getting from the end of the groyne back to the house. It was as though he blacked out and then found himself standing at the front door. He trembled so violently he could barely grasp the knob. She was gone. There was simply no way to survive in water that cold.

He pushed into the house, screaming hoarsely for his father; wild-eyed, shivering, a broken messenger bearing the news that the life they'd known as a family was over.

Lying now in his bedroom, ten stories above the East River, he experienced again his fatal paralysis. Those five seconds had expanded over seven years into a private eternity of self-loathing, his own secret monument to failure. His father, the police, the people of Rockaway Park—they thought him brave to plunge into the frigid Atlantic, to risk his life thrashing through the greedy waves after Amelia. Huddled under blankets in the precinct house, he'd told the cops that he'd gone looking for his sister and found her alone on the beach. That they'd climbed onto the groyne to goof off in the wind and spray; she'd slipped and fallen into the ocean, and he'd dove immediately after her. And it was true that once he hit the water, he'd used every last reserve of his strength to rescue her, and it hadn't been enough. But if he hadn't frozen—if he'd flung himself over the edge the instant her ankle popped free— could he have saved her then? There was no way he could be sure. It had been dark and very cold; he'd been a jittery mess. But, still, he thought he could have done it. He thought he could have saved her, and the thought killed him anew every day.

Eight

MARIA shivered as they made their way from Abraham to South Tenth the next morning. She walked with her arms folded tightly across her chest, her chin tucked into her collar. Her hair was greasy and lank, her skin oily. She was breathing heavily by the time they reached her building, and she leaned on Simon as they climbed the stairs.

Simon had slipped the keys back under the insole of her Chuck Taylor moments after Rudich had shown him into her hospital room. She'd been eating breakfast, or at least staring down at the breakfast tray, rubbery orange eggs its centerpiece, ringed by pallid fruit salad and a carton of chocolate milk. Without looking up, she'd tilted the tray toward him: "Any takers?" He'd laughed as he moved the sneakers and bag of clothes back to the floor, shielding the action with his body, hoping she wouldn't notice as he jammed the keys under the sneaker's insole. When he sat in the chair and turned around, she was still staring down into the microwaved egg patty, poking at it with her plastic fork as though it might wriggle to life and scramble, lizard-like, off the tray.

She hadn't wanted him to accompany her home. After he'd signed her out of the hospital, she'd tried, exhausted and woozy from the morphine, to convince him to leave her outside on Lee Avenue. He told her he wasn't going anywhere else until he'd seen her safely inside her apartment; if she wanted to get rid of him, they might as well start walking. She'd crossed her arms and stared him down, trying, he thought, to summon the strength to argue. But she was too weak and tired and sick, and finally she slumped against the wall of the hospital and nodded in resigned agreement.

Now he was doing his best to convey the impression that this was the first he'd seen of her building, of her dispiriting apartment. She unlocked and shouldered open the door. Inside, she headed straight for the bedroom, reappearing a moment later.

"At least it's still there," she muttered.

"What?"

She shook her head with a little flick of irritation. "Nothing."

Simon realized she must be talking about the safe. "What are you going to do now?"

"Probably stick my head in the sink and wash my hair. It feels like somebody poured a bowl of Crisco on my head."

"I mean, what about tomorrow?" he said. "Next week, next month—what's your plan?"

She looked around the empty room. "Maybe buy some furniture?"

"Tell me why you're not going back to LA."

"I'm sick of the traffic."

"Maria, please."

"I'm sorry I had to lie to you. But it wouldn't have mattered if I hadn't gotten sick, and that wasn't my fault."

"But *why* did you lie?"

"I don't have to tell you that."

"All right. All right." Simon fingered a dent in the shoddy plaster wall. "So you were just going to skip out on the follow-up care?"

"I felt all right at first. Yeah, I was tired, I was in pain, but I figured that was normal. The fever, everything with the leak . . . How was I supposed to see that coming?"

"There was probably a slight tear from the surgery. Then you aggravated it somehow, and it ruptured."

She narrowed her eyes. "So it's my fault?"

"That's not what . . ." He shook his head, exasperated. "No. But you're going to need follow-up care now. You can agree to that, right?" She hesitated. "Maria, come on." She looked away, nodded. "I have a doctor who will be discreet, but you have to promise you'll go see her."

"I'll go. I understand you can't have me getting sick again."

He heard the sarcasm. "You make it sound like it's impossible I would actually care if you did."

"You'd care because it would make things inconvenient for your job. I'm not trying to be melodramatic. It's just the truth."

"I mean personally care."

She raised her chin and looked at him. "So, do you?"

He met her gaze. "I'm here, aren't I?"

"You sure you're not here because your partner told you to be?"

"What partner?"

"You know who I'm talking about," she said. "The coordinator. Peter DaSilva. There's no other way you could've known I was at Abraham. You have to be working with somebody inside the hospital system or none of this would be possible. And I think it's him."

"That's your theory?"

"Shouldn't we start being honest with each other? If you really do care?"

"You haven't told me anything, Maria."

"Somebody has to start." She paused, then said, "All right. I'll tell you what I'm planning to do here. I'm planning to work. Hostessing at a restaurant. I put an application in at a place on Smith Street, before all this shit with the bile leak happened."

"You have $150,000 in cash, and you're going to stand at a desk and take reservations?"

"I'm not stupid. I know that money's not going to last, and it's all I have. I came here to start a life, and life means work. Or at least this life will."

"This city's a bad place to save money."

"But a good place to open a restaurant someday. That's what this money's going toward. The Mexican food here sucks as bad as I heard it would—maybe I can help fix that. Look, I've worked in bars and diners and coffee shops since I was seventeen. If I haven't figured them out by now, it's my own fault." She paused. "Your turn."

He hesitated. *Fuck it.* "Okay," he said. "I work for DaSilva. Health Solutions, it's his company. It's just the two of us. He hired me to do all the interfacing with clients. He handles everything in the hospital." Maria nodded, clearly unsurprised. He felt his switching of allegiances, from DaSilva to Maria, slot into place with an internally audible click, and he wondered, his mouth suddenly dry, if he'd made a terrible error. "I'm trusting you, Maria. Please don't make me regret it."

Hᴇ came by again the next day. She let him in, anxiousness rippling beneath her placid, opiated surface. He felt bonded to her by his confession about DaSilva, as though by so recklessly and flagrantly violating the rules of his job, he'd somehow linked their fates, strengthened the connective tissue of his responsibility toward her; as though, perhaps, by telling her, he'd sought to facilitate exactly this strengthening. The apartment was hot and dry, steam hissing angrily through the radiators. The skin of her face gave off a waxy sheen, as though she'd smeared it with a layer of Vaseline. She wore a ribbed white tank top, and he could see the bandages on her abdomen through the top's thin cotton as she pulled a sweater over her head.

He helped her down the stairs and out onto the street. Waiting for them at the curb was a black Lincoln Town Car commissioned into the service of Taxi Internacional. The driver sipped coffee and placidly absorbed the squawking of his Bluetooth earpiece as they sped over the Williamsburg Bridge and onto the FDR, eventually drawing even with Roosevelt Island.

"There's the hospital." Maria pointed at a flashing sliver of

Cabrera's turquoise glass. "I could live without ever seeing that place again."

She fell silent as the car swung off the Drive, turning into the Manhattan streets. The driver pulled up in front of a white-brick residential building around the corner from a large private hospital complex. The doctor's office was on the ground floor, off to the side of the lobby. Simon paid the driver and followed Maria out of the car. She made it halfway across the sidewalk, then abruptly stopped, wavering, as though overwhelmed by the motion and noise of the street.

"Are you all right?"

"I'll be fine." She squeezed his arm. "I'll call you when I'm out."

He killed an hour at a diner around the corner, picking at a BLT and downing cups of watery coffee. He pictured her in the examination room, sitting on the edge of a table in her paper gown, legs nervously crossed at the ankle. He saw the long, two-pronged, puckered incision, the laparoscopic scars off to the left side, three pink dime-sized punctures. He saw the safe on the floor of her closet, squat and dense, pictured the stacks of banded bills inside.

After leaving her the prior afternoon, he'd returned to the Health Solutions office and paged DaSilva. The desk phone rang just before dark, caller ID placing the number somewhere in the Bronx. On the line, DaSilva's voice competed with the thrum and bustle of street traffic as he asked for a report.

Simon told him that Maria still refused to provide an explanation for lying to them.

"Just stay on her," DaSilva said. "Maybe she'll let something slip." He coughed wetly into the receiver. "Is she talking about this with anybody?"

"I don't think so," Simon said. "I think she's very alone right now. Very isolated."

"All right," DaSilva said. An elevated train clattered by somewhere behind him. "At least we have that going for us."

On the ride back to South Williamsburg, Maria was quiet, staring out the window. The doctor had palpated her abdomen, drawn blood, taken her to the hospital next door to run her through the chattering tube of an MRI machine. The doctor found no further complications; she advised rest and patience and asked no questions. She wrote Maria additional prescriptions for painkillers and antibiotics and gave her a small bottle of vitamin E oil to rub into the scars. It was all basically good news, or at least not bad news, but Maria didn't seem particularly encouraged. Simon let her be; she didn't owe him cheerfulness. He dropped her off on South Tenth and told her he'd be back to check on her soon. "If you want to," she said, nodding, her thoughts far away.

He returned to her apartment the next night, following both DaSilva's mandate and his own impulses. She'd ordered a flat-screen television and a couch off the internet, and they'd been delivered that morning. On the muted TV screen, flashbulbs pelted a pouty-lipped pregnant woman as she walked down the front steps of a hotel. Maria sat on one end of the couch, her hands resting lightly on her lower abdomen. Simon sat down at the other end, unpacking the contents of a take-out bag from a kosher taqueria on Driggs.

"How are you doing today?"

"You're looking at it," she said. "Couch. TV. Bed. I can walk about two blocks before I feel like I'm going to throw up."

He spread the plastic bag on the cushion between them and unwrapped the foil-covered tacos. "It's going to take time." The words sounded lame, but he didn't know what else to tell her, and anyway it was the truth.

"You're not stuck here alone all day. I can't e-mail anybody. I can't call anybody. I've started talking to the fucking television."

"Why can't you call anybody?" He hadn't yet pressed her any further on her reasons for abandoning Los Angeles, but that didn't mean he'd forgotten about everything he'd found on her computer—the e-mails, the death certificate, her macabre collection of photographs.

"Number one," Maria said, "I threw away my phone. Number two, almost nobody back home knows I'm here, and I want to keep it that way."

"Can you tell me why?"

"I just . . . I had to leave. I'm sorry, Simon. I can't tell you anything more than that."

"If it was just about leaving California, then why did you come here? Why New York?"

"The idea of New York came later. The idea of the money came first. Money is freedom. In case you didn't already know that." She paused. "You have to understand. I'm not trying to *permanently* disappear. I didn't change my name. I didn't fake my own death or anything. The idea was only to get away from LA and get my hands on some money. I'd move here, work at a restaurant, build a life." She took a bite of a taco, *bistec* juice dripping down her chin. She made a face. "See, this is why I need to open a Mexican joint."

He decided to abandon his questioning for now. "Come on, these are pretty good."

"Yeah, you definitely haven't been to LA, have you?" She took another bite and grimaced as she chewed.

"The incisions are hurting?"

"It's the newer ones," she said. "When I twist too fast it's like somebody's stabbing me with a piece of broken glass." She looked down at her abdomen. "The last of the stitches were supposed to dissolve by yesterday."

"Is it leaking?"

"I don't know."

"Have you looked at it?"

"No. It . . . I'm too freaked out."

"When do you see the doctor next?"

"Wednesday."

"Maria." He tried not to sound too reproving. "You should look."

"I don't know what I'd be looking for."

"I could look at it. Or is that . . ."

"What?"

"I don't know. Too private."

"I think worrying about privacy at this point would be a little precious. I'm just sick to death of being a patient."

She put the tacos aside, went into the bathroom, and came back with a bag of cotton balls, a glass of water, a towel. She sat down on the couch, arching her back and lifting the hem of her tank top. Simon stood over her. He felt for a moment that he was back in the room at the Royal Crown, the image of what her transplant sutures had looked like then overlapping and blurring with what she was showing him now. He blinked, ridding himself of the earlier image, and saw the upside-down fork puckered and bubble-gum pink. The puffiness of the surrounding tissue had subsided. A few inches to the left, a strip of tape held in place a gauze pad. Iodine had stained the gauze and the skin beneath a yellowish brown; when she pulled the gauze away, the scars were first visible only as three raised coins of tissue the same color as the adjacent skin.

Simon watched as she patted at the scars, dipping a ball of cotton into the glass, swirls of iodine twisting like brown smoke through the water. As the iodine washed away from her skin, the wounds seemed to rise up toward him, to lift away from the rest of her abdomen like a reef bared by low tide. The circles were dark purple at their centers, shading to yellow at the edges. They were ugly, but they were not leaking and they were not infected.

"They're gone," she said. Her fingers lightly prodded one of the coins. "The stitches. They've dissolved."

"Yeah."

"How do they look to you?"

"They're fine. Just leave them alone."

She let her shirt fall back down. "It's pretty hideous though, isn't it? All of it. I'm like Raggedy Ann."

"You're not always going to look like this. It'll heal. The scars will fade."

"But you're willing to admit that right now it's pretty hideous."

"No." He sat down next to her. "It looks like what it is, that's all."

She pulled her knees to her chest. "Do people, other donors— do they ever wish they hadn't done it? Do they ever think it wasn't worth the money?"

He realized he'd been unconsciously preparing himself for some version of this question ever since he'd found her at Abraham. The answer he came up with now was truthful, if also narrow. "None of them have ever told me that," he said. "Not that I'd necessarily be the first person they'd want to talk about it with."

"How would you feel if they did?"

"I think I'm honest with people about what the surgery's going to be like, about what kind of recovery they should expect. We pay them exactly what we say we will. If they regret it afterward, I can't think of anything we could do differently to prevent them from feeling that way." He realized he was parroting language he'd heard first from DaSilva, and it gave him the discomfiting sense of being manipulated from a distance, even if what he was saying was true. He shrugged. "But that doesn't mean I wouldn't feel badly about it. I'm not trying to take advantage of anybody."

"But not badly enough to stop." She peered at him over the top of her knees. Her expression was neutral, as though she really was curious and not simply trying to challenge him.

"This isn't my life's work, Maria. Don't make me defend it too much." He paused. "And if you think you might regret having done it, you should just tell me."

"I don't regret it. I just wanted to know."

"You don't? Not even a little? After everything that's happened?"

She closed her eyes. "You don't understand what my life was like before this."

"No. I've tried to imagine it, and I've failed."

"You've imagined things?"

"I've tried."

"But you want to picture it." She seemed equal parts intrigued and wary.

"When I was a teenager, I always tried to imagine what it would be like to be my sister," Simon said. "And even though I spent every single day living in the same house and going to the same school, I had no idea what it would feel like to live her life from the inside. Eventually I had to accept that you can never truly understand another person's experience, never truly know them. But that doesn't mean I don't keep trying."

"And now you want to imagine your way inside me?"

He hesitated. "I want to try to understand how you lived before you came here."

She was silent for a moment. Then she said, "Your sister who died?"

He felt his stomach drop, as though he were hearing about Amelia's death for the first time. "How did you know that?"

"I looked you up online. This was before I came to New York. There's not much there, but it was easy to find the articles about her drowning."

Of course. Simon remembered the newspaper coverage, small items in *Newsday* and the *Post*, a larger piece in the *Wave*, the local Rockaway paper. Two Hasidic kids from Mott Avenue had spotted Amelia's body hooked around the rotted pilings near the groyne at Beach 60th, in front of the abandoned Edgemere lots, as the tide went out early on the morning after Simon lost her. Accompanying the *Wave*'s reporting of their grisly discovery was a small color headshot of Amelia, inset into a larger black-and-white photograph of the desolate stretch of beach where her body had been found. Project towers crowded the waterline to the east, where the land curved out into the ocean; in the foreground snaggle-toothed wooden pylons, remnants of an old jetty, jutted out of the water next to the more recently built stone groyne. The photo of Amelia had been taken from the St. Edmund's yearbook. Simon remembered her staring straight into the camera, her streaky blond hair piled on top of her head in a careless knot, the collar of her dress shirt askew. Her lips were mashed together as though she were holding back a laugh. Simon imagined her in the little room off the chapel where they did the yearbook shoots, trying to look bored or serious or sophisticated—anything but a goofy teenager—and yet unable to resist whatever cheesy line the photographer had deployed to get her to smile. When the photograph was taken, the spring before the accident, Amelia *had* been a goofy teenager; by the time she died, less than a year later, she had become something else, more ingrown and complex, more angry, halfway to being an adult.

"That's how you knew I grew up here," he said.

"Yeah." Maria frowned. "I'm sorry, I shouldn't have brought it up."

"It's all right. Sometimes I forget it's a public fact, you know? That she died." He paused. "It used to frustrate me, how bad I was at thinking my way into anyone else's life. It made me feel like the worst kind of narcissist. But after I started working for DaSilva, I became better at it. It's part of the job: people tell me about themselves, tell me things that sometimes only their families or closest friends might know. I don't have to ask. I don't even necessarily want to know. Anyway, I think I'm pretty good now at building an idea of somebody's life from a few scraps of fact. But you . . ." He shook his head. "I can't figure you out at all." He smiled. "Although I guess that's at least partially because you keep lying to me."

But Maria didn't smile. "Why do you care?"

He looked at her helplessly, then looked away. "I care about you."

"Don't say that."

"I mean it."

His words hung in the air, dissipating like mist.

"I've done things no person should ever have to do," she said.

This stopped him short for a moment, but he recovered and forged on: "It doesn't matter."

"It might not to you." Her voice was sharp.

"I'm sorry. I'm not trying to push you."

She sighed. "Let's stop talking for tonight, okay? Just sit here with me for a while."

He leaned back into the couch and watched her out of the corner of his eye. She stared at the television, a flush high on her cheeks. She changed the channel to a nature program about creatures that live on the floors of deep ocean canyons, in total darkness, pale limpid things clustered around vents that released boiling steam. The lights of the deep-sea probe shone, like X-rays, straight through the creatures—tiny tubular shrimp, pygmy crabs, waxen slugs. Fifteen minutes into the program, Maria's eyes drifted shut. Her head listed forward then snapped upright. She looked around, startled. Her eyes found Simon, and it was a second or two until the muscles of her face relaxed. She told him that she needed to sleep now, and so Simon left, promising to come back to see her again soon.

He rode the F train to Roosevelt Island, got out, and walked down Main Street. He stopped at the island's single bar, empty except for a drunken old man nursing a whiskey, and drank a pint of ale while watching cable news on mute. The outgoing president hunched behind a podium, looking weary and peevish, more than a little happy to be getting out of the house before the roof collapsed on his head. Simon could see that falling asleep in front of him—exposing herself like that—had made Maria uncomfortable, nearly angry. *I've done things no person should ever have to do.* The statement was melodramatic, but her delivery had been matter-of-fact, dispassionate: he believed her. But what was it that she'd done? The drunk at the other end of the bar grumbled something at the bartender, who changed the channel to a sports network, some kind of NFL analysis show. Simon sipped his beer and watched two wide-shouldered guys gesticulate in a studio that looked like an imitation of the command center of the starship *Enterprise*, done from memory. The program was difficult to follow without the sound, and Simon had mostly stopped paying attention when the screen suddenly cut to Howard Crewes sitting in his leather and bronze study.

Simon stared at the television, his brain lagging a few seconds behind his eyes. The initial shot cut to a split-screen of Crewes and one of the program's in-studio hosts. They framed Crewes from the shoulders up. He looked startled, his eyes fixed wide-open, as though someone had told him to make sure he didn't blink too much.

Simon waved at the bartender. "Can I get a little sound?"

"Different game then," Crewes was saying. "Different rules. Different attitude."

"You weren't flagged for what happened on that play," the host said.

"No. That's how we were taught. That's how we played."

The screen cut to a still shot of Alvin Plummer prone on the turf. Crouching medical staff obscured most of his body, his legs protruding with unnatural rigidity. Simon thought of the disappeared video, of the potent unscriptedness of watching the injury live.

The knit-browed host asked, "Do you think enough steps have been taken to prevent another Alvin Plummer?"

"I don't know if you can ever eliminate the chance of something like that happening. The speed on the field . . . Things move too fast." Crewes glanced away from the camera. "But I hope a player today, in that situation, maybe he uses his shoulder, or he goes low instead of high. Maybe he thinks about a fine, or a suspension, and then he takes a little off the hit."

"You never had a chance to reconcile with Alvin Plummer before he passed away earlier this year."

Crewes frowned and seemed about to say something, then changed his mind. "I never spoke to Alvin, no."

"What—"

"I tried," Crewes interrupted. "I tried, but his family, they didn't want that to take place."

"Well, and what, uh, what would you tell Alvin now, if you could?"

Crewes stared at the camera for a few uncomfortable seconds, his lips pursed. Finally he said, "I'd tell him I didn't mean for that to happen to him. I'd tell him I was just playing the game the way I always played it. It was nothing personal."

"And that's something I think he'd absolutely appreciate hearing," the host said, idiotically. "Howard Crewes, four time Pro Bowler, 1990 Defensive Player of the Year. Thank you very much for your time, Howard."

"All right," Crewes said.

The camera cut back to the studio. "Fifteen years ago this Sunday," the host said, "Alvin Plummer became the last player to be paralyzed during an NFL game. Has a new focus on helmet-to-helmet contact lessened the chances of such a catastrophic injury happening on the field again? Or are these new measures just . . ."

Simon stopped listening. Crewes had looked awkward on camera, caught halfway between contrition and defiance. Apologizing for something that could have happened to any other player made him angry, and it didn't bring Plummer back either. But Simon could tell he still craved some form of absolution. Maybe Lenny was right. Maybe Crewes had wanted Lenny to live for his own sake as much as for Lenny's. Simon drained the last of his pint and left cash on the bar. It didn't matter now. The surgery was over, and Lenny was alive, and the why of it was irrelevant.

THE next afternoon, Maria called him and said she'd decided to rent a safe-deposit box in which to store her cash. She chose a bank in Downtown Brooklyn, near the Williamsburgh Savings Bank

Tower, and Simon went with her to transport the money, hanging out in the bank's lobby while a clerk led her belowground to the deposit boxes.

Simon didn't mention that he'd met with DaSilva at the Health Solutions office that morning to deliver his update. He'd told Peter about Maria's plans to one day open a restaurant—Peter had simply rolled his eyes—and also that she'd admitted to severing all ties to her life in Los Angeles but still without telling him why.

DaSilva had frowned. "Are people back there looking for her?"

"I guess her friends are."

"Family?"

"I'm not sure she has one."

"How about the police?"

"I don't think so. At least, she didn't say anything about that." *The police?* He didn't want to admit to DaSilva that the possibility hadn't even occurred to him.

"Well, she probably wouldn't either way, right?" DaSilva paused, the heavy-lidded eyes seeking council inward. "Okay," he said finally. "If she wants to stay hidden, let's help her stay hidden. Keep checking in on her until we're absolutely sure she's not going to get sick or disappear again. At least a few more weeks. Does she trust you?"

Simon hesitated. "I think she's starting to." He felt as though he was somehow betraying her by admitting this, as though simply answering DaSilva's question had converted his honest—if not yet fully understood—impulse to protect and help Maria into a plan, just another canny tactic.

"That's good. Keep it up, and maybe we'll find out what the hell she wanted to leave behind so badly."

"What about Abraham?" Simon asked.

"They haven't called Cabrera again. Somebody's eventually going to chase her down for that bill, whether it's insurance or the hospital. I'm sure the people at Abraham think her story reeks of bullshit, but why would they want to get too involved?" He shook his head. "Still, I hate that she's in their records now. It's just another fucking thing for us to worry about, right?"

Simon and Maria left the bank together and made plans to meet the following morning. She told him she wanted to sit in a restaurant and eat a long, lazy brunch. She was feeling stronger, and she wanted to be out in the world again, among people living their regular everyday lives. In just a few days, the range of her walks around the neighborhood had grown from two blocks to five to ten; she'd lowered her Percocet dosage and her appetite had begun to return. And so on Saturday morning, Simon took her to Park Slope, which he considered the cradle of a certain kind of benign normalcy, the neighborhood equivalent of upscale comfort food. He met her outside the Seventh Avenue subway station. She got out of a taxi, wearing her leather jacket and a pair of tight black jeans he hadn't seen before; apparently she was finally feeling well enough to start spending a little bit of her money. They walked slowly toward Prospect Park. It was the first of November. The sky was bright and pale and clear, with the high, thin light of a sunny day in late fall, the air crisp and chilly. The streets were crawling with people. A man in a caramel corduroy jacket and newsboy cap walked by, holding a coffee cup in one hand and the leash for a chocolate Labrador in the other. They passed stoops peopled by parents and children sharing breakfast sandwiches and glass-bottled sodas. Maria's eyes flicked from person to person, as though she were filing away for later use details of their dress and bearing, their attitudes, their modes of being—an anthropologist jotting field notes, an actor getting into character.

They turned onto Eighth Avenue and picked a café done up in the requisite French brasserie style: lacquered wicker chairs, black-and-white tiled floors, splotchy wall-sized mirrors, wood paneling, brass banisters. They sat near the front window, sunshine slashing across their table, dust motes dancing wildly in the air between them. On the other side of the window, a pair of French bulldogs were anchored to a wrought-iron bench. Simon and Maria sipped their coffee and read the menu, not speaking, and Simon wondered if he'd somehow erred in bringing her here, if this was not at all the kind of place she'd been talking about. The truth was that they were both outsiders here, pretenders really—a pair of infiltrators, neither of them truly comfortable in this sunlit social world.

"What are you having?" He looked up: Maria was smiling at him, backlit, haloed. He felt relief at the sight of her smile. "I think I want a spinach and cheddar omelet," she said. "Or maybe the croque-madame. Or maybe I'll have both."

"Your appetite's back."

"That, and it's nice I can afford to order all this stuff. I'm used to being the one serving it."

They put in their orders and then resumed the conversation about Simon's family. Maria had asked about his parents on their walk to the restaurant, and he'd said only that his mother had died when he was very young and his father was essentially a re-cluse whose relatives all lived in England. Now he elaborated, tell-ing her that Michael was an only child whose own father was dead and whose mother was now a half-senile, sour old woman sequestered in a Bethnal Green nursing home. He explained Mi-chael's philosophy, how his father believed that the reverent ex-cavation and preservation of family history—which included any interest in genealogy or family lore—was a narcissistic waste of time, primitive, like burning offal for the ancestor spirits. Michael disparaged what he called the "tribalisms" of excessive national, religious, or ethnic identification, which was why he made a point of being an Englishman who didn't give a shit about drinking in an Irish bar—Derry Hills—with a "controversial" name. As he talked, Simon was aware that part of him hoped sharing pieces of himself like this would encourage Maria to do the same, but it was also true that he honestly wanted to open up to her. It had been so long since he'd spoken like this with anybody besides his father—Katherine Peel, he supposed, was the last other person with whom he'd shared anything even remotely personal—and he was surprised to find that he felt more engaged than anxious, more curious than insecure.

"Have you met her?" Maria said. "Your grandmother?"

"Only once. My father took me and Amelia to London to see her. She's an awful woman."

He told Maria how he and his sister had spent mornings at the home, sitting with their grandmother in the cafeteria. The old woman, a complete stranger to them, sat straight backed in her chair, engulfed by a maroon cardigan, her veiny hands folded primly in her lap, her entire being radiating dissatisfaction. Each party clearly baffled the other. Simon and Amelia understood little of what she said, her accent a thick, muffling blanket wrapped around her words, but they divined that she seemed to find it unutterably disappointing that they went to a Catholic school, that they lived in a largely Irish American neighborhood.

Amelia frowned. "But our mom was Catholic." She turned to Michael. "Wasn't she?"

"Yes, yes, of course," he said.

The old lady shook her head, pulled her sweater tight around her shoulders; Michael changed the subject.

Each morning they sat with the woman until noon, then went to eat lunch at a pub down the road, their father broodingly sipping from a pint of cask ale as Simon and Amelia picked at their coronation chicken sandwiches. Afternoons, they spent another two or three hours in the home, until their grandmother nodded off in her chair in the recreation room, under the blaring wall-mounted television. Michael seemed to experience the visit as an exercise in self-flagellation, excruciating but morally necessary, yet by the end of the week he'd realized that whatever he thought he was atoning for had nothing to do with his children, and so on the flight home he made it clear that Simon and Amelia would not be required to make the trip the following May.

"And that was the only time you met her?" Maria said.

"Yeah."

"That's sad."

"It's sad for her to be in a nursing home and to have a son who doesn't want to be around her very much. But it's not sad for me. I don't even know her."

"But she's still your grandmother. She's part of your family."

"So I should have deep feelings for an unpleasant old woman I've met once in my life? Just because we share some genes?"

Maria shook her head. "That's a fucked-up way of understanding how you fit into the world."

"Maybe. But you can also look at it this way: the family you're born into matters because it still determines the material facts of your life, at least at first. Your social class, your education. But who you are inside, your private self—you don't owe that to anybody, certainly not to your grandparents or even your parents. You're free to create it on your own."

"I wish that were true. But it's not so easy."

"It *is* true."

"You know what's funny?" Maria speared a piece of omelet on her fork and jabbed it at Simon. "That sounds a lot like your father's philosophy. Which seems to disprove the point."

"Very clever."

"Anyway, I think you're being naive."

"So did my sister. It's something we always argued about."

He told Maria how Amelia used to curl up with their father's old photo albums spread open across her lap. She turned the pages reverentially, as though they were illuminated texts, fragile and antique, while Simon couldn't be bothered to spend more than a few minutes with the things. There were Michael's parents standing in front of the old family cottage in Oxfordshire: gray people, gray house, gray sky. There was their father, no older than twenty, in a peacoat, with his hair falling across his eyes, leaning into the doorway of a pub. Later, in the basement of the Rockaway house, Amelia had found shoeboxes stuffed with more photographs, the boxes sagging, their cardboard damp and mildewy. She'd carried the boxes upstairs, displaying their contents to Michael as though they were evidence of a crime he'd deliberately concealed. Was he just planning on leaving them down there to rot? Didn't he care what happened to them? He shrugged, said she could do what she wanted with them. Didn't he want to look at them with her? He shook his head. "Do what you want with them," he said again. "I'm not short on memories."

And so she spent much of that winter organizing the orphaned photographs. Simon would find her cross-legged on the rug, neat stacks of photos arranged in front of her, an unsorted pile to one side, a family album open on the other. She'd flip a photo around, ask what he thought of it, where it might fit into her elaborate system of categorization. Most of the pictures she asked him about were of their mother. There she was, in her early twenties, leaning her elbows on a railing overlooking the Thames, her glossy brown hair gathered with a red ribbon at the nape of her neck. There she was, standing with another woman at a cocktail party, her belly giant and tight against her red sweater as the woman reached out to touch it. Here was their mother lifting the infant Amelia up to a Christmas tree, a crocheted snowflake gripped in Amelia's tiny fist. Their mother's hair was shorter here, cut and shaped into a dark bob that might have been a wig, her face washed out by the flash, her bare arms bony and milk white. Simon wanted to help his sister, but he could never stick with the project for very long. He'd been less than three when his mother died, and so he'd experienced her early death primarily as a kind of echo contained and transmitted within the character of his father, more as a part of Michael than as the passing away of a separate, discrete human being. Looking at the photos seemed to give Amelia a fierce, weepy sort of happiness, but it was depressing for him, and not in a cathartic way.

"I'm sorry about what happened to her," Maria said.

"I was very little. I barely knew her."

"I meant Amelia."

"Oh. Yes."

"You were close with her."

"That doesn't sound like a question."

"It's what the newspaper articles said."

"We spent a lot of time together. But then, so do most siblings."

"Which doesn't make what you had worth anything less."

"No."

"And I'm sure it didn't make it any easier when she was gone."

He closed his eyes, all the familiar, awful images pushing up against his lids. "Have you ever seen a dead body?"

"Yeah." The answer was immediate.

"What about somebody who drowned?"

"No."

"You'd think the skin would be pale. Bleached. At least that's what I thought." He opened his eyes. "But it's not like that. After a few days in the water, the skin turns black. Dark purple. Like a bruise covering the entire body. The person becomes swollen and bloated."

She reached across the table and squeezed his hand. "I'm sorry you saw that."

"I didn't have to go to the morgue. My father could've identified her by himself—they didn't need me. I chose to be there."

"Why?"

"I knew it would be horrible," he said. "Even if I didn't know exactly how she would look, I knew it would be horrible. So I went as penance. Because I was alive and she wasn't." He'd never talked about these things with anybody before, not even his father, and it was strange to hear his private thoughts suddenly exposed, like flower bulbs or squint-eyed moles, pale and moist and unaccustomed to sunlight or scrutiny. He felt naked, vulnerable. He'd said enough for this morning; he didn't want to talk about Amelia anymore. "What about your family? Is what you told me before true?"

Maria looked down, frowning.

"About your parents, I mean."

She sighed. "Part of it."

"Which part?"

"I lied about my father. I have no idea where he is or what he does, I've never known him. But my mother is dead. Just like yours."

He pictured the death certificate. "How old were you when it happened?" He hoped he sounded interested in the answer for its own sake, rather than as a test of her truthfulness.

"Thirteen."

He could feel her withdrawing from him again, turning her attention inward. "How did she die?" he asked softly.

She turned away from him, squinting at the bright window. "Simon."

"Yeah?"

"Don't push it."

He chewed and swallowed a final bite of steak and eggs, then excused himself to go outside and smoke a cigarette. He sat on the bench in front of the restaurant, the French bulldogs sniffing his ankles. He got up, walked to the curb, turned around. Through the window's glare, he could see Maria in profile. She bent over one of her three plates, cutting into the croissant sandwich, raising the egg-dripping morsel to her mouth. She savored her bite with almost comical relish, as though she were starring in a commercial, an advertisement, not for a brand of food but for, perhaps, a national airline, a nation itself, a way of life. She put her fork down and sipped from her coffee in that pensive, theatrical way rare in actual life: the thumb and forefinger of her free hand bracing the rim of the cup as she brought it to her lips. She'd let the waiter clear Simon's plate, and if he didn't know better, he would think, from where he stood, that she was dining alone, and happy to be. In less than a week, she'd gone from being barely able to walk to this, the satiated woman in the window. It was a happy change, of course, but he couldn't help wondering what she would need him for now. He tried to suppress this sort of thinking, to not let it ruin the unexpected pleasure of sharing his past with her, but it seeped up into his thoughts anyway, like toxic groundwater. The old jealousy, the old possessiveness. He remembered suddenly that he was supposed to have dinner with his father in Rockaway Beach that night. What could he possibly tell Michael about his life right now that wasn't a complete lie? He sucked at the last of his cigarette, tossed it aside, and rejoined Maria at the table to find that she'd already paid for their meal with a few bills peeled from a thick wad in the back pocket of her jeans.

## Nine

OVER and over, Simon had rehearsed the story in his head, preparing for when he would finally tell his father the truth. He would need to begin, he'd decided, on the evening before the first classes of the first semester. On the Great Lawn in Central Park, the matriculating class spread out across six baseball diamonds, bats slung over shoulders, gloves tucked under arms. The late August air thick as mud, coolers of beer stashed behind the backstops. Simon leaning against the dugout fence, learning names: Anita, Dan, Rakesh, Liz, Levi. His classmates in baseball caps, tube socks, faded T-shirts, the names of their colleges and high schools emblazoned across their chests in flaking letters.

At the bar afterward, Simon shared the end of a long table with a girl—a woman, really; she was older than him—wearing a T-shirt that read "I ♥ BX." This was Katherine Peel. She'd just moved to Manhattan from Yonkers; sharp and sarcastic and unimpressed, she was going to be a trauma surgeon. They went up to the bar to refill their pitcher, but Katherine decided she wanted whiskey instead, so whiskey is what they had. They sat at the bar and drank. She told him she'd grown up in the Bronx, and when he asked what neighborhood, she told him Riverdale, "but not the part you're thinking of." She said she'd been a nurse after college, before doing her premed courses at Pace. She peppered her speech with hospital jargon Simon didn't know, but he didn't want to appear callow, so he kept nodding and frowning and mumbling agreement.

A few drinks later, the other students began to drift out of the bar. Some slapped Simon's shoulder as they passed, and he felt an absurd sense of accomplishment for remembering their names. Allison, Pria, Jeff. These were to be his classmates. A looseness spread through his limbs. He smiled at Katherine, who was talking about witnessing her first open-heart surgery, the cracking of the rib cage. She paused, smiled back at him. He wondered how he appeared to her, whether he seemed like the kind of person who made friends easily, picked up girls in bars, traded one girlfriend for the next. He wondered if, instead, she could tell how private and constricted his life really was, whether that was in fact what she found appealing. Because he could see that she liked him, that she wanted to know more about him. He thought—he hoped—maybe it was a case of two damaged people recognizing the wound in each other, the way damaged people sometimes do. The skin of her throat was white as milk, a red blush creeping above the collar of her shirt; her smile was crooked, provocative, crimson lipstick like blood on snow. One drink more and they stood, Katherine grabbing his arm. He offered to take her home, but she told him she could make it alone. He helped her catch a taxi, and her lips brushed against his cheek as she slid into the backseat. As he walked uptown, to his new apartment on York Avenue, he was too high on the possibilities of this next phase in his life to be disappointed that she'd left without him. From the fourteenth floor, he looked out over the river and then south, down along the avenue. He thought he could see his old building, where he and his father and Amelia had lived before moving to the Rockaways, but he couldn't be sure he was looking at the right one.

The next morning, after listening to the semester's opening lecture, he stood with the rest of the students in a long, low-ceilinged hallway in the basement of the medical school. At the end of the hall, behind a set of steel double doors, waited the anatomy lab.

He could already smell the formalin, sick and sweet and chemical. The professors opened the doors and the students filed into the large square room. Eighteen rolling metal tables were laid out in rows. On each table rested a white body bag and numbered placard. The odor of formalin pushed against Simon's face, like a soaked rag held to his mouth. He found his assigned table. His three dissection partners for the duration of the semester were stationed there already, and he saw that Katherine Peel was one of them, her black hair tied up in a bun, her eyes red and hooded. The other two, a boy and a girl, blond and fresh faced and looking very young, exuded an air of horrible competence. Katherine leaned her mouth to his ear, her breath smelling of synthetic mint layered over alcohol: "You were supposed to be at the next table. I switched the placards. Thank me later."

One of the circulating professors unzipped their bag. The torso and legs were swaddled in beige cloth, the hands, feet, and head wrapped in gauzy white material over which clear plastic had been fixed in place with rubber bands. The professor pulled aside the cloth covering the cadaver's left arm, baring the skin from wrist to shoulder, then folded the cloth to expose the clavicle and the swell of a small breast. The skin was a noncolor: not quite white, not quite gray, not quite green. Smooth, unwrinkled—a young woman's arm, slim and hairless. Simon watched as the professor made the first cut, a shallow H at the rounding of the shoulder. The professor peeled back the skin with his gloved fingers, naming the revealed layer of greasy, yellowish tissue—the fascia—before sweeping it away to show the striated muscle underneath.

The four of them took turns with the scalpel, scissors, forceps, probe, and their fingers—mostly their fingers—picking their way through the structures of the woman's upper arm. This was a necessary task, and Simon was going to perform it as best he could. He looked across the table at Katherine. Her mouth was pressed flat; sweat beaded on her forehead. She held the dissection manual, reading the instructions aloud as Simon peeled the skin away from the bicep and dropped it into the tissue bucket at the foot of the table. The skin clung to his glove, and he shook his hand until it slid away and puddled at the bottom of the bucket. Katherine broke off in midsentence, handed the manual to one of their partners, and walked out of the room. Simon stopped, his scalpel poised above the cadaver's arm. He asked if he should go after her. There isn't time, the blonds said, we're behind already.

During their lunch break, he found Katherine eating a tuna sandwich in the cafeteria. She told him she'd needed to vomit, so that's what she went and did. One of the professors had found her in the hallway, she said, and tried to get philosophical. He told her it was normal to be upset by what they were doing; anybody in the lab who wasn't disturbed by it was the one with the problem. He said it would get better with time. She told Simon they'd had a nice moment, she and the professor, but what he didn't know was that she wasn't upset at all, she was just really fucking hungover. She laughed as she told Simon this story, as though to actually be disturbed by dissecting a cadaver would be ridiculous.

That evening they continued their work on the woman's upper arm. When they were finished, they sprayed a wetting solution on the flesh before rewrapping the torso. Simon zipped up the body bag, and as he pulled the zipper over the woman's wrapped head, he wondered what her face looked like, how she died, who she'd been.

The next week they moved on to the hands, removing the plastic bags and unwrapping the gauze. The woman's nails were painted black. The coverage was uniform, without chips or scratches, as though she'd just applied a fresh coat. Katherine cut down the center of the palm, drew a line across the base of the fingers, bisected each digit. The palm skin was thick and difficult to slice, and Katherine replaced the blade on her scalpel four times before finishing the cut.

After the arms came the thorax, the seat of the heart and lungs. They removed the cadaver's breasts from the chest cavity, along with the surrounding skin. The blonds took turns sawing through the ribs, bone dust curling into the air. When the work was done, they lifted the rib cage free of the body. Her lungs were mottled: she'd been a smoker. Simon felt a spasm of kinship. He held the woman's heart in his hands in the deep-basined sink, flushing the clotted blood and formalin out of the arteries.

Late at night, high above York Avenue, Simon twisted in his bed, from sleep to wakefulness and back again. He rolled over onto his stomach and flung out his arm, and his hand landed in a nest of fascia, yellow and clingy. He rolled over onto his back and sank down into heavy water, his hands and feet and head wrapped in thick plastic. He opened his mouth to breathe, the plastic clinging to his tongue. The smell of formalin filled his nostrils. This smell now followed him everywhere, no matter how hard he scrubbed his fingers and scalp in the shower. It was in his clothes, his skin, his hair, his saliva, his sweat. It filled his mouth; it was his air. He opened his eyes and his cadaver was lying in the bed next to him. She rested on her back, her chest cavity emptied out, the wet red walls glistening in the dim light that seeped around the blinds. Her face was covered in black plastic. He reached out and tore the plastic away. Underneath was a layer of gauze, which he unwrapped with difficulty, the gauze clinging to the damp skin. He pulled away the last of it, and it was as he knew it would be: it was Amelia, of course, it was his sister as he'd seen her in the Queens County Morgue, staring at him, open mouthed and dead eyed.

He told nobody about his dream. It didn't occur to him that other students might be having dreams of their own; if they were, they weren't telling anybody about them either.

Sometime in November, he missed his first lab. He couldn't say why he didn't go. When his alarm rang that morning, he was already awake. He had an hour to shower, eat, and walk ten blocks to the facilities, but he felt as though a giant hand were pinning him against the mattress. After the lab had already begun, he forced himself to get up and walk over to the window. He raised the shade onto a brilliant morning, onto the glittering river. He stood by the window for half an hour, then got into the shower, the water scalding hot, the smell of formalin and cigarettes rising from his body.

He attended the following day's lab. He read aloud from the manual as the blonds disentangled the cadaver's thigh muscles. The book was slippery with formalin residue and bits of fascia. The cadaver's knees were dimpled; her toenails were painted black to match her fingers, but here the paint was chipped. Katherine asked why he'd missed yesterday's lab. He shrugged, said he over-slept. But he missed another lab the following week, then a third, a fourth.

One night, over Thanksgiving break, he left the library after midnight and crossed the street to the hospital. He took the eleva-tor down to the basement. He ignored the lockers of scrubs in the hallway, because who the fuck cared, the smell was coming home with him anyway. He pressed his electronic ID card against the sensor. The lock released. He opened the door and flipped on the lights, and it was as though it were the first day of dissection, eighteen white body bags resting on eighteen steel tables, as though nothing had yet been done to these cadavers—no, these *corpses*, because that was what they were, corpses, "cadaver" just a pretty word for a disinfected corpse.

He found his table and unzipped the body bag, letting it fall away from the woman like a chrysalis. He pulled off the moisten-ing cloth, and there she was, her torso opened and emptied, her heart and liver and lungs stuffed into a garbage bag tucked against the soles of her feet. Katherine and the blonds had moved down her legs, exposing a tangle of tendons and muscles and nerves. He reached out his gloveless hands and turned her left leg to the side, and he saw that they had excavated the back of her thigh and calf as well, leaving the fat worm of the sciatic nerve running down the middle of a nest of ropey tissue. They'd stopped just above her ankles. Against his bare fingers her skin felt cold and greasy, the texture not unlike that of an uncooked chicken thigh. It was these kinds of metaphors—metaphors of meat, of animal flesh—that he had tried until now to suppress, because that was what he was supposed to do, but he didn't care anymore, he was sick of pretending.

You were supposed to think of your cadaver as a human being, because that would instill in you a proper respect for that human being's dead body as you tore it to pieces. But you were not supposed to think too much about your cadaver as a human being, because then you might wonder if she would like what was being done to her body if she could somehow see it now. Then you might imagine that she *could* see it, that she was watching you and your partners run scalpels and scissors through her skin, pull apart her muscles and organs with your hands. You might wonder about your cadaver's life, about what series of events had led to this terminus on your dissecting table. You might start to think of her as an individual with a past and a family and the collection of desires and fears and prejudices that we call a personality. You might start to see other people—people you know, people who are still alive—on the dissecting table, and you might start to see your cadaver freed from the table, outside the lab, taking the place of the living who surround you on your walk to and from the hospital, on your ever rarer visits to restaurants and shops and bars. This might happen first in dreams and then, later, in waking life. And if—as everybody else in your class seems to have less and less trouble determining the appropriate level of humanity, of humanness, to attach to their cadavers—instead you find yourself moved in the opposite direction, more and more uncertain about whether you were slicing open the belly and anus and vagina of a dead woman or a mere piece of meat, then you might find yourself standing in the anatomy lab, alone at one in the morning, caught between the need to uncover your cadaver's face and fear of what might happen if you do.

Simon couldn't do it, not yet. He stood there, looking at the bagged face. Underneath the clear plastic, gauze hugged the contours of her chin, her lips and nose, the ridges above her eye sockets. He put his hand on the bag, feeling his way across the swells and hollows. He rewrapped the wetting cloth and zipped up the body bag. As he walked home, he raised his hands to his face. He breathed in, smelling the formalin and something else beneath it: a sweet, rotting lemony scent like a soured perfume.

Katherine called to say that he was going to fail the lab. The next exam was in ten days. He said he'd take it, no problem. He said he'd been ill. She didn't believe him, and why would she? He didn't even bother to try to convince her. He asked her why she cared. "Because you're not a robot like these other people," she said. "The blonds are driving me nuts. You need to come back." But he couldn't do it. It was an impossibility to be in the lab with the other students, to hold the scalpel and cut. He stopped going to his other classes as well. A dean called, left two messages, then stopped calling. No one was going to make him do anything. He was not a child; he was free to sabotage himself as he liked.

A few nights later, he took ten milligrams of Valium, dressed, and left his apartment. The Yorkville streets were empty, a bitter wind whipping in from the river. The Valium kicked in as he crossed Third Avenue, and he felt a lightness lift through him, as though his bones had been drained of their marrow. The basement of the lab building was deserted. He unzipped his cadaver's body bag. The zipper's tab was positioned at her feet, and so it was not until he reached the far end of the seam and let the bag fall away that he saw what remained of her head, a pinkish-gray slab. The skin had been mostly removed, as had her left eye and the external structures of her nose and mouth. Her right eye was half-covered by its eyelid, as though she were winking at him. Her ears were still intact, sprouting from the sides of her head like mushrooms. Above her eye sockets, a thin strip of skin was connected to her scalp, which had been cut into four equal flaps and pried loose from her skull. The segments of scalp had been folded back, and he turned over the edge of one flap and saw that the scalp's skin was covered with a fine black stubble. The top bowl of the skull was entirely missing. He looked into its empty basin and saw the knobby floor of her cranial cavity, dotted with the stumps of nerves that had been severed to remove the brain. He checked under the table, and there it was, submerged in formalin at the bottom of a clear plastic bucket, its crenulated lobes the pale-cream color of oatmeal.

He'd waited too long. He would never know what her face had looked like, this woman on the table, this woman who had been reduced, partly by his own hand, to something that did not much resemble a woman. The Valium settled over his nerves like falling snow. Where was her face? The tissue bucket at the foot of the table had been emptied, but a larger plastic disposal bin near the door was mostly full. Inside: a gluey tangle of fascia, fat, bits of skin. He knew from his dissection manual that the skin of the face was removed in two intact pieces. He reached into the bin and gently cleared away a top layer of fascia, cold and wet to the touch, like gelatin. He saw underneath an uninterrupted expanse of skin. He lifted this carefully out of the bucket, letting gravity unfurl the tissue. It could be the lower half of her face, a semicircle with an oval gap for her mouth. He moved to the head of the table and watched his hands lay the skin on top of the exposed muscles of her cheeks and jaw. He returned to the bin and cleared away another clinging layer of fascia. Gently, he disentangled a second large piece of skin and lifted it free. This would be the skin of her forehead and temples. He saw himself lay this piece, too, down where it belonged. The edges of the skin curled back at their meeting point around her eye sockets. He smoothed them down with his thumb so they adhered better to the muscle, but still they rippled and bubbled like a poorly laminated strip of fake wood.

Of course, it was all pointless. What he'd assembled bore less resemblance to a human face than the bare muscles beneath. He left her as she was, under the pitiless fluorescents. He didn't bother to close the laboratory door. Let them find her in the morning and wonder. He was never coming back.

Two a.m. Outside the window of the Health Solutions office, the lights of the Fifty-Ninth Street Bridge stretched across the river, their reflection smeared in black water. DaSilva behind the desk, Simon in the chair across from him, a full ashtray between them.

"Bring her to the apartment," DaSilva was saying. "Keep her there until I figure out how to contain this."

"I'll try. But I can't force her to do anything."

"Are you fucking kidding me?" He jabbed his finger at Simon. "Get her to the apartment. It's for her own good, she'll see that."

"When?"

"Tomorrow." He checked his watch. "Or today, I guess. After you see Crewes."

Simon rubbed his eyes, their corners gritty, sandpapery. He was exhausted, losing concentration. This day just would not end.

The call from Howard Crewes had come late in the afternoon, as Simon sat at his kitchen table, scanning the Cabrera waiting list on his laptop one last time before setting off on the endless subway journey out to the Rockaways. He'd eyed his buzzing cell phone. There was no good reason for Crewes to be calling, and he'd considered not answering, as though he could ward off trouble simply by remaining ignorant of it. On the fourth ring, he'd snatched the phone off the desk.

"Howard," he said. "What can I do for you?"

"He's dead."

"What? Who?" But even as Simon said it, he knew.

"Cheryl found him this morning. He . . ." Crewes made a low sound, a kind of growl. "Vicodin, Ambien, and whiskey. It wasn't an accident."

"What are you talking about?"

"Are you listening to me? He waited until Cheryl and the kids were away for one night, and then he did it. He fucking killed himself. He planned this." Crewes's voice was hoarse, furious. "He tricked us all."

Simon felt the tingle of panic climb his spine. "I'm so sorry, Howard."

"You need to know this, whether you cared about Lenny or not. Because it's not going to stop here. You see that, right?"

"Yes." And Simon did see it, the whole terrible shape of the thing unfurling.

"We need to talk," Crewes said. "In person. You need to come down here."

Simon closed his eyes, wishing he could freeze this moment before DaSilva found out, before he had to tell Maria.

"Simon?" Crewes said. "Are you there?"

"I'm here."

"You'll come see me."

"Yes."

"I don't give a shit if this sounds callous," Crewes said, "but I'll be goddamned if Lenny brings everybody else down with him."

Of course Simon had never made it out to his father's house for their dinner after that. But if Simon was exhausted, he knew DaSilva had to feel a thousand times worse. Peter had arrived at Cabrera at seven that morning for a transplant surgery unrelated to Health Solutions. The donor had gone under anesthesia at eight, and the recipient had come out of the OR at six in the evening. DaSilva had spent much of that time in the waiting room, with the two families, relaying updates from the surgeons. He hadn't responded to any of Simon's pages, and so he'd known nothing when he was pulled out of the waiting room and put on the phone with a Nassau County medical examiner. Just like Simon, he must have seen it all immediately, the clusterfuck that had just fallen on his head; but unlike Simon, he'd had to keep himself together through endless conversations with Nassau County officials and, later, Cabrera administrators, all the while monitoring the transplant surgery currently under way and attending to the patients' families. For the hospital, the crucial issue was keeping the state of Leonard Pellegrini's health—that he'd been an unreformed alcoholic at the time of surgery—under wraps. Cabrera had patient confidentiality on its side, so its worry was mostly confined to what Cheryl Pellegrini or Howard Crewes or somebody else who had known Lenny well might say.

"What should I tell Crewes?" Simon asked.

"Not to talk to anybody about anything. That you have it under control. He doesn't know Maria's name, does he?"

"No. But Cheryl knows her first name and what she looks like. They met in the hospital."

"I was there, remember?" DaSilva took an angry drag off his cigarette. "There's nothing we can do about that now."

"Crewes is going to want to know what kind of trail his money's left."

"His payments to the hospital are legitimate. And his payment to Maria is untraceable."

"Are you sure?"

DaSilva stared at him. "Am I sure of what?"

"That the cash is untraceable. How do you know?"

"Because I made it that way, Simon." His voice was flat, signaling an end to this line of questioning.

Simon hesitated. He decided to leave the issue of the cash alone for now. "What if a reporter tries to talk to him?" he asked. "If the hospital payments are legitimate, that means they're on record. Somebody will find out that he was behind them soon enough."

"He's grieving. He's upset. He can tell them to fuck off."

"And when they ask him who Lenny's donor was, he says it's private, none of their business."

"Right." DaSilva coughed, a wet, phlegmy rattling. "How did he seem to you, on the phone?"

"Pissed off."

"Yeah, I would be too. Did he say anything about Lenny's wife?"

"Like what?"

"Her state of mind."

Simon looked at DaSilva. His mind flashed to Cheryl sitting in the car by the train station, her eyes searching his face as he lied to her. "Her husband just committed suicide. I don't think her state of mind is hard to guess."

"Don't be an asshole. You know what I'm talking about. Is she looking to blame you? Blame Cabrera?"

"He didn't say. I doubt it."

DaSilva shook his head. "What a sad fucker. He had no idea what kind of mess he was making."

"I doubt he would've cared."

"You're probably right." He shook his head again. "Bring Maria to the apartment. No bullshit excuses. Keep her out of sight."

"We should've seen this coming," Simon said quietly. "Lenny never wanted our help."

"Don't," DaSilva warned.

"It's true."

"Don't fucking start with that right now." DaSilva glared at him across the desk. "It's pointless. We're moving forward. You understand me?"

Simon said nothing.

"Simon? Pull your head out of your ass and focus. This is your problem too."

"I know that."

"Then don't just sit there wishing things had gone differently. Help me fix it, or we're both fucked."


FIVE hours later, Crewes greeted Simon at the front door of the house in New Jersey and led him again to the study in the rear.

He told Simon he'd been in Long Island most of the previous afternoon and well into the night. He'd driven to the Pellegrinis' house to find it still cordoned off by the police but located Cheryl and the two children at a friend's place nearby. Cheryl sat on a couch, surrounded by the owner of the house and a few other women Crewes didn't know, with the boy, Gregory, sitting by her side, his hand in his mouth. Crewes had leaned down to hug her, and she'd been as responsive as a block of wood. He went into the kitchen to get a cup of coffee, and he found the little girl, Daniela, sitting across the kitchen table from an owl-eyed woman whom he later learned was a county social worker. The woman had her hands stretched across the table, palms up, offering them to Daniela, who sat in her chair with her eyes shut and her knees pulled tight to her chest.

"She was the one who found him," Crewes said. "Dani. He did it in the master bedroom upstairs."

Simon shook his head. "Christ. They'd been away?"

"Cheryl took the kids to her mother's place for the weekend. Lenny was supposed to go with them. They were about to leave when he said one of his headaches was coming on, and he told her to go without him. She didn't want to leave him alone. But he made her go." Crewes paused, his hands braced against the edge of the desk.

Against his will, Simon imagined the scene: the kids bursting into the house, itching to see their father after a night away; Cheryl hanging back, already suspecting that something was wrong, wondering why Lenny hadn't answered her call that morning; Cheryl finally stepping inside and taking the temperature of the house, its silence, dread wrapping around her spine as Daniela scampered up the stairs, yelling out her father's name. The cruelty of inflicting such a scenario on your own children was astonishing, but Simon also understood that the pain out of which such cruelty was born had to be so relentless and crippling that it was difficult to hate Lenny for what he'd done.

"What I want to know is when he decided to do it," Crewes said, his anger like a physical thing occupying the air between them. "I want to know how long he was lying to me. Lying to his wife. I want to know how he could let her and Dani and Greg move back into the house with him, how he could look at them every day knowing what he was going to do."

"Maybe it wasn't like that," Simon said, hoping rather than believing this might be true. "Maybe he didn't plan it."

Crewes was quiet for a long moment. "He tried it before," he said finally. "About two years ago. With the same shit, pills and booze. But he swore he was past that. He told me the transplant had given him a new start. He looked me in the face and lied to me."

"Then why did he go through with it? If he already knew how it was going to end, what was the point of the surgery?"

"I don't know. I don't know if he actually believed it himself for a moment, if he convinced himself that things were going to be different, or if he agreed to it just to shut us all up."

Simon was afraid he knew the answer to Crewes's question, and it wasn't the one the man wanted to hear. Yet Simon also knew he was complicit in all of this too; he hadn't cared what Leonard Pellegrini really wanted. None of them had, not DaSilva, not Crewes, not even Cheryl, who'd understandably preferred that her children grow up with a father. The question for Simon wasn't whether Lenny wanted to live; the question was whether a man with a wife and two young children had the right to choose to die.

"The press is calling Don MacLeod already," Crewes said. "The *Times*. The *Post*. ESPN. They've covered those meetings at his house before. And now here's another retired football player killing himself. It's something more for them to write about." He paused, staring somewhere above Simon's head. "You heard about DeMarcus Rogers?"

"The name sounds familiar."

"He played linebacker for the Bears in the eighties. Won a Su-per Bowl, voted into some Pro Bowls. He used to do work for the

Players Association. I met him a few times, and I liked him. Most people did. But the word was he'd been having difficulties these last few years. He'd get so frustrated when he couldn't remember things that he'd fly into these crazy rages, smash things up at work. He got divorced, and his kids didn't hear from him much. He sold his stake in this chain of hardware stores he had up in Illinois, and then he stopped doing work for the association. Basically dropped off the map. Turned out he'd rented a condo in Miami without telling anybody. About six months ago, he shot himself in the chest with a handgun. He left a note saying he'd chosen the chest because he wanted to leave his brain intact for testing. They can take a slice of it now, put that slice under a microscope, and discover how badly your brain got fucked up when you were playing. What they're finding out is that all these guys who're dying young, in their forties and fifties—guys who are killing themselves, OD'ing, crashing their cars drunk—all these guys, their brains are ancient. They're finding these markings, the same things a seventy-five-year-old with dementia or Alzheimer's would have. DeMarcus was the kind of guy who paid attention to this stuff." He shifted carefully in his chair, as though his bones were fragile cargo within the bag of his body. "Don MacLeod is going to ask Cheryl if she's willing to donate Lenny's brain to the same people."

"What do you think she'll say?"

"I don't know. I think it might be good if she could give a name to what she saw happen to him. You know? To have somebody tell her there wasn't anything she could've done differently. That something had happened to his brain, something he wasn't coming back from. Then again, she might be sick of people cutting his body apart."

Simon looked at Crewes's hands grasping the edge of the desk, the knuckles swollen to the size of quail eggs, the left pinky skewed at a crazy angle. "What are you going to tell them when they ask you about Lenny's transplant?"

"Who's 'them'?"

"The press, the same people who are interviewing Don and Cheryl. If they make that link."

"Isn't that what you're here to tell me?"

Simon took a deep breath. "I think the best we can do is keep the donor's identity a secret for as long as we can. Until the story is dead and nobody cares enough to look for her anymore."

"'The best we can do'? Jesus." Crewes seemed more weary now than pissed off. "Well, I don't know who she is, so that shouldn't be so hard for me. What about my money?"

"The money that went to the donor? Untraceable."

"It's in cash now?"

"Yes."

"You laundered it?"

Simon hesitated. "It went through a process, a conversion to cash."

Crewes held up his hands. "Correct me if I'm wrong, but is that not exactly what laundering is?"

"I think it's actually more like the opposite of laundering." Simon paused. "Anyway, I'm not sure how it was done."

"Come on, Simon, I'm not fucking taping this conversation. Be real with me here."

Simon cleared his throat. "I am. The money, that's not my area."

Crewes stared at him, a single vertical furrow cut between his eyebrows. "But somebody converted it?"

"Yes."

"Where's the cash?"

"In a deposit box at a bank."

"And where is the girl?"

"In a safe place."

"I hope she stays there."

Crewes paused, and with Howard's tough-guy patter quieted for a moment, Simon's attention was drawn to the despair edging around the man's eyes, despair and also fury—fury that he'd been unfairly cheated out of his best opportunity for atonement, as indirect as it might have been. It was a particular strain of anger and frustration, that of a man who has tried to do the right thing and been punished thoroughly for it, and Simon recognized it with the sympathy and respect of a fellow sufferer.

"I can't be tied to paying that girl anything." Crewes rapped his knuckles against the desk. "I'm not going to jail just because Lenny was a depressive fuckup."

SIMON drove his rental car—a ridiculous candy-red Dodge, high and short like an SUV lopped in half—directly from Crewes's cul-de-sac to Maria's apartment on South Tenth. He parked across the street and looked up at her window, stalling. He didn't want to have this conversation, but he understood that DaSilva was right: too many people at Abraham, and probably Cabrera too, knew where she was. If somebody in one of the hospitals decided to talk to a reporter, she'd be quickly found, and then they'd be fucked, all of them—Simon, DaSilva, Crewes, Maria herself. Still, he hated doing this to her, dragging her out of her apartment, adding yet another absurd and difficult complication to her run of epically miserable luck. He got out of the car and crossed the street; he couldn't put it off any longer. She buzzed him in and met him in the hallway outside her front door, wearing a baggy T-shirt and flannel pants, her face still bleary with sleep.

"What is it?" she asked. "What's happened?"

He guided her inside the apartment and told her about Lenny's suicide, leaving out the fact that it was Lenny's own three-year-old daughter who'd found him facedown on the bed in a puddle of vomit.

"Oh, fuck," Maria said, sinking onto the couch. "His wife. I saw her in the hospital, I remember . . . What was her name?"

"Cheryl."

"And he had kids too, didn't he? You told me he had kids."

"Two of them."

"How could he do this to them? How could he just . . . just . . . *give up*? After everything that everybody did for him?"

"I know," Simon said, "I know." It was awful what Lenny had done, an act of sadism toward his family almost breathtaking in its spitefulness, a resounding fuck-you to the world, but what could they do about that now? They had to try to salvage what could be salvaged. "People are going to try to find out about you now, okay? This is an alcoholic ex-NFL player who killed himself a month after getting a liver transplant. People are going to want to find out who he got the liver from, and somebody in the hospital might tell them."

He knew by her expression that she saw it then—how Lenny was the first domino, how his falling could lead to her, then to Crewes, to Simon, to DaSilva and Cabrera itself. She stood up from the couch.

"That money is mine," she said fiercely. "I fucking earned it. I fucking *need* it."

"Nobody's going to take it from you," he said. "But you can't stay here."

She started to shake her head.

"Yes," he said. "We've got to leave. Too many people know you live here. We need to hide you, just for a short time."

"Where do you want to go?"

"My apartment."

She looked over at him, her face suddenly wary.

"Now you don't trust me?" he said. "It's safe. I promise you."

She screwed up her eyes and balled her fists, as though she could reverse Lenny's suicide through sheer force of will. A low, furious humming escaped her pursed lips.

"Maria?"

She opened her eyes. "I'll go to a hotel."

He shook his head. "For how long? And, anyway, hotels are too public, too many variables you can't control. Listen, we'll find you a new apartment soon, once everything's calmed down. But my place is the safest thing for now." He paused. "You've got to trust me."

She went into the bedroom, and he stood in the doorway and watched as she angrily swept her clothes into a duffel bag, throwing her laptop in with the sweaters and jeans and skirts. She squatted down, punched a code into the safe. Inside was a small mound of banded bills, and she dumped them into the bag as well, plucking out a single wad of hundreds and waving it at Simon. "The point of this was not needing to trust anybody anymore. Do you understand that?"

"I know," he said, although he didn't, not really.

She threw the wad into the bag and yanked at the zipper. "I hate this, Simon."

"I know," he said again. "How much cash is that?"

"Somewhere close to two thousand, I think."

"The rest's in the bank?"

"Yeah." She tried to hoist the bag, but she buckled under its weight, grimacing and clutching at her abdomen.

"I've got it." Simon took the duffel from her and slung it over his shoulder. "Ready?"

"My meds," she said.

He found the pill bottles in the bathroom cabinet and tossed them into the bag, then he hustled out the door, Maria following close behind. Out in the hallway, he reached back for her hand. There was a pause, and then he felt her palm, hot and slick, press against his own. He moved quickly across the hall to the stairwell, and she let go of his hand and grasped his shoulder, keeping her other hand on the banister. He'd almost gone running down the stairs, forgetting for a moment how careful she still needed to be with her body, only five days out of Abraham. He threw the duffel into the trunk of the rental car, helped Maria into the passenger seat, and jerked the Dodge out onto South Tenth, accelerating around the corner onto Bedford, driving far too fast, as though the difference of a few minutes were going to mean anything now.

They didn't speak during the ride to Roosevelt Island, Maria staring blankly off into space. Her mind seemed far away, preoccupied with some other crisis of the distant past or future. Inside his apartment, she collapsed onto the couch, her face pale, damp with sweat. Simon fetched a glass of water as she dug the bottle of Percocet out of her bag. She swallowed a pill and wiped her face with her sleeve.

"So I'm just supposed to hide out here?" she said. "For how long?"

"Until we don't think anybody's trying to figure out who Lenny's donor was."

"*Fuck* that, Simon!" Maria smacked the couch, anger erupting suddenly, shattering her opiated calm. "I'm not just going to sit around and wait and hope nobody finds me. I was supposed to be anonymous, okay? That was part of the deal."

"I know. We're trying to keep it that way."

"You're not trying—you're *hoping*. And who's 'we'? You and that coordinator, DaSilva? How can we trust that guy?"

"We don't have to trust him."

"Why not?"

"Because he can't screw me. I know too much about what he does, about how he operates inside that hospital. If I ever told people what I know, he'd have far more to lose than me. Forget his job. Forget all the money he's making from Health Solutions—"

"Which is how much?"

Simon hesitated. Naming precise figures seemed like yet another clear and definite step in what he'd come to think of now as his betrayal of DaSilva.

"Jesus, Simon," she said. "Don't you think you owe me some fucking honesty here?"

"He's taking nearly $75,000 off the top of each deal." Simon spoke in a rush, before he could stop himself. "Double on yours, since it was a liver instead of a kidney. Before you and Lenny, we'd put together a dozen pairs in the last eight months."

"That's almost $900,000."

"Right. He's taking payments for brokering transplants. He's doctoring medical records, doctoring financial records. He's laundering cash. I have no idea how much time all that could get him. Fifteen years? Twenty?"

"But don't you think he knows that?" She shook a second Percocet into her palm and studied it, as though its shape concealed some divinable solution to their problems. "Don't you think he has some kind of plan in place?"

"His plan is to not get caught. Look, you see how this all works, right? Everyone is holding something over someone else's head. Me and DaSilva. You and Howard Crewes. DaSilva and Cabrera. That's the glue that makes this whole thing stick together."

"Fear?"

"Self-interest." Saying it out loud for the first time, he saw the situation's elegance, which he'd always understood, but also its fragility, which until now he had mostly chosen to ignore. "Everybody's got what they want, and it can only be taken away if they go after someone else."

"You mean deterrence." She tossed back the Percocet. "Which is another word for fear."

"You can call it that if you want."

"That never works for very long, Simon. Somebody always upsets the balance trying to protect themselves."

"How do you know that?"

"Because I've seen it. Somebody gets greedy or panics. They try to catch everybody else by surprise."

"Seen it where?"

"It doesn't matter where. The scam changes, but people's behavior doesn't." Maria gave him a hard look, and he thought he'd just glimpsed another facet of her composite self: the scrapper, the fighter. The survivor. "Don't be the guy waiting around, trusting that the system's going to work," she said. "You need to take control. You need to do something."

"DaSilva's not going to panic, okay? It's not his style."

She shook her head in annoyance, as though he were completely missing the point. "How long are you going to do this job, Simon?"

"It wasn't supposed to be a long-term solution."

"That's not an answer."

"I'm only two, maybe three, deals short of paying DaSilva back my loan." As soon as he said it, he knew this was an irrelevant statement, borderline ridiculous.

"Wait, you owe him money?" Maria looked genuinely surprised for the first time during the conversation.

"I . . ." He was suddenly embarrassed. How could he have put himself into such a position? It had seemed so simple at the time, so logical. His shoulders slumped. "Yeah. I owe him money."

"And you'd start work on another deal?" She stared at him. "After everything? Are you fucking kidding?"

"No, you're right. Of course, you're right." Simon rubbed his eyes. "I'll quit when this is over. When you're safe. When nobody's looking for you anymore."

"Will he let you go?"

"I don't know." He looked away. "I guess we'll find out."

## Ten

THAT night, Simon took Maria on a walk around the island, circling past the lighthouse and then south along the eastern river promenade. Maria, stir-crazy and still fuming, wore a hooded sweatshirt pulled tight over her head to hide her face, a gesture that Simon thought shaded into the paranoid. They passed under the bridge, the cavernous sound of traffic rumbling overhead, and when they came out on the other side, there was Cabrera, the sooty main building genuflecting to the blue-green glass of the transplant wing. On the far side of the hospital's parking lot, a single fisherman cast over the railing into the glossy black river, a bucket of bait at his feet. Beyond Cabrera, they cut across a large hillocky field, an expanse of dirt and grass littered with colossal pieces of construction equipment. They took a gravel path hemmed in by low trees and emerged onto a narrow spit of dirt strewn with weeds, plastic trash, blocks of broken concrete. The spit rested low, only a few feet above the waterline, a rusted metal ladder descending into the murky water. They sat at the top of the ladder, their feet hanging out over the edge. The river flowed by, the incoming tide pushing up from New York Harbor to part around the island. Simon looked out over the water to his right, at the blank-faced towers of Tudor City. South, down the barrel of the river, the three bridges to Brooklyn hung like Christmas lights strung across the expanse. They sat together in the half dark, the glow of Manhattan on one side, Queens on the other.

Earlier in the evening, Simon had paged DaSilva to his cell phone. When the call came, he stepped into the stairwell and told Peter that Maria had returned with him to the Roosevelt Island apartment. DaSilva ordered Simon to keep her there, under his watch. He'd been even more curt with Simon than usual, as though every word were costing him money, as though he'd reached some rarified level of tension beyond the expression of speech. "How are things at Cabrera?" Simon had asked. "Difficult," DaSilva had said, and then he'd hung up.

"It's beautiful," Maria said quietly now.

"It'll be different soon though." Simon gestured behind them. "That field? With all the equipment on it? They're going to turn this whole end of the island into a manicured park. Level it off, plant some grass, a few clusters of trees. This spit here"—he kicked the rusted ladder—"it'll be long gone."

They fell silent, the only sounds the river lapping at the concrete under their feet and the distant hum of traffic on the FDR. The night was cold, and Maria hunched deeper into her sweatshirt, her face disappearing within the hood.

"I keep thinking about Lenny," she said. "Can you imagine how hopeless he'd have to feel to do something like that? How worthless?"

"I can *imagine*," Simon said, "but that's all I can do. I haven't been there, you know? I've been low, but not that low." And it was true: even in his darkest moments after Amelia's drowning, he'd never truly wanted to die. He could thank Michael for the idea that suffering was something to be endured, not avoided, a concept his father had taught by example.

"Yeah. I'd be lying if I said I've never thought about it. But probably everybody thinks about it at some point." She turned away from Simon, looking downriver toward the three twinkling bridges. "Big difference between thinking and doing."

"When did you think about it?" Simon said.

She turned back toward him. "You're asking what was my lowest moment?"

"I guess so."

She snorted out a laugh. "Take your pick. There's a whole fucking banquet of misery to choose from." She touched her stomach. "I'm sick of it. Sick of being miserable. Sick of being the victim. I'm done with that forever."

"You're not just talking about the surgeries. About getting ill."

"No."

"What happened to you, Maria?" He spoke softly, as though she wouldn't notice the seriousness of the question if he asked it gently enough.

She seemed to retreat even deeper within the hood, and he was afraid that he'd pushed too far, that she was going to shut him down again. Instead, she said, "What are you supposed to do when something bad happens to you? You're supposed to *process* it. *Understand* it. Right? You're supposed to work through your feelings, as if thinking about something terrible over and over and over again will make you feel any better about it. It's an idiotic idea. But I can tell you that avoiding the thing doesn't work either. You can't forget something just because you wish it hadn't happened." She paused. "You know all about that too, don't you? With Amelia."

"Yes."

"You keep reliving the night she drowned, right? You wonder if you'd done something differently that night, maybe she'd still be alive. And you know what? Maybe she would be. But that doesn't matter now. It's not your fault. You didn't *want* her to die. It was a tragedy, an accident. There's nobody to blame." *If you only knew,* he thought. "But what if there were?" she continued. "What if there was one person who caused your pain? One person who deliberately hurt you?"

"Who? Who are you talking about?"

She pulled back her hood and looked at him, her eyes searching his face for—what? He tried to show her what she needed to see, which in practice meant holding his face very still, as though he were having an X-ray taken.

"I don't know how to talk about this," she said.

"Can you try?"

She shook her head and looked away.

"Wait," he said, desperate not to lose her. "Please. You can trust me. I would never tell anybody." He gave her a rueful smile. "And even if I wanted to, you know I don't have anyone to tell."

She returned the smile. "That I believe."

"I want to understand you," he said. "Please let me try."

She stared at him, her eyes dark and shadowed. Weighing, judging. "If I tell you this," she finally said, "I'm going to start at the beginning. I want you to listen until I'm finished before you say anything. All right? Can you do that?"

"Yeah." He was suddenly nervous, as though he could somehow fail at the simple act of listening. "I can do that."

"All right." She closed her eyes, and when she opened them again she seemed nearly in a trance, speaking as though her words were already fully formed and she was simply reciting them, delivering something that had been crafted long before.

"I told you my mother died when I was thirteen," she said. "That's true. I also told you I don't know who my father is. That's also true. Of course, I asked my mother about him, and she said she could give me a name if that's what I really wanted. But she didn't know where he was and she wouldn't help me find him. She said I'd be better off never knowing him, and even though she was maybe not the most reliable narrator of her own life, I believed her about this. So for thirteen years it was just the two of us. I don't remember how old I was when I realized she was an addict. I guess I realized it before I knew the word 'addict,' before I understood why she passed out on the couch at eight o'clock every night—you could set your watch to it—or why it always seemed like she was talking to me from deep inside a plastic bubble. It was pills, pain-killers. Before I was born, she preferred to get drunk, at least according to her. But I was a difficult birth, didn't want to come out, and they ended up performing a cesarean. She was in a lot of pain afterward, so they did what overworked doctors do—they gave her a prescription, and she basically kept refilling that prescription for the next thirteen years.

"She definitely *was* an addict, but I still don't like using that word to talk about her. Not because I'm ashamed, but because I've seen addiction a lot since then and I know what it can look like. Or at least I know what most people picture when I say that word. They picture squalor. Filth. Some shitty house with a bunch of junkies sitting around on duct-taped couches, shooting up at noon on a Tuesday. And, yeah, I've seen it like that—it just wasn't like that with us. She kept her job right to the end. Our house was small and rented, and the neighborhood wasn't great, but inside it was clean. It was a home. She might have passed out every night at eight, but she was up and going by six the next morning. Getting me ready for school, getting herself to work. Things changed some in the last two years, when she switched out her Vicodin for oxy, or really in the last few months, when she started crushing the oxy. Here's a rule: if you're snorting or injecting something, it's going to catch up with you soon enough. Something I learned when I was a kid but forgot about for a few years there."

Maria paused. Simon pictured the pile of red powder on Katherine Peel's coffee table, and he felt an echo of the slow sweetness of that drug, whatever it had been, spreading through his veins. It would be easy, he knew, to want that sweetness every day, to depend upon it until it didn't matter if you wanted it anymore or not.

"My mother OD'd on a Monday," Maria said. "She was off work for some reason, and I guess she was celebrating. I spent a week at a youth shelter, and by the next Monday they'd placed me in a foster home. I was officially a ward of the state. They couldn't find my father. Maybe he's dead too, who knows. My grandparents didn't want to take care of me, and I don't blame them. They lived in East Texas—still do, I think—and they were both sick and barely getting by already without a teenager to deal with. There was nobody else. So I went into the system.

"The first family didn't work out. Neither did the second or the third. When I was sixteen, I was taken in by the Dreesons. They'd never had a foster kid before, and God knows why they took me on, a sixteen-year-old punk. Maybe Mrs. Dreeson was bored and wanted a girl around, somebody to talk with about, you know, womanly things or whatever. If that was it, I'm sure she was sorely disappointed. Anyway, they weren't so bad, the parents, just regular middle-class Southern California people trying to get through life without the whole thing collapsing on their heads. And I liked San Gabriel fine. It felt like a real neighborhood. People knowing each other's business, but in a good way. I even got along all right in the high school there."

She stopped again. Simon nodded in what he hoped was an encouraging way. She chewed her lip for a moment, and when she resumed speaking her voice was flattened out even further, emptied entirely of inflection and emotion. She would be a conduit for her story now—a neutral medium—and nothing more.

The problem, she continued, was the Dreesons' biological son, Thomas. He was a year older than Maria, a gangly kid obsessed with his dirt bike, which was perpetually half-dismantled in the family garage. At first, he seemed excited to have Maria around. And why not? He was a bored seventeen-year-old kid—bored with his parents, his neighborhood, his school, his life—a high school senior treading water until he could get the hell away from home. And here, suddenly, was a girl with dyed purple hair, a pierced nose, and a safety-pinned Circle Jerks hoodie, sleeping in the spare bedroom down the hall. Here, suddenly, was a badass younger sister—or at least that was the role into which he first cast her.

She'd lived in San Gabriel for two months when he showed her where his parents kept their petty cash. He waved her into the master bedroom, a shadowy, musky space she'd been told was off-limits. This was during the drowsy late-afternoon hours between the end of school and the Dreesons' return home from work. Thomas hadn't bothered to turn on the lights, and he stood, stoop shouldered, in the murk, his hand resting on his parents' dresser.

"Listen, M.," he said, "you keep lifting cigs from Chet's place and he's gonna bust you."

"I'm not stealing—"

"Save it. First off, I've seen you doing it. Second, Chet already knows. I had to tell him to chill and let me talk to you before he called the cops."

Was it true? Maria thought she'd been smooth at the newsstand, palming the packs while Chet—she hadn't known his name until then, the stringy white guy with the ponytail and tobacco-stained fingers—bent to the register to make change for some deliberately convoluted transaction, like a handful of pennies and nickels for a candy bar. The open-air newsstand was the only place she could pull it off, since the cigarettes were right out there with the magazines instead of barricaded behind the counter like in every other store. If the guy—Chet—had seen what she was doing, wouldn't he have stopped her on the spot? Why would he wait to talk it over with Thomas? Or maybe Chet hadn't seen anything, and Thomas had told him about it himself. But, then, how did Thomas know what she'd been up to?

"They don't give you any spending money, do they?" Thomas shook his head at such gross injustice. "Never gave me shit either." She didn't think this was true—she'd seen all the gadgets in his room, the PlayStation, the TV, the stereo—but she didn't say anything. "Anyway, I thought I'd let you in on a little secret, being that you're my new sister and all." He opened the bottom drawer of the dresser and beckoned her over. In the drawer was a simple metal cash box with a three-digit combination. "Combo's one, two, three," he said. "No joke." He opened the box. Inside was a jumble of bills, mostly fives and ones. "Rainy day cash," he said. "Car wash, carton of milk, et cetera. You know how they have that old-person thing about using a credit card for a small purchase? Anyway, they have no idea how much is in here. You take ten bucks for a couple packs of smokes every week, they'll never know."

She stared at him. "Thomas, I'm not going to steal from your parents. They've taken me in, and—"

"Gimme a break. They're not fucking saints, trust me. And this money's not going to make any difference to them."

"I don't know."

"Oh, so now you're above stealing anything, and I'm the asshole? Who was ripping off the newsstand in the first place?"

She looked down into the cash box. "But even if I take this . . . I'm too young. He won't sell to me."

Thomas grinned. "This is the good part." He told her that he'd cut a deal with Chet: if Maria paid him back double for the two packs she'd already stolen—*four*, she said silently, *but okay*—he'd sell cigarettes to her for now on, with an extra fee of two bucks per pack tacked on, no ID required. And, unbelievably, it worked: Chet accepted her mumbled apology, took her money, and gave her the American Spirits she asked for. What she hadn't told Thomas was that the cigarettes weren't really for her. She didn't care about smoking one way or another, but the school's punks, in their Rancid and Bad Religion T-shirts, did, clustering in a corner of the school lot to suck a few butts during lunch. She'd figured this was her way of getting in with them: not by smoking herself, but by being the provider of what was—for a bunch of kids—a precious commodity, almost a currency, she thought, like in prison. Basically, she was a newbie freak with dead parents who needed some friends, and the cigarettes were how she was going to get them. Thomas had been right about his parents too: they didn't notice the missing cash, or at least they didn't say anything about it to her. And after a few weeks of stealing from the box, she forgot to feel guilty about it anymore. But what about Thomas? What was in it for him? At the time, Maria left the question unexamined, but even then she understood, uneasily, that he'd both made her into his accomplice and placed her in his debt.

The change in Thomas's behavior toward her was at first subtle. The way his eyes lingered on her ass for a breath too long, the way he seemed—deliberately, she wasn't sure—to get in her way in the kitchen, contriving superfluous little jolts of physical contact. He was suddenly obsessed with whether she'd found a boyfriend, what she thought about the pickings at San Gabriel High. He himself, he took pains to inform her, had a girlfriend at the beginning of the school year but had dumped her—it was now April—for being "too clingy." As a senior, he believed it was his right to "sample the wares." She'd wrinkled her nose at the phrase, and he'd assured her, with an unnecessary squeeze of her shoulder, that he was just joking around and that she should try to loosen up.

In the beginning of May, he tried to kiss her. He'd lured her out to the garage with an unlikely story about finding a stray kitten curled up in the wheel well of his mother's Accord. She followed him out there, already pretty sure he was full of shit. His dirt bike was propped up on a lift, its engine in a dozen pieces. He led her over to the Accord and squatted down by one of the back wheels. "Come on," he said, "help me look." Maria kneeled down next to him and peered halfheartedly under the car. "It was here," he said, "just a few minutes ago." He took a small flashlight out of his pocket and made a show of pointing the light around the car's undercarriage. "Ah well." He snapped the light off. "Guess it got spooked."

He turned to her then, their faces only a few inches apart, the two of them crouched behind the Accord and hidden from the doorway that led into the house. He smelled like cinnamon gum and motor oil. *Oh shit*, she thought, and then it happened before she could stop it: Thomas pressing his face against hers—because that's what it felt like, him pressing his whole greasy, pimply, hormonal face into hers, the lips basically incidental—and his hand latching on to the side of her neck like it was a pole in a subway car. She pulled back and slapped his hand away. "Thomas, what the *fuck*?"

He gave her a slack-jawed look that suggested he was genuinely surprised by this reaction. "Hey, M.," he said, "chill out. We're just having fun."

"Speak for yourself," she said, and moved to get up off the floor.

He grabbed her wrist and yanked her back down. "M., listen—"

"Get the fuck off me." She tried to free her wrist, but he held tight.

"Hey, think about it." His eyes were bright, evangelizing. "We mess around a little, whenever we feel like it. Nobody has to know. It's perfect."

"Thomas, let go of my wrist."

"Maria—"

"Let go, or I'll tell your parents about this."

His eyes went dead. His face turned hard and mean, and Maria thought she was looking through a window into the man he would become ten or twenty years from then—pissed off and aggrieved after he'd been told, yet again, that he couldn't have every last thing he believed himself entitled to. He let go of her wrist. "You say a word to my parents, and I'll tell them about the money. Think they want some klepto gutter-punk bitch sleeping in their house?"

Maria's face went red with anger. "You wouldn't."

"What're you, sixteen? Nobody wants teenagers anyway, and definitely not a klepto. Too much trouble. Everybody'd rather adopt some cute little kid. How'd you like the shelter? Wanna go back?" Maria said nothing, just stared at him in fury. "Didn't think so," he said dismissively. He got up, walked over to his dirt bike, and started wiping down a piston, turning his back to her as though she weren't even there.

She said nothing about this episode to the Dreesons, nor to the distracted child-services rep on his pro forma visits to their household. Maria figured she only had to endure Thomas for another few months—he'd graduate in June, leave for college in August—and then she could finish high school here in San Gabriel. She would turn eighteen a week after she graduated the following spring, and after that she'd be free to—well, she didn't know what she was going to do. Get a job, she supposed. Whatever she did, though, it would be *hers*. She'd be free of the system. Nobody could tell her what to do.

After Thomas left for UC Santa Cruz, she didn't see him again until Christmas break. His few months away had emboldened and hardened him somehow. What had been run-of-the-mill teenage disrespect—for his parents, for Maria, for sluts and jocks and fags and whoever else was pissing him off at any given moment—had refined itself into a purer form of contempt. Maria sensed it as soon as he walked through the door, eyes shaded by his flat-brim Monster cap: directionless hostility. He was itching for a fight.

She did her best to avoid him. The first week, when she was still busy at school, was easy enough. Christmas fell on Wednesday of the following week. Both of his parents went to work on Monday, leaving Maria and Thomas alone in the house together. Maria left in the morning, but without a car she could only go so far, riding her bicycle around the Valley, hemmed in by freeways and mountains. She returned home in the late afternoon, exhausted. She wheeled her bicycle into the garage, her stomach sinking when she saw Thomas's dirt bike. She could hear them through the garage door: three or four of them, yelling and cursing over the PlayStation's machine-gun chatter. She hesitated at the door. She had a strong impulse to turn around and get back on her bike and ride away—it didn't matter where. But this was her home. Screw him and his dumb friends: this was where she *lived*. She opened the door and stepped inside the house.

She moved through the living room as quickly as she could, her eyes fixed on the carpet. She smelled the funk of beer and liquor and In-N-Out burgers. Ten steps to the stairs. Nine, eight—"Yo, sis!" Thomas's voice, booming, slurred. She didn't stop. Her foot on the first step, she risked a glance out of the corner of her eye: three of them on the couch, Thomas in the middle. On the coffee table, a half-empty handle of Jack Daniel's presiding over a congregation of Tecate cans. "Come hang with us for a while, little sis," Thomas said, smirking. Maria shook her head and kept walking—*slowly*, she told herself, *don't rush*—up the stairs. "What the fuck's her problem," said one of the friends, laughing, and then she was inside her bedroom, shutting the door behind her.

She lay down on her bed and put on her headphones. She turned up the volume and closed her eyes, and then she was floating inside the music, free of Thomas, free of the Dreesons, free of San Gabriel. Some time passed—four songs, maybe five—then, in the silence between tracks, she heard the knocking. She took off her headphones. "What?"

"Yoo-hoo." Thomas. "Can we come in?"

"Fuck off."

Laughter from outside the door. "Yeah," Thomas said, "not gonna do that."

The knob rattled—there was no lock; why was there no lock?—and then they were inside her room, Thomas and his two idiot friends, all stinking drunk. Thomas swayed slightly as he pointed at her. "You," he said, pausing as though about to deliver the capstone to a historic speech, "are a girl who needs to learn how to have fun."

"Get out of my room," Maria said.

"But it's not your room," Thomas said. "Remember? None of this"—he swept his arm in a wide arc—"is yours. You're a free-loader, Maria. A leech."

His two friends laughed. They were a blur to Maria, pasty-white faces floating above baggy athletic clothes. They crowded her room, shrinking the space around her.

"Yo, Tom," one of the faces said, "what's a leech do?"

"I don't know," Thomas said. "Why don't we ask Maria?"

Maria got up from the bed. "I'm leaving." They blocked her way to the door. She shoved one of the friends, and Thomas grabbed her arm and threw her back onto the bed. "Show some respect," he said.

She sat on the bed and stared at him. A dangerous charge pulsed through the room. In retrospect, she recognized this moment as the junction between Thomas choosing to be one kind of person or another—and between him choosing one kind of life or another *for her.*

"I think," he said slowly, "Maria needs to learn how to show a little gratitude."

The two friends moved to either side of the bed. Thomas stood at the foot, staring down on her with a blank, glassy look. For a second, nobody moved, and then Maria sprung up and at Thomas, catching him in the side of the head with her open palm. With a surprised grunt, he flung her back down onto the bed. She twisted as she fell, smashing her mouth into the headboard. She felt one of her teeth flare with pain—this was the origin of her gray and crooked incisor—and tasted the blood filling her mouth. "Hold her," Thomas said, and the two friends obeyed, pinning her shoulders to the mattress. Thomas pulled away her jeans and underwear, and then he stopped, his hands gripping her thighs. "Ah, shit," he said, and for a moment she thought he might have realized what he was doing, might have realized the damage he was about to cause. Then he told his friends to leave the room. They let go of her shoulders, but still she couldn't move, paralyzed by both fear and the staggering incomprehensibility of the scene, and then the door closed and Thomas's hand gripped her neck while the other yanked at his belt, and suddenly he was on top of her, pushing himself inside, and she went dead, limp as though her bones had dissolved into her blood. She stared into his face as he strained above her; she wanted him to acknowledge her. He didn't look her in the eyes once, not until after he was finished. When he finally did, he appeared startled, as though he'd woken in an unfamiliar place and didn't know how he'd gotten there. He buttoned up his jeans. "At least I wasn't your first," he said. "I would've felt pretty bad about that."

Maria stopped here, abruptly, as though she'd reached the last page of an incomplete script, its final scenes gone missing.

"Maria," Simon said. She ran the tip of her tongue back and forth against her damaged tooth. He tried to hold her gaze. He wanted her to know that he was trying to understand how shattering it must have been for her, to communicate how desperately he wished it had never happened, and he knew he'd fail with words alone. She turned away and stared stubbornly down the river. "Jesus. I'm so, so sorry."

She snorted, as though trying to undercut the horror of what she'd told him. "Don't say that until I tell you what happened to *him*."

"You didn't say anything to his parents?"

"I didn't think they'd believe me. He's their son. They'd known me for, what, a year? And I tell them some crazy fucking story about a *rape*? No."

"But . . ." Simon remained stubbornly fixated on the aftermath's details and logistics, as though he knew there was nothing he could say or ask that could touch the burning-hot, terrible core of the story, of the act itself. "What about the social worker? Or the police?"

"You're looking at things from the outside, logically, like it was a problem I could solve if I just did things the right way. It didn't feel like that from the inside. I couldn't think like that, not then." She pulled up her hood again, retreating. "I remember the main thing was this absolute terror that I would get pregnant. When that didn't happen, I felt better. At least temporarily."

"You never told anybody?"

"Not for years and years. I was so angry sometimes, I could barely see. But I was too young and fucked up then, and I turned a lot of that rage onto myself. And shame too. I couldn't believe I'd let this happen to me—that was how I thought about the thing. I didn't *let* anything happen, obviously. But it took some time before I could see that." She stood up abruptly. "So *that*, Simon, was my lowest moment. Now you know." She turned away from the river. "I'm cold. Let's get back."

"What happened to him? Thomas."

She shook her head. "That's a story for another night. Please, can we go now?"

BACK inside the apartment, Simon saw that it was later than he'd thought, nearly midnight. He brought pillows and a blanket out from his bedroom and started arranging them on the couch.

"I'll sleep out here," he said. "You take the bed."

"You don't have to do that."

"It's fine. I don't mind."

"Simon."

Her voice was sharp, and he looked up to see her standing rigid in the doorway to his bedroom, two high spots of color rising on her cheeks.

"What?" he said.

"I don't want your sympathy. That's not what this is about."

"Decency isn't the same thing as sympathy."

She stared at him for a breath, then relaxed and nodded. "All right." She lingered in the doorway. "I'll see you in the morning, then."

He nodded, unfolded the blanket. "Okay. Good night."

"Good night." She paused for a moment, as though about to

say something more, then slipped into the bedroom and shut the door.

Simon lay down on the couch. There had been something awkward about this exchange that made him suddenly and acutely aware that he was sharing an apartment with Maria and should, perhaps, feel self-conscious or strange about this, especially after she'd made herself vulnerable to him by telling her story. But he searched inside himself and found that he didn't. What he felt about her—a complex cocktail of protectiveness, respect, and fascination—was unrelated to anything erotic. He recognized that she was, objectively, attractive, and he even had to admit that he was attracted to her, but only in the literal sense of the word: he was drawn to her, he wanted to be near her. This attraction was not sexual. It was grounded, instead, in an impulse to protect her, to save her, an impulse undiminished despite the unwanted realization that soon enough she wasn't going to need his help anymore.

He was thankful for this absence of desire, because for him sex had recently become—there was no other way to say it—a fucking disaster. He thought of the last girl he'd slept with, an old hook-up from college he'd run into at an East Village bar a few weeks after he'd started working for DaSilva. He'd been drinking alone, and the girl, Sylvia, had spotted him at his back-corner table, zoning out over his third whiskey. She sat down opposite him, red cheeked, bubbling with drunken good cheer. When she asked what he was doing with himself, he told her he was in medical school, and it didn't even feel like a lie. Two whiskeys later, her friends left—they'd been drinking over at the bar, eyeing Simon with, he'd thought, rather ill-concealed suspicion—but Sylvia had waved them off and stayed, and he'd suddenly realized that she was flirting with him with real intention and not out of boredom or nostalgia. He straightened up in his chair and tried to rise to the occasion, and he must have done well enough—they'd had their genuinely lovely moments back in college, after all—because he ended up back at her apartment on Ludlow Street, a damp brick-walled three bedroom, with two roommates, two cats, and no real kitchen. Her bedroom was in keeping with those of most other twentysomething girls he'd encountered: a high, small, wobbly bed overrun with an armada of pillows; clothes and shoes erupting out of every enclosed space; no curtains on the windows and nothing to block out the cacophony of the street two stories below.

Once they'd managed to struggle out of their clothes, Sylvia produced a condom from a drawer in the nightstand, pausing for a moment before tearing the packaging open, searching Simon's face for any sign that he wanted to stop things here. He gave none, and so she shook the condom once, briskly, before unrolling it onto his cock. She pushed him up against the mound of pillows before she climbed on top and almost dismissively inserted him into her. They fucked without speaking, their bodies settling into a pattern they'd established at college years before, muscle memory persevering over drunkenness. He felt slightly incidental to the whole thing, which didn't bother him too much. Quickly and without warning, she clenched as one unified muscle, and then the tension released and her body went slack, her head slumping forward, her hair falling into his face.

After a moment, she looked down at him, two high spots of color rising on her cheeks. "Come on," she said, more playful than angry. "Are you even here?"

He pushed her off him, dutifully, flipping her over onto her stomach. She rose onto her knees and elbows, and he took what she offered, driving himself into her. Her face was pressed into a pillow, and all he could see of her head was the tangle of her blond hair spread across the white pillowcase. The knobs of her vertebrae pushed against her skin as she arched her hips up, and he thought, unwillingly, of the plastic model of a spine that had hung from a hook in a classroom at medical school, of the concave bowl of the sacrum, the coccyx's truncated tail. He looked down at her body stretched out in front of him, fused with his own, and it was as though he could see through the skin and fat and muscle down to the basic structures of tendon and bone, as though he were seeking, with his thrusting, to touch these structures.

She cried out, her voice muffled by the pillow, and he pressed her down flat against the mattress. An image came to him, of her back with its skin slit open and peeled and pinned like his cadaver's in the anatomy lab, the muscles striated, the fascia yellow and clotted. He tried to fight the image off by closing his eyes. But then he saw, in the black behind his lids, the rib cage of the girl they'd dismantled, the ribs curving away from the sternum like a pair of wings, smaller and more delicate than he'd ever imagined. He opened his eyes and saw that Sylvia had twisted her head to see him—she was smiling, she was fine—and he came then, out of nowhere, while looking at her face, a hard, mean orgasm.

He rolled himself off her and lay panting on his back. The exact moment of disentanglement was for him unbearably sad. The sensation of immense loss lasted only a few seconds, but it was real; he'd felt it every time he'd had sex, with Sylvia or anybody else. It was instinctual, a product of the reptile brain: the withdrawal of warmth. His penis lay toppled on its side, the condom crumpled around the tip. He stood up and walked to her tiny bathroom. He closed the door behind him, threw the condom into the trash and washed himself off. In the mirror above the sink, his pale face was splotchy, his colorless hair mashed to his skull; he appeared stunned, as though he'd been assaulted. The usual sadness of decoupling was shadowed for him now by shame. He'd been able to keep images of the girl from the lab out of his mind for over a month, and he was ashamed that they'd come rushing back to him here, now, during sex. He was embarrassed by himself and his undisciplined mind. He hadn't slept with anybody since that night. He was too afraid of losing control over his thoughts, too afraid of what bizarre and rotten spectacles his mind would conjure up, its compartments cracking open, the barriers between things that he worked so hard to maintain melting away as quickly as sugar held to a flame.

## Eleven

THE next morning the sky was the color of lead, the river black and glossy as crude oil. Simon got up from the couch and opened the *Times* website on his laptop, and there was the article, posted as the sports section's lead story: "Ex-NFL Player's Suicide Linked to Concussions." Don MacLeod was paraphrased as saying that Leonard Pellegrini had been "frequently in attendance" at his support group for former players suffering "cognitive and emotional difficulties." The article noted that Pellegrini had also suffered from acute liver disease "exacerbated" by alcohol and prescription drug abuse, and that a liver transplant at Cabrera Medical Center on Roosevelt Island, less than a month before, had brought "new hope" to his wife, Cheryl Pellegrini. Cheryl was quoted as saying—somewhat stiffly, Simon thought— that "we believed if we were able to solve Lenny's liver disease, which had grown debilitating and life threatening, it would have a positive, healing effect on the way he experienced life." The article concluded by saying that Cheryl had decided to donate Lenny's brain to a group of medical researchers in Boston, the same group that had examined DeMarcus Rogers's battered tissue. Accompanying the article was a photograph of Lenny from his playing days, standing on the sidelines with his hands on his hips. He looked young, strong, ready to do damage. The picture was from only ten years ago.

Looking at the photo, Simon remembered what Crewes had explained to him about offensive linemen's freakish skill set: they had to be extremely large, six foot five or six and over three hundred pounds, but also capable of rapid bursts of movement in any direction (including backward), their footwork agile, practically balletic, their hands a karate blur as they warded off pass rushers. They were the grunts of the team, the trench diggers, complimented as a unit and singled out mostly for their mistakes, for missing a block or committing a penalty. And they were also, Crewes told him, some of the players who suffered most after a retirement usually forced by injury. It's a difficult thing to be in excellent physical shape and at the same time essentially obese; it requires masochistic amounts of training and conditioning offset with equally masochistic feats of food intake. Remove the training and what's left is an obese person with the hips, knees, and back of a septuagenarian.

Simon knew from Lenny's medical files that he'd had two replacements of his left knee and one of his right, plus a pair of surgeries to repair bulging disks in his back. One of these operations had occurred while he was still playing, another within three years of his retirement, its costs still covered by the league. The rest, though, he'd had to pay for himself, with no insurance company willing to assume the future costs of such a battered consumer. The painkillers could have been first prescribed for any of these surgeries, or perhaps before, to manage the lesser pain of a broken finger or bruised rib. And this was only the toll on his body. The damage to his mind had surely been subtler, more insidious. Most likely there hadn't been one or two big hits Lenny could point to and say that's where it all started; most likely it was the accumulation, over a decade and a half, of the routine catastrophes of each snap, stretching back to whenever teenaged Lenny had discovered the power and joy in being both the unstoppable force and the immovable object.

Maria emerged from the bedroom and joined Simon at the

kitchen table. She'd piled her hair into a dark, unruly knot on the top of her head and wore a baggy wool sweater, moth holes dotting its hem. She looked as though she'd barely slept, and he feared that telling her story had weighed on her mind during the night, that she regretted opening herself up to him like that. But what could he say about it that would put her at ease, that wouldn't come off as condescending or pitying?

He brought her a cup of coffee and pointed at the laptop. "The story's out there now."

She chewed her lip as she read the piece. "No Crewes."

"No. Hopefully people will be more concerned with Lenny's brain than his liver." He paused. "Did that sound cruel?"

"Not to me. But I'm biased."

He went into the bedroom and pulled on a sweater and his winter jacket. He'd decided he couldn't wait any longer: he needed to speak to Cheryl Pellegrini. Calling seemed insufficient, a cop-out. He wanted to look her in the face and apologize for lying to her; he wanted to tell her what he'd really seen when he'd faced Lenny across her dinner table. He felt he owed her that much.

Simon didn't tell Maria where he was going. He knew she would think visiting Cheryl was a terrible idea, far too rash, and he didn't want to risk being talked out of it. Instead, he said he was going to the office to pick up some files DaSilva had left for him.

She just nodded and turned back to the laptop. "You know where to find me."

He ate breakfast in a diner near Penn Station, watching commuters pour out of the subway entrance on the corner. He thought about Maria's story and tried to imagine the rage and confusion she must have felt after what Thomas had done to her. He felt sick about what had happened, but he didn't know how to express himself to her in a way that she wouldn't find cheap or irrelevant. The rape had set her on a course that led her here, to Health Solutions, but he still couldn't understand exactly how it had happened; there was a five-year link missing between then and now. He thought of the collection of photographs on her laptop. How did they fit into this? He knew better than to press her though; the best he could do was listen if she chose to tell him anything more.

He finished his coffee, walked to Madison Square Garden, and headed underground. He boarded an LIRR train, and about twenty-five minutes out of the station, as the train pulled away from Jamaica, he realized he was an idiot: Would Cheryl really be sleeping in the bedroom in which her husband had committed suicide only a few days before? She'd have to be staying somewhere else, with the friend Crewes had mentioned, or maybe with her mother, on the North Fork. He tried to remember whether Crewes had said anything about where this friend's house was, but all he could recall was that it was supposedly nearby, a few blocks away from the Pellegrinis'. He could call Howard and ask, but he knew Crewes wouldn't tell him; he'd think Simon's visit was a terrible idea as well.

Simon had the Pellegrinis' home number, and he tried it now. It rang five times, then came a click and Cheryl's voice saying: "Hi. You've reached the Pellegrini household. If you'd like to leave a message for Cheryl, Lenny . . . ," and here a muffled mumbling, then a boy's voice announcing "Greg!" followed by a little girl saying, "Daniela," drawing it out into four distinct syllables—Dan-i-*ell*-a—and then Cheryl once more, saying, "please leave us your name and number after the beep."

Simon hung up. He pictured Cheryl on the phone, Gregory and Daniela clustered around her, the children pulling at their mother's elbow, anxious for their turn at the receiver. He imagined Cheryl's determination—cobbling together just enough fragile, self-deluding optimism—to record something suitably cheerful for this new beginning to their life as a family, and it broke his heart.

He got off the train and into a taxi waiting at the stand. He gave the driver an address a few numbers removed from the Pellegrinis. The cab crossed over Sunrise Highway, then continued past the high school football field, the grass chewed up, midfield a patch of bare dirt. This was probably where Lenny had played his high school ball, probably where somebody first told him he might make a living out of displacing other large men from their assigned spot of turf. A few minutes later, the cab pulled up outside a white Cape Cod.

"Here?" the driver said.

"Here is good."

Simon got out and stood on the sidewalk, trying to get his bearings. He walked first one way, saw the numbers moving in the wrong direction, then turned around. He again passed the Cape Cod, then a dilapidated house with a sagging porch and rusted wind chime, then a green-painted clapboard home with a For Sale sign driven into its front yard. The plots were close together, only a scraggly line of bushes or a few bare-limbed trees separating one from the next. He quickly found the Pellegrinis' place, with its peeling yellowish paint, its tire-track-rutted lawn. He stood looking up at it, hands in his coat pockets. The block, not surprisingly for eleven thirty on a Monday morning, was deserted. Nobody on the sidewalks; no cars passing on the street. The house's windows were dark, and its driveway empty. He looked around. Nobody seemed to be watching, so he walked across the spongy lawn to the porch, climbed the stairs, and paused in front of the door. He listened, heard nothing but the sound of distant traffic. He opened the screen door and tried the knob. It was locked, of course. He stepped back onto the sidewalk and looked up at the second-floor room that Lenny had retreated to during Simon's last visit, the room he had to assume was the master bedroom. The shades were drawn, just as they were behind all the windows of the ground floor.

What was he supposed to do now? It was unlikely that Cheryl would have decamped all the way to the North Fork, over an hour drive away. There were surely arrangements to be made for the funeral, or wake, or whatever they were going to have, and it would be disruptive for the children. There was a good chance that wherever she'd first thought to go was where she'd stayed, and so he set off on foot to find this friend's house that Crewes had described. He hoped to be able to recognize it by the presence of her car outside, the maroon Honda. He lit a cigarette and came to a commercial street dotted with a Dunkin' Donuts, a Subway, a few local businesses. He turned left, randomly, onto this street and then made a few more equally arbitrary turns. The houses ran out onto a weedy field, and he stopped and realized he was completely lost. He turned back into the residential neighborhood, and then, halfway down the block, he saw it, the maroon car. It was parked on the sloped driveway of a tidy two-story clapboard house painted pale blue with white trim, blocking in a Ford station wagon. The Honda was the same model, he was sure of that, and as he drew closer he saw the bumper stickers he remembered: a yellow Support Our Troops ribbon and one in which the word "coexist" was spelled out with an Islamic crescent, a peace sign, a Star of David, a yin-yang symbol, and a Christian cross. It was her car, no question.

He watched the house and saw a light in one of the ground-floor rooms, another upstairs; the shadow of movement crossed a downstairs window. The presence of the Ford suggested that some-body else was home, but he'd have to live with that. The longer he stood on the sidewalk, watching the house, the more he felt his resolve slipping away, so he tossed his cigarette aside, walked up the cement path to the porch, and rang the doorbell. A few moments later, the door was opened the slightest bit, a single eye and sliver of cheek filling the crack.

"Can I help you?" A woman's voice, Long Island accent, not particularly friendly.

"Sorry to bother you," he said. "Is Cheryl Pellegrini staying here?" He winced internally as the words left his mouth. Why did he use her last name? It made him sound like some kind of official or, worse, reporter.

"No." She started to close the door.

"Wait. Please." He put his hand inside the frame. "I need to speak with her. Please."

The door opened slightly wider. The woman eyed his hand; he removed it. She was about Cheryl's age, in her late thirties or early forties, short and trim, a flat, wide nose dominating her oval face. "I said she wasn't here."

"But that's her car outside," Simon said.

The woman glanced over Simon's shoulder, then brought her eyes back to his face, her expression curdling. "You're going to have to leave. I'm sorry."

"Can you please just tell her I'm here? If she doesn't want to talk to me, I'll leave. Okay?"

He saw a flicker of motion in the hallway, the woman turning her head slightly. Then the little girl, Daniela, rounded a corner and, as though drawn by a magnet, latched onto the woman's hip. "Dani," she said, "go back inside, okay?"

The girl looked at Simon standing on the doorstep. "Hey," she said shyly, half-hiding behind the woman's leg. "You were at my house."

"That's right," he said. "I met you and Gregory."

The woman gave Simon a sharp look, then turned to Daniela. "Sweetie, go back upstairs. I'll be up in a minute." The little girl shrugged, then wandered away, humming some half-familiar melody under her breath. The woman turned back to Simon. "What's your name?"

"Simon Worth."

"All right. I'll tell her. But I swear to God if you upset her, I will kick you off my property and call the police if you ever come back."

He nodded. "Thank you."

"Just wait here," she said, and closed the door in his face.

He stepped back and tried to compose himself, to look sober and empathetic and penitent. He could smell cigarettes on his clothes, taste their ashy staleness in his mouth. Abruptly, before he was ready, Cheryl opened the door. Her face was thinner than he remembered, skin stretched tight over cheekbones like canvas over a frame.

"Wow," she said. "You're somebody I never thought I would see again."

"Cheryl."

"What are you doing here?"

"Can we talk?"

"We are talking."

"Inside, maybe?"

"How about out here." She stepped out and closed the door behind her, sitting down at the top of the porch stairs. He sat next to her, unsure of how exactly to begin. The temperature was tumbling toward freezing; no sun, a chilly wind. Cheryl wore only a long-sleeved thermal shirt and jeans, but she didn't seem bothered by the cold. She sat perfectly still, looking out at the street, hands resting on her thighs. "Well?" she said.

"I wanted to say I'm very sorry about Lenny. Howard called to tell me."

She nodded, still looking straight ahead. "Did he tell you where I was?"

He hesitated. "Not really."

She glanced at him.

"All he said was that you were staying at a friend's. I found you myself. He doesn't know I'm here." She nodded again, and he tried once more. "I wanted to tell you how sad I was to hear what happened. I know how difficult—"

"I'm not going to say anything, all right?" Her voice was bitter. "Your outfit or company or whatever is not something I'm going to talk about. What would be the point? It wasn't your fault. Not the hospital's either. You didn't need to come out here for that."

"That's not why I came."

"No? What, then? You want an invitation to the funeral? It's Sunday. Bring a flask. It's what Lenny would've wanted."

"Cheryl, I saw it too."

"Saw what?"

"What you asked me, at the train station. It wasn't just you. I saw it. He wasn't . . . He was just showing us what he knew we wanted to see." He spoke quickly now, trying to get it all out. "But it wasn't what he was really feeling. You were right, and I saw it, and I said I didn't because I didn't want to believe it. I didn't want to get involved. So I lied."

"You know what?" She leaned forward, hunching into herself. "I don't need you to tell me I was right. I knew that when Dani came running down the stairs, asking why Daddy was sleeping in a puddle of throw up."

Simon swallowed. This was not unfolding as he'd imagined it. "I wanted to say I'm sorry. Sorry for making you think—"

"So this is for you, then?"

"What?"

She turned to face him, her eyes chips of blue ice. "How is this supposed to make me feel better about anything? You didn't owe me the truth back then, you weren't getting paid to be honest. You were free to turn away just like you did. But you heard Lenny killed himself and now you feel guilty. You think maybe if you'd said something, things might have been different. I might have— what?—demanded that Lenny see a psychiatrist again. Might have been more *vigilant*. I might not have left him in the house alone for a weekend. Is that it?"

"No, I—"

"You want to apologize, so you can say at least you're being honest now. Well, to be honest with *you*, I don't think things would've been any different if you'd said something. I doubt it would've been worth anything. Maybe, but probably not. What I am sure of is that you coming here and telling me this shit now is worth less than nothing." She stood up. "You should leave."

"Cheryl, I'm sorry. That's not how I meant it."

"Everybody's sorry. Howard drove up here from Jersey when

Lenny's body wasn't even cold to tell me how fucking sorry he was. Sorry that he didn't see it either—Lenny faking his happiness. I could tell Howard was more pissed off than sorry though. Because he'd tricked himself, he really believed in it. I wanted to believe in it too. I just never quite did. Now go."

Simon stood up. "I shouldn't have come."

"No, you shouldn't have. Especially since I already knew that you'd lied to me. I wasn't angry then—mostly I was just disappointed—because I understood why you did it. But I also understand why you're doing this now, and I *am* angry. Good-bye, Simon. Please don't come here again."

She turned her back on him then and went inside the house.

Simon pressed his forehead to the train window. Bare trees blurred into a brown strip above which the sky hung heavily, thick, bulbous gray clouds laced with black veins. It was only the first week of November, but the prediction was for snow, the earliest in the season Simon could ever remember. He'd felt the temperature drop as he waited on the platform, the bottom falling out of the air. It had been stupid to come, stupid to think Cheryl would want to hear his apology. He'd realized she was right, of course: he'd come to talk to her, not for her sake, but for his own. Even though his apology had been genuine, it was also pointless, a shortcut to an absolution she'd justifiably refused to grant. If he took her at her word, he could at least steal some consolation from the fact that speaking the truth in the first place would have changed nothing. He couldn't imagine how horrible it must have been to live in the same house, to sleep in the same bed, with a husband you knew was pretending all the time, a man who wore a happy mask and voiced happy words when you knew he meant none of it, no matter how much you wanted him to. To suspect that something terrible might be coming, and not be able to do anything about it.

His train pulled into Penn Station at quarter to three, and he headed straight for the Health Solutions office. He wanted to page DaSilva, to find out what was happening at Cabrera; if it was bad news, he didn't want to have to talk about it in front of Maria. As he let himself into the lobby and rode the elevator up, he thought of her waiting alone in the Roosevelt Island apartment. How much longer was she going to tolerate hanging around? Wasn't it likely that as soon as she healed, she'd simply cut her losses and disappear, leave New York, take the cash and wash her hands of DaSilva and Health Solutions and the whole gnarled mess, him included? Yet if things really went sour—if Lenny's transplant came under more intense scrutiny, if the story didn't simply disappear as they all hoped it would—would DaSilva just let her leave like that? Wouldn't he come after her, wherever she went, to find her before somebody else did? Still, even if this was true, what could Simon do about it?

He unlocked the office door and stepped inside, and then he stopped, for a moment not quite understanding what he saw. The office had been stripped. The computer was gone; the shelves were empty, all the files missing. He squatted down behind the desk: the safe was gone as well. The room had been emptied of everything except its furniture and the ashtray overflowing, on the windowsill, with crushed butts. Even the phone had been removed.

Simon paged Peter to his cell phone and sat behind the desk, smoking, fighting off a wave of panic, his mind animating and then quickly discarding scenario after scenario. He waited and then paged DaSilva again, adding "9-1-1" to the end of his number. Still nothing. He felt another sick lurch of anxiety roll and pitch his body. *Fuck, fuck, fuck.* He considered calling DaSilva's cell phone directly, but then he quickly decided against it. Maybe it was better if he didn't know Simon had visited the office. DaSilva had stripped the place without telling him; perhaps this had simply been an oversight, but what if it was intentional? Why would DaSilva freeze him out now? He stubbed out his last butt and locked the office behind him. He needed to get back to Maria;

she deserved to know what he'd found, and anyway, he'd left her alone long enough.

Down on the street, he hurried past the subway entrance—he didn't want to miss a call while underground—and continued on to the tram station. Finally snow started to come down, the flakes weightless and fine as powdered sugar. He climbed the concrete stairs and stood waiting on the dock, watching the revolutions of the giant blue-painted gear that winched the tram. Either somebody had already started to piece the whole chain together—from Lenny to Crewes to Maria to Health Solutions—or DaSilva had cleared the office out of an abundance of caution, a kind of paranoiac spasm. But why hadn't he contacted Simon? The tram car slipped into its berth and disgorged its few passengers. Simon secured a spot against one of the Plexiglas windows facing north before the car pulled out of the station, gliding along its cable, over the ledge and into the air. It was barely four o'clock and the sun was already starting to set, its eerie, volcanic glow lighting scalloped black clouds from below. Snowflakes were pushed and pulled by the wind, a strong gust drawing a curtain of white across the car before just as swiftly tugging it away.

On the Roosevelt Island side, Simon exited the tram with about a dozen other passengers. The group dispersed, most heading north with Simon, past the diminutive Episcopalian church and on toward the apartment complexes that crowded the upper half of the island. The snow fell steadily now, January muscling into the beginning of November. Businesses were closing early for the night, the street emptying out according to the island's own suburban-minded clock. Once Simon passed the last of the commercial blocks, the foot traffic thinned even further. He continued alone past the tennis courts and baseball diamond, reaching the point where Main Street bent west toward the river, and he saw parked there, at the mouth of the walking path that led to his apartment building, a mud-spattered gray RAV4, its engine running and lights off. The car was familiar to Simon, but he hadn't yet placed it by the time the driver's door opened and a woman bundled in a heavy winter parka stepped out to meet him, raising her hand, her glossy black hair blowing across her face.

"Katherine?"

He hadn't spoken to Katherine Peel since a few weeks after starting with DaSilva. He'd had the sense that she didn't want to know too much about what he was doing for Health Solutions, that ever since she'd stopped helping Peter, she'd deliberately maintained a degree of ignorance about Simon and his activities and that this ignorance was, for her, a kind of protection. There was also the shameful matter of his behavior in the anatomy lab, as well as the clumsy, supremely inebriated pass he'd made in her apartment—not to mention the larger shame of simply dropping out of medical school—and so, with a mild, nagging sense of guilt, he'd let their friendship slip away. He felt happy to see her now, even though he suspected he wasn't going to like why she was here.

"Simon." She smiled at him. "It's nice to see you."

"Yeah, you too." He glanced up at his apartment building, the tower enveloped in blowing snow, and pictured Maria waiting inside the apartment. "So . . . what's going on?"

She laughed. "You mean, what the hell am I doing here?" She tugged on his elbow. "Come on, get in the car and I'll tell you. It's freezing out here. Crazy fucking weather."

He hesitated. "There's somebody upstairs waiting for me."

"Yeah, I know. She'll be fine."

He stared at her. "What do you mean, you know?"

She sighed. "Please, Simon. Just get in and we'll talk." She watched as he stood, paralyzed, gazing up at the apartment building. "I'm trying to help you," she said, her voice firmer now. "We don't have a lot of time. Please."

He turned away from the building and climbed into the car. Katherine had cranked the heat, and snow melted from his hair and eyebrows, icy runoff soaking his collar. She put the car into gear and rolled them slowly down Main Street, away from his apartment.

"Where are we going?"

She glanced over at him. "The Bronx."

He took out his cell phone and started to dial the number to his apartment's phone.

"No," Katherine said sharply. "Not yet."

"I need to tell Maria—"

"I said not yet. Put the phone away."

Simon jammed it back into his pocket. "Jesus, Katherine, what is this? What are we doing?"

"Saving your ass." She leaned forward, squinting into the swirling snow. "Peter called me. Cabrera's launched an internal investigation into Leonard Pellegrini's transplant. They're in full fucking crisis mode over there, and they want to talk to Maria. Peter's stalling them, but he probably can't for much longer, and now a guy from the *Post* is sniffing around the story, digging and asking questions and working the administrators into a frenzy. This investigation can't know that you exist, obviously. Peter's still stuck at Cabrera right now, or else he'd be doing this himself."

"Doing what?"

"I told you. Protecting you." She swung the RAV4 onto the tiny Roosevelt Island Bridge and then gunned it north onto Vernon Boulevard.

"Protecting me from what?"

"You need to get out of the city, Simon. It's not just the hospital. If a reporter presses Howard Crewes, or maybe Pellegrini's wife, what's her name—"

"Cheryl."

"Yeah. If they're pressed hard enough, they're going to crack. They'll name you, and then you're fucked."

Simon shook his head. "I don't think so. I saw her today, and—"

"*What?*" Katherine turned to stare at him. "You saw her? Where?"

"I went to find her on Long Island," he said. "I wanted to see how she was dealing with all this."

"Are you out of your fucking mind?" Katherine stomped on the accelerator, the car's tires chewing up the pasty, grimy snow. "You can't have anything to do with these people anymore. Come on, Simon, you must realize that."

He shook his head. He understood, of course, that it had been a mistake to visit Cheryl, but he didn't want to hear about it from Katherine. "She just wants this whole thing to go away. She's not going to say anything about me or about Maria getting any money."

"You don't know that. And you can't risk it."

"You mean DaSilva can't risk it."

Katherine cut him a look. "What are you trying to say?"

They merged onto 278, heading north across the Triborough Bridge. A caravan of snowplows—city garbage trucks outfitted with blades and chains—rolled, hazard lights flashing, in a slow, militaristic column down the middle lane.

"If this is really about me, about keeping me safe, then shouldn't I get a say?" He traced an X into the fogged-up passenger window. "I trust Cheryl and Crewes. I want to stay with Maria."

"I'm sorry, Simon, but you can't."

"So it is about DaSilva, then. I'm the connection, the only link between him and everybody else, and now he needs me to get out of the way." But even as he said it, Simon realized this wasn't true: Maria knew about DaSilva. Maria knew about DaSilva, and yet Peter and Katherine didn't know that she knew. There had to be an advantage for him in that gap.

"It's about both of you." Katherine stared straight ahead, through the windshield, jaw clenched.

"What about Maria?"

"She stays in Peter's apartment."

"So she's a prisoner?"

"What? Jesus, Simon. Calm down, okay? She's safest where she is now, in that apartment. If people at Cabrera want to speak with her, it'll be worse for everyone if she's gone missing."

"I need to talk to her, Katherine."

"Wait until you get where you're going."

"Yeah?" Anger welled up inside him, a bilious surge. "Well, where the fuck is that?"

"I don't know. I'm handing you off."

"Handing me off? To who?"

Katherine sighed again. She seemed suddenly exhausted, less sure of herself. "You understand by now how this kind of thing works. The less each person knows, the better. Break it up into pieces, right?"

"So you're just going to hand me over to some guy because Peter told you to?"

"Yeah, some guy who's going to take you somewhere safe, okay? Some guy who's going to hide you until Peter fixes all this. Some guy who's going to keep you from getting arrested. Get it?"

"Who is he?"

"I told you—I have no idea. Probably some meathead Peter grew up with who wants to earn a few bucks, who knows."

"I thought you were done with all this," he said. "I thought you didn't want to be involved anymore."

"I am and I don't. But this is an emergency and who else could Peter call?"

"Is he paying you?"

"Jesus Christ!" Katherine gripped the steering wheel as though she were about to rip it off.

"Well, is he?"

"It's a favor, Simon. That's it."

He crossed his arms and stared out the window. Cars crawled along the highway, struggling in the slush. "This is bullshit, Katherine."

She ignored him and frowned at the ribbons of red taillights stretching out in front of them. "We're gonna be late."

They sat in silence for a few minutes, Simon listening to the soft swooshing of snow under their tires.

"Listen," Katherine said, her voice softer now, "I know I got you into all this shit, and I know I have to take some responsibility for that. I liked you, Simon. I still like you. I saw that you were desperate, and I wanted to help. You were different from all the other kids, all these overachieving robots I'm gonna be stuck with for the next three years. They're smart, all of them, we know that, but it's just one kind of intelligence, right? Hypercompetitive book smarts. They're coming straight from college, these kids, and most of them have never experienced shit, nothing real anyway." She shook her head. "Whatever, I don't need to tell you this, you were there with me. But you weren't like them. There was something different about you. So when you . . . when you had to leave, I just wanted to help you. I didn't think anything like this was going to happen."

"You didn't make me do anything."

"Yeah, fine, it was your choice, but I brought the choice to you. Just don't think it's not weighing on me, okay? This is . . . It wasn't supposed to go like this. This last deal Peter put you on . . ." She shook her head again. "He's getting greedy. He pushed it."

She exited the highway and turned into a nondescript neighborhood of small vinyl-sided houses bound together by thick tangles of electrical and telecommunications wires. Simon had no idea where they were. The Bronx was a closed box to him, as far removed—physically, anyway—from the Rockaways as the borders of the five boroughs would allow. The blowing snow made it difficult to see much beyond the hunched, swaddled houses. Under the streetlamp's pools of orange-sodium light, the parked cars were quickly disappearing, obscured by layers of flakes that stuck like frosting to the cold metal.

"Where's this guy going to take me, Katherine?" he asked.

Katherine slowed down, peering up at the street signs. "You know Peter wouldn't tell me that. A safe house, that's all he said."

"Yeah, that's what I figured."

She executed a complicated series of turns, bringing them deeper into a warren of quiet residential streets.

"This near where you grew up?"

"Not too far." Katherine was distracted, focusing on the route. She made a last turn and then pulled up to one corner of a four-way stop. She turned off her lights and peered across the intersection. "This is it." She checked the clock. "We actually made up some time there."

"We're early?"

"Just a few minutes."

Simon patted his pockets, found his Parliaments. He waved the pack at Katherine and tilted his head questioningly toward the street. She wrinkled her nose and nodded. She hated cigarettes as only a former addict could, and he knew she'd let him smoke in her apartment that one night only out of pity for his disastrous state.

"Come out and talk with me," he said. "Who knows when I'll see you again, right?"

She nodded again, unfastening her seat belt and stepping out onto the sidewalk with him, leaving the car running. He walked around to the driver's side and stood next to her. His fingers were clumsy from the cold, but he managed to pry a cigarette from the pack and get it lit. He took a few drags in silence, looking around at the nearby houses. Nobody seemed to be watching them. He peered down each of the four streets; a car approached from two blocks down on one of the avenues, some kind of low, long sedan. He prayed this wasn't the man they were waiting for, holding his breath as the car came to a stop at the intersection. The tires crunched to a halt in the salted snow. Simon stared at the car. It seemed to stop for a strangely long time, the seconds ticking by, and then just as Simon was about to ask Katherine if this was the guy, the sedan inched forward into the intersection, its tires spinning for purchase before catching and jerking the car forward, across, and away. Simon watched the taillights disappear around the next corner. He wasn't going to leave Maria behind; he wasn't going to fuck up this time. He took a last drag of his cigarette, tossed it away half-finished, and turned to Katherine.

"Katherine."

"Yeah?" She turned to him expectantly, half-smiling, her lips a dark slash across her pale face.

"I'm sorry," he said.

She looked at him in confusion for half a breath, and then he bolted to the car, yanking open the RAV4's door, pushing the gear into drive with the door still open and his body only partway on the seat. Katherine sprung after him, but her feet slipped out from underneath her on the snow-slick sidewalk and she landed heavily on her tailbone, her body meeting the concrete with a wet thump. "Fucking Christ!" She scrambled to her feet, fingers scrabbling at the running board, eyes bugging wide, screaming at him to stop the fucking car. "I'm sorry," he yelled. "I'm sorry!" He pulled the door shut with one hand, the other steadying the wheel as he coasted across the intersection and then gunned it down the block, toward the smeary blur of a busier street a few hundred yards ahead, as he blew through one stop sign and then another, in the rearview mirror Katherine receding and then finally disappearing, swallowed up by the snow-speckled darkness.

## Twelve

Simon lifted his foot from the accelerator, the RAV4 rattling violently before settling into its new speed. Signs announced the terminus of the Long Island Expressway, and he took Route 24 southeast to the Sunrise Highway, black fields constricting the narrower road. The asphalt scrolled in front of their wheels, overlaid with a writhing veil of snow. He glanced over at Maria. She was still asleep, arms tucked inside her sweater, hands lightly cradling her stomach. Her head rested against the window, her breath fogging the glass.

He'd called her while he retraced Katherine's route back to Roosevelt Island, his frozen fingers fumbling with his cell phone, and told her to pack her bag, to throw some of his clothes and his laptop into a duffel as well.

"What?" Her voice was sluggish, as though she'd been sleeping. "Where are we going?"

"Away from the city."

"Where?"

"I don't know." He had a vague notion of heading east, far out onto the island. "The ocean. Montauk."

"I don't understand. What's happened?"

"Please, just get ready." He glanced at Katherine's cell phone rattling around in one of the cup holders: this was a piece of good luck, but she'd figure out a way to contact DaSilva soon enough. "We'll talk in the car." He passed another battalion of plows, grinding along like tanks in the opposite direction. "One more thing."

"Yeah?"

"In my bedroom, on the floor of the closet, there's a lockbox. Can you bring that for me too?"

"Yeah, fine." She paused. "Simon, what the fuck is this?"

"Just trust me. Please."

She'd been waiting in the lobby when he pulled up, the RAV4 a little squirrely in the snow, threatening to fishtail as he steered to the end of Main Street. She threw the bags into the back, and then they were off again, heading east into Queens, onto the Grand Central and then the LIE. He told her what had happened with Katherine, and she'd listened in silence, absentmindedly rubbing her stomach and staring out the window as he spoke.

"You're lucky you got away," she said once he was finished.

"I hated ripping Katherine off, it's not her fault. But I couldn't leave you behind like that. And what—I was just going to be a prisoner somewhere until DaSilva decided to set me loose?"

Maria turned to him, surprised. "Prisoner? You believed that story?"

"What do you mean?"

"Simon, that guy she was going to leave you with? You think he was going to set you up in some cabin in the fucking woods somewhere? Like a witness protection program or some shit? No. He was going to kill you or take you to somebody else who'd do it for him."

"What are you talking about?" He almost laughed, the idea was so absurd, as though the specter of professional murder could just wander into his life from a mob movie or paperback thriller.

"I'm serious. Think about it."

"Katherine would never do that to me."

"She probably didn't know. DaSilva sent her because he thinks you trust her. And I bet she believed whatever DaSilva told her."

"But clearly you don't."

"Not a fucking chance. You're the only person the clients ever saw or talked to, right? So get rid of you, and then all he needs to worry about is that hospital investigation. Nobody can connect him to Health Solutions."

"Except Katherine. She worked with some of the older clients, back before I started."

She shrugged. "Yeah, and who knows what he's got planned for her."

"Still, Maria . . . Murder? Come on."

She shrugged again. "It's what I would do if I were him."

He glanced over at her. She was staring out the window, hunched in her black leather jacket, a black scarf wound around her neck. He couldn't tell if she was joking.

"So, what are we doing?" she said.

"We're driving to Montauk. I told you."

"Simon. We can't just run. There's no end to that."

"What do you want to do? You want to stay in that apartment and wait for him? You think he wants me dead—that's what you just told me, right? Even if I think you're crazy—which makes waiting around sound like a pretty terrible idea."

She curled into her seat, tucking her head into her shoulder. "You're right about that much."

She shut herself down then, closing her eyes and pulling the scarf over her face, her breath deepening as she fell asleep. Simon stared into the pointillistic swirls of snow rushing over the windshield. He remembered the first and only time he'd been to the East End before, back in high school. It had been Ray Kippler's idea: a surfing contest. Kippler had heard about a circuit of amateur events on Long Island—Lido, Gilgo, Tobay, all the way east to Montauk, where the final contest of the summer and fall season was taking place. At that point, Ray was still just a guy Simon surfed with sometimes, not yet Amelia's boyfriend, although his crush on her was already obvious to Simon and, presumably, to Amelia as well.

Michael drove the three of them out to the contest site, a

secluded wedge of beach tucked into a crease in Montauk's dun-colored bluffs. They'd found the ocean in chaos, waves running east to west across the rock reef, breaking at cockeyed angles. Simon had been overpowered by the raw swell, flaming out in the first round, while hours later Kippler lost in the finals to a lanky semipro kid from Babylon. Sometime during the blustery afternoon, Michael had driven back into town, to seek refuge at a bar; Simon hitched a ride and found him in the bar's parking lot, after dark, stretched across the backseat of the family car, head wedged awkwardly into the crook between seat and door, his mouth slack, a white crust smeared across one corner. The four of them ended up spending the night in a motel off the Sunrise Highway after Michael declared he wasn't interested in dealing with the drive home. Simon remembered the fury in his sister's eyes, fury at the embarrassment that was their father. Simon had found it difficult to summon the same immediate anger; he simply added Michael's behavior to the long list of grievances he nurtured, more water on the sickly plant of his resentment. He remembered returning from the trip more worried about Amelia and Ray than about his father.

Now, seven years later, he drove the same route he'd just traveled in his memory, stretches of dark road punctuated by clusters of one-story commercial buildings and then, every few miles, the towns themselves, their Main Streets even more picturesque in the snow, sidewalks pristine white carpets, streetlamps glowing softly like crystal balls. To Simon, the whole place still looked unreal, like the model town stuffed inside a snow globe.

"I've never seen this before."

He glanced over at Maria. Her eyes were open, sleepily regarding the depthless swarm of flakes rushing over the windshield. "The snow?

"Yeah," she said. "It's. . . . rawer than I imagined. Wilder." She sat up and stretched. "Where are we?"

"I'm not sure. Bridgehampton, maybe."

"You know your way around out here?"

"A little bit," he said. "I surfed near here once. It's been a long time though."

They spotted an open motel on the far side of Montauk, a mile past the edge of town. A single car, a Toyota pickup with a fishing-rod rack, was parked in the lot. The motel was a long, low building with two floors of rooms, their doors painted sky-blue. A small freestanding structure stood off to the side, its window glowing, "Office" stenciled onto the glass.

Simon pulled into the lot and turned off the RAV4's engine. They sat in the lingering heat. The silence was sudden, shocking. Simon's tensed shoulders fired off flares of pain as the adrenaline finally drained from his muscles. A tiredness verging on catatonia threatened to subsume him. He roused himself, afraid if he didn't move now he'd fall asleep right where he was.

They gathered their bags and trudged through ankle-deep snow to the office, which was empty, a functioning space heater the only evidence that anybody might be nearby. Maria rang a silver bell on the counter. Nothing happened. She rang it again, and finally a door behind the counter opened, a teenage boy materializing, reddish patches of dry skin flaking on his cheeks and forehead, the whites of his eyes vermillion tinted. He blinked, as though their appearance in the office might be a glitch of his stoned brain.

"Help you?" he finally said.

"We'd like a room, please," Maria said.

His eyes meandered over to Simon's face and then back to Maria. "How many nights?"

Maria glanced at Simon. "We're not sure. Does it matter?"

The kid shrugged. He consulted a weathered ledger filled with cryptic, crabbed glyphs and fussed underneath the desk before producing a key. "Room 12. They're all the same, so . . ." He put the key on the counter, then told them the rate, which was far more expensive than the place's appearance suggested.

"That's fine," Maria said.

"Solid. I just need a credit card."

"We're paying cash."

"Uh, so we need a credit card for check-in? As, like, a deposit."

"Here." Maria withdrew a wad of twenties from her pocket and placed it on the counter. "All right?"

The kid eyed the money as though it might disappear if he looked straight at it. "Um."

"That's enough for two nights," she said. "If we only stay one, you can keep it all anyway. You get me?"

A mercenary gleam flickered behind the kid's glazed eyes. "That's not our policy, but . . . maybe if you make it three nights . . ."

"I don't think so." Maria took the key off the counter and nudged the cash. "Recognize a good deal when it's right in front you."

He shrugged and quickly scooped up the bills. "You folks have a nice night," he said, already retreating behind the private door.

Room 12 was at the end of the second floor, farthest from the office. Maria unlocked its door, revealing a boxy space done in a chintzy maritime style, an oar fixed onto the wall above the television, a gloomy oil painting, of what appeared to be a capsized whaling ship, over the bed. She shut the door behind them, hooking the lock chain into place. She turned and saw Simon sitting on the bed, watching her.

"What?" she said.

"We made it. That's all."

"For tonight."

He nodded. "For tonight."

He took off his shoes and jeans, throwing them into a heap on the floor, and climbed under the blankets. There'd been no discussion of splitting up or finding a room with two beds. He closed his eyes, listening to Maria move around the room from what seemed like a great distance, then feeling the mattress shift as she climbed into the bed beside him, her body warm without touching his back. He saw, coalescing out of the black behind his eyelids, Katherine's face, her mouth a perfect O of surprise as she tumbled down onto the icy pavement. She must have already told DaSilva about his escape; he wondered how violently Peter had reacted, whether he'd taken his anger out on her. DaSilva wasn't just going to let them go—Simon understood that much. He'd be looking for them—probably he already was—and Simon thought he might finally learn the real nature of DaSilva's criminal self: a thug or just a hustler, a simple con man or an honest-to-God killer?

SIMON snapped awake from a dream of drowning. He'd been thrashing through the ocean at night, his limbs tangling with those of other unseen swimmers, the cold water roiling with dozens of struggling bodies. He'd tried with all his strength to push toward shore, but something underwater held on to his ankle, an icy hand that would not relinquish its grip, pulling him down under the surface of the waves. He fought to keep his head above water, but he wasn't strong enough, and as he opened his mouth to scream, the frigid salt water poured in, and—

He woke up, his mouth open wide, taking in huge, desperate gulps of air.

The motel room was dark and warm, womb-like. As he lay there on his back, heart kicking and eyes open, shapes became objects: desk; chair; television. He could hear the ocean on the far side of the marsh behind the motel. He turned his head to the window: dawn's gray glow framed the blinds. He felt shaky, panicky. Just because a bad dream was simple to understand—was almost idiotic in its literal-mindedness: Amelia, always Amelia—didn't make the experience of it any less terrifying. He looked to his other side, and the dark shape next to him resolved into Maria's body, covered by the sheets, and above, her bare neck, the curve of her shoulders. Her face floated within the dark mass of her hair, like a reflection of the moon on water.

She yawned, rolled onto her back, and rubbed at her eyes. She looked over at him.

"How long have you been awake?"

He shrugged. "Not that long."

"Thinking?"

"Too much."

She sat up against the headboard. "Why'd you pick this place, Simon?"

"We had to get out of the city."

"Yeah, and that could've been anywhere."

"I still had to pick somewhere, right?" He reached over and switched on the bedside lamp. "I didn't want to just start driving."

She got out from under the covers and pulled on a pair of jeans. "What's your plan here?" She sat back down on the bed, cross-legged. "We run? We hide?"

"Just until—"

"Just until what? Until DaSilva gets bored of looking for us?" She shook her head. "Screw that. We can't wait around. He's going to come after us. He tried to have you killed, Simon."

"I don't know if I believe that. And, anyway, you could leave. I'm the one he needs to get rid of. You'd be safe."

"Don't be such a martyr," Maria said. "And, yeah, maybe he can't hurt me now, not while this investigation's happening. But since I left with you, he's got to figure I know all about his gig with Health Solutions, right? I can't be looking over my shoulder for the rest of my life. I won't live like that."

"So what do you want to do, Maria?"

"I don't know." She rubbed her face. "DaSilva or that woman, Katherine—have either of them called you?"

"I'm not sure." He remembered that Katherine's phone was still in the RAV4 out in the lot; she probably didn't have his number at all now. But DaSilva had to be trying to reach him. He stretched for his jacket, crumpled on the floor next to the bed. He patted at the damp lump of wool, but he couldn't find his phone in either of the outer pockets. Annoyed, he lifted the jacket and shook it out over the bed. His cell phone tumbled out of the inner breast pocket, followed by a sheet of folded, partially crumpled paper. He picked up the phone and jabbed at its buttons: the thing was dead, its battery long drained. He showed Maria the blank screen.

"Figures," she said.

"Yeah." He reached for the sheet of paper, and as soon as his fingers touched it—even before he'd unfolded it, before he'd smoothed it out on the bedspread, the dime-sized burn hole at its top edge, and fully understood its immense value—he remembered with a jolt what it was: the wire transfer form he'd found in the office. He'd completely forgotten about it, never returning it to DaSilva; instead, he'd carried it around, ignored, in his coat pocket for over two weeks. His pulse thumped hollowly in his ears: it was pure luck he hadn't lost it. Even now, he handled the damp paper carefully, desperate not to smear the ink.

"What's that?" Maria asked.

He looked up at her, and she must have seen it in his face, his surprise and excitement, because she quickly leaned over the paper, squinting as she tried to read DaSilva's scrawl. After a few moments, she raised her head to stare at him: "Holy fuck."

"I know."

"You had this the whole time?"

"I forgot about it. I don't think I quite realized what it was before."

They looked back down at the paper together. The form authorized the transfer of $380,000 from the Health Solutions LLC account at a Citibank branch on Jerome Avenue in the Bronx. This amount, Simon realized now, was exactly what Crewes had paid for the combined cost of Maria's liver and Health Solutions' fee. Listed as the beneficiary was a company called Black Sea Holdings, located at a street address in Nicosia, Cyprus; the beneficiary's bank was the Cyprus Popular Bank, also in Nicosia. The numbers for both accounts were filled in clearly. But all of this would have meant very little without DaSilva's signature, bold and messy, overflowing its box at the bottom of the page.

"Does he know you have this?" Maria asked.

"No." He told her how he'd found it where it had fallen behind the fax machine. "He doesn't even know it exists."

"He will soon." She stood up and dug a smartphone out of her bag.

"I thought you threw away your phone," Simon said.

"I bought this last week. New number, no contract." She held the phone over the paper and snapped a photo. "I wondered how he was doing it."

"Doing what?"

"Manufacturing all that cash. Clients write out checks, right?"

"Yeah."

"So he had to figure out a way to turn those checks into untraceable cash. It's like laundering in reverse. This"—she tapped the form—"is the first step. Getting the money out of the American banks."

"And this company in Cyprus, they—what, exactly?"

"My guess is that whoever's behind it has people here in New York who will give DaSilva the amount in cash, for some kind of a fee. Probably dirty money, from drugs, gambling, whatever. Untraceable. And now this guy's company has a bunch of clean American money sitting in its account." She shrugged. "But I'm just guessing. It doesn't really matter. This paper fucks him either way."

Simon picked up the form. "We should take this to the police, Maria."

"No." She spat the word out. "No cops." She paused, and then, more measured, said, "You broke the law too, remember? You think you can get a plea deal? Maybe. But get ready to give back all the money you've made. And what about your clients, people like Crewes and Cheryl? You want to bring everybody down with you?"

He said nothing. She was right—he knew it.

"No cops, Simon," she said again, defiantly. "I've earned my cash, and I'm keeping it."

"We can still use this though." He paced back and forth from the bed to the window. "We have some leverage here, we just have to figure out what to do with it." He stopped, looked at her. "What if we offer to sell it back to him? We give him the form and he gives us—what? Forty thousand in cash? More? And then he agrees to sever all ties with us. We don't owe him anything more. We don't tell him anything about where we're going. He'll never find us."

"And if he says no?"

"We say we're going to take it to the police."

"He won't believe that."

"A reporter, then. Somebody who wants to dig into all this."

Maria nodded slowly. "Yeah. That might get him out here."

"How much should we ask for?" Simon said. "Thirty? Forty?"

Maria shrugged. "We can ask for whatever we want. He's not going to give it to us."

"What are you talking about?"

"He's not going to just pay up and leave us alone," she said. "I'm telling you. He wants you dead. He'll probably blackmail me so I say what he wants me to say during the Cabrera investigation. Or maybe he'll just get rid of me too, now that he knows I know about him. Either way, there's not going to be any exchange."

Simon sat back down on the bed. "I thought you agreed with me."

"You got it half-right." She smiled, the crooked gray tooth flashing. "We get him out here."

"Yeah? And then what?"

"And then we kill him."

He barked out a laugh. *This* was her idea? It was too insane to be serious. But she wasn't smiling. "Maria. I'm not a murderer."

"Nobody's a murderer until they kill somebody."

He shook his head. "That's circular logic."

"This man doesn't want you alive, Simon. There's no other choice."

"I just offered us another choice."

"Oh yeah?"

"Yeah. We disappear."

"You really think you can do that? And is that how you want to live the rest of your life? Invent an identity? Cut yourself off from your family, all your friends?"

"Isn't that what you did?"

"I don't have a family and those weren't real friends. What are you afraid of? Getting caught? We'll design it so that's impossible." She grabbed his arm and squeezed. "Listen to me now: killing somebody is as simple as making a plan and having the will to follow through. That's it."

"Jesus, Maria." He pulled his arm free. "What the fuck is wrong with you? Do you realize how crazy you sound right now?" She shrugged, unmoved. "And how do you know anyway?" She looked away then, down at the worn, nubby carpet. "Maria?"

She raised her head. "Because I've done it."

He stared at her. She held his eyes, steady and calm. Then he broke her gaze and laughed. "Okay, you almost had me."

"I'm not lying."

"You've lied to me about all kinds of things, from the day we met. Now you expect me to believe this?"

"Yeah, and I was protecting myself before. I think you understand that. And I wasn't lying about the rape."

"All right, but—"

"Why would I lie about this? Right now?"

"Okay," he said. "I'll play along. Who did you kill?"

"My foster brother." She spoke without hesitation, her voice steady.

"When?"

"The night I flew to New York."

"What? Just a few weeks ago?" He said this as though it was only the timing that made the whole thing impossible.

"Thirty days. But who's counting."

"You're telling me that was your plan? To kill your brother—"

"Foster brother. I don't share any blood with that piece of shit."

The venom in her voice silenced Simon. For the first time, he wondered if he should be afraid of her. "Maria, if this is true—"

She sliced her hand through the air, cutting him off: "It's fucking true."

"If this is true, why are you telling me?"

"To show you it can be done. Nobody helped me. I did it by myself and here I am. Alive. Free."

Tires hissed wetly on the nearby road; the light around the blinds brightened, suffusing the room with a milky glow.

"This was revenge?" It wasn't really a question.

"He deserved to die," she said. "He was scum, Simon. The kind of person who picks on the helpless and most vulnerable just because he thinks he'll always get away with it."

"How did it happen?" He didn't know if he believed her yet, but he wanted to hear what she would say. "How did you do it?"

She smiled a little, almost bashfully, and he could tell that she took a measure of pride in her planning, in the sheer audaciousness of her act.

"You need to understand what it was like for me after Thomas left. The fucker went back to college like nothing had happened. I stayed with the Dreesons through the end of the school year, in some kind of shock, I guess, in this sort of numb haze. All I could think about was finishing school and leaving. I turned eighteen a week after I graduated, and then I got the hell out of there."

She told Simon that the day after her birthday she moved into a crowded and mildewy share house on the east side of Venice, a room she'd heard about through the punk-show grapevine. She dipped into the Dreesons' cash box one last time and took a hundred dollars for her first two weeks of rent. When the day came, she rode the bus in a diagonal across the entire city of Los Angeles, her bike wedged between her knees, duffel bag on the seat next to her. Before she left, she told the Dreesons that they shouldn't expect to hear from her anymore. They didn't seem surprised; she'd barely spoken to them during her last five months in the house. Within a week, one of her new roommates had found her a job as a waitress at a café in El Segundo, and finally, she thought, her real life had begun.

What had actually begun, though, was a period of darkness or, rather, the desperation of staving off the darkness, of filling time and mind and attention with something—anything—else. She lived around the cheaper fringes of the South Bay, waitressing and bartending and getting high. She inhabited a world of casual, low-stakes criminality: bottom-rung drug dealers, crooked chop shops, guys fencing stolen electronics. She discovered—like mother, like daughter—that she preferred downers: alcohol, painkillers, Xanax, certain strains of indica weed. She snorted heroin a few times, but it was too expensive, and after she saw an evil batch of black tar rip through Venice, she was too scared of it anyway. The obvious point of it all, as she recognized now, was to obliterate the rape and the feelings associated with it, but at the time she just thought of the drugs as an end in themselves, just what you did when you were young. She decided, too, that Thomas wasn't going to take sex away from her, and so she fucked whomever she wanted, as a way of proving to herself that she wasn't afraid of sex, wasn't afraid of men. And it was true: she wasn't afraid of them; she mostly just hated them. But none of it—not the drugs, not the sex—made her feel better. None of it chipped away at the temple of pure anger in which she felt herself encased, to the altar of which she offered her every action, her every thought.

Four years after she left the Dreesons, she finally told somebody about Thomas. She didn't plan this disclosure; it just happened. She and two of her girlfriends—Amanda and Dalia—went to a house party in Manhattan Beach, passing a flask of Bacardi 151 between them, the party the usual blur of smoke and music and bullshit. At some point they stumbled the few blocks to the beach and collapsed in the damp sand. Amanda lit a blunt of Kush, and as they passed it, talk turned to a story going around their circle. A girl Maria vaguely knew had passed out in the upstairs bedroom of a party not unlike the one they'd just left. According to the story, the host of the party had found her there after everybody else was gone, and he'd done just about what you'd expect a shithead like him to do. "And she," Amanda continued, "did *nothing* about it."

"Yeah," Maria said, "'cause she was unconscious."

"No, I mean after. She knows what happened. But she still sees the asshole at parties and acts like everything's fine!"

"It's not that simple," Maria said.

Her two friends looked at her. "What do you mean?" Dalia asked.

"I mean . . ." Was she really going to say it? Why shouldn't she? "I mean, I was raped, and I didn't have a fucking clue what to do about it."

"Shit, Maria," Dalia said. "When?"

She told them the story, leaving out Thomas's name. She'd half-expected to feel the immediate lifting of a burden merely because she'd said the words out loud—"I was raped"—but after she'd finished the story and searched inside herself, she found that nothing had changed, not yet. Her friends, too, seemed less shocked than she might have expected them to be.

"I know what I'd do," Amanda said.

"Oh yeah?" Maria said. "What?"

Amanda shrugged. "If it were me, I'd kill him."

Dalia snorted out a laugh.

"Bullshit," Maria said.

"I would. And you should too."

Dalia cracked up, falling back onto the sand: "You are so full of shit."

Maria stared at Amanda, the weed fogging her brain. Was she joking? Maria was too fucked up to know. Amanda pulled from the blunt and exhaled a mushroom cloud of smoke. "You're crazy," Maria muttered. Amanda just shrugged again and handed her the blunt.

Maybe Amanda was crazy, and maybe she'd been joking, but her words—*I'd kill him. And you should too*—lodged themselves in Maria's mind, a burr tugging at the fabric of her attention. She'd daydream behind the counter at the café and the idea would slip into her unguarded thoughts: *I'd kill him.* She'd come to, after another night of obliterative drinking, and the words were right there alongside her hangover: *And you should too.* Slowly, subtly, over the course of a few months and without Maria quite realizing it, the idea shifted from an absurd, offhand comment to a kind of mantra to the first tracings of a blueprint. Soon enough, she thought about killing Thomas, not as an abstract concept, but as a possible reality, a reality that she could design. She thought about how she might feel if he were dead. Not just dead—dead at her hand. There was no ambivalence in the answer that came to her: she'd feel pretty fucking fantastic about it. Revenge, she thought, wasn't one of the great motivating forces in human history because it didn't work.

She made the final, purposeful decision to kill him two months before she arrived in New York. She quit drugs and drinking that same day, a renunciation she'd since maintained with only two very notable and useful exceptions before she was prescribed her painkillers at Cabrera. All her energy and focus went into planning Thomas's death. Once she'd decided on her escape strategy— she learned about Health Solutions the usual way, through internet and chat-group searching—she found out where Thomas currently worked and lived. This wasn't particularly difficult: she cruised around the old neighborhood in San Gabriel, talking to people in the stores and bars, picking up information wherever she could. He'd dropped out of UC Santa Cruz, she learned, and now worked in management at a warehouse distribution center for computer parts in Long Beach. He lived nearby, with his girlfriend, in Carson.

She drove out to the distribution center, glad for once to be behind the wheel of her crappy gray 1998 Civic, the kind of car people forget the instant they've seen it. She watched as the workers dribbled out of the warehouse into the parking lot. Thomas appeared near the back of the group. He wore an ill-fitting black suit and white dress shirt without a tie, and to Maria these clothes looked like a costume and Thomas a teenager playing at being an adult. He drove a dusty black Jeep with a Fox Racing sticker on the side window. She watched from across the street as he pulled out of the lot and turned south, and then she followed a few car lengths behind as he drove toward the 710. She was afraid she'd lose him on the freeway, but it turned out he wasn't going that far. He turned left onto Anaheim Street and pulled into the parking lot of a bar; she parked across the street and waited. He came out about an hour and a half later, swaying slightly, and got back into his Jeep. She didn't see him speak to anyone on his way in or out, and she wondered if he'd been drinking alone. Over the next few weeks, she returned to the warehouse five more times at closing hour. Each evening Thomas went to the bar on Anaheim Street for an hour or two before emerging, visibly tipsy, and climbing into his Jeep.

She sourced some Rohypnol from her old pot dealer, who also moved an assortment of pharmaceuticals for a crooked nurse's aide. He raised his eyebrows when she requested it.

"Can't sleep," she said.

"This shit is heavy," he said. "Be careful."

"Just give it to me."

He shrugged and sold her a blister pack of ten. "Whatever gets you through the night."

The gun was more difficult. She wrote down a list of all the people she knew in the South Bay who owned a handgun. She stared at the four names. She was sure all the guns were illegal, stolen, or bought on the black market, their serial numbers shaved. She'd have to steal one of them herself; she couldn't risk anybody knowing she'd wanted to purchase the thing. She picked the most careless of the four: it had to be Alvie, a young, low-level Venice heroin dealer who seemed to pour the majority of his profits back into his own habit, the worst cliché of getting high on your own supply she'd seen, and the kind of idiot who'd leave his gun out on the table just to let people know he had it.

She paid Alvie a visit under the pretense of wanting to purchase half a gram. He greeted her at the door, shirtless and sleepy-eyed at three in the afternoon, a spindly kid with a sunken, hairless chest and a wispy attempt at a mustache.

"Hey, Maria," he mumbled. "I thought you weren't down with this shit anymore."

"Yeah, well, I believe in change and personal growth."

He grinned. "C'mon inside."

It was clammy and dim in the little bungalow, the air smelling of mildew and incense and a sharp, sweet odor she thought might be opium. He weighed out the matte-white powder, poured it into a plastic baggie, slid it across the sticky coffee table. She handed him the cash.

"Listen, Alvie . . ."

"Yeah?"

"You know I don't do this stuff so much . . ."

"Yeah."

"So I was thinking . . . maybe we could do some now? Together, here in a safe place? Get my sea legs back or whatever."

"Aw, Maria, I got people coming by later, and—"

"I'm offering, Alvie. Out of my bag. Let's do just a bit."

She'd been betting that he wouldn't refuse free heroin, and she was right. He took his works out of a box under the coffee table.

"Oh no," she said, "no needles."

"Chipping, huh?" He shrugged. "Whatever you want."

She gave him back the bag, and he tapped out two points of powder, onto a smeary hand mirror. "Lucky this white just came through. It's been all brown around here, and you shouldn't be snorting that shit." He held out a segment of plastic straw.

"You first," she said.

He bent his head to the mirror and snorted. "Fuck, that's harsh." He slid the mirror across the table. "Not too much, okay?"

She nodded and bent to the straw. She took a tiny hit, as small as she could manage without tipping Alvie off. After ten minutes, she felt it creeping up on her, like the first trembling edge of an orgasm. *I remember this*, she thought. *Fuck, do I remember this.* She looked over at Alvie. He seemed basically sober, and she pointed at the bag. "Have some more." She exaggerated the slur already present in her voice. "My treat." Alvie didn't turn her down, bending to the mirror one, two, three more times. He held out the straw. She waved him off sluggishly, not quite sure how much she was acting anymore. Finally, after his fourth bump, Alvie started to nod out.

"How you doin', Maria?" he mumbled.

"Yeah, all right." She watched him through half-closed lids. He sprawled back on the couch, tried to light a cigarette, failed. He giggled and let his head fall to the side, eyes closed. She waited until she was sure he was passed out, and then she pushed herself out of the chair. She made her way into his bedroom, its air thick with a humid funk. She remembered him showing off the gun at a party. He'd pulled it from underneath his mattress, an ugly snub-nosed SIG Pro 2009, and passed it around the room, like a new father showing off baby pictures. *Idiot.* She tried to lift the mattress and failed, toppling over onto the bed. She lay there, her face pressed into his musty sheets. It wouldn't be so bad, she thought, to just take a nap for a minute. *Get the fuck up, Maria.* She laughed a little, the sound muffled by the sheets, and pushed herself to her feet. She reached under the mattress and there it was, the SIG, sitting like a black turd on the white box spring. She grabbed it and let the mattress fall.

"Maria." She froze: Alvie, calling her from the living room. "Hey, Maria?"

She shoved the gun into her waistband, right at the small of her back, and pulled her sweatshirt down over it. She walked out into the living room as casually as she could. But it didn't matter: Alvie was where she'd left him, his head lazily cocked on the pillow, eyes still closed. "Someone in my room," he slurred. She crept silently over to the chair on the other side of the couch. She sat down, the SIG digging into her tailbone.

"Nah, Alvie," she said quietly. "Don't think so."

His head lolled on the pillow and he slitted his eyes at her. "No?"

"Nope."

"Fucking gremlins." He giggled and closed his eyes again. She waited for about fifteen minutes, until the bump had mostly worn off. Then she stood, pocketed the baggie, and shook Alvie's shoulder. "Thanks, Alvie."

He looked up at her and nodded drowsily. "Been a pleasure."

Three days later, she drove her Civic to Thomas's warehouse and followed him, as usual, to the bar on Anaheim. Once she'd watched him go inside, she drove a few blocks away, parked, and checked her purse for the SIG and the pills. She had to keep moving, she knew—she couldn't risk pausing and thinking too much. She walked quickly back to the bar and stood at the door, listening to the murmur of talk on the other side. *You know what you have to do. All that's left now is to do it.* She opened the door.

The bar was dim inside, as she'd hoped, its windows tinted. She scanned the crowded room and found Thomas sitting alone at a high table in a back corner. His head was bent over his phone; he hadn't noticed her yet. She ordered herself a Tecate. She was a woman drinking alone at a bar. She waited a few minutes, sipping at her beer—the first alcohol she'd tasted in months, bright and crisp and wonderful—and pushed away the impulse to turn around. She wanted him to notice her first; she thought it would seem less staged that way. She waited a few more minutes, and when she went to take another sip of her Tecate, she found the can nearly empty. *Easy now.*

She rose from the bar stool, turned around, and looked straight into Thomas's eyes. She froze for half a breath, and then she felt her face—*thank God*—shape itself into the expression she'd practiced in front of her mirror for weeks: a kind of startled puzzlement, as though her brain hadn't quite caught up with her eyes. Thomas looked like he'd been kicked in the stomach, all the bluster knocked out of him. He recovered quickly though, his expression resolving into an ironic, slightly smug smile.

She made her way over to his table.

"I thought you were up in Santa Cruz," she said. Her voice sounded obscene to her own ears—false, too loud.

"Nah." He shook the ice in his drink—a rum and Coke, Maria could smell it. "That didn't work out."

"What are you doing in Long Beach?"

"I could ask you the same thing."

"So ask me."

He looked at her for a long moment. His face had filled out, the flesh of his neck thickened. She could see he was trying to place her into some kind of story, trying to identify the point at which he'd intersected her life—trying to figure out where she was coming from.

"I work nearby." He sipped at his drink. "What about you?"

"I live in Redondo," she said. "But sometimes I like to come over here and have a drink at a place where I don't know anybody and nobody knows me."

"Guess I fucked that up for you. Sorry."

"I'll get over it." She glanced at his drink. "Need a refill?"

"I'll do it."

She waved him off and went to the bar. She bought him a rum and Coke and herself another Tecate, and she carried the drinks back to their table. She looked around: nobody seemed to be paying any attention to them.

"You drink alone?" she asked. "First sign of an alcoholic."

"I don't see anybody here with you either."

"Yeah, well, I'm a foster child. I'm supposed to be fucked up. What's your excuse?"

"I deal with people and their bullshit all day long. If I come here and have some drinks alone, it's like a buffer, so I don't bring any of that negative crap home." He paused. "So, pretty much why anybody ever drinks after work."

"Home to what?"

"Home to my girlfriend."

"Ah." He stared at her. He was trying to figure out how he should act around her, Maria saw, and failing. "What's her name?"

"I don't want to talk about her with you." He licked his lips. "Look, maybe I should go."

"Why, do I make you nervous?"

He stood up.

"Oh, stop it," she said. "Calm down and let's have a drink together. We're adults now, right?" He hesitated, one foot on the floor. She slid his drink closer to him. "Sit. Please. I want to talk to you."

He sat down and took the drink. "My parents are going to be blown away when I tell them about this."

"They would be," she agreed, "but I'd rather you not tell them."

"Why?"

"Let's just keep it between us." She made her voice light, neutral. Maybe she was flirting, maybe not.

"Fine." He stirred his drink. "What do you want to talk about?"

"What happened in Santa Cruz? What are you doing now?"

"That's a long story."

"I want to hear it."

He started to talk. He was wary at first, and she suspected that he'd only agreed to stay because he was scared she'd cause a scene if he tried to leave. She must be crazy—who knew what she'd say! But after a while, after she kept up with the charm and he kept up with the drinks, she could sense him relaxing. She'd learned to never underestimate how much people love talking about themselves. And what did he have to be afraid of, really? She'd kept quiet for five years; surely she wasn't about to start blabbing now.

He finished his drink and went up and got them another round. She set the new Tecate next to her last one, which she'd barely touched. When Thomas got up again to use the bathroom, she reached inside her purse and popped two Rohypnol pills out of the blister pack. She dropped them into his rum and Coke and stirred the drink, watching as the pills dissolved.

He returned from the bathroom and sat down, and she could smell the gum on his breath as he started to talk again, that same cinnamon-flavored crap he used to chew around the house in San Gabriel, and she flashed to the evening when he'd tried to kiss her in the garage, his face hovering above hers like a crater-ridden moon about to crash into the earth, and then her mind zoomed forward to the afternoon she'd spent five years trying to obliterate, and the fact of its recurrence—here, now, in the bar—only proved to her, all over again, the necessity of what she was going to do: no forgetting, no acceptance, no *process* or *method*. Just revenge.

"Maria?" He was looking at her strangely.

"Yeah, sorry." She shook her head and smiled. She saw that he'd finished half of the spiked drink. "Spaced out for a second. I suppose it's my turn now."

She talked about what she'd done over the last five years, a blend of truth and fiction. She kept an eye on his drink as she spoke. He sipped it without comment until, finally, it was finished, just a few half-melted ice cubes and—*shit*—a residue of white powder. She interrupted herself: "One more?"

"I shouldn't, I gotta—"

"Come on. Who knows when we'll see each other again?"

Before he could protest, she grabbed his glass and her beer, and carried them to the bar. By the time Thomas finished his last rum and Coke, she could see the roofie working in his glassy eyes and gluey movements. She had to get him out of the bar before he knocked something over or passed out.

He didn't protest when she suggested they leave.

"Not feeling so hot," he announced. He sagged against the wall. "Fucking strong drinks."

She got him out into the parking lot without too much difficulty, trying to keep her head down as she moved through the bar.

"Which one's yours?"

He waved at the black Jeep. They made their way over to the car, Thomas weaving and stumbling.

"You're not driving like that," she said.

"I'm fine."

"Give me the keys."

"Gimme a fucking break, Maria."

"You want a DUI? Give me the keys."

"Where's your car?"

"Over there." She waved vaguely at the other end of the lot. "I'll come back for it. C'mon, you live nearby, right? I'll drive you home."

"She can't see that."

"What?"

"June can't see you drop me off."

"Your girlfriend?"

He nodded.

"Whatever. I'll park it a block away or something. Just get in."

He sighed heavily, unlocked the Jeep, and gave her the keys. He climbed into the driver's-side seat and slumped over. "Embarssin'," he said.

"What?"

"It's embarrassing. Don't understand . . ." He shook his head. "Fuck, I'm hammered."

"Happens to everybody." She started the Jeep and pulled out of the lot.

Suddenly he sat up straighter. "But why aren't *you* so drunk?"

"'Cause I was drinking beer."

He pointed a wavering finger at her. "You *meant* to get me wasted."

She flushed. "Nah . . ."

"Yeah, you did."

But when she looked over, she saw he was grinning, slackly and stupidly. He thought it was funny.

"Okay," she said, "maybe a little bit."

"Get me drunk and take 'vantage of me. Ha!" He slouched against the window. "Can't believe you're even *talking* to me."

She kept silent. She felt an enormous pressure building up inside of her. The gun seemed to pulse with radioactive heat from inside her purse.

Thomas narrowed his bleary eyes. "Hey," he said. "This isn't the way to my place."

"It's a shortcut."

"Did I even . . . ? I didn't tell you where I live, did I?"

"I know where we're going."

She drove them west, away from the commercial strip and toward the Los Angeles River. She'd memorized the directions and knew exactly how long it would take to get to the place she'd chosen. The lot was next to a shuttered warehouse, adjacent to the river and a few blocks south of the PCH. It was enclosed by a chain-link fence, but the fence's gate was busted and hung open. She drove into the lot, to a corner tucked behind the warehouse and hidden from the street.

"The hell is this?" Thomas said.

"Listen, I have something to tell you." She stopped the Jeep. "Meeting you in the bar? That wasn't luck. It wasn't random. The truth is that I can't seem to get you out of my head these days."

His glassy eyes stared at her. "You knew I'd be there?"

"I wanted to see you, Thomas."

He looked outside the car, at the deserted lot, the forlorn warehouses. "What are we *doing* here?"

"I needed some privacy."

"I don't understand. You wanna . . ." He rubbed at his face. "I mean, I can't really believe . . ."

"What do you think I want to do, Thomas?"

"I'm saying, you don't have to get me so *wasted*, take me all the way out here, if you wanna fuck, you know?"

Maria unfastened her seat belt and reached into her purse. Her fingers found the SIG, cool and solid in her hand. "Right." She thumbed the safety. "But I don't want to fuck you, Thomas." She pulled out the gun and pointed it at his face. "I want to kill you."

She'd expected him to gape and cower while she made him listen to her pain, while she enumerated the reasons he had to die. She'd envisioned a sort of dignity for his killing, something ritualistic, sacrificial. But he didn't cooperate. Instead of cowering, he fought through the sedatives and slapped at the gun, almost knocking it out of her hand. He reached for her throat, and she twisted awkwardly in the seat, trying to turn the weapon on him. He went after the gun again, and this time she pulled the trigger, not bothering to aim.

"Fuck!" he screamed. She looked down and saw blood staining his thigh. "You bitch!"

She raised the gun again, and this time he struggled to open the door and, half-tangled in the seat belt, stumble out of the Jeep. She fired, catching him in the lower back. He fell to the ground, wheezing. She got out of the car and ran around the hood. He lay sprawled on the concrete, breathing with a wet rattle. He tried to get up, failed, and then began to pull himself forward with his arms, leaving behind a smeared trail of blood.

"There's nowhere to go," Maria said.

He looked up at her. His eyes were wild, rolling around in their sockets. He wheezed louder, as though he was trying to say something.

"Try again," she said.

Finally he got it out: "Why?"

"You know why."

"Don't deserve this," he whispered.

"I decide that."

"Please."

She couldn't talk to him anymore. Couldn't look at him like this. She raised the SIG and shot him in the head. He jerked violently, his skull bouncing off the concrete. She fired into his head three more times, emptying the clip. The shots echoed off the warehouses and up into the sky. Thomas lay motionless, facedown, a pool of blood spreading around his ruined head. Maria looked down at his body, fixing the image in her mind: the position of his limbs, the shape of the blood pool, the texture of the moonlight on concrete. Then she turned off the Jeep and ran out the back of the lot, sprinting up the embankment to the river. She scrambled down a rocky and trash-hewn slope, threw the gun into the water, and then walked quickly south along the path. After half a mile, she turned in toward her car, walking along a different route from the one she'd driven. She heard the sirens just as she reached her Civic, what sounded like two or three patrol cars speeding over in the direction of the river. They didn't scare her. She was nobody, getting into her nothing car—a nonentity, a person about to disappear.

She drove back to Venice, along the PCH, and parked in front of her bungalow. She had three hours until her red-eye to JFK. She took off all her clothes and inspected them: only a few drops of blood on the cuff of her jeans. She stuffed the clothes into a garbage bag, walked to Washington Boulevard, and dropped the bag into a dumpster behind a Del Taco. Back at her bungalow, she showered for half an hour, standing under the scalding hot water until it turned lukewarm and then cold, getting out only when she started to shiver. She dried her hair and dressed. Her duffel bag was packed, her taxi to the airport booked. She looked around the bungalow: she wasn't going to miss this place, not for a second. She felt blank, but that blankness was itself a relief from her usual gnarled and agitated inner state. Her mind felt clean and smooth and feature-less, like a pebble washed for thousands of years in the ocean. She sat on the edge of her bed and waited for her taxi to arrive.

"So." Maria looked sideways at Simon. "Do you believe me now?"

"Jesus Christ." He thought of the Mori folder, all those photographs of slaughtered young men. Maria couldn't capture the scene of Thomas's death, so she'd assembled a collection of its analogues in bits and pieces: the corpse's posture in one, the lighting in another, the character of the gunshot wound in the next. Within each one of these scenes, she'd located an element of what she'd done to Thomas, how she'd left him. Encoded within the collection of photos was the precise expression of his killing. "Yes." He cleared his throat; his voice was hoarse and ragged, as though he'd been the one telling the story. "Yes, I do."

"You weren't supposed to get involved. I'd make my money, and then I'd use that money to disappear, forever." She paused. "It can be done, Simon. And we're going to do it. Today."

"I don't . . ." He stood and walked to the window. He lifted the shade and looked out over the motel parking lot. The lot's churned-up slush had hardened overnight into ridges of icy mud. Pure white snow covered Katherine's RAV4. The sky was a rich, deep blue, scrubbed clean by the storm, and the morning sunlight fired the frozen lot with gold. He turned back to Maria. She sat on the bed and looked at him calmly, watched him work through it all. It still didn't seem quite real, this talk of murder. It was as though he'd slipped, unwittingly, from one parallel reality to the next, from the world he'd inhabited his whole life into a shadow world animated by violence, betrayal, revenge. He was sharing a room with a murderer, but the truth was that he was not afraid of her. He knew, intellectually, that maybe he should be, but he didn't feel it. He wasn't repulsed or outraged either. Instead, he felt fascination and a touch of awe. And he'd thought he could save her! He had nothing to offer her; she was beyond all that now.

"Simon." She tapped the bedside clock. "We need to do this. Now."

Maybe she'd stepped fully into that shadow world, but he didn't have to. He shook his head. "I can't do it, Maria. I *won't* do it."

"You don't get it, he's going to kill—"

"I said no. We have to find another way."

"Come on, Simon." She gave him a disappointed look, as though he were a soft-brained pupil with difficulty remembering even the simplest of facts. "Don't you understand? It's him or you."

"Maria. Stop."

She stared at him, biting her lip, as though willing him to change his mind. Finally she sighed and turned away. "Fine."

He picked up the transfer form from the bed and held it out to her. "You'll help me sell this back to him?"

"Yeah. But we can't do the exchange here. We need somewhere hidden."

Simon thought for a moment, his mind churning. Then he remembered: "All right."

"All right?"

"I think I know the place."

## Thirteen

THEY waited at the foot of the bluffs, on the beach where Simon and Kippler had competed in the surfing contest seven years before. The geography of the cove fit their plan well enough, and the chances of any random beachgoers turning up were slim on such a frigid afternoon. Today the waves were flat, the Atlantic a bright, limpid green; sunlight glittered fiercely on the ocean's surface, shattered and strewn about like broken glass. The path, a steep and slippery mixture of sand and snow and crumbling limestone, ran down a hundred feet from the dirt lot. The beach was about two hundred feet long and less than twenty wide now, at high tide, the cliffs at its east and west edges extending all the way to the ocean, pinching off the sand. At the eastern end, an archipelago of rocks draped in beard-like seaweed stepped out into the ocean. The path up the bluff was the only way out, besides the water, and the bluffs were steep enough that the beach was concealed from anyone who wasn't standing right at the cliff's edge.

Maria looked at her phone again. "He should've been here an hour ago."

"He's coming." Simon stared up at the lip of the bluff. "I'm sure of it."

All morning they'd worked through their plan, but the whole thing still seemed depressingly contingent to Simon, the least bad among a wilderness of terrible options. Somehow he'd put himself into a situation in which his freedom—and, if Maria was right, possibly his life—depended upon a rickety blackmail plot hatched in a motel room with the help of a violent and damaged young woman he still couldn't say he truly knew or completely trusted. It was insane, ludicrous, but inarguably his reality.

They would ask DaSilva to hand over the money first. After he gave them the cash, Maria—she'd volunteered for the task—would hand over the transfer form. And then they'd be gone, up the path to the lot and Katherine's RAV4. They'd drive north, deep into New England, to some place Maria had chosen, although she wouldn't yet tell him anything more specific about it.

"If everything goes to shit, just run," Maria had said. "He's a fat bastard. He won't catch us."

"But your sutures—"

"I'll fight through it if I have to."

First, Maria texted DaSilva the photo of the signed form. Peter's number was locked inside Simon's dead phone, but they found it written out on the document itself, right below Health Solutions' account information. Maria waited about a minute and then handed Simon her phone. "Call him." As Simon started dialing, he experienced a strange sort of calm, a numbness settling onto his chest. This was fatalism, he realized. The sensation of having made a choice and having committed to playing that choice all the way out to its end. He hesitated, his finger hovering over the final digit, and when he at last entered it into the phone, the action felt almost involuntary, as though he were being manipulated by forces greater than himself or, rather, as though he'd suffered a sort of schism, and the self who commanded his finger to move was entirely different from the self who carried out the command.

DaSilva answered on the first ring: "Who the fuck is this?" His voice was strangled and scratchy, as though the words were being yanked from his throat by a fishhook.

"Peter, listen. It's Simon."

A long pause followed. Maria leaned close to Simon, listening in. A door shut somewhere behind DaSilva, and when he spoke again, it was with a slight echo, as though he'd moved into a large, empty room. "What the hell are you thinking?" he hissed. "That bullshit with Katherine, are you out of your fucking mind? She was trying to help you."

Maria caught Simon's eye, shook her head. "You saw the photo," Simon said.

"The what?"

"The photo. Of the transfer form."

"Yeah, I saw it. Where'd you lift that from, you prick?"

Simon hesitated. He had no idea how to do this. Maria flapped her hand at him: *just keep going.* "You want it back, right?"

"What is this? You're going to blackmail me?"

"I'm with Maria. We need—"

"Where are you?"

"Listen to me!" Simon snapped. Maria jerked her head back, eyes widening. A smile crept onto her face. Simon had surprised both DaSilva and himself into silence, but he quickly plunged onward to cover it up: "We need $40,000 in cash and your guarantee that you will not try to come after us or contact us ever again. Otherwise, I'm handing this form over to the press, to the people who are already sniffing around Cabrera."

"Have you gone completely insane?"

"I'm done, Peter. We do this deal, and then I'm gone. You'll never hear from me again."

"You think it's that easy?" DaSilva said. "You think you can just disappear like that?"

"It's what you wanted anyway, isn't it? You give me this money, and I'll do it myself."

"What, you really think I have $40,000 in cash just lying around?"

"Maybe. Or maybe it's in Health Solutions' bank account. Want me to read off that account number for you?"

Maria put her hand over her mouth, suppressing a laugh.

"You're a real motherfucker," DaSilva said.

"I'm sorry. I didn't want it to be like this."

"What about the girl?"

"Maria and I leave together."

"There's a fucking *investigation* going on here, Simon," DaSilva snarled. "People need to talk to her. Do you know what it'll look like if she's just gone?"

"I don't care. And neither does she."

A pause. DaSilva hacked out a cough, the sound of a busted generator struggling to catch. "What's gonna stop you from sending that photo around?" he said. "Even if you give me the original form?"

"You know a photo like that doesn't count as evidence." Simon was guessing, but it sounded right. "It's too easy to fake. But the real thing? That's completely different." He paused. "Maria will delete it from her phone if that's what you want. She'll do that right in front of you."

There was a long moment of silence. Maria stared at the phone, biting her lip. Simon wondered if he'd somehow screwed up, if he'd said the wrong thing.

"You think you're some kind of hustler?" DaSilva finally sneered. "You don't have a fucking clue."

"But you'll do it? Forty thousand."

Another pause, then, "Yeah, forty thousand. So where the fuck are you guys?"

They'd made the call almost five hours ago. DaSilva had told them he'd be there in less than four; he needed an hour to get out of the hospital, another to gather the cash, and then not quite two to drive out to Montauk. But he was late, and Simon could see Maria's frustration blossoming. She hunched against the chill in her leather jacket, her gloved hands stuffed into her armpits. He was trying to figure out what to say, how to convince her to be patient, when he heard the crunch of tires over dirt echoing down from the top of the bluff.

"Maria," he said, but he could see in the way she stiffened and tilted her head toward the cliffs that she'd already heard it too.

The sound of a car door slamming. Nothing for a few moments, and then DaSilva appeared at the edge of the bluff, a dark smudge against the snow and pale limestone. He carried a duffel bag slung over his shoulder. Simon lifted his hand in greeting, and after a brief pause, DaSilva returned the gesture. Peter started to pick his way down the trail, gingerly transferring his bulk from foot to foot. He steadied himself against the bluff with one hand while the other, carrying the duffel, waved wildly in the air. Simon felt the sudden, deeply inappropriate impulse to laugh. The sight was so incongruous, so ridiculous: DaSilva in his black slacks and black coat and black leather shoes—his Cabrera work clothes—his imperious gut, his giant square head; his awkward, painstaking movements along the path.

Finally he reached the foot of the bluffs. He paused for a moment, turning his head to take in the dimensions of the beach, its geometry. Then he walked toward where they stood, near the waterline, and stopped about ten feet away. Simon and Maria had kept five feet between them, at Maria's insistence, and so the three made a triangle with DaSilva its apex. He stared at Simon, his chest heaving, eyes crinkled almost entirely shut against the brightly reflecting ocean. He glanced at Maria briefly, with something like contempt or at least dismissal, and then he returned his attention to Simon. "So where is it?" he said.

Maria reached into her jacket pocket. "Here." She took out the carefully folded sheet of paper and held it up.

Peter dropped the duffel onto the sand with a heavy thunk. "How do I know that's the real thing?"

Maria stepped closer, unfolding the paper.

"Wait," Simon said.

She waved him off. "It's fine." She stopped a few feet from DaSilva and held the paper out in front of her. "Take a look."

Peter leaned forward and scanned the paper. "All right." He squatted down in the sand next to the bag, opened its zipper, and yanked back its top flap. "It's all here."

Simon looked down into the duffel: a layer of banded bills lay tight across the top of the bag. Simon's ears prickled. Peter had actually brought the money; this absurd plan was actually going to work.

"Here." DaSilva reached into the bag. He plucked out a banded wad and tossed it to Simon. Simon caught the bills and flipped through them quickly: ten hundreds, all fresh and uncreased. As he counted them, DaSilva stared at him with a fury that was only more obvious for how hard he was trying to suppress it. Simon looked over at Maria. "Okay," he said. "Get the rest."

She nodded and moved toward DaSilva. She handed him the form with one hand, the other stuffed inside her jacket's pocket.

"Maria?" Simon said. What was she doing? This was all out of order. "The bag?"

"It's all right," she said.

DaSilva took the paper from her and looked down to read it, the duffel still at his feet.

"I don't—" Simon began, but before he could finish, Maria's hand darted out of her pocket, a glint of metal winking in the sun.

DaSilva saw it too, and he hunched away at the last instant, enough that Maria's switchblade struck him in the shoulder instead of square between the ribs. He staggered sideways, bellowing. The transfer form fluttered to the sand. As she pulled back the knife for a second blow, he lifted his arm to block it. The blade caught on his jacket fabric, tearing through the wool, revealing a bright flash of blood. With his other hand, he shoved Maria backward and gained some distance. He reached inside his coat.

Simon sprang forward as DaSilva drew a handgun from a holster against his ribs and raised it to Maria's face. He slammed into DaSilva's side just as he fired, the gun's report like a crack of thunder inside Simon's skull. Maria collapsed, screaming in pain, clutching at her foot.

Simon and Peter fell onto the sand in a tangled heap, Simon swinging wildly. He connected with DaSilva's wrist and knocked the gun loose, the pistol skittering away across the half-frozen sand and into the water.

They rolled, locked together, into the shallows. Icy water filled Simon's jacket and soaked through his shirt, water so cold it felt hot, burning and prickling against his skin. He pushed free of DaSilva and thrashed his way to his knees in time to greet Peter's fist as it smashed into his jaw, knocking him back into the water. He staggered to his feet and saw Maria crumpled on the sand, blood soaking the hem of her jeans. And then Peter was on him again, sputtering and snorting, huge and relentless, his wounded arm hanging awkwardly against his side, blood leaking from gashes in his shoulder and forearm, as he tried to pull Simon under.

Simon's ears filled with the ragged huffing of their breath, the desperate sucking and hoarding of oxygen. "I didn't know," he gasped. It didn't matter anymore, but he couldn't help himself. He stepped backward and the seafloor fell away, the water quickly up to his shoulders and then his chin. "She wasn't supposed to do that."

"Fuck you both," DaSilva hissed.

There was nothing more to say; they were beyond talking, beyond explanations.

*Now*, Simon thought, and he took a breath and dove.

He opened his eyes and saw, through the murky green, DaSilva's pillar-like legs. Simon drove himself into the knees, wrapping his arms around the thick calves and rolling his body to the side. Peter's dress shoes scrabbled for purchase on the seafloor, and then he toppled over and joined Simon underwater.

Simon grabbed DaSilva's jacket, yanking at the lapels, pulling the collar over the big man's blocky head and twisting it around his face. Simon's mind was filled entirely by bright, white-hot rage, more a primal state of being than an emotion: survival was all. He kicked hard, pinning DaSilva against the bottom, driving himself down on top of the giant head. Peter's fists battered Simon's back, but his left arm was ruined and the blows fell weakly.

Simon's lungs burned; black spots crept across his field of vision.

DaSilva flailed again, and Simon's hold on the jacket loosened enough that the fabric slipped away from Peter's face. His mouth was pressed into a flat line, his nostrils flared; his eyes were wide-open, as though pinned back by invisible nails. He looked straight into Simon's own eyes. The look was one of confusion. This isn't what was supposed to happen, the look said. Or maybe DaSilva was beyond that. Maybe the look was meaningless, pure reflex. Finally Simon felt himself on the cusp of passing out, and he let go and pushed off, breaking the surface.

He stood in water up to his chin, hauling in lungfuls of cold, crisp air. DaSilva surfaced a moment later and floated, belly-up, a few feet away, wheezing and coughing up salt water. His face was red and his eyes squeezed shut. He seemed only half-conscious, unaware of where he was and what was happening to him. But he was still alive.

"Bring him in!"

Simon turned toward the beach: there was Maria, kneeling at the waterline. He couldn't imagine how she'd managed to move at all, the blinding, otherworldly pain such an effort must have demanded.

"Come on, hurry!"

Simon grabbed DaSilva's shoulders and dragged the heavy body toward shore. Peter didn't resist, his breathing wet and labored. They reached the sand. Simon collapsed onto his hands and knees next to DaSilva's prone body. He retched, hot bile and cold salt water mixing in his throat, as DaSilva began to moan and twitch.

Maria limped over to Simon and shook his arm. "Stand up. We're almost there."

Simon forced himself to his feet. DaSilva had managed to roll onto his side and was coughing blood-spattered phlegm onto the sand.

"Where's the gun?" Maria said.

Simon shook his head. His limbs were trembling with cold and exhaustion. DaSilva slowly lifted his head off the sand and looked up at Simon and Maria. There was no question now that his mind had returned to his body, that he understood what he was seeing. "Don't," he said. His lips were blue. "Don't."

"Here." Maria handed Simon the switchblade. The handle's mother-of-pearl design throbbed in time with his frantic pulse.

DaSilva tried to push himself up, gaining his hands and knees.

"Keep him down," Maria said.

"What do you—"

Maria grabbed the knife from Simon, flicked open the blade and slammed it down into DaSilva's back. Peter collapsed to the sand again, the air whooshing out of his lungs. Maria nearly fell over, her face white with pain.

"Find the gun," she said through gritted teeth. "Please."

Simon waded back into the ocean. He found the pistol after a minute of searching, its silver barrel shining in the clear and shallow water a few feet from shore. He dangled it upside-down, shaking it a few times, letting the water drain out of the barrel. He turned back to Maria and DaSilva. She stood over the large man as he twitched and muttered. Peter tried to rise again, and again she slammed the switchblade down into his back. He grunted and then lay flat on the sand, his only movement the labored rising and falling of his chest, the stubborn insistency of his breath.

"Finish this," Maria said.

Simon squatted down and pressed the barrel of the gun to DaSilva's right temple, shivering so much he had to steady his shooting wrist with his other hand. He stayed like that for one, two, three breaths, the gun pressed to Peter's temple, his left hand gripping his right wrist, his finger trembling against the pistol's trigger. He stared at his finger. He willed himself to pull, the action itself so insignificant, barely a muscle twitch.

Nothing happened. He let the muzzle drift away from DaSilva's head.

"Simon," Maria said. "Do it."

He nodded. He steadied the gun again, pressed it against

DaSilva's forehead. But still he couldn't fire. This wasn't self-defense, not with DaSilva lying here half-dead on the sand, not beyond the most existential, abstracted sense of the term. This was pure, unadulterated murder. He couldn't do it.

Simon lowered the barrel of the gun.

"Simon," Maria said.

"I'm sorry." He looked up at her. She swayed slightly, her face pinched and ashen. "It's not in me," he said. "I can't."

She didn't try to convince him again. Instead, she simply put the switchblade into her pocket and held out her hand. He stood and gave her the gun.

DaSilva stirred again. His head lifted from the sand, and his eyes widened as he saw Maria point the pistol at his face. "No," he rasped. "No, I can't—"

She pulled the trigger.

Simon turned his head away, but nothing happened. Maria lifted the pistol, shook it. A few drops of water spattered onto the sand. She bent over and pushed the barrel back against DaSilva's temple. He tried to move away, sobbing now, but he was too weak, and without hesitation she depressed the trigger a second time. This time the gun fired, jerking sharply in her hand. DaSilva's head lifted off the sand and then dropped back down. His temple was caved in, splinters of bone protruding from the edges of the hole. Maria bent down and placed the pistol into DaSilva's right hand, curling the fingers around the grip, bending the pointer inside the trigger guard. A wave surged gently across the pebbles, washing over the hand that held the gun. Simon noticed a flash of white in the water: the transfer form, soaked through and already falling apart. Another surge of water carried the paper onto shore; the wave receded and sucked it back under. Simon retrieved the stray wad of cash and stuffed it back into the duffel. He picked up the bag, and then they turned their back on Peter's body and limped across the beach to the foot of the path, Maria's arm slung over Simon's shoulder, her wounded foot dragging behind her.

## Fourteen

THEY made it to a Best Western in Jamaica that evening, a concrete box near the Grand Central Parkway. It was as far as he'd allow them to travel before tending to her foot. She'd refused to let him bring her to a hospital. "I need to disappear," she'd said, "not be processed in a fucking ER again." Upstairs in their room, he helped her onto the bed and propped her foot on a pillow. His jaw ached, tapping out a Morse code of dull pain. He held her ankle gently. "I'm going to take off the sneaker, okay?"

She nodded, staring at the foot. Her face was grayish white, her pursed lips nearly colorless. A hole had been blown through the top of the black Chuck Taylor and dried blood stiffened the sneaker's fabric. Simon loosened the laces as delicately as he could, then lifted the tongue. The blood had soaked the sock, a sticky, rusty red. He gripped the sole between his hands and looked up at her. "Ready?"

"Just do it already."

He pulled the sneaker off in one quick motion. She hissed, her fingers digging into the bedspread. Her body went limp, and he looked up and saw her eyes roll back into her head. She came to gradually, surfacing in increments. Her eyes refocused on his face and then slid, reluctantly, down to her foot. The hole was neater than he'd expected, punched right through the webbing between her first and second toes. He looked inside the sneaker. The bullet was still there, embedded in the sole. He brought the lamp over from the bedside table and leaned in closer to her foot.

"It's only nicked the bone," he said. "You're lucky."

"Yeah," she said. "I feel really fucking blessed right now."

"We're alive, aren't we?"

"There's that."

He walked to a drugstore on Hillside Avenue and bought a bottle of hydrogen peroxide, tweezers, bandages and gauze, a tub of ibuprofen. He found a replacement charger for his cell phone and threw that into his basket too. While he waited on the check-out line, he closed his eyes and saw DaSilva lying on the sand in his sodden black jacket, a hole in his head. The image presented with the dispassion of a fact, like one of Maria's collected photographs: DaSilva's skin blue white, the dried blood crusted around the lip of the wound reddish black and flaking. Beneath this image and at the same time contained within it, a palimpsest, were the half-dismantled girl in anatomy lab and Amelia in the morgue. The dead were piling up in Simon's mind. *It could have been you*, he told himself. *Remember that, it could have been you.* But although he recognized this as the truth, he couldn't simply reject his guilt, toss it aside like a smoked cigarette. He was partially responsible for a man's murder; he'd failed to save his own sister. That the man had tried to drown him and that he'd risked his own life in the attempt to save Amelia's did not change these facts. He thought of Lenny Pellegrini too, the suicide Simon had done nothing to prevent; he'd ignored Lenny's pain because it was inconvenient. He recognized that guilt would always be a part of him. He needed to learn not to fight it, nor let it overwhelm him, but to coexist with it, to make space for it, like a difficult, burdensome family member within the house of his self.

Back in the Best Western, he found Maria on the bed, hunched over DaSilva's duffel, a few stray wads of cash scattered across the comforter. She looked up when he walked into the room and gave him a seasick smile. "Does this make you feel any better?"

She tilted the open bag toward him. Inside were a few more banded wads of cash, but the rest of the duffel was filled with stacks of plain white printer paper. "He was going to fuck us too," she said.

"It's not the same thing." Simon reached inside the bag and lifted up the reams of paper. There was nothing underneath. He knew he shouldn't be so surprised that DaSilva would try something like this. But all it proved was that he was going to shortchange them on the money, nothing beyond that.

"What isn't?" Maria asked.

"Really? You're going to make me say it?"

She just looked at him, waiting, defiant.

"Ripping somebody off and killing them, Maria. Not the same thing."

"I had to do it."

"You're not going to convince me, so just stop trying."

"He was going to kill you," she said. "Probably both of us. If not today, then eventually."

"You lied to me."

"Only after you said you weren't going to do it the way I wanted to. The way we *needed* to." She picked up a handful of bills and waved it at Simon. "It's about $2,000, the cash he laid on top. He probably got the idea from a TV show or something, the trick's so obvious. Anyway, you should take it. It's all yours."

"I don't want it."

She stared at him. "Come on, Simon."

He shook his head. The money was contaminated: blood money, pure and simple.

"Here," he said. "Let me see your foot."

He cleaned out Maria's wound and wrapped the foot before taking scissors to her sneaker and cutting out the tongue. He pried the bullet out of the sole with the pair of tweezers. She held out her hand and he dropped the bullet into her palm.

"I'm going to keep this," she said. "String it on a necklace."

She asked him what she should do to keep the wound from getting infected.

"Wash it out with hydrogen peroxide twice a day," Simon said. "That'll hurt like hell, but you have to do it. Cover the hole with gauze. Take ibuprofen for the inflammation. You still have your painkillers?" She nodded. "Use them when you have to. Keep taking your antibiotics too." He paused. "What are you going to do, Maria? Where are you going to go?"

"Don't you think it's better if you don't know that?"

"You shouldn't have to do this alone. *I* don't want to do this alone."

"You don't want to hang around me for too long. Didn't I prove that already?" She closed her eyes. There was a long pause filled only by her jagged breathing. She grimaced as she shifted her wounded foot. "I'm glad you didn't pull the trigger, Simon."

"I thought you were disappointed in me."

"For a moment, yeah, maybe I was. But I was wrong. I'd crossed that line already. I'd become that person. You didn't have to." She opened her eyes. "I've felt what it's like to be powerless, and I am never going to let that happen to me again. I'll do anything to fight that feeling. And I'll tell you something else. Killing DaSilva was easier than killing Thomas, and DaSilva hadn't even done anything to me yet. You understand?"

"Are you saying I should be afraid of you?"

"What I'm saying is that you can recover from this. You can get a job or go back to school, keep your head down and hope they never tie you to DaSilva's mess. You can try to build a regular life—you still have that choice. I've already chosen a different way to live."

"You can have a regular life too." It was pointless to argue with her, he knew that, but he couldn't fight the compulsion to do it anyway. "Move somewhere remote and private. Start fresh."

She smiled gently, as though he were a child who needed to be cushioned from hard truths. "I don't think it's going to work out quite like that."

Simon sat down on the bed. "I've wanted to ask you something."

"So ask."

"Did it help?"

"What?"

"Killing Thomas. Did it make you feel better?"

"It made me stop feeling worse. It made me feel like . . . an imbalance had been corrected."

"I'm sorry you've suffered so much." Simon lay back against the pillows next to her. "I don't know what else I can say."

"So am I." She turned toward him. "Now I'm going to ask you something." She reached over the edge of the bed, to his bag, and came up holding Amelia's lockbox. "I know it's private. But you asked me to bring this. It was the only thing you wanted from your apartment, so it made me wonder what's inside. What you care about that much."

Simon looked at the box. He didn't say anything.

"I'm sorry," she said. "I'll put it back. I guess it's none of my business."

"No. I'll show you." He spun the lock and opened the lid. "It's a few of my sister's things."

The hemp bracelet, grayed and ragged, lay next to the red diary, both resting on top of the Venus flytrap drawing. The objects appeared small and sad, drained of their magic as he looked at them now in the presence of another person.

"Do you have a picture of her in there?"

"I don't need to be reminded of what she looked like," he said, hearing echoes of his father in his words.

Maria reached toward the box. "Can I?" He nodded, and she lifted the three objects out and placed them on top of the comforter, smoothing out the drafting paper. "She drew this?"

"Yeah. She wanted to get it tattooed on her back."

Maria laughed, then covered her mouth. "I'm sorry."

"I know, I know." Simon found himself smiling. "She was fifteen, remember."

Maria looked back down at the paper. "It's a good drawing. I just wouldn't want it on my body my whole life." She brought it closer to the light. "What's the flytrap?"

"What do you mean?"

"She's the fairy, the Tinker Bell, right? So what's the flytrap? Or *who's* the flytrap?"

"I don't think it's a symbol. She probably just liked the way it looked."

"You weren't a teenage girl," Maria said. "Believe me, it meant something." She plucked the band that held the diary shut. "Is this her diary?"

"Yes."

She moved as though to open it.

"Don't do that," Simon said. "Please."

She stopped. "No, sorry, of course. It's private."

"I just think that if I haven't read it, neither should anybody else."

"You haven't read it?"

"I'm afraid of what it might say about me." He'd never articulated his reasons for not reading the diary before, but as soon as he spoke the words, he knew they were true.

"I'd never have the discipline. I'd be too curious." Maria put the diary back into the box and lifted the hemp bracelet. "What's the story behind this?"

He suddenly didn't want Maria looking at these objects anymore, didn't want her touching them. He felt foolish, ignorant, secreting these things around like fetishes. "It was just her bracelet, that's all."

Maria read his irritation and returned the bracelet to the box. He reached over, closed the lid, and spun the lock.

He lay back on the pillows and stared up at the ceiling. "We shouldn't have done that," he said softly. "DaSilva. How could we have done that?"

"He was never going to let us go."

"We don't know if that's true."

"Yes," Maria said firmly. "He deserved it."

"Nobody deserves that."

"Better him than us, Simon."

How could he argue with that? And yet Simon's own potential death seemed to him an abstract concept next to the blunt facts of DaSilva's blown-out temple, his sightless eyes, all that heavy, dead-white flesh anchored, forever inanimate, to the wet sand. The equivalency didn't seem equal, or fair.

MARIA Campos exited his life at 7:13 the next morning. He looked at the clock the moment the door closed behind her, as though fixing the exact minute in his mind would mean something. She wouldn't let him take her downstairs; she didn't want them to be seen leaving the hotel together. This was the first move in the game of her disappearance, and she would make it alone. He sat on the bed and waited until all traces of her presence had dissipated, until he could feel nothing remaining of her in the room.

As she was leaving, she'd turned to him in the doorway and said, "What we did to DaSilva, it only exists in our minds. Do you understand?" He'd shaken his head that he didn't. "Only we know exactly what happened," she said. "Everybody else will just be guessing. The truth lives and dies inside our heads. Okay?" He nodded. She was telling him to keep his mouth shut, and, of course, he would. "I'm sorry," he said, "for everything you've had to do." She leaned in. "You'll survive this," she whispered. She smiled at him, the gray tooth flickering, dark eyes shining, and then she'd turned and walked to the elevator and didn't look back.

He got up from the bed, took the elevator to the lobby, paid their bill in cash, and went down into the garage under the hotel.

Katherine's RAV4 was still parked where he'd left it the night before, a filthy snow- and salt-spattered incrimination. He started
up the car one last time and pulled out onto Jamaica Avenue. He
drove slowly, on local streets, to the nearest A train station, a mile
or two away. Thick black clouds had rolled in again overnight and
it was bitterly cold. Traffic was sparse, and he made it to Liberty
and Lefferts in under ten minutes. He parked the car around the
corner from the station, on a quiet residential block. A few figures
hurried down the street, hunched inside puffy jackets, and nobody paid him any attention as he hauled his duffel bag out of the
backseat, left the car, and walked to the subway station.

As he waited for the train on the elevated platform, he took his
cell phone out of his jacket pocket. He'd charged it overnight, but
he was only looking at his messages for the first time now. He
found a text from DaSilva, from the night he and Maria had driven
to Montauk. He read it with the sensation of plunging down a
well, the bottom falling out from under him: "Where the fuck did
you go? Call me." He deleted the text, his fingers shaking.

The only new voice mail was from Howard Crewes. Simon
pressed the phone against his ear and, hunching against the wind
and the clatter of the tracks, listened to Howard's message.

"Shit, Simon." Crewes spoke in a voice almost comically fatigued, like that of a healthy man calling in sick to work. "How
could you go see Cheryl like that? I'm sure she was pretty damn
clear, but in case you didn't understand: do not contact her again.
Get it? You and Cheryl, you've never met, never spoken, nothing.
Same thing with you and me now. I just want to forget this ever
happened." There was a pause before Crewes finished: "Maybe
I'm being naive, but I'm praying it all ends here. I just hope you
weren't lying about that girl. I hope she really is someplace where
they never find her."

Simon erased the message. He didn't know what DaSilva's
death would mean for Crewes and Cheryl. Probably it would help
them. Without Simon and DaSilva, the hospital was never going

to find Maria; any worries about the money Crewes had paid her could probably end there. Simon felt sorry for Howard, all the man's best intentions in ruins, but he couldn't do any more for him now. Crewes was right: from this point forward, they'd never known each other.

He peered down the tracks: still no sign of his train.

He wondered what Katherine Peel would do when she found out DaSilva had been killed. She might assume the murder was somehow connected to Simon, but what would she do about it then? He knew how important medical school was to her, how ambitious and stubborn she was. Was she really going to risk derailing all that by going to the police with what she knew about DaSilva's scam? Wouldn't she rather just leave it alone? Her car though—the kid at the Montauk motel had seen it, maybe somebody at the Best Western as well. If she were reunited with the RAV4, she might be dragged into things whether she wanted to be or not.

Simon ran down the platform stairs and around the corner to the block where he'd parked the thing. It was right there, of course, exactly as he'd left it. He still had the keys in his pocket, and he unlocked it, rummaging through the glove box until he found Katherine's registration and insurance. He shoved the papers into his bag—he'd shred them later, at his father's house—along with her cell phone, and then he hunted around the cluttered trunk until he found a small screwdriver. He looked around the block: there was nobody to see him. Quickly, he removed the license plates and stuffed them into his bag too. He locked the car again and forced himself to walk slowly and calmly back to the train station. They'd eventually be able to link Katherine to the RAV4's VIN, but he figured she would be smart enough to say the car had been stolen. He tossed the car keys and her cell phone into one garbage can and his own phone into another, and then he trotted up the stairs, a Rockaway-bound A train pulling into the station just as he reached the platform.

————

Wind cutting across Jamaica Bay. Whitecaps slapping against the base of the tracks. White line of sky pressed thin between black clouds and black water. On Beach 116th, snowbanks worn down to icy gray nubs. An upended trash bin spilling Styrofoam cups and soda cans onto the sidewalk. The pizza parlor, the shuttered surf shop, the fogged windows of Derry Hills. At his house on Beach 113th, a single yellow lamp glowing in his father's bedroom.

As he climbed the stairs to the porch, a shadow moved behind the glass. The kitchen light switched on, and Simon saw his father backlit—a cutout, an absence. Then Michael turned toward the light, and he looked exactly like what he was: a middle-aged man who lived alone, tidying his kitchen.

Simon didn't wait any longer. He crossed the porch and knocked on the door.

Michael didn't ask Simon where he'd been, why he'd skipped their dinner earlier in the week without explanation, why he hadn't returned any of his messages. Instead, he pulled his son inside the house, sat him down at the kitchen table, and made him breakfast: fried eggs and sweet Italian sausage and white toast. He poured the last of the carafe's coffee—weak and slightly burnt, just like always—into a mug, set it on the table, and leaned against the counter to watch Simon eat. Simon knew it must be obvious he was in some kind of trouble, and for once he was immensely grateful for his father's circumspection. After Simon finished his breakfast—devouring every last scrap of food, his body abruptly realizing it hadn't been fed in almost twenty-four hours—Michael retrieved the bottle of Jameson from the sideboard and poured them each a tumbler, two fingers, no ice. It wasn't yet ten in the morning, but neither of them much cared.

Where do you start? How do you begin to be honest when there are still so many truths you cannot afford to reveal? Simon wanted to tell his father how Amelia drowned—the real story, leaving out nothing, not their argument, not his spying, not his shameful moment of paralysis before he jumped in after her—but he thought his actions would seem so alien, so inexplicable, that he wanted first to build a bridge, to give that night context and meaning, to show where both he and Amelia were coming from when they arrived together on that beach. He first needed his father to understand how it felt when Simon realized that Amelia was going to grow up to hate him. If Michael could understand this, maybe he would be able to one day understand what had eventually followed from it, how those few seconds of hesitation on the groyne had colored the balance of Simon's life, insinuating themselves into every calibration of self, all those countless subconscious adjustments to his own understanding of who he was; how those few seconds had made him out into a coward, a failure; how a sense of inadequacy had become the imperative force in his psyche, a kind of perverse lodestar guiding him into the embrace of its darker cousins, shame and guilt.

There was no direct causative line from any one point in Simon's life to the horrible scene on the beach in Montauk, to the fact that he was now, in all but the most literal reading of events, a murderer. But there was a course to be mapped nonetheless, a chain, no matter how tangled, that bound the Simon who had pointed a gun at DaSilva's head to his younger and more innocent self. If he couldn't ever explain where the course had ultimately led—and he couldn't; he would forever protect Maria with his silence—at least he might help his father understand who he had become and how he might now change, if it was still possible, into someone better.

"Want more?" Michael nodded at Simon's plate.

"I'm all right now," Simon said. "It's just like high school, remember? How if I was stressed out over a test or something, you had to force-feed me spaghetti before I realized I was hungry?"

Michael swirled his whiskey. "You want to tell me why you're stressed?"

"Not really. Not yet anyway." Simon paused. "Right now I want to talk about Amelia."

Michael shifted almost imperceptibly in his chair, like an antenna recalibrating to better receive some distant, obscure signal. "I'm listening."

"Remember when you asked me to watch over her, right after we moved out here?" Simon said. "I took what you said very seriously."

"I know you did."

"Yeah, and that was mostly because you were telling me to do something I already thought I should be doing. I thought she needed my help and that I wasn't giving her enough of it. But I was wrong," Simon said. "What she needed was for me to start letting go, not to hold on any tighter."

"You're being too hard on yourself."

"You don't know that," Simon said sharply. He took a breath. "I'm sorry. I just . . . I never really listened to her. That was the problem. Taking care of her—even when she didn't want me to—it gave me a purpose. I did it for me more than I did it for her." He finished his whiskey. "Even back then, I realized I was always going to disappoint her. Over and over and over again. The harder I tried not to, the worse it would be. I knew this, and yet still I refused to accept it."

"You were doing the best you could." Michael looked steadily at his son. "I could see that."

"It wasn't right. It wasn't good enough."

"Sometimes it's not going to be, and that's just the way it is." His father stubbed out his cigarette. "I obviously know all about that."

Silence then, interrupted only by the rasp of Michael striking a match, the crackle of the new cigarette catching.

"Dad, listen to me," Simon suddenly blurted out. "I dropped out of med school, okay? I've been lying to you. It's been almost a year already."

His father focused on the lit end of his cigarette, puffing until the cherry glowed a healthy orange. He inhaled and then let a long, thin stream of smoke out the corner of his mouth, prolonging the moment, Simon thought, maybe even relishing it. Simon braced himself for anger or disbelief, even pity. Instead, his father said, "I thought you had."

"What? You did?"

"Give me some credit, Simon. I'm not an idiot."

"But then . . . why didn't you say anything? Why did you let me lie to you like that?"

"Because I wasn't going to shame you into telling the truth. You'd tell me when you needed to." He paused. "And isn't that what happened?"

"Jesus, Dad." Simon had to laugh. Of course his father would sit silently by and watch Simon dig himself into such an absurd and unnecessary hole, the behavior fitting Michael in its passive-aggressive combination of tact and cruelty by omission.

"I don't know why you dropped out though," Michael said. "I was hoping you'd tell me that sometime."

"I had some difficulties with anatomy lab." His father tapped his cigarette expectantly against the ashtray's edge. "I, uh, well . . . I guess I kind of had a breakdown." *Why not call it what it was?* "I saw Amelia everywhere. The way she was in the morgue, I mean, that Amelia. I still see her like that sometimes, in dreams mostly, sometimes just when I close my eyes."

"But it was worse then?"

"Yeah. Much worse. The girl we were dissecting . . . I guess, for me, she *became* Amelia, and I couldn't stand what we were doing to her."

Michael stared down at the kitchen table. He rubbed his thumb across the wood, smearing spilled ash into the grain. "What have you been doing since you left school?"

"I don't want to talk about that. But it's over. I hope it is, anyway."

Michael nodded as though he'd expected this answer. "Could you go back if you wanted to?"

"Not to that school, no."

"A different one?"

"I'm not sure. Maybe."

"Then do it." Michael lifted his eyes from the table. "You look at my life and you see a waste, don't you?"

Simon flushed. "No, I—"

"Stop." Michael raised his hand. "I know you do. You think I've given up, and it's true, in some ways I have. But I also hoped I might put my ruin to some use. I thought I could take on most of the grief and pain over what happened to Amelia so you wouldn't have to. You'd be free to live."

"Wait," Simon said. "It's not like there's a fixed amount of suffering, and if you take on more, there's less left for me. It doesn't work like that."

"It can if you let it. My life is done changing or improving, Simon. This"—he gestured as though to take in the house, Rockaway, the available world—"this is what's left for me." The words bordered on hyperbole, but the way his father spoke was restrained and shorn of self-pity. "I'm not telling you to forget her. But, you want to make your sister's death mean anything? Go out and do something good with your life."

Michael fell silent then. Simon felt the warmth of the whiskey spread through his body. The kitchen smelled of burned coffee and sausage, a cocooning thickness to the warm air. Frost edged the windowpanes, and the sky outside was heavy and gray as poured concrete.

"Dad," Simon said.

"Yeah?"

"Is it all right if I stay here for a while? Just until . . . I don't know exactly. Until I don't have to anymore."

"You don't have to ask." Michael stood and brought Simon's dirty plate to the sink. "Stay as long as you need."

Simon left his father in the kitchen and carried his bag up the stairs, to his old bedroom. He turned on the lamp and sat on the mattress. He wondered where Maria was at that exact moment. It was difficult to imagine her progress when he didn't know where she was going, what her plan was. What they had done together—what she had forced him into doing—was unforgivable, and their complicity would bind them forever, no matter how far the physical distance between them. An invisible, unbreakable string. She was strong—he knew that—stronger than he could have imagined, but still he feared that her suffering wasn't finished. He hoped, despite everything, he was wrong about that. He hoped that her wounds, all of them, of body and psyche and spirit, would heal with a perfection he knew wasn't often granted. He hoped she might one day discover a peace that didn't rely upon the promise of violence, that she might one day be happy. But he also knew that what he hoped for her—what he wanted for her—didn't matter anymore. This was her own life. It wasn't about what he wanted, and it never had been.

Simon pulled Amelia's lockbox out of his duffel and held it for a few minutes in his lap. He spun the combination and removed her diary. He ran his thumb over the red cover, the edges of the pages wavy and brittle. Then he removed the elastic strap and opened the book, and he began to read.